THE SEAFORT SAGA

"A ripping good read – the sort of thing that attracted us all to SF in the first place"
S. M. Stirling

"Something special indeed . . . Feintuch has at last captured for the science fiction community the quintessential spirits of greats such as C. S. Forester and F. Van Wyck Mason" *Bill Baldwin*

"An excellent entertainment" *Analog*

"Feintuch has constructed a fascinating story . . . You'll find his adventures highly entertaining"
Science Fiction Chronicle

"An excellent job of transferring Hornblower to interstellar space. A thoroughly enjoyable read"
David Drake

The Seafort Saga

Prisoner's HOPE

DAVID FEINTUCH

An *Orbit* Book

First published in Great Britain by Orbit 1997
Reprinted 1997, 1998, 2000

This edition published in arrangement with
Warner Books, Inc., New York

A CIP catalogue record for this book is
available from the British Library.

ISBN 1 85723 439 1

Printed and bound in Great Britain by Clays Ltd, St Ives plc

Orbit
A Division of
Little, Brown and Company (UK)
Brettenham House
Lancaster Place
London WC2E 7EN

DEDICATION

To Rick, Betsy, John and Beth Grafing, friends, to Ardath Mayhar, for unstinting support, Betsy Mitchell, for her sagacity and nearly infinite patience, Don Maass for helping a miracle come to pass, and as always, Jettie. Especial thanks to the staff and musicians at Ragtime Rick's of Toledo, Ohio, for serving and sustaining that odd character in the corner booth tapping at the keys of his computer.

PRISONER'S HOPE

*Being the third voyage
of Nicholas Seafort, U.N.N.S.,
in the year of our Lord 2200*

PART 1

April, in the year of our Lord 2200

1

Admiral Tremaine drew himself up, jowls pursed in indignation. "Who would you believe—this young scoundrel or me?" Ignored for the moment, I held the at-ease position.

"That's not the issue." Fleet Admiral De Marnay gestured at the holovid chip I'd brought on U.N.S. *Hibernia* across sixty-nine light-years of void. "Captain Seafort is but a messenger. Your recall was ordered by Admiralty at home."

Through the Admiral's unshuttered window, the late afternoon sun of Hope Nation illuminated his Centraltown office with dazzling brightness. A muted roar signaled yet another shuttle lifting off to Orbit Station from the spaceport behind Admiralty House.

I sighed; I'd docked *Hibernia* at the Station just hours before, and my trip groundside was proving no respite from the tensions of the bridge. I'd had no idea Geoffrey Tremaine would be in the office when Admiral De Marnay received my report.

"Messenger, my arse." Tremaine swung toward me, glowering. "You arranged it!"

I decided it was a question, so I could respond without fear of contradicting my superior. "No, sir, Admiral Brentley made the decision and I wasn't consulted."

"A patent lie." Tremaine dismissed me with an airy wave and turned back to the Admiral Commanding. "Georges, be reasonable—"

"It is no lie!" The savagery of my snarl startled even me. The two Admirals glared, astounded at such an interruption from a mere Captain, the youngest in the U.N. Navy. I rushed on, abandoning the shreds of my discipline. "Mr. Tremaine, Lord God knows that if anyone should be removed from command, it is you. But I say again, I had no part in it. Admiral De Marnay, as my verity has been ques-

3

tioned, I demand truth testing!" Drugs and polygraph would quickly confirm my statement or expose my lie.

Georges De Marnay got slowly to his feet. "You demand, Captain?" His tone was glacial.

"Sir, I have never lied to a superior officer!" It was the one remnant of honor I'd retained in my slide to damnation. "Three times he's accused—"

"Seafort, get hold of yourself. Be silent!"

"Aye aye, sir." Midshipman or Captain, there was no other possible reply to a direct order.

Admiral Tremaine's choleric face shook with wrath. "You see the insolence I had to put up with, when he had *Portia*? He—"

"Before you stole her from him." De Marnay's acid reply sliced through Tremaine's diatribe.

"Stole her? What are you saying?" Before De Marnay could answer, Tremaine rushed on. "The facts are clear from *Portia*'s Log, which you reviewed when I docked. I had to threaten to hang him before he'd transfer to *Challenger*!"

Better had he done so. Many would live who now were lost.

De Marnay said nothing.

Tremaine's voice took on a wheedling tone. "Recall or no, you're the Admiral in theater. Those bloody aliens of Seafort's may strike at any time. You need a commander groundside as well as aloft, and Admiralty didn't appoint my replacement. As Admiral Commanding, you could reconfirm me until my tour's up. Or try me yourself, for that matter."

"Yes, I could well do that." De Marnay swung his chair, fingers tapping at the edge of his desk.

I closed my eyes, my jaw throbbing with the effort to hold it shut. My commander had ordered me to be silent, and silent I would be. In any event, nothing I said could prevent Admiral De Marnay from reinstating Tremaine, the man who'd taken my *Portia*. His own U.N.S. *Challenger* had been disabled by the huge goldfish-shaped aliens that I'd discovered three years before on my first interstellar voyage. Tremaine transferred his flag, leaving me, as well as the aged and infirm passengers and the young transpops he loathed, drifting on *Challenger*, deep in interstellar space, unable to Fuse.

After he fled, the fish had come again. We'd been testing the fusion drive, and they seemed to sense the N-waves on which our ships traveled the void between stars. Over and again, they'd Defused alongside *Challenger* to hurl their acid tentacles at our hull.

I took a sharp breath, realized I was clammy under my stiff jacket.

"After all, Admiralty is far from the scene, eh, Georges? They don't know—"

Admiral De Marnay said, "I could reinstate you, Mr. Tremaine. But I won't."

Tremaine said slowly, "You'd believe that"—he spat out the words—"that trannie Captain over me?"

"I believe the evidence in the Log, and in your conduct, sir." De Marnay's tone was icy. "Admiral Tremaine, you are relieved. Mr. Seafort, you may go."

"Aye aye, sir." I saluted and quickly made my escape.

I trudged across the back yard of Admiralty House to the spaceport perimeter and the terminal building seventy yards beyond. Other than the hum of a distant engine, all was silent.

At the far end of the tarmac, freight was piled high. My *Hibernia*'s cargo would soon be added to the supplies and equipment stockpiled here for the U.N. forces defending our colony from the aliens.

When last I'd seen Hope Nation I'd been so young, and innocent of the shattered oath that damned me.

Though I was fully recuperated from my physical ordeal on *Challenger*, my appalling misdeeds left me subject to fits of black despair. On our long journey to Hope Nation my companion and lover, Annie Wells, had done her best to allay them in the solitude of our cabin.

I wondered if Annie knew how I relied on her ministrations. Now even she would soon be gone. I'd come to know Annie on *Challenger*; she'd been among the transients from the slums of Lower New York bound for faraway Detour as part of a foolish social welfare program. After *Challenger*'s ill-fated voyage, we'd sailed again on *Hibernia*.

We'd made the sixteen-month cruise in one interminable Fuse, with a tiny corrective jump at the end. I'd docked at massive Orbit Station, taken the shuttle groundside, reported to the now bustling Admiralty House, Admiral Tremaine's recall orders among the packet of chips in my case.

Now I looked around, wondered what to do with my day before going back aloft to Annie.

I wished I could talk over the morning's encounter with a friend like Midshipman Derek Carr, one of the officers I'd forced to stay behind when I was transferred to *Challenger*. But Derek was stationed on U.N.S. *Catalonia* en route to Detour, and not expected home for months. So I was alone, on my mandatory long-leave, free of responsibilities. I had time to look up Vax Holser and the others.

As I crossed the terminal a whoop split the air; I turned to see Lieutenant Alexi Tamarov bounding after me. "You're here! Thank Lord God, you made it!" He snapped a crisp salute, grinning with pleasure. Then he saw my face and blanched. "My God, what happened, sir?"

My scar had that effect.

I offered him my hand, relieved beyond words to see him safe and well. "A laser, on board *Challenger*. It's healed."

"You look—" He remembered his manners and bit it off. Friend or no friend, I was Captain.

"Awful. Yes, I know." I deserved a ruined face. Lord God in his time would do worse. An oath is sacred.

"Well, er, different, sir." He quickly changed the subject. While he chattered I reflected on all that had passed since our days as midshipmen in *Hibernia*'s wardroom, when Alexi was a young fifteen and I, at seventeen, struggled toward manhood.

After *Hibernia*'s officers had been killed and I was catapulted to Captain, I'd left Alexi in the wardroom. We'd shipped together afterward on *Portia*, but since then we'd gone our separate ways for two long years. He was—what? twenty-one?—and I was tired and numbed at twenty-three.

"God, I'm glad I ran into you, sir. I'm off duty today, but tomorrow it's back to Admiralty House." He shrugged and smiled wryly. "They have me working in Tactics." Like any lieutenant, Alexi wanted ship time, which would give him a leg up toward promotion. His grin faded; his eyes drifted from mine. "About what I did on *Portia*, sir, I'm so—I'm ashamed."

"Did?" I tried to remember what he might be ashamed of.

"I wanted to volunteer for transfer, sir. I meant to ask the Admiral, but I couldn't. I sat in my cabin for hours before I gave up pretending. Now I know how cowardly I am."

"Stop that!" My anger thrust him back a step. "I told you then I wouldn't accept you on *Challenger* under any circumstances. You're no coward."

"I should have volunteered." He turned away. "Whether you took me or not. You had the courage to go."

"You fool!" I spoke so savagely he winced with the hurt. "If Amanda and Nate hadn't died, perhaps I'd have wanted to live. I wasn't brave, I was running away!" His look of dismay only goaded me further. "If I'd died I wouldn't have become what I am now."

Alexi's eyes met mine, troubled. What he saw there made him shrug and try a tentative smile. "Whatever our motives, sir, we've done what was in us. I won't let you down again."

"I absolve you, for what it's worth." To distract him I said, "They've relieved Tremaine."

"Thank Lord God, sir. But what about your challenge?"

"You heard about that?" Livid with rage when Geoffrey Tremaine had off-loaded *Portia*'s transient children before fleeing to safety, I'd sworn an oath to call challenge upon him, to fight a duel that would destroy one of us. Now that he was relieved it was legal for me to do so. But what did that oath matter? I'd already forsworn myself.

"Yes, we knew," Alexi said. "The Admiral wasn't alone on the bridge when you radioed. And Danny recorded. He'd have told us if we hadn't already heard." *Portia*'s puter liked to gossip, no doubt to ease his loneliness. What a joy it would be to visit with Danny again, as on so many deadened days on the bridge after my wife's death. We'd become friends, if such a thing was possible between man and machine. But I didn't even know where in the galaxy my old ship had been sent.

"I suppose I have to call the challenge, Alexi." At the time I'd yearned to cast my life against Tremaine's. Yet, Philip Tyre and the rest were dead, and nothing would bring them back. With an effort I thrust recriminations aside. "What happened to Vax?"

Alexi bit his lip. "He's here, sir. They have him running back and forth between Admiralty House and the Station."

Lieutenant Holser was alive and well. My old rival, once my enemy, now my friend. Twice he'd saved my life. "It will be good to see him."

After a moment Alexi spoke of other things. Restless, I invited him to wander Centraltown with me. He accepted with delight, and proudly led me to the electricar he'd managed to acquire. They were in short supply thanks to the population increase. I stared out the window as he drove downtown along Spaceport Road.

Centraltown had grown since my last visit, but the town had no sights I hadn't seen before, and what I saw reminded me of Amanda. For Alexi's sake I fought my depression, and eventually settled with him in a downtown restaurant. He respected my lapses into glum silence, and the evening provided more companionship than I'd had in many months. When finally we left, Minor was full overhead, and Major, Hope Nation's second moon, was just over the horizon. I looked up, imagining I could see Orbit Station passing above.

"Have you a place to stay, sir?"

I shook my head. "I'll bunk on the ship for a few days, I suppose."

"I meant tonight. Would you—" He hesitated. "Sir, would you, ah, care to stay with me this evening?" I understood his unease; the gulf between a lieutenant and a Captain was normally unbridgeable.

"Annie is waiting on *Hibernia*." Still, it was late, and I had no idea whether another shuttle would lift tonight; if not, I'd find myself sleeping at the terminal or in Naval barracks. "Well . . . for the night. I'd like that." I was rewarded with a shy grin of pleasure.

Alexi's flat was in one of the dozen or so prefabs that had sprung up along Spaceport Road since my last visit. Sparse, tiny, and clean, it reminded me of the middies' wardroom I'd once occupied on *Hibernia*, though it was far larger.

He said, "The bedroom's in there, sir. I'll take the couch."

How could I have not realized he'd have but one bedroom? "I prefer the couch." My tone was gruff.

"You can't!" He was scandalized.

"I won't take your bed, Alexi." Rank or no rank, I wouldn't put him out of his home.

"Please, sir." He patted the couch. "It's comfortable; I'll be fine. Anyway"—he rushed on before I could object—"I won't sleep at all if you're bunked here while I've got the only bed. Please."

Grumbling, I let him persuade me, wondering if his respect was for my rank or for myself. Then I marveled at my foolishness. I was Captain, and he was but lieutenant; what else could he do?

In the morning Alexi dropped me off at the spaceport and I handed the agent a voucher for the early shuttle. Two hours later I was back on *Hibernia*. I debated whether to check the bridge.

By naval regs, all crew members were entitled to thirty days long-leave after a ten-month cruise or longer, and during that leave only a nominal, rotating watch was kept, in which no one was made to spend more than four days aboard.

Nonetheless, my footsteps carried me along the Level 1 circumference corridor, past my cabin to the bridge beyond. The hatch was open; normally, under weigh, it would have been sealed. Lieutenant Connor, in the watch officer's chair, was leaning back, boots on the console. Her eyes widened in alarm as I strode in. She scrambled to her feet.

"As you were, Ms. Connor." Had I found her lollygagging on watch while under weigh I'd have been outraged. Moored, it didn't matter.

I glanced at the darkened simulscreens on the curved front bulkhead. Normally, they provided a breathtaking view from the nose of the ship. And under our puter Darla's control, they could simulate any conditions known. My black leather armchair was bolted behind the left console, at the center of the compartment. Lieutenant Connor, of course, was in her own seat. No one dared sit in the Captain's place.

"All quiet, Ms. Connor?"

"Yes, sir. The remaining passengers went down on last night's shuttle, except for Miss Wells."

There was nothing I need do. "I'll be in my cabin."

"Yes, sir. Miss Wells, ah, seems to miss the other passengers, sir." She looked away quickly, as if she'd gone too far in speaking of my personal affairs. She had, but I let it pass.

As I slapped open my cabin hatch a lithe form flew at me, knocking my breath away. I hugged Annie with heartfelt warmth, grinning until I realized she was sobbing softly into my shoulder. "What's wrong, hon?"

Annie clung. "All'em gone. Dey be downdere, all'em joeys. No one up here 'cept me." Only under stress did her hard-won grammar and diction lapse into her former trannie dialect.

I squeezed her tighter. She'd known that all the transpops awaiting transshipment to Detour would be leaving, including herself, and had chosen to stay with me a few extra days. I thought better of reminding her. "Sorry I couldn't get back last night, hon."

She sighed, disengaging herself from my damp shoulder. "I unner—understand," she said carefully. "Did yo' Admiral say where they sending you next?"

"No." I hung my jacket in the bulkhead closet. A third of the entire Naval fleet was now protecting Hope Nation system. There was little chance *Hibernia* would be the next ship to Detour colony.

Annie and I would have to part, and we both knew it. The only way we could stay together was to marry, if she'd have me, and that would almost certainly cost me my career. Admiralty was notoriously conservative; my disregard for regulations and my youth already worked against me. Were I to marry a former transpop—one of the ignorant and despised hordes who roamed most of Earth's sprawling cities—I'd be blackballed. Though I'd never be told the reason, I'd be unlikely to see command again.

"I met Alexi," I said. Both he and Annie had shipped on *Portia*, but she'd known him then only as a distant, handsome young figure occasionally glimpsed in the corridors of Level 1.

"Nicky, I been thinking." As she calmed, her diction returned, and despite myself, I smiled. "This staying on ship, it be no good," she said. "I ain—I'm not ever going to see Hope Nation again, and you need time on real land. Would you show me dis place?"

"It's full of memories." My tone was gentle. How could I take her where I'd gone with Amanda? The comparison could only be cruel.

"I wantin'—I want to know your memories." I frowned and she rushed on, "Nicky, yo' wife is dead. She ain' never coming back. You got to live. I won' be 'round, but you got to go on."

That she was right didn't make it easier, but I owed much to her. "If that's what you'd like," I said. "We'll rent a room groundside and I'll show you the sights." The Venturas, perhaps; the breathtaking mountains of Western Continent, where Amanda and Derek and I—no, this would be a different trip.

We could visit the plantations. Emmett Branstead, a passenger I'd impressed into the Service on *Challenger*, had returned to Hope Nation while I was recuperating at Lunapolis from my injuries. Despite his condescending and irritable manner before enlisting, Emmett had proven a loyal and conscientious sailor once he'd taken the oath. He'd left word at Admiralty House that I was invited to his family's plantation whenever I could come.

His invitation rather surprised me; I'd have thought he'd be anxious to put his involuntary servitude behind him. I'd met his brother Harmon, three years before, on my long-leave with Derek Carr.

I put aside the throb of memories. "When would you like to go?"

"Today?"

I groaned; my chest still hurt from the morning's liftoff. Still, diving into Hope Nation's gravity well wouldn't be half as bad as clawing out of it. "Very well." I reached for the caller, set it down again. "No, let's walk to Dispatch; I'll show you Orbit Station."

"I don' want to go to dat place."

"The Station is just like a ship, only bigger."

"There ain't no air around it. I don' like it." Groundsiders.

"It's as safe as *Hibernia*, and I'll be with you. Come, I'll show you around." Protesting, she let me take her through the locks.

Imagine an old-fashioned pencil stood on end, with two or three half-inch-thick disks slid halfway down and pressed together. That's a rough model of an interstellar ship. Forward of the disks is the hold, in which cargoes for our settlements are crammed, along with the supplies consumed during the ship's long voyage.

The passengers and crew live and work on the disks. Each disk is a Level, girdled by a circumference corridor, connected to the other disks by east and west ladders. The bridge is always on Level 1. Hydroponics and recycling are below. Aft of the disks sits the engine room, whose great Fusion motors terminate at the drive shaft comprising the stern of the ship.

Orbit Station was like a stack of these disks, only without the pencil. And more and larger disks. The Station had five levels, enough to get lost in, which to my embarrassment I soon did.

"You ain' no better than a groundsider," Annie scoffed when we passed the commissary again. "Jus' ask someone."

"Dispatching should be down this corridor."

"It wasn't the last time."

She could be maddening. "Come on." We passed a sign pointing to Naval HQ but I ignored it; though they could arrange shuttle seats for us, I could have done as much from the caller in my cabin. My goal was to find Dispatching, somewhere on Level 4.

Annie seemed as relieved as I when we finally arrived at the dispatcher's office. A shuttle was leaving in two hours; time enough for us to pack. I let the dispatcher provide us detailed instructions back to *Hibernia*'s bay.

I came on a young officer lounging in the entryway of Naval HQ, and I stopped. "Excuse me, Lieutenant, are you assigned here?"

He stiffened. "Yes, sir."

"Do you know Mr. Holser?"

"Holser? Oh, yes, Vax. The big joey." He grinned. "He's posted to tactics. I believe he's at Admiralty House this rotation, sir."

"Please check."

A few moments later the man returned, another lieutenant a few steps behind. "As I thought, sir. He'll be groundside another week."

"Very well. Thank you."

"Uh, Captain Seafort?" The lanky officer who'd followed. I returned the lieutenant's salute. "Yes?"

"I thought it was you, sir, from the holozine pics. Second Lieutenant Jeffrey Kahn."

"What do you want?" My voice was sharper than I'd intended.

"I—nothing, sir, except to speak with you. I wondered if—what it was like to see the aliens, sir. For the first time." Those damned holozines. Just as the notoriety of my discovering the aliens had begun to fade, my return with *Challenger* had fanned the flames.

Annie gasped, wrenching her hand free. My face was hot, my scar throbbed. "Where are you assigned, sir?"

"I was on *Valencia*, sir. Sorry if I—"

"If you were under my command you'd be sorrier, Lieutenant. Dismissed!"

"Aye aye, sir. I apologize."

I stalked down the corridor, pulling Annie with me until she protested. "Nicky, you hurtin' me."

I let go of her arm. "The damn—blessed insolence! Interrupting a Captain!" She scurried to keep up. "Just so he could say he'd met me!"

Annie spoke with dignified care. "There no harm being famous. You're lucky."

"*Is* no harm," I corrected, my pace slowing. During our year on *Hibernia* I'd labored, at Annie's request, to teach her Uppie speech and civilized ways. She approached the English language as the study of a foreign tongue, which in a way for her it was.

"Anyway, that's not the point," I said. "If one of my lieutenants felt free to annoy a Captain I'd—"

I'd what? I didn't know. I recalled Alexi offering me the use of his apartment, though it was a blatant breach of protocol. But we were friends, weren't we? Shipmates.

No, that shouldn't matter. I sighed. Perhaps I'd been a touch hard on Mr. Kahn.

I browsed through listings in a spaceport caller booth and arranged apartment showings. The furnished flats were expensive, especially on a lease of weeks, but on a ship in Fusion my pay gathered unspent, so I could afford it. As it happened, the second apartment we saw was but two blocks from Alexi's and for some reason I liked it enough to take it without looking further.

We unpacked our few belongings and sauntered around our block. Annie devoured the texture of Hope Nation with eager eyes. I promised her a tour of downtown, we bought a few groceries for the micro, and sun still setting, we went home to bed. As we snuggled under the covers she made it clear that I'd get little sleep that night.

In the morning, surprisingly rested, I strolled downtown with Annie, pointing out buildings I knew. We passed Circuit Court, where years before I'd confronted Judge Chesley in defense of my authority to enlist cadets. Near downtown, several blocks had been set aside for an open park; we wandered amid its greenery.

She caught her breath. "What's that, Nicky?" A Gothic spire lanced upward through the genera trees ahead.

"The Cathedral, hon."

"It's beautiful."

So it was. On my previous landfall, I'd visited Reunification Cathedral, to pray that the burden of command be lifted. "Shall we go in?" I took her hand.

The Cathedral's spires soared from thick buttresses of cut stone, each testifying to the dedication and fervor in which the Cathedral had been born over a century before. When Hope Nation was founded, the Reunification Church had already become our official state religion. Though we tolerated splinter sects, our U.N. Government was founded in the authority of the One True God, and I, as Captain, was his representative aboard ship.

Annie and I knelt before the altar. I gave silent prayer, sad at the knowledge that it must go unheard.

Annie waited behind me, in a pew. When I stood she whispered, "Look up."

I gazed upward at the ornate gilt-edged craftsmanship of the buttresses. "Yes. Beautiful." I squeezed her hand.

"Place is so strong. I feel . . . safe. Don't wanna go."

Yes, she'd feel secure in Lord God's house, if anywhere. I stopped myself from saying it aloud. "Detour has its own churches, hon." But none as beautiful as this. Detour was too young, too raw.

"Let me stay here awhile." She ran her finger along the sturdy, burnished wood of the pew.

"All right." I sat, took a missal, idly thumbed through it. Annie wandered.

"Sir? Is that you?" A plump youngish man.

I peered. "Mr. Forbee!" An old acquaintance. We shook hands. "I'd have thought they'd let you retire again."

Three years ago, when I first arrived with *Hibernia*, Forbee was floundering as Commandant of the tiny Naval station, eager to be relieved. "I suppose I could if I wanted to," he said. His eye flicked to my scar, and away. "But with the invasion, and all . . . as long as there are senior officers so I'm not left in charge again . . ."

"Of course."

He paused. "I'm with the tactical group now. Enjoy the work."

"Isn't that where Vax Holser's posted?"

"Yes, sir. He's at Admiralty House this rotation." For a moment his eyes clouded. "What are your plans, sir?"

"Miss Wells and I are taking in the sights." I beckoned to Annie, introduced her. "We're lunching with Lieutenant Tamarov, then I'll stop at Admiralty House."

He hesitated. "Sir, about Vax . . ."

"Is he well?"

"Oh, yes, fine. Couldn't be better."

I said, "He's a good man, very good, but I'll admit he takes some getting used to." I glanced at my watch and stood. "Annie, we'd better get going; Alexi's waiting. Nice to see you again, Mr. Forbee." I extended my hand.

We met Alexi at a restaurant I recalled from my previous visit, and afterward he drove us back to our apartment. At Annie's urging I accompanied Alexi back to Admiralty House; she wanted our dinner to be her own accomplishment. I went eagerly.

Alexi said little during the short drive, as if preoccupied. After he parked, we climbed the steps to the double doors, past the winged-anchor Naval emblem and the "Admiralty House" brass plaque I'd known from my first cruise.

The lanky duty lieutenant stood from his console to salute. "You're here for Admiral De Marnay?"

"No, Vax Holser."

"He's upstairs in the tactics office, sir. Shall I call him down?"

I grinned. "I'll run up. We're shipmates."

Alexi followed me up the ladder. "Sir, I think I should tell you—"

"Later, Alexi. Let me say hello to Vax."

"But—"

"Vax? Are you there?"

"STAND TO!" Vax Holser's bellow made me flinch. The roomful of lieutenants and midshipmen snapped to attention.

Eyes locked front, the brawny lieutenant stood ramrod stiff.

"As you were." I hurried forward, my hand out. "Vax, how are you? Good to—" I stumbled to a halt.

Vax Holser, his face an icy mask, had swung into the at-ease position, hands clasped behind him. His eyes were riveted on the bulkhead past my shoulder. He pointedly ignored my hand.

I gaped. "What's wrong?"

"Nothing, sir." His gaze remained fixed on the wall. He said no more.

"I'm so glad to see you, Vax!"

"Thank you, Captain." His voice was remote.

Alexi cleared his throat. "Mr. Holser, Captain Seafort's been through hell. He came to see you as soon as he—"

"Be silent, Mr. Tamarov," I snarled. I wouldn't have Alexi beg on my behalf. "Leave at once!"

"Aye aye, sir." Alexi wouldn't argue with a direct order, even if I wasn't his commanding officer.

I approached my former first lieutenant with trepidation. "Are you speaking to me, Vax?"

Vax Holser said slowly and distinctly, "Yes, sir. We're on duty."

His reply told me what I needed to know. I turned on my heel and left.

Alexi waited below in the anteroom. "I tried to warn you, sir, before—"

"Why?" I demanded. "What's he so angry about?"

"When you were to be left behind on *Challenger*, you wouldn't let him relieve Tremaine or transfer to join you."

I was stunned. "He won't forgive my saving him from harm?"

"No, sir."

Numbly I went out into the heat of the day.

We paused on the steps. "I tried talking to him," Alexi offered. "He wouldn't listen. He said you had no right to refuse our help, to face that nightmare alone."

"Lord God damn it!"

Alexi drew back, shocked, knowing it was blasphemy. For the moment I didn't care. I hated the Navy that had cost me my wife, my son, my friends.

"So, you young whelp, I suppose you're smirking over your revenge."

I spun. Admiral Tremaine glared from the foot of the steps.

Alexi echoed, "Revenge?"

"Thanks to him I've been relieved, as I'm sure you know." Tremaine's expression was sour. "Despite your sniveling, Seafort, you made it home and back again. So your whining about *Challenger* was for nothing."

I was in a foul temper. "Admiral Geoffrey Tremaine, you are on inactive duty; before witness I do call challenge on you to defend your honor!"

The Admiral's eyes narrowed. "You'd go through with it, then? Very well. You're aware the choice of weapons is mine?"

"Of course." I'd practiced with the dueling pistols Admiral Brentley had given me, but not nearly enough.

"Very well, then. If you find someone to act as your second, have him call on me to arrange the details. I'll be at—"

"With your permission, sir, I will be your second."

"Thank you, Alexi." I saluted the Admiral. "Please make your arrangements, gentlemen." I stalked off.

They had tried to stop me. Annie begged, and when that failed, used all her wiles to divert me. "But what good it do, you be killed? Dey bury you here, and dat Admiral goin' home free?"

I made my voice gentle, for her sake. "Hon, I have to."

"But why? You know he shoot better than you!" Antique powder weapons were the Admiral's particular hobby.

She couldn't understand, of course. In some things, the striving is important, not the achieving. And I'd sworn my vengeance to Lord God. Though I'd already forsworn myself in other things, my misery made me anxious not to do it again.

Four days after my challenge, we met on a grassy meadow outside the town, Alexi stiff and formal at my side, a staff lieutenant an unhappy second to the Admiral. Other officers waited in hushed groups a distance away; news of our duel had spread.

I hadn't allowed Annie to attend.

While our seconds conducted the preliminary ritual I stood sweating in dress whites, conscious of every quivering leaf of the great genera tree in whose shadow we stood, aware of every tremulous beat of my heart.

I hadn't prayed Lord God's help; my soul was forfeit and my prayers must go unanswered. I was afraid, though. Not of death, but of what was to come afterward.

I had much to account for.

The Admiral's second stepped forward. "Gentlemen, I appeal to you to forsake your quarrel and declare that honor is satisfied, that this matter may be put to rest."

Admiral Tremaine's smile was almost a sneer. "You will recall that Mr. Seafort initiated this quarrel. I do but respond." At his lieutenant's frown he added, as if reluctant,

"However, I declare that honor is satisfied, if the Captain is so minded."

The Admiral's second turned to me. "Captain Seafort?"

The sun beat down on the stillness of the meadow. Alexi, young and handsome, spoke softly. "What shall you do, sir?" I hesitated. He blurted, "Sir, he's ordered home for trial. You told me how Admiral Brentley spoke of him. He's finished."

I felt my legs tremble and spoke loudly as if to stop him from noticing. "You care that much if I live?"

Alexi looked down, but with an effort returned his gaze to mine. "Very much, sir."

My legs steadied. Alexi cared, as did Annie. If they truly understood me they wouldn't have such feelings, but I was glad nonetheless. As Alexi said, Tremaine was done for. Honor didn't require me to sacrifice my life to accomplish what the law itself would achieve.

Admiral De Marnay would also be pleased if I called it off. A day before, he had summoned me to his office to demand that I withdraw my challenge.

"Is that an order, sir?"

He waved it away. "You know perfectly well I can't give such an order. You're on leave and he's inactive." His fingers drummed the console at his mahogany desk.

"Then, sir, I—"

"There's no point to fighting him, Seafort. You're needed on *Hibernia*."

"Yes, sir. On the other hand, I gave my oath."

"That bloody dueling code should be amended. A Captain fighting an Admiral . . . it looks bad." He glanced at me, said quickly, "Oh, I know in your case it has nothing to do with promotion or advancement. But people won't understand."

"Captain Von Walther fought a duel with Governor Ibn Saud, sir." Generations ago, but Captain Von Walther was the idol of every officer in the Navy. I'd once stood in his very footsteps.

"The Governor wasn't his superior officer. And you're not Von Walther." His tone was acid.

"No, sir." It was presumptuous to compare myself to the legendary Hugo Von Walther, who'd discovered the derelict *Celestina*, become Admiral of the Fleet, and twice been elected Secretary-General. "Still, there's the matter of my oath."

"I could put you back on active duty." It would effectively bar me from a duel.

"Yes, sir. But I'm entitled to long-leave."

De Marnay's stare was cold. "I know that. But Tremaine isn't. I can recall him."

I swallowed, glad of the reprieve. "If that's what you wish, sir."

His fingers drummed. "No, I won't, even to save you. I wasn't free to beach him myself, but now that he's recalled, I'll let it stand. I still want you to withdraw your challenge."

"Yes, sir, I understand."

His tone softened. "Seafort, you've been through a lot. You're coiled tight as a spring. If you were thinking clearly, you'd find a way to let this go."

"I understand, sir," I repeated. By giving no more, it was a refusal.

"Very well." He studied me. "That's all." As I left, I could feel his eyes pierce my back.

"Sir?"

I blinked, back on the dueling field. Alexi awaited my answer.

Again I swallowed. For Annie, and for Alexi. For Admiral De Marnay. "Tell him—tell him I agree—"

Father's stern voice, as I sat over my lessons at the creaky kitchen table. "Your oath is your bond, Nicholas. Without it, you are nothing." Yes, Father. But I am already damned. For some sins, there can be no forgiveness.

Father faded to distant disapproval.

The young voice had a catch in it. "I'm glad to have served with you, sir. Godspeed."

Blanching, I whirled. "What did you say?"

Alexi stepped back. "Nothing, sir. I didn't speak."

"Not you. Philip Ty—" I snapped my mouth shut. Was I out of my mind? Philip Tyre was dead, thanks to the cruelty of the man I faced. A troubled boy who'd striven to do his duty.

I spoke to the Admiral's second. "Sir, tell your principal that upon his humble apology to the memory of Lieutenant

Philip Tyre and the passengers and crew of *Challenger*, I will consider my oath fulfilled. And on no other terms."

Tremaine didn't wait for his lieutenant to repeat my speech. "Get on with it, then."

I picked up the round-barreled pistol, its grip vaguely familiar in my hand. Admiral Brentley's parting gift. I turned to Alexi. "Thank you for your assistance, sir. I'm most grateful to you."

Alexi's formality matched my own. "And I to you, sir." He saluted.

We paced and turned. I saw the savage glint in Admiral Tremaine's eye as we raised to fire.

2

"Honor is satisfied. For God's sake, get them to a doctor!"

"The Captain, yes." The lieutenant looked up from Tremaine's inert body. "It's too late for the Admiral."

I stood swaying, glad of the shade of the red maple. My chest was numb. I put my hand to my side. It came away wet.

"It'll be too late for Captain Seafort as well, unless you hurry." One of De Marnay's staff; I didn't remember his name.

"I'll help you into the heli, sir," said a solicitous voice.

"I'm all right, Alexi."

"You aren't, sir. Let me help you."

Numb, I let Alexi lead me to the waiting heli. Bending to get in jarred something in me; a wave of pain carried me off to a far place. I coughed and it blossomed to fiery agony.

"Christ, get moving!" someone shouted.

I thought to rebuke the blasphemy, but choked and couldn't find my breath. I spat salty red liquid. The whap of the heli blades merged with my ragged breath in a red crescendo that slowly faded to blessed black silence.

The bridge was white, too white. "Have we Defused? Plot a course to Orbit Station."

"It's all right, sir."

The middy knew he was required to say, "Aye aye, sir." It was the only permissible response to his Captain. Well, he'd learn after a caning; the barrel was a quick teacher.

But weren't we still Fused? "I didn't order a Defuse!" It emerged a feeble whisper instead of the bark I'd intended. And what was draped over me? A tent?

"We're groundside, sir. You're in hospital."

Why was Alexi here? He'd gone on to Hope Nation with Admiral Tremaine.

"When did we dock?" I whispered, groggy. "We just Defused for nav check."

"That was weeks ago, sir."

God, how my chest hurt. I slept.

Shadowy figures kept me company. Walter Dakko, master-at-arms on *Challenger* and on *Hibernia*. Eddie Boss, the transpop who'd responded to my call for enlistment. Annie Wells, her face worried. Even Philip Tyre came to sit with me for a while, before I recalled that he was dead.

I drifted in and out of consciousness as the sedation eased. Doctors and nurses loomed, disappeared, reappeared. The fires of hell burned.

"The infection's spread," someone said crisply. "Yank the lung, replace it, and be done with it." Two doctors conferred as I gazed passively through the vapormask.

A medipulse pressed against my arm. Solicitous aides lifted me from my bed to a gurney. The ceiling slid smoothly past, and I struggled to stay awake. I failed.

The officer across the desk quickly looked away from my face, but I was used to that by now. "Do you know where you are?"

The tube had been in my throat too long; it still hurt when I spoke. "Centraltown General Hospital." I read the nameplate on his desk. "And you're the psych officer, Dr., uh, Tendres." I coughed, flinching as a lance of pain stabbed.

He smiled briefly. "This interview is to see how you're orienting yourself. Your name."

"Nicholas Ewing Seafort, Captain, U.N.N.S. I'm twenty-three. Six years seniority."

"What else do you remember, before your recent cruise?"

I said grimly, "I sailed on *Portia*, part of Admiral Tremaine's relief squadron to Hope Nation. My baby son died in an alien attack and my wife Amanda followed soon after." Then we'd encountered the Admiral's flagship, disabled by the fish. "Tremaine off-loaded the elderly passengers and the young transpops. I swore I would call challenge on him. You know the rest."

"Tell me."

My throat was sore and I wanted to get it over with. "The fish attacked again." My tone was dull. "Our remaining lasers were knocked out. I used the last of our propellant to ram the biggest fish just as it tried to Fuse. We were Fused with it, and starved for several weeks in a derelict ship. The fish Defused outside Jupiter's orbit." But before the stricken fish had brought us home, I'd broken my solemn oath.

"Your memory seems intact, Seafort. You know how long you've been here?"

"Three weeks, they tell me." Enough for *Hibernia* to sail without me. I'd lost her, and what little home I had.

"Much of the time you were delirious or under sedation."

"They gave me a new lung."

"Which your body is accepting well, so far. You're loaded with antirejection drugs, of course. You're familiar with anti-rejection therapy?"

I nodded. "The time-release meds last a month or so. The second treatment will pretty well cut out any chance of rejection."

"That's right. Routine replacement, a lung."

I fingered the skintape covering my healing incision, wondering when I'd be released. And more important, when I'd be fit for active duty. Before I could get a ship, I would need clearance from the man I confronted.

As if reading my thoughts Dr. Tendres said, "You've faced a lot for a joey your age, Seafort."

I didn't reply.

He read from my chart in his holovid. "You still have the nightmares?"

"Which ones?" I asked despite myself. Well, my medical records would indicate the recurrent dream I'd had for years. Father and I were walking from the train station to Academy, where I was to begin my first term; I'd never left Cardiff before, except for day trips. When we arrived, Father turned my shoulders and pushed me toward the gates. Inside, I turned to wave good-bye, but he strode away without looking back. I was thirteen.

It was as it had happened. It was Father's way.

Perhaps my records also mentioned the dream in which

Tuak and Rogoff, men I'd hanged for mutiny, shambled into my cabin, dead.

I doubted he knew about the others.

He raised his eyebrow. "Tell me your nightmares."

"I dream sometimes," I said uneasily. "I'm all right."

"You've seen a lot of death." His flat statement gave me no clue to read his thoughts.

"Yes." I'd caused a lot of death.

He suddenly asked, "How do you feel about what you've done?"

"The killing?"

"Everything."

I hesitated a long moment. "I betrayed my oath, you know."

"That bothers you."

"Bothers me?" I half rose from my wheelchair, subsided when the pain stabbed. The man must be a freethinker. How else could he not understand my desolation?

"Your oath is what you are," Father had taught me. It was my covenant with Lord God Himself. I'd deliberately broken my sworn pledge. In doing so, I'd damned my soul to everlasting hell; no act of contrition or penance could save me. Now the thread of my life was all that stood between me and the eternal torment of Lord God's displeasure.

Yes, it bothered me.

And even if I should somehow be granted the miracle of Lord God's forgiveness, I must live with the knowledge that I was a man without honor, a man whose word could never be trusted, a man of expediency.

I waved my hand irritably. "I've learned to live with it," I said. Surely he must understand. If not, there was no point in laboring to explain.

"Lookidaman be sleepindere!"

The familiar voice recalled me from my doze. "Hi, Annie," I said. Automatically I added, "Don't talk that way," though I knew she did so only to tease me.

"Feeling better today?" She was beautiful in a new sky-blue jumpsuit, perhaps one size snugger than absolutely necessary. Annie had adapted with enthusiasm to the latest fashions and hairstyles.

"Yes, hon," I said dutifully. I felt a pang of regret that she would soon be gone to Detour.

"Good." I was rewarded by a chaste kiss on the forehead. Annie was restraining herself, lest undue excitement cause me breathing problems. She curled into the chair alongside the bed. "I been shopping."

"Oh?" My throat hurt hardly at all today.

"Mira!" She emptied the shopping bag on my stomach. Frilly garments tumbled out. Gauzy, gossamer, weightless ones. Chemiwear. The material responded to changes in skin chemistry. Certain changes caused them to become translucent.

"I don't wear silk underwear," I said, pretending crossness, which had the effect I intended.

"I c'n see you on your bridge in these, sure," she snorted.

I raised myself carefully, aching; this morning they'd made me promenade the corridors for an hour. I took Annie's hand in mine and lay back, wondering if my revenge against Tremaine was worth the cost: my health, my ship, Admiral De Marnay's goodwill.

Ashamed, I recalled the misery my crew and passengers had endured after our abandonment. I thought of Philip Tyre, sailing bravely to his death aboard *Challenger*'s fragile launch. Yes, it was worth it.

My reverie was interrupted by Annie's soft voice. "Where are you, Nicky?"

I smiled. "Just dreaming, hon. Nothing important."

I glowered at the young lieutenant until I was rewarded by a look of nervous anxiety. I turned away; it wasn't his fault. I swung my legs out of bed. Annie, sitting quietly in the corner, shot me a worried glance.

"Very well," I growled. "Where do they want me to stay?"

"Shoreside, in the Centraltown area, sir. That's all Admiral De Marnay said."

I glowered at the orders in the holovid before snapping it off. "Inactive duty until certified as fully recovered . . ." Well, that was fair; it had been my own doing. If I hadn't chosen revenge, I wouldn't have spent weeks in a hospital trying to avoid a cough that might dislodge my lung.

I didn't like at all the phrase that followed. ". . . from disabling physical injury and continuing emotional stress." The orders were signed by Georges De Marnay himself.

"Very well, Lieutenant. Thank you." The young officer saluted and left with obvious relief.

I'd killed De Marnay's fellow Admiral; was that why he was beaching me? He had a reputation as a fair man, but . . .

No, my careless answers to Dr. Tendres's probing questions had caused my grounding. I should have pretended a relaxation I didn't feel, and denied my nightmares.

Still, I'd come this far without having lied to a superior officer. I had little else to be proud of; I would keep that shred of honor, even if it cost me my posting.

I smiled at Annie. "They gave us more time together, hon. Would you like that?"

Her grin of delight was answer enough. I wondered when she'd be called for Detour. By unspoken agreement we never mentioned our parting.

The door swung open. "Why all the smiles, sir? Oh, good afternoon, Miss Wells."

"We have a vacation, Alexi." I reached for my shirt.

"For how long, sir?"

"Awhile." I dressed myself slowly. "Until they say I'm recovered. I'll need a place to stay. At least they haven't taken my pay billet; could you two find me a home?" Annie had closed our apartment when it was clear I'd be a long while in hospital.

"Of course, sir," Alexi said automatically. "We'll look this afternoon, if Miss Wells is ready."

"You knowin' my name be Annie," she said disdainfully. "All that Miss Wells goofjuice be for records an' all." She tossed her sweater over her shoulder. "I be ready now, Mist' Tamarov." At the door she turned regally. "Good afternoon, Nick." Now her diction was flawless. "I'll be back to see you after dinner." With a scornful toss of her head she was gone.

Alexi, at the doorway, shrugged ruefully. "Sorry, sir." He followed. Alone, I wondered what strings Alexi had pulled to be assigned as my aide during my recovery. Well, it was a soft shoreside billet . . .

On the other hand, perhaps he hadn't even volunteered. After all, why would he want to be posted with me?

"Do you know how many capital ships we have in system? Thirty-eight! And we've seen not a single fish." Captain Derghinski stared morosely into the setting sun.

I turned away, my hand tightening on the rough-sawn balcony railing. But for my self-indulgence in challenging Tremaine, I would have a vessel of my own. Absently I fingered the scar on my cheek.

"Is that bad?" Annie asked.

His visage softened. "I realize you've met the aliens, ma'am, and it wasn't pleasant. But we can't beach the fleet in Hope Nation forever, waiting for fish."

I sipped at a cold drink, feeling the welcome sting of the alcohol. Being grounded had advantages; alcohol, like most drugs, was contraband aboard ship.

"I'm surprised at how much of the fleet Admiralty committed here," I admitted. In addition to Tremaine's squadron, two others had arrived while I was in hospital. They provided Admiral De Marnay with more firepower than had been massed anywhere for many decades.

Derghinski nodded. "Eventually we'll have to go home. What if the fish show up near Terra or the Lunar bases? And while we've diverted squadrons to Hope Nation, our interstellar commerce has gone to hell." Naval vessels carried most of our cargo and all passenger traffic between the stars. Schedules had been sparse enough before the alien invasion. Now, they were almost nonexistent.

That was one reason Annie was still with me. In the past, the lone supply ship that visited Hope Nation would have continued to Detour, taking her to her new home.

The apartment Alexi and Annie had found was in a row of connected town houses on the outskirts of Centraltown. From our balcony I could just glimpse Farreach Ocean in the distance. It wasn't far from where my wife Amanda had once roomed, in another time, another life.

"A fine party, Mr. Seafort."

I smiled back at Captain De Vroux. "Thank you, ma'am."

To my surprise, my home was becoming a shoreside refuge for off-duty officers. The constant replenishment of drinks and food ate into my savings, but I didn't mind. At least it helped keep me informed. The lieutenants and Captains, for their part, liked to unwind without guarding their speech as they'd have to among civilians. They probably enjoyed Annie's good looks and careless charm as well.

I breathed deep, glad to be free of pain at last. I turned back to Captain Derghinski. "We can't hit them until we find them," I said. "So far we've never found a fish . . . they've always found us."

A confident young lieutenant from *Resolute* spoke up. "Well, sir, if your theory is right that the fish hear us Fuse, they should be swarming over us by now. All our ships dropping into normal space as they arrive . . ."

"It was only a suggestion," I muttered. "And anyway— what's your name, again?"

"Ter Horst, Ravan G., Lieutenant, sir," the young man said cautiously. I could understand his anxiety. Though I'd never been a lieutenant I remembered the awe that a Captain—any Captain—inspired in me as a midshipman. For all this fellow knew, I consorted with Admirals, if not Lord God Himself, and a word from me could do him inestimable harm.

"Well, Mr. Ter Horst, we have no idea how long it takes the fish to respond once they hear us. Or even where they come from." I shivered despite the afternoon warmth. "They might be on their way even now."

"Yes, sir."

"You needn't be afraid of me," I snapped. "I don't bite, at least off duty."

He attempted a grin. "Sorry, sir. Anyway, we're ready for them this time. Thirty-eight ships, all armed to the teeth with laser cannon. I'd like to see the fish that can run that blockade."

"Not a blockade, Ter Horst." Captain Derghinski was gruff. "We're scattered all over the system; we have to protect miners' ships and local commercial craft as well, you know. And ten of our ships are posted near Orbit Station; we can't afford to lose the Station under any circumstances."

No, we certainly couldn't. Our huge interstellar vessels, assembled in space, couldn't heave themselves out of a planet's gravity well. The ships were floating cities and warehouses that carried passengers, crew, and cargo across the immense reaches of interstellar space, on voyages that took months or years to complete. Hope Nation's cargo and passengers were off-loaded at the huge, bustling Orbit Station, where they transferred to shuttles for reshipment groundside.

If Orbit Station and its shuttles were destroyed, only the starships' frail launches would serve as lifelines to the colony. Hope Nation's trade would be crippled.

"Still, sir," said the lieutenant, "we've got more than enough force to handle any imaginable attack."

"I hope so," I said. Though I wished I were aloft, part of me silently thanked Lord God I was ashore; the thought of the fish appearing to hurl their acid globs at my ship sent chills down my spine. I turned away, ashamed of my cowardice.

Captain Derghinski stared bleakly at the lieutenant. "U.N.S. *Resolute*, hmm? I don't remember that she encountered any fish on the way out."

"No, sir," Ter Horst agreed.

"I remind you, sir, that you speak to Captain Nicholas Seafort of *Hibernia*, *Portia*, and *Challenger*. He discovered the aliens and fought them three times. He hardly requires your advice."

Lieutenant Ter Horst wilted under Derghinski's rebuke. "Please forgive me, Captain Seafort," he said quickly. "I spoke without thinking."

I tried not to show annoyance at Captain Derghinski; after all, he was my guest and my senior as well. "No matter, Lieutenant. I'm glad you're eager to do battle for us." I turned to Derghinski as Ter Horst gratefully made his escape. "Thanks for your concern, sir. I'm really all right, though."

"Hope so," Derghinski said bluntly as we drifted toward the buffet. "Not according to rumors I've heard."

"Oh?"

He sized me up with a glance. "They say you're at the end of your tether. Not just your wound, but the word is the psych report blew you off the bridge."

"Dinner, Nick. Gentlemen?" Annie's blessed appearance at the door saved me from the need to answer.

"Wouldn't hurt you to get a word in at Admiralty House," Derghinski muttered, as we drifted inside.

No, it wouldn't, if I could get through to Admiral De Marnay. I'd already tried twice for an appointment.

I suppose dinner was delicious. I didn't notice.

I pointed to the prefab going up across the street. "Last time I was here, all that was open land."

Annie shrugged. "It better havin' somethin' on it." I nuzzled her hand as we strolled toward the spaceport, and Admiralty House beyond. She'd survived the streets in Lower New York, where every lot held either a decaying building or rubble; to Annie, open spaces were dangerous jungles to be crossed to the safety of abandoned tenements. She added, "What's so special about a piece of land, anyways?"

In those thickets Alexi Tamarov had hidden two dirty and disheveled cadets, waiting while a loyal sailor lured me to their hideaway, unable to reveal his secret. "Nothing, hon." Once I'd passed Judge Chesley in the street. If he recognized me, he gave no sign. I was content to leave it so. Another voyage, another time.

I would miss Annie, when the transpops were shipped onward. I suspected, though, that the Centraltown authorities would be glad to see the last of them. Freed from shipboard discipline, the rash young streeters had been involved in more than a few incidents. Now, most of them were gathered in a temporary camp on the edge of town.

The iron gate to Admiralty House creaked as I opened it. Two lieutenants on their way out saluted; I returned their salutes automatically, my mind on the interview I sought. I brushed back my hair.

"Yes, sir?" The lieutenant paused at his console.

"I'd like to see Admiral De Marnay."

"Have you an appointment, sir?"

"No." I couldn't get one.

He looked dubious. "I don't know if I can get you in, sir. The Admiral shuttles back and forth to Orbit Station. When he's groundside the quartermasters, supply officers and tacticians line up waiting." His eyes darted to my cheek. "You're Captain Seafort, sir?"

"Yes." My scar was ample identification.

"I'm Lieutenant Eiferts. Glad to meet you. If you'll have a seat I'll pass the word you're here."

"Thank you. Let's sit, Annie." Though I wouldn't admit it, the long hike from Centraltown had winded me. I picked up a holozine and flicked through it.

"Mr. Seafort?" It was Captain Forbee. "Here for a meeting?"

"Not exactly. We—Miss Wells and I—took a long walk today, and I thought perhaps Admiral De Marnay could see me."

"Did Eiferts say you haven't a chance?"

"The Admiral's that busy?"

"Well, I might be able to get you a word with him. Depends on his mood at the moment. Come upstairs." He touched his cap to Annie. "Nice to have met you, Miss, uh, Wells." Was there a second's hesitation before he acknowledged the name? He led me up the red-carpeted stairs and along the paneled hall.

Forbee's office was bigger than the one I remembered from my first visit to Hope Nation. He parked me in a comfortable chair and disappeared.

I was looking for something to read when a head appeared in the doorway. "Excuse me, sir. Midshipman Bezrel. The Admiral will see you now."

"Very well." I followed the very young middy down the hall, through a waiting room filled with officers, some of whom I recognized. I saw speculation in their faces; was I summoned back to active duty? If not, how had I managed to slip past them?

The midshipman knocked and opened the door. He snapped to attention, as did I. "Captain Seafort, sir," he said. His voice hadn't quite settled into the lower registers.

"As you were, Bezrel. That's all." Admiral De Marnay

stood from behind his desk. "Hello, Seafort. Stand easy." He put out his hand.

"Thank you for seeing me, sir."

"You're supposed to make an appointment for this sort of thing," he said irritably.

"Yes, sir. I've tried several times."

"Did it occur to you that I wasn't ready to see you?"

"I hoped it wasn't the case."

"Well, it was." The Admiral's scrutiny was neither friendly nor hostile. "Sit down. What do you want?"

"A ship, sir."

"No."

"Return to active duty, then. In any capacity."

"No."

"May I ask why, sir?"

"No."

"Aye aye, sir." I was finished. I wondered what I was suited for, other than the Navy.

He relented. "You're not recovered from your ordeals, Seafort. You were near death for a long while." That was true. I'd been around death for longer than he knew. Much of it I'd caused by my ineptitude.

"We walked here today, sir. From downtown."

"We?"

"A friend and I, sir."

"Well, that's good. But physical recovery is only the half of it. You're overstressed, Seafort. You've had more tragedies—catastrophes—than most Captains see in their entire career. You're not fit."

I tried to keep my voice calm. "In what way, sir?"

"Emotionally, Seafort. You're a bundle of nerves."

"That's goofjuice," I said, regretting it almost instantly.

He ignored the impertinence. "You're wound so tight you wouldn't even answer the psych officer's questions. What if you cracked under the strain of command? You could lose a ship, or even suicide, as your wife did."

"That's not fair!" I cried. "Amanda was distraught. Her baby—"

"You're distraught too, whether or not you know it."

"No, I'm not! I—"

He came to his feet in one supple motion. "Look at your-self!" he bellowed. "Why do your eyes glisten? Your fists are clenched, did you know that? Do you realize how you've been talking to me?"

I was shocked into silence.

"You've done more than anyone could ask," he said more gently. "You've proven yourself over and over again. I'm not going to let you drive yourself into a hormone-rebalanc-ing ward. You've earned a rest, Seafort. Take it."

I sat in abject misery, not daring to speak further. Finally I whispered, "I can't lie about and do nothing, sir. Please give me a job. Anything."

"If you can get clearance from Dr. Tendres in psych, I'll find you a shoreside billet. Later we'll see about a ship. That's all."

I opened my mouth to protest but realized I would only work against myself. I saluted and slunk out.

It was a long walk back to the apartment; past the space-port, past the prefabs alongside the road, past bars and restaurants, offices and homes. Annie tried to chat at first, but my grim and uncivil replies reduced her to silence.

"I'm sorry," I muttered, pressing my thumb to the door lock. "It's not your fault."

"Damn ri' it ain't," she responded. "So why you acting like it be?"

I smiled despite myself. "Because there's no one else to take it out on."

"He said he'd put you back to work, didn't he?"

"When I get clearance from the psych officer."

"You'll go see him?"

See him, and face his probing questions. I could lie to res-cue my career, or hold to the truth and stay beached. So grounded I would remain. "Sure, hon. I'll call tomorrow."

She busied herself rummaging through the freezer for a dinner we'd like. "Yo' problem is you afraid of seein' him," she announced. "My Nicky, he be'ent—isn't—as brave as we thought." She put the dinners in the micro. "Two minutes on high, then broil for a minute," she told it, then turned to me, wrapping her arms around me as I slumped exhausted in an easy chair.

"I never was brave," I said, pushing away her caress.

She regarded me thoughtfully. "You really be unzark, huh? Do this my way, then."

"Do what?"

"Promise you won't call ol' doctor man for a few days."

"Huh? What are you talking about?"

"That psych man, promise you won't call."

"I've got to—"

She fell into my lap. Her lips pressed against mine, while her hands wandered down to my waist.

"Hey, you have dinner on. Maybe later, after we—"

"Promise."

3

The walk to the hospital was farther than to the spaceport four days earlier, yet I was hardly winded. I squinted in the bright sunlight, forcing my pace to slow. A full hour before my appointment, and I was striding like an anxious middy at Academy. I grinned.

At the hospital I put a zine in the holovid while I waited. Two years old now, the holozine had reached Hope Nation no more than eight months before. Almost too recent for a doctor's waiting room. I flipped through the pages on my screen.

"You're the first article, Mr. Seafort."

Startled, I looked up at the nurse. "I—what?"

"The lead story, right after the ads. See it?"

I flipped to the first few pages. Aghast, I saw my haggard face staring back. "I wasn't looking for—I mean—"

"At first you were in all the zines. The hero of Miningcamp, savior of *Hibernia*, all that. Then it kind of died down." She smiled.

"Yes." I snapped off the holo.

"But they started again when you rescued *Challenger* and fought off all those fish," she said without remorse. "*Holoweek* calls you the Navy's most eligible bachelor, even with that silly scar."

"God in heaven." I stumbled to my feet, dropping the holovid on the coffee table.

"If you're collecting clippings, Mr. Seafort, I'm sure we could help—"

"No!"

"Hello, Seafort, you're looking fit."

I turned to see Dr. Tendres waiting in the doorway. "Thank you, Miss, er, um, Miss. Thank you for asking. Offering." I fled to his office.

"So, then, how do you feel?" His office lights were off. Though the blinds were open, his desk was in shadows.

"Better." I sat in a straight chair in front of the desk, cap on my lap, knees tight.

"Still having the dreams?"

"None lately." For the past few days, at any rate. I'd been too busy at night for dreams.

"What were your nightmares about?"

I recognized his test: a few weeks ago, I'd refused to talk about them. I took a deep breath. "The one about Father bringing me to Academy, you've seen in my record. I also dream about men I've killed—Tuak, Rogoff, and others—coming to take revenge on me. And about how brutal I was to Philip Tyre, a lieutenant I shipped with."

"How do you feel about that?"

"Mr. Tyre? I regret I wasn't kinder. I wish I could apologize to him. The other men?" I considered. "I don't know. I had little choice but to execute them." How glibly the words rolled off my tongue.

"How badly do you want a ship, Nick?"

"Badly." The word slipped out before I could stop it.

"Enough to tell me what I want to hear?"

"What I've said is the truth."

"Yes, but do you feel it true?" He went to the window, clasped his hands behind him. "Tell me how you feel about yourself."

It was my turn to stand. "Sir, must I do this?" I twisted my cap in my hands.

He turned. "You find it painful?"

"Excruciating." I forced myself to meet his eye.

He regarded me. "You may choose whether to answer or not. I only ask that you tell me the truth or nothing."

Slowly I sat. "Very well." It was a moment before I was able to summon the words. "I feel myself a failure, in that I've been unable to carry out my duties without terrible cost to those around me and to myself. I know the Navy doesn't see it that way, sir, but I do."

"What cost?"

"Pain, death, and damnation."

After a long silence I realized he wouldn't speak, and went

on. "I've hurt many people, and caused the death of people I wasn't alert enough to save. And I've dishonored and damned myself."

"Your oath?"

"My oath." I willed my irritation away. If he didn't understand, it was my task to make it clear to him. "I shot a woman whom I'd sworn I wouldn't harm. I gave her my oath so that I could get close enough to shoot her. I knew when I gave my pledge that I intended to break it."

"Your purpose doesn't matter, then?"

"My motive was to save my ship, yes. You people—Admiral Brentley, back home, and others at Admiralty—seem to think my duty to protect *Challenger* was an excuse. I do not." And surely Lord God does not.

"Our Government is founded on the Reunification Church and we all serve the One True God," he said carefully. "But there's more than one interpretation of His will in the matter."

My fury welled forth. "I don't engage in sophistry."

"That's not—"

"Or heresy!"

That silenced him, as well it might.

After a long moment he said coldly, "I won't argue theology with you, Captain Seafort. It is not germane to our purpose."

I scowled back at him, knowing I'd destroyed any chance that he'd give me clearance.

The silence dragged out. At length I said with more calm, "I'm sorry, sir. I know you view my outburst as more evidence that I'm unfit."

"I view it as evidence that you have strong religious convictions." He sat again. "How will your supposed damnation affect the way you function?"

"My soul is forfeit; duty is all I have left." Whatever satisfaction this life gave me would soon be ended; what was to come did not bear thinking about.

"Can you ever be happy?"

I considered it. "I was once. For a brief time."

"When?"

"On *Portia* with my wife and baby son. Before they died."

"And now?"

"Now I have duty. Perhaps with Lord God's grace I will see contentment again, but I doubt that."

"So, again, how do you feel?"

I closed my eyes to seek an honest answer. What I found surprised me. "Not happiness, exactly, but . . . a sort of peace. I know the worst that will happen to me, and all other dangers pale before it. I have a—a companion now, and I enjoy her company."

"Miss, ah, Wells."

"Yes, sir." Just how much I'd enjoyed her company during the past three days, I didn't intend to tell him. Hour upon hour of bedplay, soft caresses interspersed with dizzying bouts of passionate love at odd and frequent intervals . . . Omelettes at the kitchen table, a quick trip to the head, Annie's hand pulling me insistently back to the bed, her lips and hands exploring, her feverish thighs pressing me tightly, until at last I begged her only half in jest to let me die in peace. It just made her smile, and lay her head against my chest, and . . .

I blinked, back again in Dr. Tendres's office. "Sorry, sir. My mind was wandering."

"From the look of it, a pleasant memory."

I smiled. "Yes."

He snapped on his holovid. "Well, whatever the cause, you're more relaxed than when I last saw you." Relaxed? That was one word for it. "I'll recommend limited shoreside duty, Mr. Seafort. Three months, and then we'll see."

"Three months?" Had my honesty cost me this? "I was hoping to be assigned a ship—"

He waved impatiently. "No, Mr. Seafort, you'll get nowhere by pushing me. Three months."

"Liaison, sir?" I repeated. "Surely you can't mean it."

"Why not?" Admiral De Marnay glowered. "The planters respect your accomplishments; you've been here before, you've even visited their plantations."

I stared glumly at the carpet. "I've met some of them, yes, but as for their respecting me—"

"Harmon Branstead, and his brother Emmett from *Chal-*

lenger. They've been singing your praises to the other families. You're well regarded."

I said doggedly, "Whatever talents I have, sir, public relations isn't among them."

"There's not much public relations involved. The planters are agitating for self-government. We want someone to listen sympathetically without committing himself. With a war on, it's important to keep communications open." The Admiral checked his watch. "Anyway, that's your assignment. Feel free to travel."

"Isn't there any other duty, sir, that I could—"

De Marnay roared, "Damn it, Seafort, why won't you let me be diplomatic about finding you makework? You'd stay beached for the rest of the year if I hadn't promised you something!" His fingers drummed his holovid. "You talked Tendres into a clearance, so I'll keep my word, but don't ask for more."

Shocked, I could say nothing.

A knock at the door. The same young middy I'd seen earlier said urgently, "Sir, excuse me, *Resolute* reports ambig-ambiguous contact at edge of radar range. It may be a fish."

"Very well, Bezrel, I'll be right there. Look, Seafort. I have nothing against you." He got to his feet. "You'll get a ship in good time. But first you need rest." He accompanied me to the door, clearly in a hurry. "I've got to run. If that's one of the aliens . . ." As I left he called after me, "Take an aide and a driver to help out."

I spent several days nursing my resentment in the isolation of my apartment; even Annie's wiles couldn't lure me out of my sulk. It was only when Alexi asked permission to put in for a transfer that I was shaken into awareness.

"Apply whenever it suits you," I said, trying to make my voice toneless.

"Yes, sir, thank you." He bit his lip, troubled. "It's just that, now you're recovered and inactive, there's nothing for me to do."

"I know that," I said, relenting. "You know about the glorified vacation they've forced on me. Do you want to be part of it or to go back to ship duty?"

"I want ship duty, of course."

"Very well."

He blushed up to the roots of his hair. "But, ah, I was hop-ing . . ."

"Spit it out."

"Aye aye, sir. I hoped you'd ask me along, when they give you a ship."

"Oh, Alexi." I wandered to the balcony doors. "I'm sorry. Of course I'll have you. Shall we wait it out together?"

He grinned. "Whatever you say, sir."

"Admiralty House is even busier than before since that false alarm with the fish, so we'd better organize our own jaunt. Admiral De Marnay said something about a driver. I don't suppose we really need one."

Alexi said, "Pardon, sir, but the larger your detail, the more you'll impress the planters."

"Um." I thought it over and sighed. "Very well, put in for a driver."

The following morning I was ready to leave. I'd vetoed putting in for a heli; we had little enough to do as it was, and I wanted to keep our mission low-key. An electricar was ample. Alexi loaded our luggage, along with maps, callers, and, just in case, camping gear, while I said my good-byes to Annie. Her idea of farewell was different from mine; as I changed clothes afterward I said, "We'll only be a few days, hon. Sure you can manage without me?"

She rewarded me with an impish grin. "You be surprised how well I can manage without you, Cap'n."

"Belay that," I growled with mock severity, and bestowed a final kiss.

Outside, I hurried to the electricar. "Sorry to keep you waiting. Let's get—" I stumbled to a halt. The driver came to attention, grinning. I managed, "What are *you* doing here?" Eddie Boss, like Annie, had been one of the transpops set adrift in *Challenger*. He'd chosen to enlist, and remained in the Navy after we were rescued.

"I be assigned to drivin' you, sir." The huge petty officer's smile was wider than usual.

"But how—why—"

"Dunno, sir. I was on *Kitty Hawk* and I got orders. Come on down and drive for the Cap'n, they say."

"I put in for him, sir," said Alexi. "As a surprise." He regarded me with misgiving. "Maybe it wasn't a good idea."

"You surprised me, all right." I felt myself smiling. "As you were, sailor." Eddie relaxed. "Do you drive?" I asked. In Lower New York, the only cars seen were gutted hulks.

"*Hibernia*'s joes taught me on long-leave, sir."

I settled into the front seat. "Well, let's see what you learned. Mr. Tamarov, brace yourself." I made a show of gripping the dash.

"Aye aye, sir!" We were off.

I didn't need to study the map; only one road led west out of Centraltown to the plantation zone, and I'd driven it before. Bulldozed through the rich red earth, Plantation Road ran more or less parallel to the seacoast. An hour or so out of town, it narrowed and the smooth pavement gave way to gravel.

"You went this way with Derek Carr?" asked Alexi from the back seat.

"To visit his family holdings. As I remember, we had lunch at Hauler's Rest. The meals are big enough to fill even Mr. Boss." Eddie grinned his gap-toothed smile.

Derek and Alexi had served together as midshipmen on *Hibernia* and were friends. Now Derek was on a run to Detour, eleven weeks away. Even if he returned safely, I might not see him again if I gained a ship first.

After a time Alexi took the wheel. With three drivers we could continue until well after dark. Along the road grew thickets of unfamiliar ropy foliage through which an occasional massive genera tree thrust its mighty snout. On my last trip I'd enjoyed the drive. Today, the woods projected an ominous silence that disturbed me. What was different, other than myself?

By midafternoon we were still long hours from the plantation zone. I took the wheel. As evening fell Minor rose first, followed by Major. I had to concentrate on my driving; their twin shadows made me dizzy. I glanced occasionally at the map to see how far we were from the vast estates that supplied so much of Terra's foodstuffs.

Alexi said, "The Bransteads aren't expecting us until tomorrow, sir. We can stop at any plantation for the night; we'd be welcome in a guest house."

"I know." All plantations offered food and lodging without charge to travelers; it was the local custom and they could well afford it.

We drove another hour before we came on the marker for Mantiet, the first of the many plantations that justified Hope Nation's existence. I slowed, biting my lip. "I hate to ask hospitality at this hour of the night."

"We be campin', then?" asked Eddie.

Alexi snapped, "Speak when you're spoken to."

His manner helped me decide. "Why struggle with a tent when we're tired and irritable? Let's find the guest house."

I turned down the long dirt drive, past fields of corn and wheat radiant in the soft moonlight. Eventually we came to a circular drive that curved around the front lawn of a sprawling mansion.

A dog barked. A light went on; a moment later the door swung open. The man who strode toward us had obviously dressed with hurry. He peered into the car.

"Sorry," I said. "I didn't mean to wake you."

"Then why drive past my home at midnight?"

"I was hoping to find the guest house."

"You don't think it's a bit late to be calling?" Without waiting for an answer he pointed to the drive. "Behind the manse. You're welcome to breakfast in the morning, then be on your way." He turned on his heel and strode to the door.

Alexi called, "This is Cap—"

"Quiet." I slammed the vehicle into gear.

"Cap'n, the house be over—"

"I heard him, Mr. Boss!" The car lurched over the rutted drive toward the main road.

Alexi asked mildly, "I take it we're not staying?"

I growled, "The temperature isn't right."

"Sir?"

"Hell hasn't frozen over." I spun the electricar onto the highway, muttering under my breath. Alexi and Eddie Boss knew me well enough to remain silent.

I drove at a fast clip until my adrenaline faded, leaving me tired and shaky. "Look for a good place to pull over," I said. "We'll camp the night."

A half hour later we were parked alongside the road pulling out our duffels. I'd forgotten just how easy our pair of poly-mil tents were to assemble, or I'd have been less reluctant to use them. After we pounded in the stakes, Alexi, Eddie, and I quickly spread the tough plastic over the poles and staked it. Alexi rummaged in the cooler and came up with softies for all of us; I swigged mine greedily.

Alexi asked, "Shall I bunk with Mr. Boss, sir?"

I hesitated. A lieutenant didn't share quarters with a seaman; it wasn't done. But he wouldn't share quarters with his Captain, either. We should have brought three tents.

I felt a wistful longing for times past. "If you had your choice?"

He shifted uncomfortably. "I—um, as you wish, sir."

I raised my eyebrow, realized he couldn't see the gesture in the dark. "If you'd like to bunk with me, I don't mind." My tone was gruff.

"If you're sure—I mean, thank you, sir." He tossed his duffel into the tent. "Take the other, Mr. Boss."

"Aye aye, sir." Eddie stared up at the unfamiliar constellations. "Never slept in no outside place before."

"Not even in New York?" I asked.

He shrugged. "On roofs, sometimes. But didn't see no stars from there."

"They won't hurt you, Mr. Boss."

"I know." He sounded scornful. I left Eddie contemplating the majesty of the heavens.

Alexi had unrolled our self-inflating mattresses and was getting ready for bed. "Almost like old times, sir," he said softly as I undressed.

How many years had it been since *Hibernia*'s wardroom? "I was thinking the same," I said.

Huddled in our beds we recalled old shipmates: Vax Holser, Derek Carr, and poor Sandy Wilsky, long dead.

"I'll never know how you had the guts to stand up to Vax, sir. He could have broken you in half."

It had been a memorable fight. But it was the Navy way;

wardroom matters were to be settled between the middies. "I had a secret weapon, Alexi."

"What was that, sir?"

"I didn't care."

"I felt that way after Philip Tyre was put in charge."

"I'm sorry. I shouldn't have done that to you."

A long pause. "That's what makes you different, sir. Other Captains would have no regrets."

"It's worse, then. I knew better, but still did wrong."

"He was senior." Alexi turned onto his other side. "After Tremaine off-loaded you and the others onto *Challenger*, it was . . . odd."

"Oh?"

"Captain Hasselbrad was in charge. A ship has but one Captain."

"Of course."

"But the Admiral wouldn't leave him alone. He'd stay on the bridge for hours at a time. The Captain would give an order and Tremaine would countermand it in front of us all. I almost felt sorry for Hasselbrad."

"Almost?"

"He assented to what Tremaine did to you."

"You all did, Alexi. You had to!"

He said fiercely, "No, we chose to!"

"It's over and done with."

His voice wavered. "It isn't. It never can be. We let you down." He struggled for words. "When you . . . Some wrongs cannot be righted. We only learn to live with them."

I mused, "Derek Carr's gone, in Lord God's hands. Vax hates me. You're my only friend. Please don't do this to yourself."

A long quiet. Alexi said with a catch in his voice, "God, sir, I've missed you."

4

We got up late, washed as best we could in an icy chuckling stream, and sipped steaming coffee while we repacked the electricar. I drove; after an hour we came to a dirt road that wound away into a heavy woods, under a homebuilt gate whose sign read BRANSTEAD PLANTATION.

When we pulled up to the house a youngster lounging on the porch got up to greet us. "I'm Jerence." He sounded sullen. "Pa told me to say hello if he was still out back."

"You've grown, boy."

"Yeah, I guess. I'm thirteen now. I was ten last time you came." He opened my door and gestured toward the house. "Go on in. I'll call him."

"Thank you."

He kicked disconsolately at the red earth. "You're welcome." He loped away, disappearing behind the house.

Sarah Branstead was at her door before we reached the steps. "Welcome back, Captain Seafort. To Hope Nation and Branstead Plantation." Her smile was warm and genuine.

"Thank you, ma'am."

"No, you must call me Sarah. It's good to see you again, Captain. I've heard you've had . . . difficult times."

"Yes." I cast about for a way to change the subject. "Who'll be here today?"

"Tomas Palabee, old Zack Hopewell, Laura Triforth. The Volksteaders, do you know them? I know you met Plumwell, the manager of Carr Plantation. Some others; I'm not sure just who Harmon invited. And Mantiet, of course." A momentary annoyance passed across her features. "Mustn't leave him out."

We strolled into the manse. Moments later Harmon Branstead hurried in to greet us, two youngsters trotting alongside.

"Sorry, Captain. I was working on the new silo." We shook hands, and I introduced Alexi.

When he heard we'd camped out for the night, Branstead was appalled. "After passing half a dozen plantations? Hospitality was all around you!"

I grunted, catching Alexi's eye before he could speak. "I camped on my last trip," I said. "I was looking forward to it."

I'd have waited until dinner hour to eat, but Eddie Boss, offered refreshments, accepted with alacrity despite my scowl. The housekeeper, noting Eddie's enthusiasm, disappeared into his kitchen. The tray he brought us a few minutes later—savory sliced meats and steaming fresh vegetables— was more a meal than a snack, and I ate with gusto.

I was just mopping the last of my gravy when the whap of heli blades sounded in the distance. As a lightweight private craft settled on the front lawn the Branstead family moved outside to greet their guests. A burly, unsmiling man jumped out before the blades stopped whirling.

He gave Harmon Branstead a perfunctory handshake and scrutinized us as he approached the manse. "You're Seafort, the imperial envoy? I'm Palabee." His clasp was firm. "Did they instruct you to keep us pacified at any cost, or to tell us to go to hell?"

"Tomas, don't harass him. He's just arrived from a night in the woods. Imperial envoy, indeed!"

"Isn't that what you are?" Palabee was blunt.

"I—"

Harmon Branstead said firmly, "No. He is my guest."

Palabee had the grace to blush. The corners of his mouth turned up. "Very well, sorry. But the sooner we get to business, the better."

"What business is that?" I asked.

He shot me an appraising glance. "Didn't they tell you?"

"They told me I got along well with the planters," I said coolly. "Apparently they were mistaken."

He ignored my tone. "Just why *are* you here?"

"As liaison between the Government and the plantation owners." I glowered. "Why are *you* here?"

"To negotiate, of course. If they haven't prepared you for that, we're wasting our time."

"What's to negotiate?"

His reply was forestalled by the throb of another heli. We went outside, where I was introduced to Seth Morsten: flabby, middle-aged, affable. Awaiting the rest of the guests, we retired to the parlor and drinks.

The Volksteaders farmed the next plantation west; they arrived by land. So did Lawrence Plumwell, manager of Carr Plantation. He eyed me with disfavor. "It seems we've met before, Captain."

"Yes, sir. Three years ago."

"You traveled with your retarded cousin, I recall." His tone was acid.

I flushed. We'd thought the deception necessary to get Derek Carr safely in and out of the plantation he owned but did not control. "I'm sorry, sir."

"As am I. It would have been good to speak candidly with Mr. Carr."

"If I see him I'll tell him so."

With a sardonic smile Plumwell moved on.

Zack Hopewell looked old enough to be Harmon Branstead's grandfather. Given the intermingling of the old Hope Nation families, perhaps he was. He nodded shortly to Palabee, shook hands warmly with Branstead, and turned to me. "So this is the hero of Miningcamp."

I flushed.

"Seriously, Captain Seafort. My granddaughter instructed me not to return without your autograph. Your exploits are well known here. And admired."

"An honor I'd be happier without."

The old man's tone was severe. "Lord God chooses your destiny. You do not."

He sounded so much like Father that I glanced up, half expecting to meet Father's stern visage. "Lord God provides choices," I said slowly. "We may turn toward Him or away from Him."

Zack Hopewell studied my face. "You're troubled."

I blurted, "I am forsworn of my oath and have no honor."

An astounding admission, but he'd sounded so like Father . . .

He blinked. "Well, I asked for it. Teach me to meddle. Sorry I intruded."

"Better all should know." I didn't bother to hide my bitterness.

"Is that why you wear the mark of Cain?"

My hand went to my face. "It was given in a fight. I have no reason to remove it."

He frowned. "Get rid of it, lad. Men will judge your soul without need of external markers."

I had to turn away: memories of Father's hearth were so strong. Ashamed of my indiscretion, I wandered the ornate parlor, examining the ancient imported furniture. At the buffet I helped myself to a glass of wine. Sarah Branstead said, smiling, "I didn't know you Navy men were allowed alcohol."

"Aboard ship it's contraband, ma'am. Ashore we're free to partake." I sipped from my glass of wine. "I'm not much of a drinker."

Mrs. Branstead waved away my comment. "Oh, no criticism intended. I just wish it were the case in Centraltown."

I thought of a sailors' bar I'd once patronized, outside the spaceport. "I wasn't aware of a problem, ma'am."

"It's getting worse. In part because of the war, partly thanks to the farmhands we've imported over the years. Downtown gets very nasty at night."

"My neighborhood seems peaceful enough."

"You're fortunate," she said primly. "Mrs. Volksteader was accosted on the way from a restaurant to her car. If another couple hadn't come along at the right moment, she might have been in great trouble."

I felt a touch of sadness that Hope Nation was going the way of old Earth. "The civil authorities don't respond?"

"Oh, they try, but what can they do? Centraltown's just a small town. The men ran away. Our police don't have fancy tracking tools, like your—" Her face lit as a couple entered the parlor. "Oh, look, the Mantiets. Excuse me a moment."

Frederick Mantiet strode into the room, his breathless wife a step behind. Mrs. Branstead gave him a scant nod but bestowed a warm hug on the woman. The greeting completed, she brought the Mantiets to the buffet and introduced us.

"Glad to meet you, sir." I held out my hand.

His stare was hostile and contemptuous. "That was you last night, eh?" He looked me up and down. "Force us into discourtesy, to put us at a disadvantage? Well, it won't work."

I said evenly, "It hardly seems necessary to force you into discourtesy, sir."

Mrs. Branstead intervened. "Oh, I do so want you to be friends. Frederick, have you heard Emmett's stories of Captain Seafort on *Challenger*? He was absolutely marvelous."

Mantiet muttered something under his breath. I managed to busy myself with my glass until the moment passed. After a time Alexi drifted closer and said quietly, "Do you sense hostility, sir?"

"From some, yes."

"But why?"

"I don't know yet."

"How many of these joes did you meet three years ago?"

"Just Branstead and Plumwell."

"When Ms. Triforth joins us, the planters in this room will account for about eighty percent of Hope Nation's revenues."

"So?"

"If they're hostile, it's something to worry about, sir."

"Thanks for telling me my business, Lieutenant."

Alexi gulped. "Sorry, sir." He retreated.

From time to time I caught contemplative glances from the planters. I tried to keep my face a mask as I studied them in return. Palabee was skeptical and faintly combative, expecting some sort of negotiating session. Mantiet was thoroughly antagonistic, but I couldn't tell whether that was because I had driven away from his manse in a rage, or from a deeper cause. Plumwell was unfriendly, but then, I'd once abused his hospitality with Derek.

On the other side of the ledger, Arvin Volksteader seemed eager to get along with everybody; and old Zack Hopewell seemed friendly enough, in his stern, righteous way.

Only Laura Triforth was absent.

Sarah Branstead conferred with her housekeeper and called us in to an early dinner. The long plank table was ample even for a gathering as large as ours. I sat next to Harmon, who was at the head of his table. Alexi was across from me, and the other planters and their wives farther down the table. Some guests seemed disgruntled by their placement; it made me appreciate all the more the round tables at which officers and passengers sat aboard ship.

Jerence, used to eating with the adults, was directed to the kitchen with his younger brothers and Eddie Boss; he obeyed with a disdainful toss of his head.

While the food was passing I leaned toward Harmon. "I thought this was to be an introductory meeting, a social occasion."

"That's what I had in mind, Captain Seafort." He looked perturbed. "But some of them don't want to wait; they're ready for serious talk."

"I'm not quite sure—"

"Pity I didn't meet you on your last trip, Mr. Seafort." Tomas Palabee, from the other end of the table. "An eighteen-year-old Captain would have been a sight to see."

My smile was perfunctory. "It was. I was lucky to bring *Hibernia* back home."

"And skillful." Sarah Branstead. "Emmett says—"

"Emmett, Emmett, Emmett." Mantiet sounded sour. "You quote your brother-in-law as if he were Gospel, Sarah."

"Not Gospel, Frederick," she rejoined. "But he's the only one of us who's seen Captain Seafort in his element."

"As he never tires of reminding us." Palabee's tone was dry.

Harmon looked annoyed. "My brother is proud of his—"

"Don't bother to get up!" The door swung wide as a lanky middle-aged woman strode in, cape flowing. "Late. Business to attend to."

Harmon Branstead rose smoothly. "Captain Seafort, may I present Laura Triforth, of Triforth Plantation."

I stood. "Glad to meet—"

"Yes, and all that. Well, well. The official Naval liaison to the locals." She shot me an appraising glance. "So you're the one who discovered the aliens?"

"Unfortunately."

"Get on with your dinner. I've eaten, but I'll sit." She un-clasped her cape and tossed it over the back of an empty chair. "Got the damp-rot licked, Palabee?"

Conversation resumed.

After the huge dinner we adjourned to the parlor, which had been cleared of the afternoon's hors d'oeuvres. Alexi arranged our chairs so that he sat alongside and a bit behind me.

Arvin Volksteader asked, "Just what do you know of our situation, Captain?"

I said slowly, "Hope Nation supplies hundreds of millions of tons of foodstuffs for Earth. Most comes from the plantations represented in this room."

"That's right. Now, we've tried for years to get proper representation in the U.N. Several years ago we sent Randolph Carr as a special envoy, but he got nowhere."

"Why do you need representation?"

"Who ships our grain?" demanded Frederick Mantiet.

"The interstellar liners carry some," I answered carefully. "The barges take most of it." Larger even than passenger vessels such as *Hibernia*, manned by skeleton crews, the huge, slow barges carried home grain from Hope Nation and ores from Miningcamp. A chain of barges was always in the pipeline, en route between the mother world and her colonies.

"Yes, but who runs the barges?"

"They're under Naval jurisdiction."

"Right!" He shook his head angrily.

"I don't see the problem."

"The rates, man!" Mantiet paced the open area in the center of the parlor. "You've been systematically gutting us for years. You set the charges for our grain shipments and for the return shipment of our supplies."

"The Navy doesn't set—"

"Not your damned Navy, the U.N. tariff office!"

Zack Hopewell said quietly, "This was to be a discussion, not a confrontation."

"We've had discussions, Zack! We've been having discussions since you were a boy. What good are they?"

"Then why are you here, Frederick?" Hopewell's voice was mild.

"Don't patronize me, you old fool!"

Amid shocked murmurs Zack Hopewell came slowly to his feet. There was nothing mild in his manner when finally he spoke. "Frederick Mantiet, I do hereby call chall—"

"Wait!"

Hopewell brushed off Harmon's restraining arm. "No, I choose not to wait. Mantiet, I—"

"This is *my* home!" Branstead's tone made even Hopewell go silent.

Harmon Branstead appealed to Mantiet. "I've lived on Hope Nation all my life. It's been a good life, all in all. We were brought up as gentlemen, we taught our sons the graces, expanded our holdings, did well for ourselves."

He turned to the rest of the planters. "But something is changing in us. Can't you feel it? We're becoming . . ." He groped for a word. "Imperious. We're losing our civility of speech, as well as our patience. And I . . ." He broke off, apologetically wiped his glasses. "I won't have it. In my house there will be civility. There shall be grace. Your remarks are unacceptable, Frederick, though I'm sure you couldn't have meant them as they sounded. So I'll have you apologize to Zack, or I'll have no choice but to call challenge on you myself."

Mantiet looked from one to the other. "Are you both mad? You'd have us waste strength dueling each other rather than fighting them, the real enemy?" He gestured at me with contempt. "No, he's not worth that. It's evident I can't work with you, but I'll not waste my blood or yours. Zack, I withdraw my remark. Good day to you all."

He stalked out. His wife scurried after.

"Hotheads." Harmon Branstead shook his head. Late in the evening we sat over steaming spiced drinks at his plank table. The guests had long since departed; Alexi and the others of the household had gone to bed. "They don't stop to reason."

"Not all of them," I said.

"Enough. Even Zack, when he gets his dander up."

"They're strong-willed. Especially Ms. Triforth."

"Laura's one of a kind." Harmon shifted in his chair. "She's the first woman who's ever headed a plantation, you know."

"How did that come about? You have primogeniture here."

"Yes, of course." He pursed his lips. "Her older brother Armistad was to inherit. A tragedy. A stroke at thirty-two."

"And she was the heir?"

"Oh, he didn't die. Not for many years. But he was—well, there wasn't much left of his mind. He had no sons; there were no younger brothers, so Laura stepped in. She faced down the banks, expanded the acreage . . . did a hell of a job. Armistad finally died, a few years back. It's all hers now."

"How many of you feel as she does?"

Harmon looked a touch apologetic. "The grievances she cited are legitimate. You have to admit the shipping rates are abominable; our shipping costs are twice what you charge your own merchants to send their goods here."

"Ah." I hadn't known that.

Tariffs weren't all they'd brought to my attention. After Mantiet's departure the discussion had ranged far and wide. Some planters were infuriated by the paternalism of the colonial Government; others worried about the quality of settlers arriving from Terra.

What had disturbed me most of all was Laura Triforth's sardonic description of the waste and mismanagement of our war effort. She'd paced the parlor as she spoke, emphasizing her words with sweeping gestures, while the others nodded agreement.

"Since you were last here, Seafort, they've sent more ships than we've seen since Hope Nation was founded. Ships loaded with unnecessary machinery, useless supplies, and foolish men."

"Be specific, please." I'd made an effort to sound conciliatory.

"Fine. They've sent thousands of soldiers. Why? The planet hasn't been under attack, and if it were, I doubt we could defend it from the ground. Your troops were sent to the Ventura Mountains, halfway across the world from our settlements. And to top it off, the holds of at least three of your ships were filled with—" Laura paused dramatically for effect.

I allowed her a moment of theater. "Yes?"

"Food! Food that we here on Hope Nation grow and send to Earth, they send back as rations! If there's one thing we could provide your armies, it's enough food."

"I agree."

She smiled without mirth. "A pity you weren't in charge of planning the expedition. But there's worse. They intend the army to be based here a long while, so they sent a huge prefab factory on one of the ships. It was supposed to turn out modular housing."

I sighed. All this was outside my brief and well beyond my competence. "Go on."

"Unfortunately, they forgot that we have no landing craft specifically designed to bring such heavy machinery down from orbit. So, we've had to divert cargo shuttles we needed to haul our produce, and modify them for you. Your factory was to crunch genera trees, of which God knows we have an abundant supply, and spit out celuwall." She stopped her pacing to face my chair.

"Unfortunately, they forgot we have no roads in the Venturas to bring raw trees to the factory or carry the modular housing units to their bases." She glared as if it were my fault.

"I'm sure all that can be—"

"The factory was cleverly designed; it's powered by any heavy-duty electric power source. Unfortunately, they forgot we have no generating plants in the Venturas."

I listened with growing uneasiness.

Laura smiled again. "Oh, we didn't let your soldiers freeze or go homeless, though we had to divert valuable manpower during our harvest season. I won't mention the laser installation built in the Venturas, also without a proper power source. If we hadn't sent them an emergency fission generating plant . . ." She sighed. "And perhaps you noticed the vast stockpiles of war matériel sitting on the tarmac at Central-town, with no convenient way to get it to the Venturas and no need for them when they arrive?" She paused for breath.

"The worst is that our land taxes have more than doubled to pay for it all!"

"It's only fair for you to help defend—"

"What defense? Your army sits safe and useless in the Venturas!" From the other planters, sounds of agreement.

I asked, "Have you brought all this to the attention of Unified Command?"

"Once. They patted me on the head and told me to mind my own business." She ran her fingers through her short, curly hair. "I'll tell you what *is* our business. It's the loutish, unmannerly sailors and soldiers and greedy civilians who are taking over Centraltown."

"Now, Laura—"

"I didn't mean him, Harmon. Sorry, Captain, if that seemed personal. But Centraltown was a small town, and we liked it that way. Now, it isn't even safe after dark."

"You people are more of a menace than your mysterious aliens!" Plumwell, my old adversary at Carr Plantation.

"Be fair," Harmon Branstead interjected. "Centraltown's problems were on the rise for years before the military buildup. Ever since we started hiring temporary workers for harvest rather than keeping resident field hands. All winter, they—"

Laura said wearily, "All right, Harmon, the migrants contribute. But the soldiers make matters worse."

I got slowly to my feet. "I can't respond to all you've told me, but I'll take your complaints to my superiors. I promise I'll get you answers."

"When?" Zack Hopewell was blunt.

"I don't know. I have to go through Admiral De Marnay, and he's a busy man. As soon—"

"I told you we're wasting our time!" Laura Triforth knotted her fists. "Mantiet may get carried away, but essentially he's right. They haven't listened, and they never will."

Zack Hopewell said, "Sit down, Laura." His tone brooked no argument. Surprised, she turned to face him. Their eyes locked, and after a moment the woman gave way. Muttering, she sat.

"The lad deserves a chance," Hopewell said gruffly.

"We've waited so long there's little to be lost by waiting a few days longer."

"Days?" said Laura with scorn.

"Or weeks. He knows our grievances, and he knows we want things put right. Let us see how he handles himself." He glowered until he heard murmurs of assent.

Now, at night, sitting across the plank table from Harmon, I doubted I could be of any help. If only they knew how hard I'd found it to get through to the Admiral . . .

Harmon checked his watch. "I was hoping Emmett would be back this evening, but it doesn't seem likely."

"Perhaps I'll see him in the morning, before I go." I bade him good night and went to my room.

In the morning, Mr. and Mrs. Volksteader drove over to join us for breakfast and see us off. After an ample meal we strolled along the drive, chatting. Mrs. Volksteader attached herself to me, chatting with animation about matters of no consequence. I noticed her husband take Alexi aside and speak urgently, glancing once in my direction. After, Alexi, his lips compressed, hurried to rejoin us.

After our stroll we said our good-byes, piled into our electricar. As Eddie drove down the long, shaded lane toward the main road Alexi said, "Sir, I had the oddest conversation with Arvin Volksteader."

"Go on." Just ahead I spotted a slim figure trudging down the drive. "Who's that, walking this far from the manse?" As we approached I recognized Jerence, a bulky knapsack strapped to his back. Eddie slowed, and the boy waved us down. I bade Eddie stop.

"C'n I have a ride?"

"Which way?"

"I'm going east, same as you." Jerence seemed far more animated than the previous afternoon.

I was dubious. "What are you doing on foot?"

"Thought I'd walk to Cary Mantiet's, since it's a nice day, but since you're headed that way anyhow . . ." He paused, then said politely, "I'd appreciate a lift, if you don't mind."

"Of course." I made room for him next to me in the back seat.

"Thanks." He hopped in, unstrapping the knapsack.

"What are you lugging?" I asked, to make conversation.

Jerence shot me a suspicious look. "Nothing. Just stuff."

With a pang of nostalgia I remembered my thirteenth year, running free with my friend Jason, before the football riots of '90. We had our secrets from the adult world, as did this joey.

"Very well." We turned onto the main road. There was no traffic in sight; outside of Centraltown I expected none.

Alexi said, "We've time to make it home tonight if we try, sir."

I thought of Annie, and found the idea appealing. As if reading my mind, Eddie Boss drove a touch faster.

Alexi ventured, "About that other matter I mentioned, sir?"

I glanced at Jerence. "Later, when we're alone."

"Aye aye, sir." Alexi stared out his window, brooding. "I'm glad to be out of there," he muttered. "Too much antagonism."

"They have cause."

"But some are looking for trouble."

I grunted, not wanting to discuss the matter in front of the boy.

"Ms. Triforth and Mantiet are odd ducks. I wouldn't trust them any—"

I said sharply, "Another time, Lieutenant."

"Aye aye, sir." Alexi subsided.

We reached the end of Branstead lands, and as the road curved we came upon the Mantiet marker that signaled the border of his estate. "Where should we drop you, boy?"

"Outside the main gate, please," said Jerence.

Eddie slowed for the curve, then pumped the brakes hard. Ahead, a grain hauler was jackknifed across the road, blinkers flashing. "Careful, Mr. Boss," I said.

We neared the accident. The scene was deserted.

"Where's the driver?" asked Alexi.

I snapped, "How should I know?"

"Odd that no one's here." Jerence.

"He's probably gone to the manse for—"

"Get us *OUT* of here!" Alexi reached across, jammed his

foot on the gas, twisted the wheel. We lurched away from the truck.

"Alexi! What in hell are—"

A flash of white light. Stupendous pressure. A giant hand tossed our electricar into the air. A rending crash. We slammed into the bole of a huge genera tree.

Pitched from the broken vehicle, I lay dazed, my ribs aching abominably. I coughed, waiting for the salty taste of blood, but none came. It seemed too much effort to sit. Minutes passed.

The squeal of brakes. A door slammed, then footsteps.

"Good Christ!"

"Don't blaspheme," I mumbled.

Someone poured water from a canteen onto a cloth, and held it to my head. I struggled to prop myself against the genera.

"Are you all right, sir?"

I started at the familiar voice of Emmett Branstead. "Yes, I think so." I leaned against the trunk.

"We've called a heli ambulance from Centraltown."

"I don't need one."

"Not for you," Branstead's tone was grim.

Oh, Lord God. "Help me up. Please."

Clutching his arm I staggered to my feet. Eddie Boss sat dazed, nursing a broken wrist. Alexi Tamarov's head was cradled in his lap.

"Alexi?" I fell to my knees.

No answer. Blood oozed from Alexi's nose and ear. His mouth was half open, and his breathing was ragged.

"No!" I eased my arm under his head, felt something soft and wet. My hand came away red. I closed my eyes.

"What happened, sir?" Though Emmett Branstead was no longer a seaman, discipline died hard.

I blinked. "I don't know." Frowning, I tried to recall. "A hauler had jackknifed. An explosion . . ."

Branstead snorted. "I'll say." He pointed to the road. "Look at that crater."

"Never mind that. Look to Alexi."

"I'm no med tech, sir. Are you?"

I bit back a vile reply. "No."

Eddie said, "My han' all broke up." He sounded plaintive.

"I know, Mr. Boss."

"Hadda carry Mist' Tamarov outadere, only one han'."

I snarled, "Why did you move him?"

Eddie shrugged. "Dunno if be fire in dere."

"Electricars don't blow up, you trannie fool!"

He stared at me without expression. "Neither do roads," he said with meticulous enunciation.

After a long moment I had to look away. "I'm sorry," I muttered. "Mr. Boss, Mr. Branstead, I beg you both to forgive me."

Eddie grinned mirthlessly. "Cap'n shook up, all of us be." He pointed to his lap. "I put my coat unner his head, make him as comf'ble as I can."

"Thank you." It was hard to meet his eye. I cleared my throat. "Where's the bloody heli?"

"It'll probably be a good half hour." Emmett Branstead.

I cursed under my breath. My ribs aching, I paced helplessly until at last we heard blades beating in the distance. A small heli set down in the center of the road.

But it wasn't the ambulance. Harmon Branstead jumped out, ran toward us. "I was in the granary when you called, Emmett. What in God's grace is going on?"

Emmett Branstead returned his brother's quick embrace. "I'd say an ambush. Someone tried to kill Captain Seafort."

My mind reeled. "What?"

Emmett gave me a strange look. "You think we blow up roads for amusement? What did you imagine happened?"

"Some sort of accident. The truck, dangerous cargo . . ."

"We don't use explosives here. The dirt is soft; we just sculpt it with a bulldozer. Anyway, look at the hauler."

The abandoned cargo hauler was twisted by the force of the blast. "What about it?"

"It's still there," Emmett replied, impatient. "If the cargo had exploded, there would be nothing left of the hauler. The explosive must have been buried in the road. The hauler was there to make you stop."

"But why—how do you know it was me they were after?"

Harmon said, "Who else? Your driver?"

I swallowed, trying to take it all in. "Harmon, can you take us to a hospital?"

Emmett said, "Wait for the medevac heli, Captain. Don't try to move him." I looked down at Alexi and nodded with reluctance.

Harmon's eye roved past Eddie to the genera under which Jerence stood quietly. Harmon crossed the distance in quick strides. He studied his son without expression. Abruptly he slapped the boy's face. Jerence recoiled, his hand rising to his reddened cheek.

Harmon slapped him again. "Into the heli!" Jerence bit back a sob, ran to the open door. Emmett Branstead looked grim.

"What's going—what was that—"

Harmon asked, "Why were you taking my son to Central-town?" His eyes were hard.

"Centraltown? Nonsense; he asked for a ride to the Mantiet place."

"Why?"

"To see his friend Cary Mantiet."

Harmon glared at me until Emmett intervened. "Frederick Mantiet has no children, Captain. Harmon, he didn't know."

I took a deep breath, ignoring the pain in my bruised ribs. "What in Lord God's own hell is this about?"

Harmon's shoulders sagged. He shook his head, walked back to the waiting heli.

Emmett said softly, "My nephew was running away, Captain. He's done it twice before." I gaped; he shrugged, as if in apology. "I assume he asked for a ride to Mantiet's because he figured you wouldn't take him to the city. He probably meant to hop a grain hauler the rest of the way."

"But why?"

Emmett said quietly, "For the family's sake, keep this to yourself."

I nodded.

"He can't buy goofjuice out here. Only in Centraltown."

I said bleakly, "His life wasted, at thirteen."

Emmett stared at the open heli door. "Lord God knows why. Or how he gets it. He's on the edge: habituated, but not yet fully addicted."

Goofjuice. I'd seen the results of its use, years ago on *Hibernia*, when crewmen had smuggled some aboard. The user is quite happy while he's sailing high. He may, with perfectly good cheer, slaughter his best friend. Perhaps afterward he might feel remorse.

"Haven't they tried . . . I mean, doctors—"

"Everything short of having him committed."

Harmon emerged from the heli and hurried toward us. "Sorry about that. Personal problems. I called Centraltown; the ambulance will be here in five minutes."

Emmett crouched next to Alexi. "He's still breathing, sir. He may have a chance. It's amazing what modern surg—"

I grated, "Who did this?"

Harmon shook his head. "We're crossing Mantiet land. Frederick left yesterday in anger, but I can't believe—"

"Why isn't he here? Didn't he hear the explosion?"

"I don't know. I called the house, but he's out. His wife didn't know where, or how long."

Emmett asked, "Whose hauler is that, Harmon?"

"I don't recognize it. We can trace it by the transponder number or the engine serial number, if it comes to that."

The welcome thump of a heli grew audible. "Make sure it's done." My voice was tight.

If the hauler was his, Frederick Mantiet could be seized for questioning under polygraph and truth drugs. Thank Lord God that the Truth in Testimony Act of 2026 abolished the ridiculous right to silence that had hampered criminal investigations for centuries. These days, once we had a suspect, we got answers.

If Mantiet was guilty, the sophisticated drugs would force him to admit it, and of course we could then use his confession as evidence in his trial. If he was innocent, he'd suffer only a headache and nausea. After I'd returned home with *Hibernia*, reporting the death of her officers, I'd submitted to extensive questioning with the drugs and poly. It wasn't pleasant, but it cleared me of suspicion.

Harmon was grim. "Oh, yes, we'll find whose hauler that is. My son was in your car too."

The heli landed; med techs scrambled out and hovered over Alexi. His head bandaged and supported, they eased him onto a stretcher and bundled him into the heli. Eddie Boss and I climbed aboard.

"Find out," I shouted as we lifted off. From Harmon, a grim nod.

5

"Sorry, the Admiral isn't here."

I scowled at Lieutenant Eiferts as if it were his fault. Then I sighed. "When will he be back?"

"Probably not for a while, sir. He went up to Orbit Station, and from there he may take a ship to review the squadron positions."

"Why bother? They're in the puter." I regretted it almost instantly, but it was too late.

The lieutenant said carefully, "I wouldn't know, sir." I wondered if he'd repeat my disparaging remark to De Marnay.

"I've been trying to reach him for three days, Mr. Eiferts."

"Yes, sir."

"Very well." I left Admiralty House with as much dignity as I could muster.

Outside, Annie crouched at the flower beds, gently fingering the geraniums. She straightened. "Will he see you?"

"He's not here." I slipped my hand into hers as we walked to our rented electricar.

"Oh, Nicky."

"Can't be helped."

Annie had met us at the hospital, showered my face with kisses amid sobs of relief. She'd waited outside the operating room, pressing against my side, while they'd worked to save Alexi. During the five days since, she had followed me wherever possible, unwilling to let me out of her sight even for a trip to the grocer's. "Where to?" she asked now.

"The hospital."

"I called this morning. He no better."

I knew. I had called too. Nonetheless, I could sit at Alexi's side. Tubes in his nose and throat, waste lines attached below the sheets, his monitors maintained their vigil. His brain waves weren't flat; there was hope. I gathered not much hope, though the doctors, as all doctors, were reticent.

At Centraltown Hospital we signed in at the nurses' station and hurried to Alexi's room. He lay unmoving. In the corner Eddie Boss stirred.

"Eddie? What are you doing here?"

"Wanted to wait wid him." The seaman was gruff.

"There's nothing you can do," I said gently.

"Nothin' you can do, neither." Insolence, from a sailor to a Captain. And yet . . . His eyes met mine until I broke contact.

"Very well, Mr. Boss." We sat together, and waited, hoping.

Annie sat next to the hulking sailor. Her hand strayed to Eddie's cast. I'd watched a med tech apply the bone-growth stimulator; Eddie wouldn't have to bear the cast long.

After a silent hour in Alexi's sterile room we left. Eddie followed us to our car. "How often have you been to see him, Mr. Boss?"

"Every day." His look challenged me to object.

"I didn't think you knew Alexi that well."

"Back on *Challenger*. When dem—those Uppies were makin' fun of us. He chase them away, sometimes."

"Ah." More I hadn't known.

Annie opened the car door. "You gonna go see the planters, Nicky?"

It was foolish to visit until I had news to report, but soon they'd decide I was ignoring them. "I suppose I ought to."

"In a heli this time." It was more a demand than a question.

I sighed. "Yes, Annie, in a heli." I looked at Eddie Boss. "I'd like you to look after Annie while I'm gone."

The huge seaman broke into a slow smile. "Aye aye, sir. No joe be messin' wid Annie. I see to dat."

They'd taught me piloting at Academy, and I'd flown a civilian craft on my last visit to Hope Nation. Now, on duty, I rated a military heli. It took me a while to acquaint myself with the heavier machine and its unfamiliar equipment. A miniputer chattered bearings and weather information until I flipped a switch to silence it; I preferred to fly by dumb instruments.

I had no anxiety as I raised the nimble craft off the tarmac and headed for Zack Hopewell's plantation. None about flying, that is. I had no idea how the planters would react when I admitted Admiral De Marnay had made no time for them. I worked out diplomatic phrases in my head: Investigating the allegations. Reviewing their information. Deciding how best to alleviate their grievances.

Zack Hopewell had set on a radar beacon for me, and I let the autopilot home on it. Hopewell and Harmon Branstead were waiting on the lawn when I set the machine down. Hopewell Plantation was similar to the others I'd visited, though there was a sternness, a lack of frivolity about the place that reflected its proprietor.

I followed Zack Hopewell into his manse. Unlike Branstead, he offered no hors d'oeuvres, no liquors, but mugs of hot, steaming coffee and good soft pastries. I chewed on a roll and sipped my coffee gratefully.

They waited.

I addressed Zack Hopewell. "Since I spoke to you last," I began. If only he didn't look so much like Father . . . "I haven't accomplished a thing," I blurted. "I've made several tries but I can't get in to see the Admiral."

Hopewell snorted. "Well, at least he doesn't offer the usual bullshit."

"I'm sorry."

"Your candor is refreshing." He shrugged. "We haven't been able to do much, either. No one knows where Frederick is. With Dora's permission we even searched his house, and I can verify he wasn't there. We traced the hauler; it belongs to him and was supposed to be in Centraltown."

"What could Mantiet gain by killing me?"

Harmon's face darkened. "He called you the real enemy, remember? Said we shouldn't waste our blood fighting among ourselves instead of you."

"Still, how does he benefit?"

"If he wants to disrupt the Government, eliminating a reasonable voice would be in his interest."

"That's treason!" I could conceive of murder for personal

gain. But rebellion against the lawfully ordained Government of Lord God Himself? On Terra, we'd had no revolution since the Rebellious Ages ended, over a century ago. I tasted bile.

Harmon said carefully, "I didn't say treason. I said disruption."

A distinction without a difference. I was about to say as much when Zack Hopewell intervened. "In any event, Mantiet will confirm the truth when he's caught."

"Yes." I sat again, slowly. "I wish I could tell you Admiralty was anxious to correct its mistakes. Perhaps they will be, when I manage to inform them."

"You didn't submit a written report?"

"Of course. I dropped off my chip the day after I returned. But still . . ." I doubted De Marnay would take action unless I personally warned him of the planters' vehemence. Perhaps not even then.

"I don't know what Mantiet thinks, but Laura wants to revise the Planetary Charter," Harmon said. "Eliminate the Governorship, elect a council from among the planters."

"She needs to take that up with the U.N. at home," I said stiffly. "It's not my province."

"No," said Harmon. "But you should be aware of it."

We broke for a light lunch, and afterward I stopped at the Palabees for a brief visit before returning home. I was revving the throttle when a call came from Hopewell.

"A Miss Wells called, Captain. She wanted urgently to speak with you."

I muttered under my breath. It was folly to allow my personal life to mix with duty. I thought of returning her call, but I was leaving anyway, and would be home in an hour or so. I relayed a message to that effect and started my engine.

Annie met me at the door, her eyes red. "Dey call here coupla hours back, sayin' *Concord* be leavin' in morning. I gotta be ready go, ten o'clock."

"Oh, Annie." I took her into my arms. I'd known it was to come, yet . . .

She sniffled. "I be all ri' on Detour, Nicky. Be wid trannies, 'n all."

"With, not wid," I said automatically. We'd struggled so hard.

"With," she said dutifully.

We wandered into the bedroom. Her bag was on the bed, half packed. My voice was dull. "I wish you could stay."

"I know, Nicky."

"They'll give me a ship soon, and you couldn't go with me."

"I know." She smiled through tears. "How I get all my fancy clothes in? Gonna need 'nother case."

"We'll get one. The best that money can buy." I grabbed her hand. "And that ruby necklace you liked, at the jewelers."

Her eyes widened. "Really? Oh, Nick, you don' have ta do that."

I was already regretting my impetuosity; the bauble would cost me almost two months pay. But what would I spend it on, alone? "I don't mind," I said manfully. I led her to the door and the waiting car.

Hours later, necklace shining against the pale satin of her dress, we came back to the apartment, my pleasure already dampened by her impending departure. I keyed the lock. "Just a minute," she said, and went to the bedroom.

I sat disconsolately, knowing I would soon hate this place. Perhaps I would move into Naval barracks.

She called, "C'n you help me with this, Nicky?"

"Can't close the case, hon? Should we have bought the bigger one?" I went into the bedroom.

Nude, she stood outlined against the window, ruby necklace sparkling in the soft evening light, hands cupping her breasts. Slowly she raised her hands to the clasp. "Show me how this works, Nicky."

I came behind her, touched the clasp. She turned, slid into my arms, soft, vulnerable, irresistible. Our lips met, then our tongues. I clawed my way out of my jacket and we fell onto the bed.

Later, in the darkened room, I roused myself to pick up the buzzing caller.

"Captain Seafort? Lieutenant Eiferts. I got you a few minutes with Admiral De Marnay in the morning, at ten."

"Very well." I rang off.

"Who was it?" Annie sounded heavy with sleep.

"The Admiral will finally see me tomorrow. I'll drop you off at the spaceport and walk to Admiralty House."

"That's good, you gettin' talk wid him."

"Yes." I lay back.

A moment later, a sob.

My arms provided what comfort I could. I knew that after tomorrow, I'd never see her again. She'd settle into her new life in one of Detour's many new factories, producing goods so urgently needed by the new-settled colony. We'd write, or at least I would, for a while. Then we would forget each other.

With Lord God's help, I might forget.

In the morning I called the hospital. Alexi remained in coma. His chances of recovery dimmed each day it lasted.

I dressed, inhaled hot coffee at the kitchen table, stared moodily at a holovid copy of the report I'd left for the Admiral. Annie put the last of her gear in her fancy new case.

Somewhere above waited *Concord*, moored at Orbit Station. I puttered about the apartment until it was late enough to justify leaving. We drove past the spaceport, parked in front of Admiralty House, got out of our electricar. The brass plaque gleamed in the bright morning sunlight. Beyond, on the tarmac, the shuttle was already loading. An hour and a half from now, it would dock at Orbit Station.

"Annie, I don't—"

Her smile was radiant. "No, Nick. No good-byes, otherwise I'll cry again."

"I'll miss you so much." My voice was hoarse.

"We was good fo' each other." Despite her resolve her eyes glistened as she hefted her two cases. "Bye, Nicky. Take care a yo'self." Without looking back, she hurried across the tarmac. I watched until she reached the shuttle and disappeared from sight.

I climbed the steps, opened the door. Lieutenant Eiferts said, "I'll tell the Admiral you're here, sir. He'll be a few minutes."

I checked my watch. Five minutes to ten. I sat, stared list-lessly at a holozine.

Lieutenant Eiferts said something. I grunted a reply. I had no idea what either of us had said. I stood abruptly.

"Pardon, sir?"

"My apologies to the Admiral. I've been unavoidably detained."

His jaw dropped. "Been what?"

"Detained." Out the double doors, down the steps three at a time. I sprinted across the yard to the tarmac.

The shuttle hatch was closing; I waved frantically as I ran. It reopened. One of the larger shuttles, with row upon row of seats. The pilot raised her eyebrow. "You're too late; our weight is already in the puter."

I climbed aboard. "I'm not going."

She looked at me quizzically. "Then you'll have to dis—"

I peered past rows of heads. "Annie?"

"Captain, we leave in two minutes."

"This won't take two minutes."

"I have to seal my hatches!"

"Yes, ma'am." Where was she? "Annie!"

Slowly she stood, several rows back. Her eyes widened in fear. " 'Bout Alexi? What happened?"

The pilot's protests faded.

I cleared my throat, fumbling for words. As Annie's fingers darted to her necklace, I blurted, "Marry me."

"I—what?"

"Please. Stay with me."

She bit her lip, turned away to hide the tears. "You sure, Nicky? I be'ent righ' kinda joeygirl fo' Cap'n."

I said huskily, "You be joe fo' Cap'n. I sho'."

"Oh, God, Nicky!" She flew into my arms.

I said to the Pilot, "Is there time to off-load her luggage?"

She grinned. "The lady is disembarking?"

My tone was firm. "Yes."

"Then there's plenty of time. I have to recalculate the weight." I gathered she didn't mind.

Annie clung to me, sobbing. I didn't know whether to laugh or cry; I did both.

It took some doing, waiving the banns and all, but we were married the next afternoon in a hastily arranged ceremony in a chapel of the Reunification Cathedral. Eddie Boss was best man. Annie stood radiant in a traditional white-fringed jumpsuit; I wore my dress whites. From time to time during the service my glance strayed upward to the majesty of the domed roof. My only sadness was that though our marriage was in the name of Lord God, my damnation meant He would not bless our union.

Over the caller, Admiral De Marnay listened to my apology without comment. Afterward, Lieutenant Eiferts called to reschedule my appointment for two days later. I'd been forgiven my unthinkable rudeness. Perhaps even my unthinkable marriage, to a despised transpop.

My escapade became known throughout Centraltown, and beyond. Cards of congratulations came from the nurses at the hospital, from Harmon Branstead, from Captain Derghinski on *Kitty Hawk*.

Alexi Tamarov stirred, his eyes vacant, and sank back into deep, unending sleep.

Lieutenant Eiferts was apologetic. "He had to run up to the Station, sir. I'll have to arrange something when he gets back."

Well, it was my own fault; I'd missed my best chance for a meeting. "When will that be?"

"I have no idea, sir."

I hung up, brooding. More days wasted, if not weeks. I'd have to explain the delay to Harmon and Zack Hopewell, a matter I'd rather not dwell on. "Come on, hon, let's go see Alexi."

Annie proudly put her hand in mine, her gold ring glittering.

We found Alexi still unconscious. The floor nurse assured us his brain waves were steady. As usual, Eddie Boss sat glumly in the corner. I realized I'd have to put him to work soon, or transfer him back to regular duty. The silence lengthened.

"I'll get us all some coffee. Be right back." At the other end of the hall, I strove to balance three cups of coffee for the long trip down the corridor.

"Captain Seafort?"

I turned. "Hmm? Oh, Mr. Forbee."

"Here, let me help with that." He held a cup for me.

"Thanks. What are you doing here?"

"Antiviral booster. It was time again." Forbee gestured toward the door. "Seeing your lieutenant, sir?"

"Yes." I was brusque. Forbee could have no idea how I yearned for Alexi's reassuring presence.

"Admiral De Marnay was livid when he heard about the attack on your party. Said to give whatever help you need to investigate."

"We have to find Mantiet." The planter had disappeared with clothing, cash, papers, and supplies. Dora Mantiet seemed panicked, and professed complete ignorance. The Centraltown police had circulated Frederick's picture, hardly necessary in so small a town.

"What are they up to?" Forbee gestured vaguely toward the plantation zone.

"There's going to be trouble. The Admiral should be briefed, but I blew the appointment he gave me."

"I heard." Forbee's eyes twinkled. "He's a busy man. Why don't you meet him at Orbit Station?"

I stopped dead in the corridor. I hadn't thought of that. "Thank you, Forbee. I think I will."

Annie wrapped herself around me tearfully. "You be careful, Nicky. Don' go gettin' yourself hurt."

"I'll be safe, Annie. It's just Orbit Station. You were there yourself."

"Safe!" She sniffed. "Way out in space . . ."

"I'll be back as soon as I can. Visit Alexi tomorrow for me." I swallowed a lump, trying to convince myself I wasn't abandoning him. If anything happened while I was gone . . .

"Eddie will take me," she said. I nodded. She'd be as safe with him as with a platoon of Unie troops, notwithstanding his injured arm.

"I have to run." I gave her a last squeeze, nodded to Eddie Boss, and loped across the field to the waiting shuttle. A few technicians returning from shore leave were the only other passengers. The pilot nodded briefly and returned to his instruments.

Moments later we hurtled down the runway and were airborne. At five thousand feet the pilot raised the nose into a stall and fired the rockets. Pressed into my seat, I gritted my teeth, willing my body to relax as the shuttle roared toward the Station.

As often as I had endured the boost, still I tensed rather than riding with the pressure as my instructors had tried to teach me. I could hear Sarge now. "Ease up, Seafort! Relax your chest muscles. Feel it press you. Just like a woman lay atop you, but I guess you wouldn't know about that." I could feel the blush that heated my face, neck, arms. Sarge's chuckle echoed still.

And then we were free, floating weightless, thrusters silent. Nothing to do but wait. I planned my long-delayed presentation to the Admiral.

As we neared the Station I glanced out the porthole. Most of the bays were closed and empty. Well, we hadn't sent a third of our ships to Hope Nation to keep them moored at Orbit Station; they'd be out patrolling. I noticed a few vessels undergoing repair in the drydock bays. We were too far away to see anyone working.

Strapped in my seat in zero gravity, I leaned into the aisle to watch the pilot, his entire attention on the meticulous docking procedure. When at last our airlock seals were mated with the Station's, the cabin lights brightened and I got gratefully to my feet, flexing my muscles.

Technicians bustled past in the bright station lights. I knew my way to the Commandant's office; I'd been there several times before. I assumed that's where I'd find Admiral De Marnay.

In the reception area for the Commandant's office a sergeant looked me over, unimpressed. He was U.N.A.F., not Navy.

"Your Admiral? No, if he's on station he'd be in the Naval corridor."

"And General Tho?"

"In a meeting," the sergeant said. "May last awhile. I could page you when he's free."

"Don't bother him. I'll find the Admiral."

He grinned without humor. "Don't get lost, Navy."

"No problem," I said immediately. "I like it groundside." I

slipped out before he could reply. Interservice rivalry didn't bring out the best in me. Not much did, these days.

Despite my bravado it took me over an hour to locate the Naval corridor, and I had to backtrack at least once. I'm not sure about the second time.

A lieutenant I'd seen before greeted me at the entranceway. "You had an appointment, sir?"

"No, but I need to see the Admiral anyway." I spoke with a confidence I didn't feel.

"Yes, sir. Sorry, but he went with *Vestra*. They're somewhere outside the orbit of Planet Four."

"I see." Any idiot would have known to call ahead; why didn't I?

"He's not due back until tomorrow." *Vestra* could Fuse here in minutes, in an emergency, so De Marnay wasn't really out of touch. But why did he keep taking these jaunts? Was he hungry for ship time, like me? The lieutenant chewed at his lip. "Sir, would you like me to signal him you're here?"

"No thanks," I said quickly. Such presumption would not go over well, especially after I'd broken my last appointment.

"You're welcome to stay in Naval barracks overnight, sir. I'm sure the Admiral would authorize it."

"Thank you." I tried to lift my flagging spirits. "It'd give me time to look around."

"The Level 4 restaurant isn't bad, or you could try the officers' mess. And if you'd care to listen to traffic, you could visit the comm room."

Was it an invitation to leave? I couldn't tell, but in any event there was no point in hanging around the Admiral's office. "Page me if *Vestra* docks," I said.

"Of course, sir."

I wouldn't go to the comm room, not immediately. I wandered along the circumference corridor until I found Naval barracks and signed myself in. They gave me a private room, almost as large as a Captain's cabin aboard ship.

I wandered through Naval territory, stopped at the mess for a quick supper, then tramped back to General Tho's wing of the Station. He would remember me, if I could arrange an appointment. These days I was having trouble getting to see anybody.

"Mr. Seafort, is that you?" He stood in the entryway to the Commandant's wing, chatting with an officer.

I gawked. "Uh, yes. Yes, sir." I shook hands with the short, elegantly groomed man. "How are you, General Tho?"

"Fine, fine. How long have you been on station?"

"A couple of hours. I was hoping to see the Admiral."

"He's on *Vestra*."

"So I learned."

"Come in." He led the way to his comfortable, spacious office. We passed through the reception area. His arm on my shoulder, the General ushered me past the astounded receptionist.

"I missed you when *Hibernia* came in, Mr. Seafort. And then you, ah, were injured."

Nearly killed in my foolish duel, he meant. "Yes." Politeness demanded something more than that. "I'm recovered, and on shore duty now."

"With our beloved planters."

"Yes, sir."

"They think the planet revolves around them." He sighed. "Well, I suppose it does. Hope Nation's agribusiness is the reason we're here. It's why we can afford a station as huge as this." He waved me to a chair. "The planters are a Naval problem, thank Lord God. Not mine."

I gazed at the simulscreen filling one wall of his office. It offered a view of Hope Nation system, from the periphery of the Station.

"Basically, they stuck with your plan, you know."

I said, "Pardon?"

"When you left here three years ago, you told Forbee to accept my orders so we'd have a unified command. They kept the unified command, but Navy has more pull than U.N.A.F., so your Admiral's in charge. He ranks even over the civilian Governor." He fished in his desk drawer, brought out glasses and a bottle. "Drink? Good. I don't mind about the command, actually. I've got my hands full running the Station, with the traffic your squadron brings. Don't need Naval jurisdiction or civilian oversight to keep me busy."

I said, meaning it, "Not many men could turn away power with as few regrets, General."

He smiled, handing me a glass of Scotch. "Oh, I won't say I didn't have some choice words for William when the news came, before I had a chance to reflect on it."

"For whom?"

"I'm William, sir." A confident baritone voice from all around me. I jumped, spilling my Scotch.

"Sorry, Captain." General Tho grinned. "Multiple speakers. They're rather startling, at first."

"Permit me to introduce myself," said the baritone. "W-30304, at your service. Colloquially known as William."

"Your, ah, ship's puter?" I brushed beads of liquid from my knee.

A short silence. William's tone was frosty. "I am to a ship's puter what your puter is to an Arcvid."

"Uh, pardon me."

A microsecond's pause before he relented. "I understand your confusion, sir. You're Navy, and according to your personnel file you've never spent extended time on a station. No offense taken. You're aware of all the functions your puter monitors aboard ship? Hydroponics, recycling, and so on?"

"Of course." I felt foolish. General Tho listened with a grin.

"Well, I do all that for the Station on a much larger scale, but I also record and evaluate all tightbeam transmissions from the puters in each of your ships, as they arrive. In addition, I monitor all Station traffic and cargo selection, storage, and loading."

"I see." He would have stupendous data banks, and a RAM that was breathtaking.

"Before I leave you to your conversation, may I say I've heard a lot about you, Captain Seafort."

"Oh?" Did they program the holozines into him?

"From Darla."

"I see."

He chuckled. "Darla is quite opinionated, but I take her conclusions with a grain of salt."

I thought of asking what data from my old ship's puter

William viewed skeptically, but decided against it. "Uh, thank you."

William said nothing.

I turned back to General Tho. I might as well make use of my visit. "Sir, have you heard much about the groundside base?"

"In the Venturas? Never actually been there. I gather U.N. Command wanted to land a force capable of defending the planet itself, in case of invasion." He shook his head. "Can't see it, myself. Groundside could only be invaded if the fleet were destroyed, and then the aliens would have air superiority to wipe out a ground force."

"Lord God forbid." I repressed a shudder.

"And why put our forces halfway across the planet from Centraltown?" He grimaced. "See what happens when you try to run a war from a distance? They should have left it in local hands."

"What kind of invasion is the base designed to counter?"

He sipped moodily at his drink. "They're equipped with all sorts of antiviral synthesizers and pandemic vaccines. But mainly they're a laser installation. Got a hell of a battery of cannon, if they finish setting it up. Could knock out just about anything."

"Lasers don't seem to do much good," I reflected. "The fish Fuse as soon as we get their range."

"Well, what else should we use?" he snorted. "Atomics?"

Lord God forbid. General Tho skated on thin ice even joking about it. Not only the use of atomic weapons but any proposal to employ them carried a mandatory death penalty. Ever since the Last War, the national governments at home were united in enforcing the ban. A hundred forty years after the last horrid bomb lit Terran skies, frightful scars remained.

We finished our drinks. When he glanced at his watch I knew it was time to go. We shook hands again; I went directly to the barracks and to bed.

I slept surprisingly well. In the morning I downed powdered eggs and burnt toast while I sipped at my coffee. My breakfast was interrupted by a midshipman bringing me a chip faxed from Centraltown. With sudden anxiety I snapped open the case and slipped it into a holovid.

"Your Lieutenant Tamarov is out of coma. Dazed but apparently lucid, according to initial reports. I thought you'd like to know immediately. Forbee." Thank you, Lord God.

"Any reply, sir?"

I looked up. The boy was waiting. "No. Dismissed." Gratefully he hurried away.

My breakfast was delicious.

After leaving the mess I couldn't help myself; I checked with Naval HQ in case the duty lieutenant had forgotten to page me, but Admiral De Marnay hadn't returned. I paced the sterile corridors until I remembered the lieutenant's suggestion of the previous day. The comm room was halfway around the disk. On a large station, a good distance. I set out, my step jaunty. Alexi was healing.

In the comm room the Navy techs gave me an informal salute but stayed at their places, as was proper when the Station was at a high degree of alert. I pulled up a chair. "Anything doing?"

"No, sir. A few puters on tightbeam with each other, but nothing for us." He hesitated. "Sir, you're, ah, Captain Seafort?"

"Yes."

"Do you think . . ." He fumbled in his pocket. "Sorry if I'm out of line, sir, but could I have your autograph?"

I bridled. What was Naval discipline coming to? At my frown he quickly thrust the paper back into his jacket and bent to his console. "Sorry, sir."

I sighed. "Never mind. Give it here." They had few enough diversions, on extended station duty. I scribbled my name. Shamefacedly, the others crowded round, scraps of paper materializing from pockets and consoles.

"I saw you in the zines, sir. Did you know you made the cover of *Newsworld*?"

Another tech gave the speaker a nudge in the ribs. "Of course he knows, you idiot." I smiled politely. I hadn't. We sat in uncomfortable silence for several minutes.

A console light flashed. The voice on the speaker sounded

weary. "Station, we're about to test the airlock again. Disregard signals, please."

"Very well, *Portia*."

"*Portia*'s here?" My heart beat faster.

"Yes, sir. In the repair bay."

I stood. "I'd like to see her. Which way?"

I followed their directions to the repair bays. *Portia* had been my first assigned command. I'd sailed with such high hopes, with my unborn son, my wife Amanda, with Vax Holser, with Alexi.

I found the bay, cycled through the Station's lock to *Portia*'s, and pressed the entry pad. A moment later the lock slid open and a young middy came quickly to attention. "Good afternoon, sir."

"As you were," I said gruffly. "I'm Captain Seafort. May I enter?"

"Captain Akers isn't aboard, sir. No one is, except my lieutenant, and he's sleeping. And the Chief, doing repairs."

"I didn't want Captain Akers." I felt foolish. "*Portia* was my ship once. I just wanted to . . ." My voice trailed off. How could I explain the whim that had overtaken me, without seeming an idiot? "I wanted to see her again," I said firmly. "Visit her bridge."

The boy swallowed, nervous in the presence of such exalted rank. Well, that was as it should be. A word from me could have him caned without a moment's pause. "I don't think they'd mind, sir, while we're moored. The bridge is this way."

I suppressed a smile. "I know."

He colored. "Yes, of course, sir. Sorry. If you care to go ahead, I'll inform the duty lieutenant."

"Very well." He scurried off while I made my way to the bridge. My chest tightened as I passed my old cabin. Within its confines, tiny Nate had died. I could almost feel Amanda's presence. I hurried past the first lieutenant's cabin, once Vax Holser's. I had spurned his help, at the cost of his friendship. Past the wardroom, where Philip Tyre had struggled manfully to redeem himself. The second lieutenant's cabin, where Alexi savored revenge against Philip until its taste soured in his mouth. Oh, Alexi, what have we done to you?

The bridge hatch was open; docked and under repair, *Portia* was virtually decommissioned.

I glanced at the simulscreens that dominated the bridge. They were blank, of course. On the console, an airlock light blinked.

I cleared my throat, suddenly shy. "Danny?" At one time the eager young puter had been my only confidant. No answer. "Puter, respond by voice, please."

A dull, machinelike voice said, "D 20471 responding. Please identify yourself."

"Captain Nicholas Seafort, U.N.N.S. Uh, reactivate conversational overlays." How could they have locked him inside for so long?

A warm contralto issued from the speaker. "Thank you, Captain. How may I help you?"

I blinked. "Danny? You sound different."

"I'm Diane, sir. Ship's puter."

Unthinking, I dropped into the Captain's seat, no longer mine to occupy. "Where's Danny?" I asked.

Diane hesitated a microsecond. "I have all Danny's memory and data banks, sir."

My hand tightened on the chair. "Where's Danny?"

An irate voice, in the corridor. "Middy, let anyone board without permission again and I'll have you over the barrel so fast you'll—"

I turned to the hatch.

"Lieutenant Tolliver repor—" We gaped in mutual astonishment.

Edgar Tolliver. A year older than I, senior by one class. My persistent tormentor at Academy, where he'd been nominated cadet corporal and put in charge of our dormitory. Sour memories welled.

His eyes flickered to my insignia. He came to attention.

"As you were," I grated. "What happened to Danny?"

Tolliver said carefully, "Diane has been the puter since I've been aboard, sir. I understand Admiral Tremaine ordered complete powerdown after he took *Portia*."

"Why?" My voice was hoarse.

He started to shrug, remembered he was in a Captain's presence. "I believe he was making sure you hadn't sabotaged the puter, sir."

I swung to the speaker. "Diane, what happened to Danny? His personality?"

"It's gone, disassembled with powerdown."

"Is he retrievable?" But I already knew the answer.

Her tone held a note of finality. "No, sir. He is not."

I sank back, dazed. My friend Danny, who'd pondered whether he had a soul. Who'd comforted me after the death of Amanda. Gone.

Derek, Danny, Vax, all lost.

I began to cry.

From the hatch Tolliver watched impassively. I fought to control myself. "Sorry," I mumbled. "It was a shock."

"Quite all right, sir."

"Thank you for having me aboard." Humiliated, I stumbled off the bridge, drying my eyes as I fled down the corridor. Tolliver and the young midshipman saw me off at the airlock.

I trudged back to the comm room. Was it blasphemy to pray for Danny's soul? I decided that regardless of the risk, I would. If Lord God could listen to one such as I.

At the comm room the tech waved me to my seat, his ear to his headphones. "Confirm, *Freiheit*, two sightings quadrant seventeen."

"What's afoot?" I asked.

The speaker crackled. "Station, *Calumet* en route to sector four, quadrant sixteen as per orders."

The tech's voice shook with excitement. "Fish! Confirmed, no false alarm. *Freiheit*'s engaging, with *Valencia* coming on. The rest of the fleet's moving into position."

I sat listening as the great ships reported their locations. Orders flowed and were instantly confirmed and obeyed. The speakers crackled with a flood of data.

"*Freiheit* reporting. Two fish, alongside! We're under attack. They're launching those, uh, outriders. Permission to Fuse!" Captain Tenere sounded anxious, as well he might.

De Marnay. "Where's *Valencia*?"

"*Valencia*, here, sir. Coordinates eighteen, one thirty-five, sixty-two. About half an hour from *Freiheit*."

"Very well, *Freiheit*. Set coordinates and Fuse to safety, minimum distance, then report immediately."

"Aye aye, sir. Engine Room, Fuse!" Tenere's radio went dead.

"*Valencia* reporting. Where do you want us, sir?"

"Mr. Groves, wait for *Freiheit* to reappear. If she's close enough, go to her on thrusters, else Fuse to her."

"I'll need an hour to reach Fusion clearance, sir— Whoops!" The voice tightened. "Three more fish, two ahead, one alongside, matched velocities! Engaging!"

"*Kitty Hawk* here. I've got three sightings." Derghinski read his coordinates.

Admiral De Marnay. "All ships, execute Maneuver B!"

Fists knotted, I watched the screens while the armada moved ponderously, our ships expending prodigious amounts of propellant to reach their new stations, hours distant.

"*Freiheit* Defused and reporting. New position quadrant eleven, grid coordinates eighteen, two oh three, fifteen."

"Very well, Mr. Tenere."

"Where do you want us to—Good Christ!"

"*Freiheit?*"

"Four, five, half a dozen fish! They're all over us! We're taking hits. Decompression. Sealing—"

The caller went dead.

"*Valencia* under fire. Two fish. We're firing back. There goes one of them, by Christ. Spewing his guts!"

My throat dry, I listened to snatches of disaster and success.

Behind me, in the Station, an alarm wailed. "*NOW HEAR THIS!* Battle Stations! All off-duty personnel and all visitors disembark Orbit Station at once! Shuttles departing in three minutes!"

I jumped to my feet and ran to Naval HQ. The outer office was empty; I opened the inner hatch and found myself in the plotting room. "Can I be of help?"

A harried Captain shot me an annoyed look. "Stay out of the way. You're off duty."

"Can I plot—"

"You'd better get groundside, Mr., ah, Seafort. If we come under attack there's nothing you can do here."

Reluctantly I said, "Aye aye, sir." It wasn't time to argue.

I reached the shuttle bay just as the safety hatches began to close. On the shuttle I dropped into a seat, struggling to catch my breath.

"Passengers, prepare for launch, please. Departure Control, Shuttle Charlie Fox four oh six ready to launch."

The reply was almost immediate. "Cleared to launch, Four oh six."

The huge shuttle bay hatch slid open. Gently at first, our thrusters drummed propellant against the launch bay's protective shields, ejecting us from the Station. I peered through the porthole. Behind us, the bright-lit Station sailed placidly through empty space.

A moment after flipabout our pilot kicked in the jet engines and we became a jet-powered aircraft. As the runway slid into view, the shuttle's stubby wings shifted into VTOL mode. We bled off speed and dropped to the tarmac, the shuttle's underbelly jets cushioning our fall.

I scrambled out of my seat the moment the engines died. When the hatch opened I jumped out to dash across the field. I galloped across the Admiralty House yard and took the front steps two at a time.

Lieutenant Eiferts looked up from his desk.

I gasped, "You have a comm link with Orbit Station?"

"Yes, sir, in the tactics office."

"What Captains are here now?"

"None, sir, other than yourself." For a moment I imagined a reproach.

"Very well. I'm going up." There was none to stop me. I hurried upstairs, bracing myself for an unpleasant encounter with Vax Holser.

"Attention!" A voice rang out in the enclosed space.

Lieutenants and midshipmen came out of their chairs. "As you were." I saw with relief that Vax was not among them. I found an empty seat. "Brief me, someone."

A familiar face. "Lieutenant Anton, sir. We're under attack. Hostiles, Fusing in at random intervals."

I already knew that. "Go on."

"The fleet's deployed, sir, as per Maneuver B. You're familiar with the plan, of course."

"No, you bloody—" I bit back the rest. It wasn't his fault I so desperately wanted a ship. "I was on shoreside duty when the plan was issued."

"Yes, sir. The fleet was divided, lightly patroling all sectors to maximize our chance of making contact. When the fish appeared, the Admiral ordered our ships to regroup into flotillas at preassigned locations within each sector. That's Maneuver B. Any ship under attack automatically became the locus for the flotilla in that sector."

"Very well."

"We count about thirty fish in all, sir."

"But that's—" Lord God. More than we'd ever seen before.

"Yes, sir."

"What are your standing orders, Lieutenant?"

"The Admiral's running the show from *Vestra*, sir. He communicates with Orbit Station by tightbeam. If he'd been here, it would be our office sending out fleet signals. While De Marnay's in orbit, his commands are relayed from the Station. Our job is to record them and serve as a backup, should—should . . ." He faltered.

"Yes?"

"Should the Station be damaged, sir."

"Lord God grant that it is not." I stared at the screen, trying to make sense of the blips. "What else do we know, Lieutenant?"

"*Freiheit* reported decompression. *Kitty Hawk* caught a transponder beam from her launch but hasn't had time to home on it. *Valencia*'s snuffed two fish, and *Hibernia*'s taken out four."

"Good."

The speaker crackled. "This is *Resolute*. We're engaging two fish. I—damn, make that three! Am firing."

The Admiral responded, "Very well, *Resolute*. *Kitty Hawk* is your closest support."

"Yes, sir. Derghinski, I'll ring if I need you." Gallows humor. I knew the impulse.

"Belay that!" The Admiral.

"Aye aye, sir." *Resolute*'s Captain, chastened.

"*Kitty Hawk* here. The bastards keep Fusing when we line up a shot." Derghinski swore. "Here come two more!"

I stared at the screen. Was I watching a coordinated attack or a feeding frenzy? Perhaps I'd never know.

"Admiral, *Kitty Hawk* reporting. We've taken a hit. Lost our portside thruster but otherwise undamaged. Got the fish." Without port thrusters Derghinski's maneuvering would be infinitely more complicated, and far slower.

"Very well."

"*Resolute*, here. We've got four beasties Fused in. Two amidshi—Oh, Jesus, they're—" Silence.

Lord God, save our people.

Lieutenant Anton pounded the console. "Where the hell are they coming from?" He glanced, saw my disapproval. "Sorry, sir."

I grunted. I too would like to know. More important, *why* did they come?

De Marnay's voice, calm. "Station, *Vestra* is under attack. Only one fish at present. Taking evasive—He's let a tentacle fly. Think he's going to miss." A long pause. "If I fail to respond for ten minutes, assume I'm out of commission. Captain Vorhees is senior, on *Electra*. Station, do you acknowledge?"

General Tho himself answered. I could sense the small, dark man pacing his office, fingers smoothing his neat little mustache. "Yes, Admiral, we do. It's in your standing orders."

"Admiralty House, do you copy?"

Lieutenant Anton keyed the caller. "Yes, sir."

"Who's on duty?"

"I am, sir: Anton. With Mr. Zalla and the techs. And three middies. Mr. Eiferts is below."

"You're senior, aren't you?"

"Uh, yes, sir. But Captain Seafort's with us."

"Seafort? What's he—Put him on."

I scrambled for the caller. "Yes, sir?"

"They know the drill, Seafort. Don't interfere."

"Yes, sir." My cheeks burned.

He hesitated. "Still, it's good you're there. If anything happens to me, you're in charge at Admiralty House until the chain of command is reestablished."

"Aye aye, sir."

He broke the connection.

We sat through the interminable afternoon, long dull periods of inaction, punctuated by terse reports of fish sighted, ships engaged, positions reached.

The fish kept coming.

We'd lost *Resolute* and *Freiheit*. *Kitty Hawk* broke off and limped back to Orbit Station, emergency patches on her hull.

We lost *Valencia*.

As inconclusively as the attack had begun, it dwindled. Finally, hours had passed with no further reports of attack. The surviving ships searched grimly for enemies, without success, but their sailors couldn't be kept at Battle Stations indefinitely. Our armada stood down.

It was late into the night before I left Admiralty House, drained and exhausted. We'd done nothing but listen and record, yet I felt as if I'd been in the thick of battle. My nerves tingled with the rush of adrenaline and fear.

Disoriented, I looked for my electricar, realized that Annie had dropped me at the spaceport the day before for my trip aloft. Without qualms I ordered a midshipman to drive me home in an Admiralty car. After all, I was acting Head of Station.

I brooded while we rode in silence through deserted streets. No one knew from where the fish came. Our xenobiologists suggested a large, low-density planet near a hot sun, but that was merely guesswork. We had no idea whether the fish themselves, or their outriders, were the dominant species. Perhaps they were symbiotes. They might even be different elements within one species. Both fish and outriders appeared to be unicellular organisms on a hitherto unimaginable scale. Were either species intelligent, or did they attack instinctively, without reason?

The middy cleared his throat. "Pardon, is that your building, sir?"

I nodded, realized he couldn't see in the dark. "Yes. Let me out in front."

"Aye aye, sir."

At the curb I got out, waved him off. In the distance boisterous shouts echoed. Some drunken melee, downtown.

So, what were we to do about the invaders? The U.N. had seventeen major colonies on hospitable worlds, and more planned. We mined a number of less-livable worlds for ores and fissionable elements. Our Navy couldn't possibly defend all our colonies at once; it would require ten times the ships we had, and each represented a colossal investment.

I trudged slowly up the walk, absently noting the twin shadows cast by Major and Minor. Could we abandon our colonies, withdraw to home system? Even retreat wouldn't free us from peril, unless our fleet stopped Fusing. Perhaps even that was too late; at least one fish had appeared in home system, mortally wounded, speared by *Challenger*'s prow in our last desperate attack.

I touched my thumb to the lock and let myself in quietly so as not to wake Annie.

Until we learned how many fish existed, we couldn't know if our fleet had the strength to protect Hope Nation, or if we'd be overwhelmed and annihilated. Today we'd lost three ships, and on them men I'd entertained in this very apartment. Captain Tenere of *Freiheit*, missing and presumed dead. Lieutenant Ter Horst of *Resolute*.

I groped my way to my favorite living-room chair, slipped off my shoes. Well, Mr. Ter Horst had met his aliens, and his optimism hadn't been justified. In the bedroom Annie stirred, moaned; a bad dream. Would she have been safer on Detour? For that matter, would *Concord* ever reach port there, or would the fish ravage her en route? Had I saved Annie's life, or held her back in greater peril?

Annie moaned again. I stood, my limbs weary. I was the one accustomed to nightmares; if my wife began having them too . . .

I padded to the bedroom door. Morning would be soon enough to worry about the fish. I heard Annie thrash against the sheets. I'd wake her, comfort her.

I opened the door. "Hon, are you all—"

A bare back, broad hips thrusting against upturned thighs, flesh gleaming in the light of two moons, frozen in a petrified moment of silence. As one they turned in shock, stared at the door.

Annie. Eddie Boss.

For an endless moment the tableau held.

I spun, slammed the door, bolted through the darkened living room, fumbled for my shoes. The sound of a window sliding, in the bedroom. I felt along the floor, pawed under the chair.

Eddie. Annie. I barked my shin on the coffee table. Where were the God-cursed shoes?

A shaft of light; the bedroom door opened. My shoes were near the couch where I'd left them.

Annie, a robe thrown over her nakedness. "Nicky?"

I tugged the laces tight on the left shoe, thrust my foot into the right.

"Nick . . ."

I stumbled to the door, opened it, lurched outside, fighting not to retch. The moonlight blinded me after the dark of the house. Mechanically I set one foot in front of the other. The walkway stretched to eternity. I reached our car. I couldn't trust myself to drive, not yet. The sidewalk, then. I strode, faster and faster, until my breath rasped and the darkened houses began to give way to the offices and stores of downtown.

I tried to think of nothing. Images intruded. My footsteps echoed, surprisingly loud.

I walked with head down, hands in my pockets. I heard a rasping sob, realized it was my own, cut it off. I crossed a street, then another. I passed an alley. Again I heard the footsteps, understood they weren't mine.

"Well, looka we have here!" A hand spun me around.

"What do you want?" I spat out the words.

"How 'bouta little loan? Few unibucks, 'til payday?" A brutish face leered in reflected moonlight.

Behind him, two broad-shouldered hoodlums snickered. "Skip the bilge, just do him!"

I slapped the hand from my shoulder. The other two joeys circled, their mirth vanished. A knife glinted.

"Hey, for an Uppie, you're kinda—whuf!"

I'd put everything I had into the uppercut. He reeled backward, slammed into the brick wall. His eyes rolled up as he slid to the ground.

"Get the motherfuc—"

The voice sounded like Eddie's. With a howl I hurled myself under the knife, wrenched the joey's arm, butted him in the stomach. He doubled over. I kneed his face with all the strength I could muster. A bone snapped. The third man backed away, hands extended, waving me off. He fled as I charged.

We sprinted through an alley, across an empty lot. Gradually he pulled ahead. Despite my frenzied efforts I fell back, until at last I lost him in the distant shadows. I fell to my knees, chest heaving, heart slamming against my ribs. Slowly the mists cleared.

When I could breathe again, I walked, until the first rays of daylight crept over downtown. I found a restaurant that opened early, sat at the counter sipping at steaming coffee, all I could afford. I'd left my jacket with my ID and money in my living room.

I couldn't abandon all my clothes; I had to go home. I would have to see her, if only for a moment. Where would I stay? Another apartment, perhaps. Or Naval barracks; they were open to me. I dropped a bill on the counter and plodded to the door.

Our apartment was many blocks to the west. Filthy and exhausted, I stumbled along the road, willing the streets to pass. My feet ached.

Ages later I trod the walkway, under a balcony whose view I'd once relished. I pressed my thumb to the lock, took a deep breath, walked in.

Annie lay curled on the couch, eyes red. "Nicky?"

My jacket first. I thrust in my arms. Now I had my papers, my pay, my insignia. An officer again, I felt a shade more secure.

"I'm sorry, Nicky." She sat hunched over, eyes wary. "I din' wan' hurt you."

I would need clothes. I went to the bedroom, opened the closet, slung my duffel on the bed. She'd put on fresh sheets, blanket folded down from the pillow, Navy corners. As if clean sheets could—I forced down the thought. Underwear, shirts, socks. I traded my grimy shirt for a fresh one.

She came to the bedroom door, sagged against it. "Talk to me, Nicky. Please."

I zipped the duffel.

Defiantly she stood in the open doorway, blocking my exit. "You got to unnerstan' one thing," she said. "I din' mean hurt you." Her beseeching eyes met mine. "Eddie an' I, we tribe. We knowed each other since N'Yawk! Tribe alla time doin' it, doncha unnerstan'? Even onna ship. Eddie wasn' only one."

I focused on the closet, desperate not to hear her words. What else would I need in barracks?

She fell into a chair by the door. "If you won' talk, listena me, then. I don' wan' you to go. You be my husban'."

"Until the Church grants an annulment."

She flinched as if struck. "Nicky, there anything I can do, make it up?"

"No."

She cried, "But I love you! Din' mean nothin', what we was doin'!"

My slap knocked her sideways out of the chair, onto her knees. Her fingers crept to her reddened face. I strode to the door, and beyond.

6

I drove through downtown looking for the barracks. I'd never had occasion to visit them but I knew they were behind Centraltown Hospital.

After a few twists and turns I was hopelessly lost. Finally I managed to reorient myself, but seeing the hospital reminded me two days had passed since I'd heard Alexi had wakened from his coma.

I parked, signed into barracks. The bored petty officer at the desk assigned me a room; I saw it had a bed, dumped my duffel on it, closed the door behind me as I left.

At the hospital I trudged wearily to Alexi's room. I opened the door cautiously, lest he be asleep. Alexi, bundled in a robe, sat by the window, hands crossed in his lap.

My heart leapt. "Oh, Alexi! How are you?"

"Not too bad, today." His eyes were on mine, as if awaiting my tidings.

"Thank heaven. We were so worried." Awkwardly I sat on the bed. "You were unconscious for so long . . ."

"Eleven days, they say."

"Does your head hurt?"

"No, but I'm weak as a baby."

I smiled. "We'll take care of that." Annie and I could fatten—My smile vanished. "You'll get your strength back." I stared at the floor. "There's something I need to tell you."

"Yes?" He watched me warily, as if he already knew. Had Annie been here first? She couldn't have. Eddie Boss, then?

"Things aren't going well, Alexi." I stared through the window. "The planters are disgusted that I haven't done anything for them, and at home—"

"I think you'd better—"

"No, let me finish," I said urgently. It was hard to speak, but I knew I must, before I burst. "Annie and I . . . while you were in coma, she and Eddie Boss and I sat with you almost every day. They called her for embarkation on *Concord*, and I married her. I wanted you there, but we didn't know when you'd recover." Or if. My eyes stung.

"Uh, I—"

I blurted, "Alexi, she's been with Eddie. I found them coupling in the bedroom. I took a room in barracks, but I don't know what to do." My voice was unsteady. "Help me. Please."

A moment's silence.

Alexi said, "Could you perhaps tell me who you are?"

An hour later we sat across from each other, Alexi on the bed, me in the chair. "You can't remember Academy either?"

"I'm trying. Don't you know how much I want to remember?"

"I'm not criticizing," I said gently. "Help me understand."

"I've been over it all with the doctors."

"Would you tell me too?"

"Why?"

"For old times' sake. For our friendship."

"I don't have any old times," he said bitterly. "Don't you realize?"

"No!" I flared. "And unless you help me, I never will!"

He recoiled from my wrath. Then, a sardonic smile. "Well, perhaps I deserved that; I wouldn't know. All right. When I woke up, I couldn't figure out where I was. A hospital, obviously, but where?" He shook his head. "They told me Hope Nation. It was . . . I'd heard of it, someplace, like a book I'd read years ago. When they called me 'Alexi,' I knew it was my name. At least I have that."

I ached for him. "Go on."

"They told me I'm a lieutenant in the Navy. It's not that it feels wrong. I can accept being a lieutenant. I just don't remember becoming one. You have to be a midshipman first, don't you?"

I nodded.

"I remember my mother; she lives in Kiev. Before I left

for school in the morning she'd thaw my lunch." His eyes showed alarm. "Is she still alive?"

"I don't know, Alexi."

"You said you were my closest friend."

"We were apart a year and a half. And we're a long way from home."

"If anything's happened to her . . ." His eyes filled.

"I'm sure she's all right," I said.

"The snow crunched under my feet on the way to school . . . you had to jiggle the switch to make our classroom holo work. I'm not a boy any longer, but those are my memories!"

"The others will come back."

"How do you know?"

I sighed. "I don't. Not for certain."

"I'd rather die than live like this!" He turned his face.

"Oh, Alexi." I squeezed his shoulder. "You'll be all right."

Alexi turned. Coldly he said, "Take your frazzing hand off me!"

I trudged back to the barracks, reeling from exhaustion. Above me loomed the spire of Reunification Cathedral, where Annie and I were married. I tried to block out her radiant smile, the sparkling ruby necklace, my answering grin of pleasure as we knelt at the altar to take our vows.

Until death do us part. Unless, of course, the marriage was annulled. I grimaced. Even if the elders permitted it, annulment made a travesty of our vows. The Church granted divorce for adultery, though several constituent sects consented to the rite with utmost reluctance. I would have to apply through the diocese and wait for approval. I headed up the barracks steps. What choice had I? I couldn't live with what she'd done.

For better or worse, until death do us part. I paused, my hand on the door.

Not adultery, Lord. That was too much to ask. Even the Church doesn't expect it.

"Ahh, Nicholas . . ." Father, his eyes bleak and disapproving.

In sickness and health, for better or worse . . . The barracks door swung open; two enlisted men came out, laughing until they spotted my insignia.

Regardless of the Church's toleration of divorce, I still knew right from wrong; Father had taught me well. I couldn't leave Annie without again betraying an oath. Yet, why did that matter, now that I was damned?

I cursed long and fluently. Then I went to my room, grabbed my duffel, got in my car, drove home.

She sat in the kitchen, sitting over a cup of tea. Her eyes raised slowly, hope dawning. "Nicky?"

My voice was like gritty sandpaper. "I won't divorce you. I swore to stay until death, and I'll fulfill my oath. You may divorce me, if you wish. I won't stop you."

"That's not what I wan'."

"Then we'll live together. What happened in the bedroom, we will not speak of. Not ever. That's all I have to say." I turned to put my duffel back in the bedroom.

"That's not all you swore." Tremulously she came to her feet. I stared at her. "Love, honor, and protect. You promised that part too."

The words caught in my throat. "I don't love you now. I—can't help that."

Her eyes brimmed. "What's marriage for?"

"I swore to it." Would that I hadn't.

"About Eddie—"

"Don't speak of him. I warn you."

"Will we sleep together? Share a bed? Talk?"

I sat heavily. "I don't know. It's all too much."

"You can't live here, hating me."

I rested my head on the table. "I don't hate you." Lord God, burn what I saw from my memory. Let me take Alexi's place, blessed with his forgetfulness. "Alexi has amnesia," I said. "He doesn't know me."

"Oh, Nicky."

I tried to speak, failed.

Her hand went to my neck, stroked me. "Nicky."

Jezebel, don't touch my flesh!

She gathered my head into her arms. Despite my resolve, I clung to her, buried my head in her soft breasts, clutched her as to a liferaft while my shoulders heaved with sobs.

PART 2

May, in the year of our Lord 2200

7

My outburst resolved nothing; after an hour I pulled myself together and went about my business. I could not put aside Annie's unfaithfulness even if I was grateful for her comfort. I realized I should have stayed in barracks; life in our apartment would be unbearably tense.

I roomed alone in the tiny spare bedroom, and I slept badly.

Daily, I visited Alexi. Sometimes Annie came along. Though Alexi seemed to like her, he had no memory of her.

A few days after the attack on our fleet, Admiral De Marnay returned to Admiralty House; we held our conference at last. He heard my account of the planters' grievances without interruption.

"And your conclusion?" He leaned back in his chair.

I pondered. "The planters' anger is one issue. The other is how the war effort has been handled."

"I told you to deal with the planters, not the war." His fingers drummed the desk irritably.

"Yes, sir. But I don't know whether their complaints are valid. If they are, and we seem to be ignoring them . . ."

"With any military buildup there's inefficiency, you know that." He glowered. "Especially when they insist on running the show from home, and informing me by holovid chip."

"I understand, sir."

"Don't you think I know it's madness to put our major base in the Venturas?" His fist rattled the table.

"Yes, sir. The complaints aren't mine."

After a moment the Admiral's glare faded. "I know." He sighed. We waited through the roar of a departing shuttle. "I could appoint you inspector-general," he mused.

"What?" I blushed. "Sorry, sir. There's no such post as inspector-general."

"Unless I create one." He tapped the papers on his desk. "Son, we've lost four ships. The enemy may strike again at any moment. The last thing we need is discontent on the home front; we *have* to keep the planters happy."

Again his fingers drummed. "Laura Triforth is right: without their help we'd never have been able to activate the Venturas Base, and we may need their aid again. Tell them you're appointed to check into their complaints so we can put them right."

"What authority would I have?"

"Authority to report to me. Don't scowl; it's a public relations title. If I decide anything needs doing, we'll take care of it."

I shook my head. "Those joeys trust me. Some are my friends. I won't pretend to be something I'm not, to mollify them."

De Marnay leaned forward, his warmth vanished. "They told me you had an insubordinate streak."

I was too tired to be diplomatic. "Yes, sir, I think I do. I'm sorry about it."

For the first time a hint of amusement flickered at his mouth. "Well, we understand each other. Take the job, and keep the planters off my back."

I stared at the floor, unready for the sudden crisis. After a time I said, "I'd rather resign, if you'll allow me."

"Resign what? Your liaison post?"

"No, sir. My commission." I met his eye.

He growled, "Don't threaten me; I'll take you up on it."

I took a deep breath. "Very well, sir."

He studied me intently, then sighed. "A lot *that* would do for morale. All right, Seafort, you've been demanding a real job, and I haven't obliged. Have it your way. I'll appoint you inspector-general. You have authority to inspect all installations and remedy any inefficiency or incompetence you find, subject to my veto. Your theater is the Venturas Base, our accommodations and arrangements in Centraltown, and Orbit Station. The fleet is off-limits; that's my bailiwick." He hesitated. "Are you aware I'm making you one of the most powerful men on the planet?"

"I'd prefer a ship."

"I told you, you'll have one. You still have two months of shore duty."

I capitulated. "Very well, sir. Where should I start?"

He stood. "How in hell would I know? That's your worry." He indicated the door. "My waiting room is packed. I need to get on with my appointments."

I said, "Pardon, sir, but why do you call me insubordinate, then hand me such power?"

"I have to work with the material at hand, Seafort. My other Captains are all shipboard, and I suppose the job really needs doing if the plantation zone is in such turmoil. Put in for a lieutenant or two as staff. And middies, if you want them." He sighed, then stuck out his hand. "Good luck."

I smiled, amazed at his largesse. "Thank you, sir."

In the outer office I asked the ubiquitous Lieutenant Eiferts where to apply for personnel. He directed me up-stairs.

The lieutenant in BuPers didn't bother to rise from his console. "Captain, you already have an enlisted man and a lieutenant."

"Lieutenant Tamarov is on sicklist. The enlisted man is . . . not available."

"Unfortunately, sir, the Admiral gave your liaison duty low priority. There's no way I can augment your staff. Sorry." With a perfunctory nod, he turned to his files.

I glowered. If he refused to give me staff I'd have to go over his head, and De Marnay would know I couldn't even put together a work detail. "I see."

His fingers tapped at the keyboard. After a time he looked up. "Is there anything else, Captain?"

"Yes. I'd like a lieutenant—no, make that two—assigned to my department forthwith."

"I've already told you why—"

"Stand at attention."

He complied, though slowly. "I'm on Admiral De Mar-nay's personal staff, sir. I'm not subject to outside orders."

"Be silent until I tell you to speak."

His position was awkward. As he'd said, he was on De Marnay's personal staff. Yet I was a Captain and he a mere lieutenant. And a Captain is obeyed, always.

I sat, leafing through a holozine. Several minutes passed, during which the lieutenant became more and more uneasy. I could see him readying himself to object to my high-handedness.

I asked abruptly, "Have you ever been to Miningcamp, Lieutenant?"

He looked confused. "No, sir."'

"You've heard of it?"

"Of course."

"Think you'll like it there?"

He said cautiously, "I'm afraid I don't know what you mean."

"U.N.A.F. runs the miners' station, you know, not the Navy. They don't have much in the way of amenities. The Station is more pleasant than the asteroid, though. At least Miningcamp Station is aired."

I browsed through the holozine. A glance told me I had his full attention. "Unless I get my staff in the next two minutes, you'll find yourself the new Naval liaison to Miningcamp, and you'll spend years wondering how you were transferred and shipped off-planet on less than an hour's notice." I switched off my holozine. "Do I make myself clear?"

"Quite, sir." He was sweating. "If I may, sir? I think I can make some changes." I nodded. With relief he dropped into his seat. His fingers flew over the keyboard. "I'll post the assignments immediately, sir. Have you any specific personnel in mind?"

I remembered the time I'd requisitioned staff at Hope Nation, years ago. "No behavioral problems. Top-rated fitness reports only."

"Aye aye, sir. They'll report to you tomorrow. Is that soon enough?"

"It will do."

"Shall I put your Mr. Tamarov on disability leave?" On general disability, Alexi would languish in the hospital, among uncaring strangers.

"No, leave him with me." Perhaps I could find a way to keep him busy. Some way to summon his memories.

I stood, strode to the door. "One more thing."

"Yes, sir?" The lieutenant was all ears.

"The enlisted man on my staff, Eddie Boss. He's in barracks now. Transfer him to the first ship going outsystem."

"Aye aye, sir." He saluted as I left.

On my way to the car, I tried to imagine Admiral De Marnay's response had the BuPers officer complained I was reassigning him to Miningcamp. Foolish joey, the lieutenant. After all, it was he who posted the assignments.

While waiting in my apartment for my two new staffers I reviewed my notes. True to his word, Admiral De Marnay had cut orders authorizing me to "investigate and correct abuses and inefficiency of whatever nature with respect to the state of readiness of U.N. Forces in the Hope Nation theater." With surprise, I realized that my writ ran to U.N. Armed Forces as well as Navy; De Marnay was in charge of the whole show and he'd chosen to give me a free hand.

My first need was office space. I couldn't very well be inspector-general from my living room.

I paced. I had promised Alexi I'd visit at noon. Annie, anxious to please, had left the apartment for the morning so I'd be free to meet with my lieutenants.

Should I start with the Venturas? A quick trip would give me a picture of what I faced. Hopefully, Laura Triforth had exaggerated the problems there. In any event, I'd like to glimpse the Venturas once more, though Amanda was long dead and Derek was light-years distant.

The doorbell chimed. I answered it, and recoiled.

"Lieutenant Tolliver reporting for duty, sir." He saluted.

"I know your name," I snarled. "Did you request this posting?" Disgusted, I turned away.

He followed me inside. "No, sir. Orders came in transferring me off *Portia*. That's all I know."

Was the BuPers lieutenant exacting his revenge? No, he had no way to know of my resentment of Tolliver.

"I'll get someone else," I muttered. "This must be as awkward for you as for me."

He looked surprised. "Awkward, sir? Why?"

"Don't tell me you can't remember."

"When we were cadets, sir?"

I nodded.

"I was a class ahead of you."

"Yes." You made life so much more miserable than need be.

"I'm sorry you're uncomfortable with me, sir. I certainly have no objection to working with you."

I peered suspiciously. Apparently he meant it. "You don't recall Academy?"

He stared, uncomprehending. "The hazing, you mean?" He shrugged. "Part of the drill, as far as I was concerned."

"I hated you." And still do.

He shrugged again. "I'm sorry, sir. I was hazed too, my first year."

My angry reply was forestalled by the chime. Lieutenant Eiferts. I let him in. "A message from the Admiral?"

"No, sir. I've been assigned to your operation."

"What?"

"I'm to join your staff."

"But you work directly for the Admiral."

"I did until today."

I hadn't known De Marnay was so devious. Whom could he trust to keep an eye on me, if not his personal aide?

"I see. I suppose if I asked for another lieutenant, they'd all be unavailable?"

The corners of his mouth turned up. "Perhaps, sir. I'm not in BuPers."

I could work with him, even if he was a spy for the Admiral, but I had to know. "Mr. Tolliver, outside."

"Aye aye, sir." Tolliver's obedience was automatic; he'd just come from a ship. Eiferts, on the other hand, had served in a soft shoreside berth. We would see.

"Well now." I paced, as if on a bridge. "Who engineered this, you or the Admiral?"

"Engineered what, sir?" Eiferts was the soul of innocence.

I said nothing. After a time, he shifted uncomfortably. I let the silence drag on.

"I'm to help however you see fit," he ventured.

"To whom is your loyalty, Lieutenant? Me or the Admiral?"

He looked puzzled. "Is there a conflict, sir?" Good question. What did I have to hide?

I smiled grimly. "Will you report to him?"

"I presume you'll expect me to do your staff work, sir. That would include processing your reports."

I roared, "Tell the truth, you insolent sea lawyer! All of it! At once!"

He flushed. "Yes, sir!" He thrust out a palm, as if to ward off my fury. "I'm to be of whatever assistance I can, sir. I'm also to report to the Admiral at my own discretion. Anything I think he should know."

I resumed my pacing. "Were your orders to report to him in secret, Lieutenant?"

He hesitated. "Not specifically, sir. I think that was understood."

"Very well. Report to the Admiral as ordered, and inform me each time you report to him. Acknowledge."

"Aye aye, sir. I will inform you each time I report to Admiral De Marnay. Orders received and understood, sir." His forehead glistened.

"Very well, then. Welcome to my staff, Lieutenant Eiferts."

"Thank you, sir." He smiled weakly.

"I'm going to the hospital to visit Mr. Tamarov. You know the ropes; how long will it take to get office space?"

"Do you want rooms in Admiralty House, sir?"

"Um, no. Downtown, I should think."

"Perhaps near Naval barracks . . . I could make a couple of calls, sir." He brightened at the thought of dealing with matters he understood.

"Very well. In the morning we leave for the Venturas. I want office space by the time we're home." I ushered him out.

Tolliver, hands clasped behind his back, was examining the flowers along the walk. I growled to him. "We'll need a couple of holovids, a day's rations, and a heli for the Venturas in the morning. See to it."

"Aye aye, sir." Tolliver cleared his throat. "Does that mean I'm to stay on your staff, sir?"

"It means you have your orders." I strode away. Driving to Centraltown Hospital I sighed with exasperation. I'd thoroughly alienated both my new staffers, to say nothing of the BuPers lieutenant at Admiralty House. A fine start.

"What are the Venturas?" Alexi frowned.

"The mountain range of Western Continent," I repeated patiently. Awesome peaks they were, which towered over vast tracts of unspoiled wilderness.

"And we—your Navy—have a base there?"

"Yes, Alexi."

"Am I required to go?"

"No."

"Then I'd rather not." He stared down at the manicured lawn below his window.

"Very well." I tried not to feel hurt. "I'll see you when I'm back."

"If you wish."

As I headed for the door he blurted, "What will they do with me?"

"You're on sick leave until you get well."

"The doctors say I may never get my memory back . . . if I don't, am I still in the Navy? Do I have to follow orders?"

"You haven't been discharged, Alexi. But if you don't recover, I'm sure they'll allow you a medical release."

"And then?" He turned, with a bitter smile. "I have nowhere to go and haven't the faintest idea what I should do."

It was as close to an appeal as I'd heard. "I'll look after you, Alexi."

He turned back to the window. "I don't want to be looked after."

"I'm sorry." I thought to touch his shoulder, refrained. "Good-bye, then."

"Good-bye, Mr. Seafort." He hesitated. "Am I supposed to call you 'sir'?"

"Of course. But I won't hold you to it until you remember why."

"Thank you." When I left he was staring out the window.

8

The flight west to the Venturas was as I remembered it: uneventful hours droning over the shallows of Farreach Ocean. Lush submarine vegetation sent tentacles groping for the surface, where they contested for sunlight with water lilies that rose and fell gently with the swells. Hope Nation had no animal life, so the ocean was a vast soup of competing herbage.

I piloted the military machine with relaxed enjoyment. One hand on the collective, the other on the cyclic, the puter switched to passive mode, I had ample time to recall which switches operated the various missiles and antimissile gear with which the heli could be armed. About two hours from Western Continent our radar homed on the Venturas Base beacon. I switched on the autopilot and leaned back, glad of the rest. I'd been flying for six hours.

In the rear seat, Tolliver dozed. Next to me, Lieutenant Eiferts studied his holovid. "Sir?"

"What?"

"I've been looking over the material and supplies we poured into that base, sir. In theory the plan made sense, but I don't think it worked out too well."

"Pity you weren't in charge of strategic planning," I said acidly. He fell silent, until I relented. "I gather the idea was to be able to defend both hemispheres."

"When Orbit Station is over Eastern Continent, Western Continent has a clear shot at any invaders above it. But that meant we had to split our resources. We should have put the base where we could support it."

"That's what we're here to learn," I reminded him.

"Anyway, ships make better laser platforms than land installations."

"But ships are so vulnerable to attack. Look how many

105

we've lost." My *Challenger*, among them. "And fish don't operate groundside."

"Unless it was they who brought the Hope Nation virus."

"They probably did." I shivered, despite the afternoon warmth. "There was a fellow, years ago, who claimed he saw them spraying."

"Captain Grone."

I looked up in surprise. "You knew about him?"

He nodded. "Used to live near the Great Falls area."

"What happened to him?"

"Nobody knows, sir."

Poor, demented Captain Grone. When I'd met him, his wife Janna was due to have a child. I wondered if the baby had survived. I thought of Nate, who would be three now. My throat tightened.

The speaker crackled. "Incoming heli, course two oh nine, identify yourself."

Lieutenant Eiferts reached for the caller. "Ventura, this is Naval heli two four nine Alpha, ETA your base forty minutes."

"We don't show a flight plan filed, two four nine Alpha. Who are you?"

"Captain Nicholas Seafort and staff. We're here to insp—"

I switched off the caller.

"Sir?" Eiferts gaped.

"Aboard ship my lieutenants knew their place," I growled. I pried the caller from his hand, keyed it on. "Ventura Base, this is Captain Seafort, U.N.N.S. We're on a sightseeing trip through the Venturas."

"Unauthorized visitors aren't allowed, sir."

I recalled our carefree flight to the falls, Derek, Amanda, and I. No flight plan, no authorizations.

The voice hesitated. "You're, uh, Captain Seafort? *The* Captain Seafort?"

"Yes." Again, my cursed notoriety.

"I'm sure the General—I'll have to confirm, sir, but I'm certain it will be all right. Do you have our beacon?"

"Affirmative."

"Please stay on your present course. I'll be back to you." The line went dead.

Eiferts looked abashed. "Sorry, sir. I thought it was customary to check in with Base Command."

I'd learn more from an unannounced trip, even if it meant we'd travel under false colors. But still . . . I sighed. "I'm on edge, Mr. Eiferts. Pardon me."

He looked startled. Captains did not apologize to lieutenants, even when wrong. "Yes, sir, of course. Sorry I interfered."

We flew in silence, a knot forming in my stomach. The speaker crackled. "Captain Seafort, General Khartouf welcomes you to Venturas Base. Would you join him this evening for dinner?"

I keyed the caller. "I'd be happy to accept." Eiferts shot me a glance, but was silent.

"Very well, sir, we'll expect you."

We were coming over the coastline. Great hills swept down from the highlands to plunge into the sea. Behind them the sun was drifting toward the horizon.

"Wake Tolliver."

"I'm up, sir." He leaned forward from the rear seat.

"Listen, both of you. When we land I'll go with the top brass. You two get a look around. We'll meet later and compare notes."

Eiferts said, "Aye aye, sir. What are we looking for?"

"Anything odd. Evidence that the base isn't well run. Sloppy security or lack of readiness."

"We already know their security is sloppy," Tolliver said.

I scowled. "How so?"

"They're letting us land, though we're unexpected and have no flight plan filed."

"I'm a U.N.N.S. Captain," I snapped.

"They only know you *said* you are," he replied coolly.

I bit back an irate reply. He was right.

When we were a few miles from the airfield I took over from the autopilot. I followed the beacon until the base was in sight, and set down on their parade ground, as instructed.

The field was a parade ground in name only. Around it, red earthen roads gouged from the plain were a mass of ruts; after a hard downpour the base must be a morass. Prefab barracks and stark operations buildings lined the perimeter road.

I straightened my jacket, tugged at my tie as a handful of officers approached, ducking under the slowing blades.

"Captain Seafort? General Khartouf." I shook the proffered hand. "My adjutant, Major Rinehart." He introduced me to the rest of his staff.

I took a deep breath; time for work. "Impressive place you have, General."

"A bit rough, still." He grinned through even white teeth. "But we manage." His eyes flickered to my scar. "We've heard a lot about you, Captain."

I grunted. I wasn't here to talk about myself. "How many men do you have, sir? Last time I was in Western Continent I saw nothing but wilderness."

"Three thousand. And they're hardly enough." We strolled toward the main building. "Join me for a drink, Captain. And your officers too, if you wish."

"My lieutenants can look after themselves," I said offhandedly. "Eiferts, Tolliver, you're off duty until the morning."

"Aye aye, sir." My two aides watched me saunter off with the Base C.O.

Dinner was served by an enlisted steward. Though I'd dismissed my lieutenants in cavalier fashion, the General's dining hall was crowded with his own officers. It was only after the soup, while we were engaged in animated conversation, that I realized they'd all come for a glimpse of me. Dismayed, I forced my attention back to General Khartouf's comment.

"They'd be easier to fight if we had weapons designed specifically for them."

"Pardon? The fish, you mean?" I toyed with my second course. It happened to be fish, imported frozen from home, and I felt my appetite subside. "Unfortunately, we don't know what weapons would work best."

"That's what I was saying." The General eyed me askance.

A middle-aged colonel cleared his throat. "Pardon me, sir, but what was most effective in your own encounters with the fish?"

His neighbor turned his head, so as not to miss a word. I

stopped, fork halfway to mouth, realizing the entire table was hanging on my answer. Did they expect a blow-by-blow account of my battles? Was that the price of my dinner? Nausea battled with disgust. I wouldn't have it. Not for all the fine Terran wines on the starched white tablecloth.

No, it wasn't the price of my dinner. It was the price of my two lieutenants having the run of the base, free to ask innocent questions. I forced a smile. "Well, on *Challenger*, they attacked three times . . ."

Unnoticed, the forkful of fish returned to my plate.

"So?"

My two lieutenants exchanged looks. Eiferts gave a small nod, and Tolliver began. "Venturas Base has been in operation over a year, sir. They've had the prefab factory set up for half that time, but the enlisted men are still living five to a two-man unit."

I thought of the transients, shipped to Hope Nation six to a cabin, packed like sardines. "Go on."

"The prefab factory was run by civilians brought from Terra on six-month contracts. They agreed to an extension, but demanded and got return passage after nine months. By then the Army was supposed to have men trained to replace them. Because it took so long to get the factory operating, the workers weren't well trained. Apparently production is minimal at best. No one's seen any celuwall leave the plant in months. I couldn't ask too much more without making the sergeant suspicious."

I waited, but that was all Tolliver had to say. I turned to Eiferts. "And you?"

"I took a long walk, sir. None of the roads are paved. Someone told me in winter they're virtually impassable."

"That's all you learned?" My tone was scathing.

"No, my stroll took me to the laser control building. I was enthralled, so the lieutenant on duty showed me through." Wearily, he made as if to sit, realized he was in my presence. "The base has four huge puter-aimed laser cannon powered by the emergency fission station the planters hauled from Centraltown. The actual cannon are on that rise south of the base. Their combined firepower would be staggering. Unfortunately, they can't be fired together."

"Why?" I gestured to the seat.

Gratefully he eased himself into a chair. He must have had a long hike. "Thanks, sir. Because the power step-down lines haven't been hooked properly. Only one laser can be fired at a time."

"Christ!" Tolliver, with feeling.

I glared. "I don't condone blasphemy."

"Your pardon, sir."

"Though I share the sentiment. The only real purpose of this base is to man those laser emplacements." I brooded. "We need to know if Khartouf mentioned these shortfalls to Admiral De Marnay. I'll call in the morning."

"He didn't, sir," said Eiferts.

"Oh?"

"Khartouf's progress reports passed over my desk, sir. I brought everything of importance to the Admiral's attention."

"That smug bastard!"

Eiferts's jaw dropped.

"Khartouf," I growled, "not Mr. De Marnay." I paced the length of our tiny cubicle, my chest tight. "What do we do?"

Eiferts said, "How do your orders read? 'Investigate and correct abuses and inefficiency'?"

"You saw them?"

"I posted them." He smiled apologetically.

"Call their office and get me an appointment with General Khartouf for the morning."

"Aye aye, sir."

I went into my adjoining bedroom and took off my jacket. A moment later, a knock. Lieutenant Eiferts, his mouth set in a grim line. "There's no answer at Base HQ, sir."

"What?"

"I can't get through."

I swore fluently. Lieutenant Tolliver raised an eyebrow.

Eiferts said, "I ought to mention, sir, that I'll be reporting this to Admiral De Marnay."

"Never mind that." I thrust my feet back into my shoes. "Let's go."

"Where, sir?"

"Out." I stalked down the corridor, the two lieutenants dogging my heels.

"HQ building, sir?" panted Eiferts.

"No. The laser control station first."

He winced at the prospect of another long hike. "Aye aye, sir." He pointed down the perimeter road. "It's that way."

It took several minutes at fast pace to reach the laser installation. The night air was chill, and though the exercise warmed me I felt the tickle of a cold coming on.

We approached the darkened building. It seemed deserted but as we neared I saw a dim light in a side window. "What's in there?"

"I don't know," said Eiferts. "I used the front gate, and the sergeant took me directly to the control room."

I stopped beneath the window. From that vantage point all I could see was a ceiling. "Boost me up."

Tolliver gaped.

"Boost me. How else am I supposed to see?"

"Aye aye, sir." He made a cup with his hands and braced himself.

I hoisted myself up to cling from the window frame. After a moment I dropped down again.

"What did you see, sir?" Eiferts whispered.

I shook my head, unable to speak.

"What, sir?"

"They're playing cards," I snarled. "Two men in the comm room, sitting over a deck of cards."

"On duty?" Tolliver was scandalized. On ship, such conduct would bring down the Captain's almighty wrath. With a twinge of guilt I recalled my chess games on the bridge, during the long dreary hours of watch. But we were Fused then. Wasn't that different?

"Freeze!"

I looked up. The sentry's gun pointed directly at me.

"Easy, soldier," said Tolliver. "This man's—"

"What are you joeys doing?"

A face appeared at the window. "Sarge, what's—"

The sentry snapped, "Call HQ, stat. We've got intruders."

"I—"

"Move it, Varney!"

The face disappeared. "Stay put, all of you," the guard ordered. He waved his laser rifle at me. "Well?"

"I'm Captain Nicholas Seafort."

"I know who you are. I asked what you were doing."

I approached him, ignoring the weapon he brandished. As I neared, I could see the stereoplug in his ear.

"What's that?" Without warning I snatched it from him.

"Hey, give it—"

"A stereoplug? On sentry duty?" Slap music emanated faintly from the plug.

"You've got no right—"

With my heel, I ground the plug into the dirt. Over seventy unibucks, in Centraltown, and that a continent away.

The sentry, wary now, looked back and forth among us. "Just what's up, here?"

"I'm acting with the authority of Admiral Georges De Marnay, head of Unified Command. Where is your C.O.?"

"General Khartouf?" He pointed up the road we'd just followed. "Officers' barracks."

"Very well. Take us there."

He shook his head. "I can't leave my post."

"You may now. You're relieved."

"What's your authority to give me orders?"

My opinion of him went up a notch. "Mr. Tolliver, your holovid." Tolliver pulled a portable from his pocket, switched it on, snapped in a chip. "Read this," I said to the guard.

By moonlight, on the laser building steps, the sentry read carefully through my orders. At length he said, "Well, sir, I guess they put you in charge. I'm Sergeant Trabao. If you'll follow me to officers' barracks . . ."

The officers' dormitory was a hundred yards from the HQ building, not far from our own rooms. Outside, a lone sentry slouched in the shadows. At the sight of us he thrust something in his pocket. "Hey, what are you—"

"It's all right, Portillo, they're with me." Uncertain, the second sentry stood aside.

Trabao said, "The General's—"

"—right here." Khartouf stood on the top step, hands on hips. "What in bloody hell are you up to?"

I said, "You'll want to discuss it privately, General."

"Nonsense. Why are you skulking around my base in the middle of the night? Your answer better be good, or you'll find yourselves in the guardhouse."

"I'm here by order of Georges De Marnay, Admiral Commanding." Not quite true; De Marnay had authorized my jaunt but he certainly hadn't ordered it. I pressed on. "I'm inspecting your readiness."

"By standing on your flunky's hands peering into windows?"

I felt an idiot. "My conduct is not at issue."

"It bloody well is, Captain!"

"Tolliver, show him the chip."

Lieutenant Tolliver proffered his holovid. "Here, sir."

Khartouf took the holo, let it fall to the dirt. "You men, escort them to the guardhouse. By force, if necessary. We'll deal with them in the morning."

The second sentry reached for his pistol. Sergeant Trabao shook his head. "No, sir. I think you'd better read the holo."

"Portillo, put Sergeant Trabao under arrest with the rest."

I protested, "If you'll just read my orders—"

"Prong your orders. I give you the hospitality of my table, and you sneak around betraying us in the night. I won't have—"

Something snapped within. I snarled, "What you'll have no longer matters. You're relieved of command."

Tolliver, Eiferts, and even Trabao gaped, but I was past caring. "Eiferts, take Sergeant Trabao's pistol. Move when I give an order! Now, cover Mr. Khartouf. Mr. Trabao, we'll adjourn to the Commandant's office. Lead the way."

A few moments later General Khartouf slammed the holovid down on his table. "All right, Seafort, I've read the bloody thing! You have authority to relieve no one."

"You're wrong." I turned to the Sergeant. "Mr. Trabao, we'll be leaving first thing in the morning. Make sure my heli is ready."

"We'll see who ends up relieved," the General jeered.

"The moment you're gone I'll be on the caller to Admiralty House."

"No, you won't. I'm taking you along."

Eiferts stirred, his uneasiness apparent. "Who'll run the base, sir? Someone has to be in charge."

"True."

"Who, sir? I ought to put it in my report."

"You."

"I—WHAT?"

"You're acting Base Commandant, as of now."

He spluttered, protocol abandoned. "But—me, sir? Why?"

"You know the problems; you've seen the reports General Khartouf sent. And I don't know who else to trust. So it's you."

"I'd need the Admiral's approval for that, sir," he said slowly. "I don't know if—"

"Have you heard of a chain of command?" My tone was savage. "Does a Captain outrank a lieutenant?"

He stared until he comprehended, then his eyes fell. "Aye aye, sir. I'm sorry. Orders received and understood, sir."

"Very well." I paced the office. "We're too keyed up to sleep. Turn on the office holo. Find the files on the prefab plant. You'll need what help the General will give you. I think you'll have your hands full cleaning up this fiasco."

"The only fiasco here is attempted kidnapping," the General shouted. "You think I'll help you rifle my files? I'll watch your hanging, Seafort! This is mutiny!"

I turned. Something in my eyes gave him pause. "Hanging?" My voice was odd. "Don't bring up the subject, General. I could stretch my authority even further."

"You wouldn't da—"

"Try me." I held my gaze until he looked away. "Mr. Eiferts, the General will show you his files now. I'll be outside. Mr. Trabao, come along."

In the hallway, I confronted the guard. "I don't think much of a stereochip on sentry duty."

He reddened. "Things have been sort of slack around here."

"You like it that way?"

He studied me. "The truth? No. I was a drill sergeant back

in Rio. But when no one backs you up, it's hard. You end by doing what the others do. I wasn't always like that."

"You don't have to be, any longer."

"Sir?"

"Mr. Eiferts will need an aide who knows his way around. Can we trust you, Trabao?"

He let out a long, slow breath. "Yes."

"I will, then. Show Mr. Eiferts the ropes."

"Yes, sir."

"I'll be outside." Shivering, I coughed. The room seemed chill.

"Stand at attention!"

I complied at once. Admiral De Marnay, red-faced, planted himself inches from my nose. "What in Lord God's own hell are you up to, Seafort? Are you power-mad?"

"No, sir." At least, I didn't think so. I felt exhausted. It had been a long, sullen trip back. Lieutenant Eiferts must have radioed ahead; after we landed I had no trouble getting an appointment with the Admiral. Not this time.

He bellowed, "The hell you aren't!"

"Sir, I—"

"Quiet, you presumptuous young—you upstart! You lunatic! You—" He spluttered to a halt.

Spine rigid, hands pressed to my sides, I stared at the wall behind his desk.

"Who gave you authority to remove a commander in the field, you insolent pup?"

"You did, sir."

"Be silent, I said!" That was unfair; when he asked a question I was obligated to answer. He growled, "Khartouf was appointed by the U.N.A.F. Chief of Staff! Am I supposed to tell Staff a baby-faced Captain, acting without orders, removed his man from office?"

I assumed the question was rhetorical.

"Answer!"

I'd assumed wrong. "No, sir."

"Oh? You're suggesting I lie to him?"

Wearily I said, "No, sir."

Admiral De Marnay flung himself into his seat. "I ought to court-martial you, Seafort!"

I knew there'd be trouble, but I hadn't expected quite so much. Well, I'd often considered resigning; now the Navy would save me the trouble. "On what charges, sir?"

"Insubordination, incitement to rebellion, mutiny . . . Don't worry, we'll find ones that fit!"

"Very well, sir."

He roared, "Is that all you have to say for yourself?"

"No, sir."

"Then say it, before I throw you out of here!" His jaw jutted.

I said, "Khartouf's base is a shambles. His lasers sit unready, his barracks unbuilt, while he dines in luxury with his officers. He's a fool."

"That's not your judgment to make."

"He's also a corrupt fool."

"I told you—eh?"

"Lieutenant Eiferts spent the night going through Khartouf's puter accounts. According to Mr. Trabao, the men have had nothing but Q-rations for the last six months."

"Well, it's a war zone. What of it?"

"There were indents for tons of supplemental foodstuffs purchased in Centraltown and supposedly flown to the base. No one knows where it went."

He was observing me closely. "Go on."

"The food may have been imaginary, or it may actually have been sent to the Venturas and resold from there. I have no idea; we didn't have time to trace it."

He shifted in his seat. "All right, assume Khartouf had his hand in the till. Perhaps he should have been removed and tried. But not by you, Seafort. Not by you."

"I understand that now, sir. I made a bad mistake."

"In removing him?"

"No, sir. In taking your orders literally."

It brought him out of his chair, hands closing into fists. I was still imprisoned at attention, my back aching, and I felt dizzy. I shouldn't have taken that long walk in the cold Venturas night.

"By God, Seafort, you're an arrogant one!"

I no longer cared. "That may be so. You knew what I was when you appointed me!" It was breathtaking insolence, for which I would have instantly broken a subordinate. I ignored his stunned amazement and rushed on. "You ordered me to investigate and correct abuses and inefficiency. Tell me how Khartouf's abuses could have been corrected without removing him!"

"You could report to me. I'd have removed him."

"You didn't order me to report abuses! You said to correct them!"

"Don't be a sea lawyer," he growled. "I had no idea that meant stripping a Base Commander of his post."

"Neither did I, sir," I said truthfully. We lapsed into silence while I fought to remain at proper attention. His anger abating, the Admiral sank back into his chair. At length I said, "Will you court-martial me?"

"Eh? No, of course not. You knew I was just letting off steam."

I'd known no such thing. "Very well, sir." I hesitated. "It's clear you don't want me to continue as inspector-general."

"I'm the Admiral here, Seafort! I'll tell *you* what's clear."

"Yes, sir."

"Stand easy."

I sagged with relief. "May I sit?" At his nod I dropped into a chair. "Sorry, sir. I don't feel well."

He tapped his desk, lost in thought. "Khartouf's brother is Assistant Deputy SecGen, as you no doubt knew." He shook his head. "Have you any idea of the trouble you've made?"

"You can always veto my acts, sir."

"You know I have to stand behind you. Reinstating him now would be a license to steal. And the Navy has to look after its own."

"I see." It was the wrong reason to back me.

His annoyance flared again. "And you've taken my chief aide as well."

"Mr. Eiferts? I needed someone immediately, and uh, I had to work with the material at hand."

"Don't be insolent!"

"Aye aye, sir. Eiferts knew the problems, and he had your confidence. He was ideal."

"I know. You were right. I can't see who else to put in charge, so now I'm without his services."

"Sorry." He couldn't have it both ways.

"Don't get in a huff, Seafort. It's all my fault; I wrote your blessed orders myself." For the first time his eyes held a glint of humor.

"What should I do now, sir?"

He tapped his desk. After a time he sighed and said, "Go on with your business."

"As inspector-general?" I sounded incredulous.

"That's your post," he snapped. "While you're at it, check the shipping records on Orbit Station. See if you can figure out why we have such a pileup of supplies at Centraltown."

"Aye aye, sir."

The Admiral's thoughts were elsewhere. "We won't try him here, of course. Send him to Earth with a full accounting."

"Yes, sir." The hot potato would be handed on.

"You'll have made enemies at home, Seafort. That's out of my hands."

"Yes, sir."

"Very well, dismissed." As I headed for the door he added, "You relieved Khartouf before you found he was stealing."

"Yes, sir."

His eye met mine. "Someday you'll go too far."

I held his gaze for a long moment.

"Dismissed."

9

Early in the morning I drooped over my kitchen table inhaling coffee, struggling to wakefulness, still bothered by my
cold. Tolliver was due at our new office near the barracks in
an hour; I needed something to keep him busy. Arrange an
inspection trip to Orbit Station? No, if I alerted the Station I
wouldn't see regular operations, I'd find a station made
ready for inspection. Though I detested it, I would have to
keep skulking about.

I tied my shoes. Annie had gone out to shop, giving me
the distance I obviously wanted. Why, then, did I feel miserable? I left for work.

We'd been assigned a three-room suite: my office, a room
for my two lieutenants, and a waiting room for visitors.
Plush, by naval standards. Tolliver was waiting.

Inside, I sat drumming my desk. I had a report to prepare,
but nothing else to do.

"I'm going to the hospital for an hour or so."

"Yes, sir. Do you have an assignment for me?"

I thought of piling him with drudgery, in revenge for the
hazing which he'd once inflicted. Abstract the quartermasters' reports for the last eighteen months. Detail the labor
that the planters supplied to Venturas Base. Count the bricks
in the top thirty feet of the building.

"Nothing for now." I added reluctantly, "Would you care
to visit Mr. Tamarov?" I knew I'd prefer to see Alexi alone.

"I'd like to meet him, sir."

"Very well." I sighed.

At the hospital, Alexi's glance flitted between us as if assessing our relationship. Our conversation was stilted. After
a while Tolliver wandered to the coffee shop, to give us time
alone.

Absently, Alexi rubbed at the stubble covering his scalp

where his bandage had been, while I told him about my escapade in the Venturas. When I was done he ventured, "Relieving him won't hurt your career?"

I shrugged. "I already have enemies. I make them wherever I go."

"Really?"

"Does that surprise you?"

He studied me. "Well, yes."

I shook my head. "I have no talent at dealing with people."

"But you're kind."

I snorted with derision. "You can't be serious."

"I am, Mr. Seafort."

"How little you remember." I was immediately sorry, but it was too late.

He reddened, but said, "You've certainly been kind since I woke. Was it once different?"

"Yes." I wished the subject hadn't come up. "When you were a midshipman."

"I seem to have survived."

I grunted, looking to change the topic. "You're gaining your strength."

"Yes." He stood, walked to the window. "What do I do now?"

"You're on sick leave. Wait for your memory to return."

"It won't, you know." He spoke as if certain. "The doctors tell me that after so long a coma, there's only a small chance."

I groped for a way to help him, found none. "I'm sorry."

"They've room here. They're in no hurry to eject me." He slumped back on his bed.

Tolliver returned. I shivered, reminding myself to find some meds for my cold. "I'll see you again in a day or so."

"Nice of you."

Something in Alexi's voice gave me pause. "Don't you want me to visit?"

He was silent a long while. "You don't understand. You come, and talk about people I should know and places I ought to remember. It's excruciating."

I said stiffly, "I won't bother you, if that's what you'd prefer."

He spoke as if Tolliver weren't present. "You still don't see. I sit in this damned room day after day, listening for your step. If it wasn't for you, I'd have nobody who cared. I'm dependent on you, and it's terrifying!"

"Oh, Alexi." I squeezed his shoulder. This time, he didn't pull free. "I'm so sorry. I'll visit every day until you're better."

"Until they give you a ship, you mean. Then I'll be alone."

True. A warship was no place for a confused and injured officer. "That won't be for a while," I said. "You'll be well by then."

"Will I?" He stared at the window.

The silence stretched. Tolliver said, "Mr. Tamarov, these things take time. I had an uncle once—"

"I don't give Christ's damn about your uncle!"

Tolliver and I exchanged glances. I said, "We'd best go. We're upsetting you."

"As you wish." Alexi still hadn't moved.

"Come, Mr. Tolliver." I drifted to the doorway, motioned for Tolliver to pass. Alexi turned. In two strides he was at the door, clutching my wrist. "Mr. Seafort, I—"

Tolliver thrust himself between us, sent Alexi sprawling onto the bed.

I caught his arm. "Tolliver, no!"

"He handled you!"

Alexi leaped to his feet. Tolliver raised his fists.

"BELAY THAT, BOTH OF YOU!" My bellow tore at my throat, but it halted the melee.

"Aye aye, sir," Tolliver said at once. He trembled slightly as he brushed the neatly creased pants of his uniform.

"Tolliver, by the door! Alexi, sit!"

Alexi made as if to object, sank onto the bed. "He shoved me!"

"Yes. You touched me."

"So? You touch me at times."

"I'm a Captain."

"What does that have—"

Tolliver's tone was harsh. "It is a capital offense to touch the Captain."

"I wasn't fighting, just—"

"He's right, Alexi. Tolliver, he didn't know."

"He's a Naval officer."

"Who suffers from amnesia. You will make allowances."

Tolliver swallowed. "Aye aye, sir."

Alexi sat, his knees shaky. "Will I be executed?"

"Alexi, for God's sake!"

He flung himself across the bed. "I don't understand your world! I can get killed doing what seems perfectly innocent!"

My voice was husky. "Sit up." I waited for him to comply. "What were you saying when Mr. Tolliver interrupted?"

Alexi blinked. "It's hardly . . . I didn't want you to go. I knew I'd been taking out my frustration on you."

"Neither of you meant any harm." I held Tolliver's eye, then Alexi's. "I want an end to this."

Tolliver was the first to respond. "Mr. Tamarov, I bear you no ill will."

Alexi stood shakily. "I'm sorry I touched your Captain; I understand you were protecting him." They shook. After a few awkward moments, we left.

"You were correct." I coughed.

"About what?" Laura Triforth asked. Her voice was distorted over the caller.

"The Venturas Base was a mess. We're reorganizing it now." I peered through my office window at the streets below.

"Where else have you been?"

"Nowhere, yet."

"I see." Her silence spoke volumes.

"I've been trying to shake off a cold." It sounded a lame excuse.

"What will you do about our shipping charges?"

"I have no authority over rates."

"I'd have thought you had no authority over General Khartouf."

"I'm not sure I did." The less said about that episode, the better. "What about Mantiet?"

"Frederick's disappeared. No one knows where."

I tried to keep my frustration in check. "You all know

each other, Ms. Triforth. Surely there aren't so many places to hide."

"There's Centraltown, the plantations, the whole continent."

I said, "Most of it undeveloped wilderness."

"Which has thousands of glades where a heli could be hidden, its transponder turned off."

My chest was tight. "Mantiet nearly killed Lieutenant Tamarov. We've got to bring him to justice."

Laura's voice softened. "He nearly killed you too. We want to find him just as much as you, Mr. Seafort."

I doubted that was possible. "Very well." We rung off. I glowered at Tolliver.

"Are they pacified, sir?"

"When I want your questions, I'll tell you." My head throbbed; all I wanted was to lie down.

"Sorry." He didn't seem perturbed. How could a man such as Tolliver feel about his assignment? He claimed to have nothing against me, yet I hated every moment of his company. I knew I wasn't being fair; he was performing his duties conscientiously and showed no resentment at my curt manner. But seeing him constantly recalled my misery at Academy.

I muttered, "Ms. Triforth insists I do something about shipping rates." I gathered my holochips to take home.

"Yes, sir."

"Is that all you have to say?"

In a patient tone, as with a child, he answered, "Yes, sir. I'm sorry if I offend you."

I slammed the door on the way out.

I decided I might as well deliver my report chip in person, in case the Admiral wanted to confer with me.

He didn't. I presented my chip to Lieutenant Eiferts's replacement and wandered to the spaceport terminal across the tarmac. The gift shop displayed low-priced tourist goods made on Hope Nation, and expensive ones shipped from home. I lunched at the spaceport restaurant. After, I dawdled, not wanting to go back to my office and cope with Tolliver.

I was glancing at the holozines in the rack when a lieutenant peered over my shoulder. "Hello, Captain." He seemed vaguely familiar. "Lieutenant Kahn, sir. I met you on the Station."

"Ah."

"Have you heard the news?"

I felt a stab of alarm. "Another attack?"

"Nothing like that, sir. A ship docked this morning."

"Oh." I shrugged. Once, the arrival of a vessel such as *Hibernia* was major news, but now ships came and went almost unnoticed. "I'll bet they're looking forward to long-lea—"

"She left Lunapolis nine months ago."

"What?"

Kahn grinned at my astonishment. "Nine months. One Fuse straight from home system."

"But—why—I mean, how—?"

"Something to do with how the fish Fuse. Our engineers went to work on it. I don't know the details, but they're calling it Augmented Fusion."

"Good Lord." What a change. No longer would we endure interminable journeys to the stars. Nine months was a—an instant.

"*Victoria,* they call her. She's small, but God, she's fast."

I frowned at his blasphemy. "How small?"

"Twenty-four crew, forty-two passengers. Not much more than a sloop. No one knows what class to name her."

I smiled. "Call her a fastship."

"Yes, sir." He grinned, sharing my delight in the extraordinary news. "She docked this morning with dispatches for the Admiral."

"Should you be gossiping about that, Lieutenant?"

For a moment he looked worried. "Well, sir, you're inspector-general. If I can't tell you, who's to trust?" His face brightened. "I heard they stripped her bare to reduce mass. Only two laser emplacements, one fore, one aft."

I said, "She'd better be fast, then. You can't fight fish with only two lasers."

"I'd love to see her. In fact, I'm putting in for transfer this afternoon."

I thought of the long slow days. Sixteen months from Lunapolis to Hope Nation; now we would cut that time almost in half. How would it affect a Captain's authority? What if the scientists shortened the journey even more? Would a Captain eventually be made to defer all important decisions to Admiralty? What if I'd been forced to brig my mutineers, to prosecute them when we reached port? Could I have maintained discipline had I not hanged them?

I paid my bill, went back to the office.

"I'm going to Orbit Station."

"Do you have a program in mind, sir?" Tolliver.

"To look around." Perhaps I'd get a glimpse of *Victoria*. Perhaps not.

"That's all?"

"Mostly." And to see what trouble I could stir up. I tried to imagine the Admiral's reaction if he heard I'd relieved General Tho as well as Khartouf.

"When will you meet with the planters?"

"After I get back." I made a note to ask BuPers to replace Tolliver; his very voice drove me to distraction. "Book us on a shuttle."

"Aye aye, sir. There's one at nine this evening." Time enough to go to the apartment, pack my duffel for overnight.

"Do we have the quartermaster's report yet?"

"No, sir."

"Go to the spaceport and get it."

"Aye aye, sir. If the quartermaster says it isn't ready?"

"Have him give you what he's got. We want to know what supplies are sitting on the runway and how long they've been there. I'll meet you at nine."

The apartment was silent and dark; at first I thought Annie was gone. I found her lying facedown on the bed, fully dressed.

"I'll be at the Station tonight."

"I see." Her voice was muffled.

I threw a couple of shirts and my toilet articles into my duffel. "I'm not sure when I'll be back. Probably tomorrow."

" 'Kay."

"Good-bye, then." For some reason, my chest ached.

"Good-bye."

I stood at the door a moment, decided to say no more. I

left. I drove our electricar to the spaceport; Annie hated to drive and wouldn't need it.

I negotiated the streets with care. Though I was in the outskirts of the city I didn't feel as comfortable as I would on Plantation Road; too many vehicles were about. I kept a wary eye for haulers or buses that might lunge at me.

Few people walked along the roadway; I eyed each pedestrian with suspicion, half expecting him to dash across my path. I passed a sailor waiting to cross the street. A lady and her dog. A youth with a knapsack.

I jammed on the brakes. The boy, startled, stared at me.

I rolled down the window. "Jerence? What are you doing here?"

He backed away. I put the car into reverse to follow, glancing nervously at the mirror. "Does your father know you're—"

He sprinted down the sidewalk, away from the spaceport.

I watched as he disappeared around a bend. Shaking my head, I drove on. The boy wasn't my problem. As a courtesy, I would radio Harmon and tell him I'd seen his son. He could heli to Centraltown and search. By that time, of course, it would be dark and the boy would have vanished.

I parked at the spaceport. I'd made it with a half hour to spare. The field was only a few steps distant.

I coughed. Jerence wasn't my concern. As inspector-general my task was to check our military readiness. On the other hand my posting as liaison to the planters hadn't been canceled. But that didn't mean . . .

Damn. I restarted the car, wheeled out of the lot. Unmindful of traffic I hurtled down the road toward Centraltown, watching both sides of the street.

Something moved. I slowed, peering between houses. Nothing. I drove another mile. Jerence couldn't have run so far yet; I stopped, turned around. When I reached the house where I'd seen movement I got out, walked up the drive. All was quiet.

The house seemed empty, unlit in the twilight. The side yard was overgrown with weeds. No sign of the boy, and I didn't want to trespass. I started back to my car, hesitated, turned again. Cursing my foolishness, I loped to the rear of the house, praying an enraged homeowner wouldn't charge at me with a stunner.

The boy bolted from the back porch, tore across the yard.

I lunged and missed. He dashed out the drive, raced toward downtown, knapsack thumping his back.

I galloped after.

Jerence was the swifter runner. My jacket pulled at my chest. I fumbled at buttons. The boy glanced back, spotted me, ran faster. I pulled one arm free, then the other, and tossed the jacket aside. At Academy we'd run the four-forty, the six-sixty, the mile. I was never the fastest in my squad, but I'd usually managed to keep ahead of the instructor who brought up the rear. If he tagged you with his baton, it meant the barrel.

My vision narrowed to the sidewalk ahead, I strove to maintain rhythm. Another block. At least I was keeping pace. It was all I could do to keep my legs pumping. My breath came in racking sobs; my heart pounded.

Slowly the gap began to narrow.

A woman weeding her yard gaped as I raced past. I hoped she'd call the police, thought of telling her but knew I was too winded to speak. I couldn't keep this up much longer.

Ahead, Jerence stumbled. He rolled to his feet, raced on his way, but I'd gained precious yards. Now, he too was slowing. I pictured my drill instructor, summoned the dreaded baton, managed to pull within feet of the fleeing boy. Abruptly he veered to the left. I lunged, caught his waist, held tight as we rolled in unmown grass.

Jerence kicked desperately in an effort to break free. My chest heaving, lungs on fire, I rolled on top of him to sit on his back. Sweat poured from my face while I panted. Below me, the boy was firmly pinned.

At length I felt able to speak. "Get up!" I kept a tight grip on his arm.

"Lemme go! You don't have a right—"

I hauled him to his feet. "Walk." My legs trembled; I hoped he wouldn't notice.

"Why?" A sullen voice, a look of hate.

"You were running away." It wasn't a question.

"Mind your own business!"

"It's not my affair." I sucked in more air, thrust him toward my car, blocks away. "But I know your father."

"So?"

"I saw his face when he found you at the car wreck." Jerence stopped, braced himself against my pushing. I shoved violently with both hands; he staggered and fell. "Up, boy. And don't try running, or . . ."

"Or?" It was a sneer.

"When I catch you I'll break your arm."

He eyed me, sizing me up as I approached. Reluctantly he nodded, fell into step beside me. "Yeah, you're big enough to beat me up. I suppose you would, too; you're just like the rest of them."

I still hadn't caught my breath. "Rest of whom?"

"Pa, and the others. 'Do what you're told. Be a farmer. Live out on a plantation, in the middle of nowhere.' "

I snorted. "You have so much to feel sorry about." Eventually he would inherit more than I'd earn in a lifetime.

"You don't understand." He trudged ahead. "No one does."

After what seemed like hours we reached my car. I opened the passenger door, shoved him in. "Touch the doorknob and see what you get," I said, striving for confidence I didn't feel. I tottered to the driver's side. Jerence slumped in his seat while I drove back to the spaceport.

"What you gonna do?"

"Call your father."

"Thanks a lot."

"You're welcome." That ended the conversation.

I parked, got out, opened his door. Jerence came out, shivering. He buttoned his jacket against the night air. I steered him to the terminal.

"This way, sir." Tolliver hurried toward me. "The shuttle's about ready to—are you all right?"

"I'm fine." I spotted a public caller and headed toward it, a firm grip on Jerence.

I let go of the boy and settled in the booth, grateful for a chance to sit. I punched Harmon Branstead's code. I'd have an airport official hang on to the boy until he arrived. Outside, Jerence watched in sullen silence.

Tolliver rapped on the transplex. "We only have a minute. Shall I ask them to hold the shuttle?"

"No, I'll just be—"

Jerence bolted.

Tolliver stared. I surged to my feet. "Get him!" I shoved him toward the fleeing youngster. "Move!"

He blinked, slow to understand, then wheeled and charged after Jerence.

Tolliver always ran ahead of me in Academy drills.

He caught the boy in the parking lot, grappled with him, twisted his arm behind his back, frog-marched him inside. Jerence lashed out in vain.

Tolliver snarled, "The Captain wants you *now,* joey!" He hurled the boy forward, almost into my lap.

I glanced at my watch. No time to call Harmon, no time to arrange a baby-sitter. "God"—I caught myself—"bless it! We'll miss the shuttle!"

"What's this about, sir?"

"He's Branstead's son. A runaway."

"Should I stay with him and join you in the morning?"

"No, I need you along." I made up my mind. "Bring him. We'll call Harmon from the Station."

Jerence looked sulky. "Kidnap me and Pa will throw you in jail!"

Tolliver wheeled on him. "You'll do what the Captain says."

"I'll scream!"

"Hang on to this ruffian." I hurried to the gate.

Tolliver's tone was as savage as I'd ever heard at Academy. "I'll give you a reason to scream! Move, while you're able!"

Jerence scurried alongside Tolliver, his defiance gone. "Don't make me go off-planet," he begged. "I've never been in one of those buses. They're dangerous."

I saved my breath for walking. At the hatch the steward waited. "Have room for an extra?" I asked. Jerence tried to twist loose. Tolliver collared him.

"We have seats, sir. The boy too?"

"Yes." From Jerence, a yelp of protest. I controlled an impulse to look back. "Naval business. He's my guest."

The steward glanced at my pass, nodded. "Have him stand with you on the scales." Jerence complied, rubbing his arm, a reproachful eye on Tolliver. Our weight computed, we took our seats. I set Jerence between us and strapped in, settling myself for acceleration.

Jerence twisted and squirmed, peering down the aisles, out the portholes. "What will happen? Does it hurt?"

"Yes," Tolliver growled.

I lowered my seat. "Don't do that to him." The joey would be frightened enough. "Jerence, lie back. A few moments after takeoff you'll feel a great pressure. Ease up. Relax your chest muscles. Let it press down on you without fighting back."

Tolliver's lips twitched. "You sound like Sarge, sir."

I smiled despite myself. One learns from one's betters.

We lifted off, the shuttle's stubby wings biting the air. At a few thousand feet the wings shifted backward, the nose flipped up and the thrusters caught. Jerence whimpered. Before the acceleration became too great I reached over and squeezed his hand. Then, I gripped my armrests and tensed my chest.

"Are you all right, sir?"

I thrust away Tolliver's hand. "I'm fine."

He leaned over me, worry in his eyes. "You passed out."

"Where are we?"

"Falling toward the Station."

My chest ached. Running after Jerence had done me no good. Blinking, I looked about. Jerence was green. He swallowed over and over, clutching the armrests as if to keep himself in his seat.

Tolliver followed my gaze. "Puke on me, boy, and I'll wrench you inside out and stuff the pieces in the recycler." Jerence moaned.

I snarled, "Don't brutalize him."

"Aye aye, sir." Tolliver seemed puzzled.

I closed my eyes, heart thumping. When we docked, I would face endless walking, through and about the Station. I would also face the certain hostility of General Tho when he discovered the purpose of my visit. I'd have to tell Harmon

Branstead I'd shanghaied his son off-planet. And I'd have to find a place to park the boy while I did my work.

If only I hadn't spotted Jerence and his bloody knapsack.

I dozed, wishing I felt better. Eons later the airlocks mated and the hatches hissed open. I got cautiously to my feet, waited for dizziness to pass. "Come along," I muttered. Under the influence of the Station's gravitrons, Jerence's color slowly began to return.

"Where, Mr. Seafort?" In the unfamiliar environment, the boy hovered close.

"To tell your father what we've done."

"Must you?" Docile, he trudged along the corridor to the ladder.

"Yes."

His protest died when he saw my expression.

We plodded through endless corridors, descended to Level 5. From there, it was a long way to the comm room. Though it was nearly midnight, occasional lieutenants and middies still trod the corridors on their errands. As we passed, I returned their salutes absently, hardly aware of their curious looks. Civilians were rare in these precincts; children unknown.

I made Jerence wait outside with Tolliver while the comm room tech patched me through to Branstead Plantation. In a moment Harmon came on the line.

I hadn't thought to ask for a private line; our conversation crackled from the speakers while the two techs listened. Now the station staff would learn of my folly in kidnapping a planter's child. "Captain Seafort? I really don't have long; I was on my way to Centraltown. Family business."

"To look for Jerence, by any chance?"

A pause. "How did you know?"

"I have him."

"With you?" He seemed astounded. "Why would he follow you?"

"That's not quite how it happened." I explained.

"So he's on Orbit Station now?"

"Yes." I waited for the explosion.

"If you'd left him in Centraltown I could have come for him."

"There wasn't time, and he was in a mood to run."

He sighed. "I suppose he's better off there than roaming downtown. Ever since he got the notion he didn't want to be a planter, he's been impossible." A pause. "Let me know when you'll be down; I'll meet your shuttle."

"Very well. In the meantime, have you a message for Jerence?"

His tone was grim. "Yes. Tell him when I'm done with him he'll regret he was born." The line went dead.

Jerence waited anxiously under Tolliver's vigilant eye. "What did he say?"

I gave him the message.

He grimaced. "That's how I usually feel." He said no more.

At General Tho's office the duty sergeant shook his head. "He's gone to his apartment for the night, sir. Shall I ring him?"

"No." I would serve the General ill enough, nosing in his affairs. "Let it wait to morning." I led my flock to the Naval barracks and signed us in for the night.

Exhausted, I tossed and turned for hours. Finally, giving up on sleep, I wrestled into my clothes and went out.

The mess was closed, as were most offices. Naturally the comm room was manned, as was Naval HQ, but I had no business in either office. I wandered the corridors, hoping to make myself tired enough to sleep, paying little attention to where I went.

"May I help you, sir?"

Disconcerted, I stared at the U.N.A.F. sentry. "Um, where am I? What's in there?"

"This is *Victoria*'s bay, sir. You're on Level 3."

My breath caught. "*Victoria*. Could I get a peek?"

He gestured to a nearby porthole.

"Thanks." I peered through the transplex hatch into the docking bay beyond, but couldn't see much of the fastship moored alongside. From what I saw of her disks she looked like any other vessel.

The bell chimed. A light flashed red as *Victoria*'s inner lock cycled; someone was coming through from the fastship to the Station. Though the seal between ship and station was tight, inner and outer locks were never left open at the same time.

The station lock cycled. A young middy in crisp, fresh uniform stepped through. He saw my uniform, saluted, and stiffened to attention.

"As you—Ricky!"

Ricardo Fuentes, *Hibernia*'s ship's boy during my first voyage, struggled to maintain a solemn expression. He broke into a pleased grin.

"As you were, Mr. Fuentes." I hesitated, held out my hand.

"They told me you were somewhere in Hope System, sir." He gripped my hand with obvious pleasure.

"Groundside, unfortunately. You've grown, boy." Ricky Fuentes had been thirteen when I'd last seen him, just promoted from cadet to middy, and off to Academy for a year of coursework.

"I'm almost sixteen, sir."

"Good Lord."

"*Vicky*'s my first posting. Isn't she zarky? Commandant Kearsey got me the berth as a reward for first in nav class."

"Wonderful!"

"Thank you, sir." He paused. "What are you here for, sir?" Though it was none of a middy's business, Ricky seemed unaware of any breach of protocol.

My smile faded. "I'm on business for the Admiral."

"Yes, sir. I meant here outside our lock."

I smiled. Ricky had lost none of his youthful exuberance. "Getting a look at the new marvel."

We fell silent. I said reluctantly, "I'll be on my way, then."

"Yes, sir. It's good to see you again." As I turned he blurted, "Would you like to see her? Inside, I mean?"

Would I? I'd give a few fingers, if not a whole arm. I pointed to a corridor notice. "She's restricted, Ricky. Authorized personnel only."

"Let me ask Lieutenant Steiner, sir. He has the night watch. After I deliver these reports to HQ." He waved his chipcase.

"Don't bother him. It's not that important." I tried to sound nonchalant.

"Aye aye, sir. But Mr. Steiner is a good joe, sir, and he'll probably let me show you around."

"Well . . ."

"Let me drop these off, sir. I'll be back as quick as I can."

I surrendered. "Very well, Mr. Fuentes."

"Right, sir. I'll try to hurry, but if I get any more demerits for running I'm in big trouble." He saluted again, scurried off. His pace . . . well, it wasn't quite a run.

Half an hour later I was shaking hands with *Victoria*'s officers. "I'm sorry, Captain Martes, I had no idea Mr. Steiner would wake you." As a full Captain I was senior to him, but I had no rights aboard his ship.

The young Commander grinned, waved away my apology. "He had to, sir. I'm the only one authorized to allow visitors."

"I'm sorry."

"Well, sir, you've had three ships of your own. What would you think of a Captain who minded being awakened in the night?"

"Good point." I relaxed somewhat. From midshipman on, we learned to catch our sleep when opportunity came, and never to expect a full night undisturbed.

"Besides, it's a great honor to meet you, Mr. Seafort. We've heard all about you. I'll show you the bridge first, if you like. That will be all, Mr. Fuentes."

Ricky's face fell. "Aye aye, sir." He saluted, spun on his heel, and left. Vax Holser, once his senior, had taught him well.

The bridge was much like *Challenger*'s. I stood behind Captain Martes's chair to peer at the instruments while he and Lieutenant Steiner stood by. Only the fusion drive screen was different from ones I knew. Where I'd traced my finger down the screen from OFF to ON, the controls now read OFF, PRIMED, and ON. I raised an eyebrow.

"It's Augmented Fusion, Mr. Seafort. We begin by priming the drives, firing them but holding their output just short of Fusion. Then we mesh the Augmentation wave with the fusion drive's N-wave, and let her go."

My head spun. I had never fully grasped the technical aspects of Fusion, no matter how hard I tried. "Holding short . . . that sounds dangerous."

He grinned. "Very. You're heating the drive shaft walls while you prime, so you've only got about twenty seconds to synchronize the waves, or you'd better shut down."

"I would turn it off automatically," said a cold female voice from the speaker.

"Yes, of course." He made a rueful gesture. "Captain Seafort, our puter, Rosetta."

"Hello," I said awkwardly.

"Good evening, Captain." A fractional pause. "Or good night, as it were. Isn't it rather late for social contacts?"

"Rosetta!" Martes was scandalized. "Mr. Seafort is a U.N.N.S. Captain!"

"I'm aware. William tightbeamed me his dossier. My question was for informational purposes only. No disrespect was implied or should be inferred."

"Enough. Rosetta, put the aft view on the simulscreen, please."

"Aye aye, sir," she said primly. Almost instantly a camera view from aft of Level 2 flashed on the huge simulscreen that filled the front bulkhead of the bridge.

Large ships, such as *Hibernia,* had three Levels. Smaller vessels like *Challenger* had only two. The Navy had a few cutters with but one Level, but they were obsolete; it was more economical to build vessels that could transship the volumes of cargo the larger ships supported. *Victoria* was a two-decker.

At the moment the simulscreen pictured the wave-emission chamber astern of the engine room. Where a normal ship's stern tapered outward in a graceful curve, *Victoria*'s was thick and stubby. Nor did her drive shaft extend as far aft as I expected.

"Looks odd, doesn't it?"

"Yes, Mr. Martes."

"She's not much for looks, but she goes like a bat out of hell."

I frowned at the phrase, but ignored it for politeness' sake. "What other changes did they make?"

"Other than reducing us to minimal hold capacity, none. Of course, we're sadly lacking in lasers."

"Why?"

"To conserve mass, sir," said Steiner. "With the added mass of the laser mountings we wouldn't be able to put her into Fusion."

"I see." Fusion was a mystery whose depths I'd never be able to plumb.

"Bram is our Augmentation expert," said the Captain. "Anything happens to him and the Chief, it's back to the manuals. Anyway, they've made us into a sitting duck. Or rather, a sprinting duck. We can run, but we can't fight. That's the only reason I'll be glad to leave her."

I looked up. "Oh?"

"Transferred as of next week." His eyes sparkled. "To a fighting ship, I hope."

"Who's your replacement?"

"Don't know." He pointed vaguely beyond the hull. "I haven't been groundside yet. What's it like?"

I had to force my mind to my reply. "Hope Nation? It's lovely. Don't you have long-leave coming?"

"Deferred 'til our next run, sir. We've only been out nine months."

I let them walk me through the rest of the ship. The only time I pulled rank was when I insisted that Martes not wake the off-duty crew or officers. At length I found myself at the airlock, saying my good-byes.

"Your hospitality is appreciated, Captain. And yours, Lieutenant."

The young Commander grinned. "It's worth an hour of sleep to be able to say I met Captain Seafort."

I cleared my throat. "Yes. Well." I paused at the airlock hatch. "Your Mr. Fuentes. I commend him to you. An exemplary officer."

"Ricky? He's a good joey. And he's told us all about you."

"Ah." I saluted and made my escape.

10

"Inspect my shipment records?"

"Yes, sir." I tried to meet General Tho's eye. He had greeted me effusively when I'd entered. Now his manner was something else entirely.

"But—why?" He stood abruptly. "Never mind. You have the Admiral's authority. Why is none of my concern."

"I just want—"

"William has all our records on file. You may study them here, if you wish."

"I don't need to take up your office. I can—"

"It may not be my office when you're through."

I gaped, trying to get his meaning. I ventured, "You mean General Khartouf? He—"

"That too is not my concern. Review the records at your leisure." It was a dismissal. Cheeks flaming, I left.

In the outer office, Tolliver and Jerence waited while I stopped at the sergeant's desk. "Where can I find a console?"

"If you need to be private, use the quartermaster's office, two hatches to the east."

"Thank you. Come along," I snapped. My lieutenant and his charge followed as I stalked down the corridor. Under my breath, I cursed the ambition that had saddled me with this meddlesome job. I was short of sleep, ill-tempered, and still not recovered from my mad dash through Centraltown.

Jerence sullenly scuffed the deck. "Where are you taking me?"

"Tolliver, keep him out of my hair."

"Aye aye, sir." Tolliver smiled. "Say something, boy. Anything."

Jerence swallowed. In silence we marched to the quarter-master's office. The corporal in the outer office came to his

137

feet. I growled, "General Tho sent me. Where's your console?"

"Mr. Cary's office, in there. But I don't think you should—" I was already slapping open the hatch. The console rested under a large screen that resembled the simulscreen on a bridge.

As I sat I realized I had no idea how to activate the Station's puter. On ship I would enter my ID code, of course. I tried it.

"May I be of service, Captain?" I jumped at the hidden voice.

"Uh, yes, William. How do I enter a request for data?"

"You might try asking me." I'd have sworn he smiled.

"Right." I glanced at Tolliver. Whatever humor he saw, he knew to keep to himself. "William, put the incoming cargo manifests for the last year on the screen, please."

"Certainly, sir." The screen was full before he finished speaking.

I tried to take in the overwhelming mass of data. "Um, show me arrival dates."

"Here you are, Mr. Seafort." He highlighted them.

I hadn't realized how much cargo flowed from home system to the Hope Nation colony. The screen was crammed with data, and had space to show only the first two months.

I remembered that I didn't have to examine it all. "Only military cargoes, please."

The screen shifted. Now, with less data, I could scan four months at a time. William's display ran across many columns, hundreds of lines deep. Each line represented a consignment ferried sixty-nine light-years from Earth to support our vast military buildup. Our strength here was second only to home system.

"Show the consignee of each cargo, please, and the intended destination."

"Right, Captain."

I puzzled through the data. "Now, where delivered and when."

"You've got it. What did you do to irk the Commandant?"

"Now add—I beg your pardon?"

"General Tho seemed put out after you left his office. I wondered why."

"You were there. Didn't you hear our conversation?"

He sounded offended. "No, of course not. I can't listen in unless I'm invited."

"I see."

"After you left Mr. Tho delivered a few remarks. He didn't order me to erase them."

"Don't repeat his private conversations," I said quickly. "Show two more months."

"Right." It sounded like a sigh.

I studied the shipping data. Many consignments had been dropped at Centraltown. A few had gone directly to Venturas Base, but most of the Venturas cargo had—

"I have to go to the bathroom."

Tolliver was already out of his seat. In one swift motion he snatched Jerence's arm and swept him toward the hatch. "Sorry, sir." They were gone.

Most of the Venturas cargo had been set down at Centraltown, where much of it still waited. Well, the Venturas Base didn't even have a proper landing strip; only the smallest of the Station's shuttles could drop cargo directly there. Mr. Eiferts would soon remedy that.

"William, show supply requisition dates and actual delivery dates." I studied the chart he generated. It looked as if General Tho had met his delivery schedules; cargo was offloaded from incoming ships and barges and brought down to Centraltown when expected.

The hatch opened; Jerence and Tolliver went to their seats. The boy sat hugging himself, crying softly. I raised an eyebrow. Tolliver stared back impassively. I decided to let it pass unobserved, as with a middy.

"No problems here," I said to Tolliver. He crossed the room to read the screen from behind my seat.

"How far back did you check, sir?"

"A year."

"And how recently?"

His questions annoyed me. "To the present."

The speaker crackled. "Until *Victoria*, *Cordoba* was the last ship to dock, Captain. Four weeks ago."

"Thank you, William." I studied the chart; *Cordoba's* cargo was listed as delivered to Centraltown as requested. "Well, that wraps it up. We could have done all this from groundside." I stood and snapped off the screen.

"It's good that General Tho's records aren't as confused as the quartermaster's," Tolliver said.

"True." My head ached, and I didn't want to be side-tracked. "Tho stays on top of his paperwork." I grimaced at Tolliver. "We could visit the cargo bays, I suppose. Just a formality. Get up, Jerence, we're done here."

The boy leapt to his feet, with an anxious glance at Tolliver. I opened the hatch, recalling the endless frustration of paperwork on a ship such as *Hibernia*. "William, how often are deliveries updated?"

"Actual delivery, Captain, or the request dates?"

"Actual, of course. The request dates wouldn't be updated."

"I post actual delivery dates immediately after the shuttles land with their cargo."

"Who posts the dates on which the quartermaster requests his supplies be delivered?" I crossed back to the console.

An infinitesimal pause. "Which time, Mr. Seafort?"

I held my annoyance in check. "You said they're only posted once."

"No, Captain," William sounded prim. "You said that."

It was like pulling teeth. "When else is the requested delivery schedule updated?"

"Approximately monthly, Captain."

Tolliver whistled under his breath.

I frowned. "But why?"

"To conform to actual deliveries," said William.

I blinked.

Tolliver said with awe, "The son of a bitch rewrites his delivery requests to match what he actually delivers!"

"That's approximately correct," agreed William. "Minus the expletives."

I grated, "What fool orders that?"

"I do." A voice came from the hatchway.

I whirled. "General? But . . ." I sank into my seat. "Who told you what we were reviewing?"

"William mentioned it." The diminutive, neatly dressed man fingered his razor mustache.

"Mr. Tolliver, take Jerence outside." The moment the hatch was closed I demanded, "Why fudge your delivery dates?"

"To make the reports I send home look better." General Tho held my gaze until I had to look away.

I said bitterly, "For that, you made a shambles of our supply operation?"

"No. Supply was already a shambles. I move my cargoes groundside as fast as possible. Changing the schedules retroactively did no harm."

"Except to your integrity."

"Except that." He looked about uncertainly, chose a chair across from the console. "You're an innocent. If you knew politics, you'd understand."

My chest ached. I coughed, wishing I hadn't chased after Jerence. "I know what signing my name to a lie means."

He nodded. "Yes. I'll resign, if you like. Save you the trouble of dismissing me."

I tasted bile. "I have no authority to dismiss you."

"Odd, your dismissing General Khartouf, then." His stare was unflinching.

I gestured toward the screen. "Why was this charade necessary?"

"Necessary? I don't know that it was." He left his seat, stared moodily at the console. "Advisable, perhaps. Expected."

"By whom?"

"Seafort, you're Navy. You're the senior service. Naval appropriations sail through the General Assembly, and your Academy is deluged with applications. You steep your cadets in honor and tradition." He focused on something deep within the screen, perhaps light-years distant. "The Army's . . . different. U.N.A.F. has to fight for scraps after Navy's done feeding. So, we have to do a better job. Appear to do a better job."

"Who cares about delivery schedules at a colony sixty-nine light-years from home?"

"The General Staff cares." His tone was fierce. "They present thousands of figures like those I send, when they go hat in hand to the U.N. appropriations committees. What you see as falsifying records, personal dishonor, is a way of life for us. As long as no one is hurt . . ."

His hand flicked in a gesture of helplessness. "How did I come to this? When I bicycled across the hills to Vientiane to drop off my application at the recruiting station . . . I don't know." With a shrug he drew himself up to his full meager height, eyed me bleakly. "Do as you will. I'll be in my office."

"General, wait—" He was gone.

I sat motionless in the silent room. After a time I got to my feet, opened the hatch. Tolliver and Jerence waited in the corridor. "Let's go."

"What will you do, sir?" Tolliver fell in step beside me.

"Visit the cargo bays."

"I meant about General Tho. Now we have to go through all his records with a fine-tooth comb." He shook his head. "Lord God knows what corruption we'll find. Where do we start?"

I stopped short. "Do *we* make decisions now?"

Tolliver looked startled. "No, sir. I just thought—you obviously have to do something about him." Jerence glanced back and forth between us.

"Is that your order?"

Tolliver gulped. "No, sir, not at all. Excuse me."

My tone was savage. "I don't excuse you, Lieutenant. In future when I want your opinion I'll ask for it. Is that clear?"

"Yes, sir. Aye aye, sir."

Jerence shot him a vengeful look. I wheeled on him. "Behave!"

"Me?" He was indignant. "I didn't do anything."

"Yes, you did. If I see that look again, I'll set you in a cabin alone with Mr. Tolliver." That silenced him. It was handy having a bogeyman on staff. In mutual outrage we all trudged down the corridor to the cargo bays.

Hours later I sat in the officers' mess with Tolliver comparing notes. We'd found several cargo booking procedures that would benefit from change, but we'd uncovered no serious problems. A memo to the quartermaster would be the end of it.

"What about supplies to the fleet?" Tolliver asked.

"The fleet is out of my jurisdiction. The Admiral made that quite clear." I picked at my food. Across the table, Jerence wolfed his sandwich.

"Yes, sir." Tolliver cleared his throat. "And the General?"

"Is out of your jurisdiction, Lieutenant. As the fleet is beyond mine."

"Aye aye, sir." His eyes fell to his coffee, and remained there.

"Anyway, we still have to—" I fell silent.

Tolliver looked up. "What, sir?" He followed my gaze. Lieutenant Vax Holser carried a tray from the line, searching for a table.

I stood. "Wait with Jerence." I crossed the room. "Vax?"

The burly lieutenant looked up, startled. Emotions flitted across his face, quickly suppressed. "I didn't expect you here." He added as if an afterthought, "Sir."

I ignored his manner. "I'd like to talk with you."

"I wouldn't like that."

I closed my eyes, willing away the pain. "Please."

His lips compressed. "Whatever the Captain orders."

"It's not an order, Mr. Holser." I looked around. Most of the tables were occupied; I saw no private place to talk. "I'll wait in the corridor, Mr. Holser. Come if you wish. If not, I'll accept your decision." Without waiting for a reply I strode out.

Naval personnel of all ranks walked the corridor, going about their business. I paced.

Vax wouldn't come. I'd begun years ago by brutalizing him, and ended by spurning his friendship. He would never forgive me; it was painful for him even to speak to me. Anyway, what could I say to him? That I was sorry? That I'd meant only to save him? I thrust my hands in my pockets, paced with head down.

"I'm here." It was a challenge.

I whirled. "Don't sneak up on me! What's wrong with you?" Thoughts of conciliation were forgotten.

Vax eyed me steadily. "Nothing. What's wrong with you, other than the mess you've made of your face?"

I bit back an angry retort. "Vax, why won't you speak to me?"

His glare could have melted an alumalloy hull. "You know God damned well why."

"Don't blaspheme!" My fury matched his own.

"That's no longer your concern, Captain Seafort. I'm on the Admiral's staff now."

"Vax," I said hoarsely. "Tell me what you won't forgive."

He was silent for a long time. When his eyes finally met mine, they were cold. "You bastard."

I gaped. Even in informal conversation, a lieutenant couldn't—I thrust down my indignation. "What did I do?"

"You saved me," he said simply.

"But I—"

"On *Portia,* whenever Alexi sent Philip Tyre up to be caned, I beat him with especial relish, because he was what I might have become without you. He was cruel and sadistic, and unappeasable. You saved me from that."

"I'm glad."

"We were friends."

"Yes."

"And then you discarded me." The words slashed.

"Challenger?"

"Yes, *Challenger.*" He glanced around, saw that nobody was looking, shoved me against the bulkhead. "I could kill you, Seafort."

"Vax," I said in anguish, "I wanted you to live. No more than that."

He bellowed, "I wanted to be loyal! No more than that!" Stunned, I could say nothing. "I wanted to follow you, even if it cost my life. What right had you to make that decision for me? Who appointed you God?"

"I was Captain." I knew that wasn't enough. "Vax, I didn't care any longer. I'd lost Nate, and—and—" I found it hard to speak. "And I'd lost Amanda. I was going to my death. I didn't want you swept up in that."

"You had no right to make the choice for me."

"As Capt—"

"Not if we were friends."

The words hung heavy in the silence. I forced myself to meet his eye. "Forgive me, Vax."

"No, not ever." The finality shook me.

"I've been through—you don't know what I had to endure on that cruise. I'm damned, and have no one but myself to blame. Please, Vax. Be with me."

"No. You made your choice." His eyes burned like lasers. "And I've made mine." He strode away.

I walked the corridor until I was composed enough to face Tolliver and the boy. At length I took a deep breath, went back into the mess. Vax Holser was nowhere in sight.

"Tolliver, book us seats on the next shuttle groundside."

"Aye aye, sir." He spotted a caller, went to it. I sat heavily at the table, across from Jerence.

"Is something wrong, Mr. Seafort?"

"Yes."

"Can I help?"

I was enraged at his sarcasm, until I realized he meant it. "There's nothing you can do."

"What happened?"

"An old friend I betrayed. He . . . told me what he thinks of me."

"You didn't betray him."

I smiled without mirth. "How would you know?"

"I've seen you with Pa and I've heard Uncle Emmett. I know."

I cleared my throat. "Thank you."

"There's always goofjuice." His tone was bitter.

I raised my gaze from the table. "Why do you use it, Jerence?"

"What else is there for me on a frazzing plantation? The world is different when you're juiced. You'd have to try it to understand."

I didn't tell him that I had, once. On Lunapolis, many leaves ago, as a green and stupid midshipman. I never touched the juice again. Not because I didn't like how it made me feel, but because I knew that given another taste of euphoria I might never give it up.

He stared at his empty plate. "Anyway, it's better than having to face farming all my life."

I smiled despite myself. "That's not written in stone, Jerence."

"There's Pa." He looked sullen. "I'm firstborn, so Branstead Plantation goes to me. I've told him I don't want it, but he won't listen. I don't think he even hears."

"A shuttle leaves in about an hour, sir." Tolliver.

"Very well." I stood. "We might as well head toward the bay."

We left the mess and wandered the endless corridors. To pass the time I showed Jerence the comm room. Some of the techs I'd met previously were on duty. The boy perused the rows of consoles, most of them silent now. After a while we left for the shuttle bay.

I would be glad to depart the Station, happier never to return.

We passed the cutoff for U.N.A.F. Command. I slowed, hesitated. "In here, first."

"The shuttle is past—"

"I know where the shuttle bay is." I stalked to the General's office, Tolliver and Jerence hurrying to keep up. I slapped open the hatch.

The desk sergeant eyed me uncertainly. "General Tho's in conference, sir."

"Get him out."

"What?"

"You heard me!"

A moment later General Duc Twan Tho stood in his outer office, hands on hips. His stare was icy. "Well?"

"This is private, sir."

He pursed his lips. "Very well. In my office." He turned on his heel.

I thought it better not to sit. "I'm leaving for Centraltown."

"So I understand."

"I don't expect to be back."

"Very well."

"We've made a few recommendations about cargo storage. Mr. Tolliver will prepare a memo to your quartermaster."

"Very well."

I turned to leave. "Another matter. You needn't update your delivery paperwork so often; it's inefficient." His eyes bored into me. Reddening, I mumbled, "I'll write you a memo when I have the chance." I fled.

"Thank you." His soft voice pursued me into the corridor. "Thank you, Mr. Seafort."

Harmon Branstead struggled with his disapproval. "I wouldn't have chosen to reward him with a tour of Orbit Station."

My cold had settled into my chest. "I'm sorry I interfered, Mr. Branstead."

"No, I'm glad you caught him. I already told you that." He stared at the heli parked on the tarmac, in which Jerence waited, slumped in the passenger seat. He sighed. "Forgive my manners. This whole business—I don't know what to do."

"I understand."

He brooded, then snapped his fingers. "By the way, Emmett says one of our hands saw Frederick Mantiet in Centraltown."

My fist clenched. "Where?"

"Downtown, near the sailors' district."

"Did you alert the authorities?"

"Governor Saskrit? On Hope Nation, we handle these affairs ourselves. Laura Triforth and I took a few men and searched. We couldn't find him."

"I see."

He gestured to the cargo stacked at the far end of the runway. "What did you learn about that situation?"

"Orbit Station downloads cargo as fast as it can. They have little contact with the quartermaster groundside. Loads end up here whether they're needed or not."

"As Laura said, then."

"Yes."

"What will you do about it?"

I said stiffly, "We're working on it." My glance flickered to the heli. "What about Jerence?"

Harmon shook his head in exasperation. "I've no idea what to try next. Between the goofjuice and his nonsense about ceding the plantation to his younger brother . . ."

"He's a bright little joey." If it weren't for the goofjuice, a tour in the Navy might do him wonders.

"I'm considering an abuse program at the hospital. I'd hoped it wouldn't come to that."

"It'll come to worse if the authorities catch him first." Society wasn't lenient with substance violators, and hadn't been since the end of the Rebellious Ages. Rightly, the law made no distinctions for age; even at thirteen Jerence could land in a penal colony for possession of the contraband drug.

After Branstead's heli receded into the late-afternoon sun I checked in at Admiralty House to drop off my reports. Then I dismissed Tolliver and headed home.

Annie was waiting in the living room, dressed, her coat across her lap. Wearily I stripped off my jacket. "Going out?"

"I don't know." I looked at her, my eyebrow raised. "It depends. Nicky, we have to talk."

"About what?"

"What happened with—about me and Eddie."

"We've spoken about it." I wanted only to lie down.

"No, we haven't." Her vehemence surprised me, yet seemed oddly familiar. I realized it reminded me of Amanda.

"Talk, then." I sat.

"Nick, I did a wrong thing. I know I did, and I can't take it back. You don' understand tribe, an' I hurt you." She paused, marshaling her diction. "But we're married. You say it's for the rest of our lives. I want you to care for me, to love me. If not—" She mumbled something into her hands.

"I didn't hear the last." My voice was wooden.

"I said if you can't, I'll move out."

"Where would you go?"

She shook her head. "I'd find someplace. Or live on the streets, if it came to that. I'm a trannie, remember?"

"Not anymore."

Her eyes filled with tears. "What are we to do, Nicky?"

"I don't know." Images overlapped on the canvas of my mind: Annie sitting in my cabin, struggling to become more than she was. Annie crying in my arms. The pair of us coupling with unending passion, before she sent me back to the hospital for my interview with Dr. Tendres. Annie clutching the broad white back of Eddie Boss.

We sat miserably in the darkening room. At length she stirred. "I'll be leavin', den," she said with forlorn dignity. "My things be packed."

I said hoarsely, "Don't." I didn't know why.

Her mouth twisted into a sad smile. "Why, you gonna say you lovin' me?"

I thought a long time. "I don't know."

"I be leavin'," she repeated.

There was an unbearable tightness in my chest. "You stay. Let me go away for a while, to think things through."

That brought a flash of anger. "An' how long you hav'n me wait?"

"As long as you want to." I forced myself to meet her eye. "I'm unfair to you, I know. But I need time."

She nodded and began to weep. I yearned to go to her, hold her. Images of Eddie Boss came unbidden, and I did not.

I crossed to the bedroom, threw clothes into my duffel. "I'll be in Naval barracks. We'll talk in a few days. All right?" She nodded again. I left my home.

Tolliver showed no reaction when I told him I'd moved. That was understandable; a Captain's personal life was none of a lieutenant's business, and I'd already made my animosity to him clear. I thought again of having him transferred. Though I abhorred his company, I took no action. Perhaps I deserved him.

When I was leaving to visit Alexi, Tolliver asked to come along.

We found Alexi scrolling through a holo in the patients' lounge. I told him about our trip.

"Orbit Station? Have I been there?"

"*Portia* docked at the Station when she came in."

"I wouldn't remember." He sounded especially bitter.

"All incoming ships moor at the Station, Mr. Tamarov." Tolliver was trying to be helpful. I shot him a look of annoyance, but he appeared not to notice.

Alexi got up to stare out the window. "What do you do next?" he asked.

"I'm leaving this afternoon to see Zack Hopewell and the planters." I hesitated. "I wish I could bring them better news. We can clean up the supply mess, but I can't do a thing about shipping rates, or the influx of sailors and soldiers in Centraltown, or the structure of their government."

Alexi's gaze was fixed on the walkway below. "While you were gone I spent a whole evening sitting in the chair you're in now, just trying to remember."

I got up, went to stand at his side. "And?"

"Nothing." He turned, and his smile was bitter. "I tried to remember you, before I was injured. I can recall your sitting here, that first visit, telling me things you expected me to know. But nothing before."

"I'm sorry."

He rounded on me. "You're always sorry, but you don't have to live with it!"

"I'm sor—" I floundered. "Alexi, I don't know what to say."

"Then say nothing! Save your pity for someone else!"

Wounded, I said stiffly, "I wish I could give what you want." From the corner of my eye I saw Tolliver's disapproval, whether of Alexi's behavior or mine I couldn't tell.

"How can you—Christ, I'm doing it again!" Dejected, Alexi slumped on his bed. "Forgive me."

"Alexi, staying in the hospital does you no good."

"What else is there?"

"You can come with me. You were part of my staff. I want you back."

"On active duty?"

I smiled, shaking my head. Even I couldn't arrange that. "On therapeutic leave."

Tolliver inquired, "What's that, sir?"

"I'm not sure. I'll pull strings to make it happen. Alexi, would you like to go to the plantation zone with us?"

His eyes were eager. "Very much."

"Then you shall."

I checked Alexi out of the hospital and drove to the space-port, where Tolliver had secured a heli. During our preparations Alexi stayed pathetically close to my side, though he looked just like the confident young lieutenant with whom I'd sailed on *Portia*. I wished I could allay his fears; all I could do was squeeze his arm in reassurance. We boarded the heli.

"You know how to fly, Mr. Seafort?"

"Yes, Mr. Tamarov. I learned at Academy."

"Did I?"

"As I recall, you were heli-rated. It's been some time since I saw your personnel file."

Alexi lapsed into moody silence. I finished my safety check and we lifted off toward the plantation zone. The heli's puter displayed our flight plan. Our ETA was approximately an hour and a half. Alexi craned to see the terrain below. After a time he asked, "Do you like Hope Nation, Mr. Seafort?"

I pondered, unsure of the truth. At length I said, "I've spent most of my career traveling to or from Hope Nation."

"But do you like it?"

I grimaced.

"Leave the Captain be." Tolliver.

"No, I don't mind. Hope Nation has a lot of memories. Some are painful."

Alexi said only, "It's hard to imagine memories being painful."

"They can be." The day I'd learned that Captain Forbee had no Captain to replace me, which meant I'd command *Hibernia* for another cruise. The evening I'd gone to Amanda's house to say good-bye, but instead persuaded her to join my vacation to the unspoiled Venturas.

"Amanda lived here, Alexi." Before she'd returned to home system with me, to sail to her death on *Portia*. It was she who'd turned Alexi from his bitter course of vengeance against Philip Tyre.

Alexi asked, "Who was Amanda?"

I said shortly, "My wife." The mother of my only son. Now she drifted with him in the endless gulf of interstellar space.

"You loved her a great deal."

"You remember?" I asked hopefully.

"It's in your face," he said.

I cast about for another topic. "Do you remember Hauler's Rest?"

"No. Should I?"

"Last month we thought of stopping there, on our trip to Branstead Plantation. You and I and . . ." I trailed off, wishing I hadn't summoned memories of Eddie.

"And Mr. Boss?"

"You remember him?"

"He was in my room when I woke." Alexi studied me. "You were friends?"

"I don't care to speak of him." I concentrated on navigation until I could be sure of calm.

"What is Hauler's Rest?" Alexi.

"A sort of inn, the only one on Plantation Road. I've eaten there more than once."

"On your first cruise?"

"Yes." With Derek Carr. More memories stabbed. Innocent days: Derek forced to masquerade as my retarded cousin so he could safely visit Carr Plantation; he retaliated by calling me "Nicky" every chance he got. If only I could be that youngster again, and blot out what had come after.

"Would you like to lunch there?" I asked.

"Sure." His face fell. "I have no money, Mr. Seafort."

"Haven't you been drawing your pay?"

"I couldn't even tell you how much I'm paid, much less how to get it." He grimaced. "What should I do?"

"I'll sign for lunch." I checked the maps and turned to a new heading. "Tolliver, make a note to retrieve Mr. Tamarov's back wages when we get home."

"Aye aye, sir."

I homed in on the Hauler's Rest transponder and brought us down at the edge of the strip bulldozed through the lush vegetation. Half a dozen cargo haulers were scattered about.

Inside, we ordered from the ample menu. I explained that

Hauler's Rest was all but self-sufficient; it grew its own meat and vegetables and was powered by an atomic pile buried in the back lot.

"Not an automated fusion reactor, like Orbit Station's?"

I smiled with surprise and pleasure. "How did you remember, Alexi?"

"I don't know." He concentrated. "I learned it somewhere; I've no idea where."

"Second year physics at Academy," said Tolliver impatiently.

Alexi's brow furrowed. "These automated fission piles are safe, but the fusion reactors our ships use are even safer."

"That's right," I said. "But even the fission reactors can't be made to malfunction without a series of deliberate missteps. They have intricate safeguards."

Alexi looked around. "If this pile ever did blow, it would make quite a hole in the ground."

"Vaporize everything for about a mile," Tolliver agreed with relish. "But that's nothing to the mess you'd make if you made a fusion engine blow. You wouldn't want to be anywhere near."

"Change the subject, please."

"Why?" Alexi.

We were skirting dangerous ground; if someone overheard us we might even be subject to a capital charge. U.N. Security Council Resolution 8645, passed back in 2037, had provided . . . I closed my eyes and concentrated.

"The threat of nuclear annihilation having for generations terrorized mankind, it is enacted that use, attempted use, conspiracy to use, proposal to use, or discussion of use, by any persons in any forum and for whatever purpose, of nuclear energy for the purpose of destruction of land, goods, or persons, shall be punishable by death and by no lesser sentence, and that the sentence of death may not be suspended or mitigated by any court, tribunal, or official." They'd made us memorize it, as cadets, and no other discussion of the topic was permitted.

"You can't even discuss it?"

"No!"

Our food arrived and we fell to. Between mouthfuls Tolliver said soberly, "Before I left home system, there was talk in the Assembly of amending the resolution."

"It'll never happen."

"God forbid they change it. But—"

"Even those dolts in the Rotunda wouldn't be so stupid! Two nuke wars were enough; the people wouldn't risk another, even for a minute. Don't even speak of such abominations!" I stabbed savagely at my meat.

Alexi gestured across the room. "Are all those joeys haulers? I didn't see that many cargo vehicles in the lot."

I tried to take the edge from my voice. "Some must be laborers." I regarded the tables crowded with rough-looking workers. "Harvest is near."

"Aren't the plantations largely automated?" asked Tolliver.

"They are, but they're so huge it takes a lot of men to run the machinery." Our uniforms seemed to be attracting the haulers' attention. One burly fellow stared at us for a while, then got up and left the hall.

The meal was huge, and though I still wasn't recovered from my cold I took advantage of a hearty appetite. It was nearly an hour before we crossed the lot to our heli. I slipped behind the controls; Alexi got in back. Tolliver, moody, stared out the window from the seat next to mine. I lifted off and headed west. As I pulled back on the collective and gave her more throttle, Hauler's Rest shrank below.

It was a beautiful day. Flying high, we'd have a better view. At the controls of a heli I felt none of the trepidation I knew driving an electricar. Airborne, I wouldn't have to contend with other vehicles careening alongside; perhaps that made a difference.

"Mr. Tolliver, advise Hopewell Plantation of our ETA, please."

"Aye aye, sir." He keyed the caller. A red light on the control panel began to blink. He froze.

The puter came alive. *"Enemy radar lock! Commencing evasive action!"*

"What—?" I gaped.

"Reset the puter," Tolliver said. "It caught a radar from one of the plantations."

"Yes," I said doubtfully. The heli was military transport, programmed to be wary of hostile attack. If we'd entered Hopewell's radar field the heli would assume enemy sensors had locked on us. "Disregard radar signal," I told the puter, switching off the warning light. "Do we have Hopewell's transponder yet?"

"We should pick it up any—"

The heli lurched. *"Missile launched! Automated evasive action sequenced! Transponder off!"*

I said, "Listen, puter, there's no missile out—"

"What's that flash, sir?"

I peered. "Lord God! It can't be!"

"Contact estimated fourteen seconds!" The puter's tone was calm.

"Jesus." Tolliver.

Should I let the heli do the evasives or take manual control? The puter could run evasive maneuvers faster than I could and more accurately. But its reactions were programmed, and the missile's attack program might anticipate them.

What was after us? A heat seeker? Laser lock? I tried desperately to recall our lessons at Academy.

In the back seat Alexi clutched the safety bar as the heli swooped. The attacking missile was a dim speck, a dot, a stubby black slash hurtling toward us.

"Take over!" Tolliver shouted. "Don't wait for the puter!"

"Contact eight seconds." The puter. *"Evasive program C12!"* The jet engines whined as the puter put us to full power in a shallow climb.

"Four seconds."

Tolliver shouted, "Seafort, do something!"

I stabbed at the manual override. Before I touched it the engine noise fell; we dropped like a stone. The missile flashed past the cockpit. The engine roared. I twisted around. Behind us, the missile was executing a long, slow turn while it climbed.

This time it would come at us from above. The speaker blared, *"Radar lock reacquired!"* The missile had found us anew.

I switched off the automatics, holding us in a tight turn to the left. I couldn't find the missile. My eyes darted between the screen and the horizon. Was there time to set us down?

"Contact sixteen seconds."

No time. Where had the missile come from? Who fired it? Never mind that. I jammed my foot on the tail rudder, yanked back on the collective. We veered suddenly to the right and climbed.

"Radar lock. Contact eleven seconds."

"Christ, Seafort, let me take it!" Tolliver leaned across the seat.

I throttled down, slammed the stick forward. We dropped. The missile made a slight correction to follow us.

"Contact eight seconds!"

"You'll get us killed! Give me the frazzing controls!"

I shook my head. "No time."

Tolliver unhooked my seat belt, hauled me out of my seat with manic strength. "Move!" He threw me aside, swung into the pilot's seat. At full throttle, he spun us a hundred eighty degrees to face the missile.

I screamed, "Are you crazy?" Flung against Alexi, I clawed at the handholds.

"Shut up!" Tolliver's every muscle was tensed.

"Contact four seconds. Three."

I braced for the inevitable.

"Two."

My heart shot through my throat as we dropped. I could hear the throb of the missile's engine past the roar of our own. It missed us by scant inches.

"We have a few seconds to put down," Tolliver shouted. "Jump the instant we hit!"

I peered out. "It's all forest!"

"There's got to be someplace flat!"

"Radar lock!"

"Christ damn it." Tolliver banked to get a better view of the terrain. "Look ahead, about half a mile." A small clearing, light green against the dark of the trees.

"We don't have time!"

"It'll be close," Tolliver acknowledged.

"Contact twelve seconds."

"Seafort, get on the horn, tell Centraltown!"

I cursed; I should have thought of that myself. I reached over the seat, grabbed the caller, trying to remember Naval frequency. No, idiot, use the emergency channel. I thumbed the caller. "Centraltown Control, this is Naval heli eight six oh Alpha, Captain Seafort, we're under missile attack from unknown source, location approximately one hundred twenty miles west of Hauler's Rest. Mayday! Mayday!" No answer.

"Contact nine seconds."

We were a few hundred yards from the field, closing with dreamlike slowness. "Hurry, Tolliver!"

"If I don't bleed off speed we'll crash."

"Contact six seconds!"

"Crash, then!" Better that than dissolve in a ball of fire.

"Hang on!" We swooped toward the field. A hundred yards.

"Contact three seconds! Two!"

Tolliver hauled back on the collective. We shot into the air. Through the rear transplex I saw the missile turn upward to correct course. Tolliver slammed down the stick and we fell toward the edge of the field.

The missile had no time to correct again. It shot over the cab of the heli. A thud, a burst of light. Fire. The engine screamed. The heli lurched, spun, dropped. Tolliver slapped off the switches. "Brace yourselves!"

We slammed into the ground on our landing gear, bounced, struck again. Flames soared from the mast above the cab.

"Out! Get out!"

I flung open the door, stumbled out, rolled away from the blazing heli. Tolliver pushed Alexi out, leaped to follow. He dropped on top of Alexi, jumped to his feet, thrust Alexi clear of the flames.

We ran.

Sixty feet away, we turned to look at the fiery wreckage.

"Jesus, Lord Christ!" I gasped for breath.

"Amen." Tolliver was grim.

"Keep moving, there may be more coming!"

"Radar showed only one missile, Mr. Seafort."

"But who in hell was shooting?"

Tolliver shrugged. "Mantiet?"

"But we're the Government!" I realized how fatuous I sounded. "You're probably right. He tried to kill us before."

Alexi stared at the debris.

Tolliver asked, "How could he get hold of a missile?"

"The planters helped move supplies to the Venturas Base." I kicked at a smoking piece of rotor blade. "Someday I'll settle with him."

"Mantiet may come looking. Let's get out of here, sir."

"He'll have heard my Mayday. He'll expect U.N.A.F. to send a heli, fast. I doubt he'll risk showing himself."

Alexi fell to his knees, retching. Tolliver put his hands on Alexi's shoulders. "Easy, Mr. Tamarov," he said gently. "We're safe."

I stared, realizing, as I calmed, what Tolliver had done.

Alexi coughed, wiped his mouth with his sleeve. "Sorry. God, I'm so sorry."

Tolliver released him. He glanced up, saw my expression. He faced me and sighed. Slowly he unholstered the laser pistol at his belt, handed it to me, butt first.

"Follow me." I turned, strode to the edge of the field without looking back. When we were out of Alexi's earshot I stopped. My voice grated. "What charges should I file, Lieutenant?"

"That's for you to decide, sir." He was pale.

"Answer."

"Mutiny. Insubordination. Striking a superior officer. Uninvited physical contact with the commanding officer. Three of them are capital. Does it matter if there are more?"

I snarled, "If I say so, it matters!"

"Aye aye, sir!" His eyes held mine. "Disrespectful speech and conduct. Unlawful usurpation of authority. I can't think of others, sir."

"Your excuse?"

"I have none, sir."

"Belay that! Answer!"

His smile was bitter. "You were always a lousy pilot. You had the lowest ratings in our barracks." And I'd spent many hours working off demerits as a result.

"So?"

"My taking over was our only chance."

"You were so sure I couldn't outmaneuver that missile?"

"Yes. Weren't you?"

I was silent, then sighed. "I should have handed over to you immediately." I bunched my fists. "But I didn't."

He shook his head. "No, sir. I made a split-second decision. I know the consequences."

"Do you?"

"You'll have me tried for mutiny or the other capital charges. I have no defense. I'm dead."

"Yes." He winced, but didn't look away. I turned my back, thrust my hands in my pockets, paced with head down. I wanted so to hurt him, to revenge the humiliations he'd inflicted on me as a cadet. He'd given me an unparalleled opportunity. I could have him put to death, and no one would question my motive. None would know how much my hatred moved me.

The temptation was unbearable.

I whirled. "Do you demand court-martial, or will you accept summary punishment?"

"Summary—?" He gaped, hardly daring to believe his fortune. "Yes, sir. Thank you, sir." Had he chosen court-martial his execution was a foregone conclusion. On the other hand, a commanding officer might issue summary punishment without a trial, but the penalties were far less severe.

"Very well." I faced him, hands clasped behind my back. "When were you commissioned lieutenant, Tolliver?"

"On the way out to Hope Nation, about a year ago. Captain Hawkins—"

"You're back to middy, as of today." My voice was harsh.

"I'm twenty-five, sir." Midshipmen who hadn't yet made lieutenant by that age rarely did so after, and we both knew promotion to lieutenant was the ambition of every midshipman's life.

"You heard me," I said. He'd unceremoniously hauled me from my seat. That couldn't be borne.

His jaw clenched. "Aye aye, sir."

"You're docked two months pay, and I reprimand you for insolence. You'll have to sign acknowledgment, of course. If you prefer, you go to court-martial."

"Aye aye, sir." He stared at the ground. "Thank you," he

muttered at last. I understood. Though the reprimand and loss of rank would blight his career, he was fortunate to escape with his life.

I blurted, "God, I despise you!"

A momentary look of dismay flitted across his features, but he said only, "Yes, sir." I held his eye a moment longer, then stalked back to the clearing. Tolliver followed.

Alexi waited, pale but composed, near the wreckage of our heli. "What do we do now, Mr. Seafort?"

"We—" I looked around. "Anyone know where we are?"

"About thirty miles south of Hopewell Plantation," said Tolliver. I marveled that while jinking the aircraft to avoid an incoming missile he still kept track of his position.

"Too far to walk," I said.

"Did you hear an answer to your Mayday, sir?"

"No." I found my legs trembling; I squatted against a tree. "We should wait, I suppose." As soon as I spoke I realized it was foolish. As my Mayday hadn't been acknowledged, help lay elsewhere. "Which way to Plantation Road?"

"It should be north, sir."

"How far?"

Tolliver looked at me strangely. "About thirty miles, sir." Of course. The road ran directly in front of Hopewell Plantation, and he'd just told me the distance.

I got to my feet. My chest ached. "If they didn't catch our signal we'll need to hike out. The sooner we start, the better our chances."

Tolliver ventured, "But if they did hear us, we'll lose them in the woods."

"It's my decision, Midshipman." My tone was curt.

Tolliver's look was sullen, but he said at once, "Aye aye, sir."

"We have no food or water," Alexi said.

"No." We hadn't carried much in the way of supplies, and the heli's emergency kits were lost in the fiery wreckage. We would probably run across a stream, but we'd have to do without food. Two days walk. Surely we could manage that. "Let's go, then."

Tolliver looked back at the smoldering heli. "We should leave a signal."

He was right. "An arrow, scratched into the turf?"

"There's scrap metal from the rotor housing. We could use pieces to make a sign."

"Very well." He gathered the scraps and arranged them in an unmistakable arrow, pointing north. When he was done we trudged across the clearing. I stopped at the far edge to stare back at the wreckage. If it weren't for Tolliver we'd be cremated in what was left of the heli, yet I'd savaged him for saving us.

We hiked into the silent woods.

11

I set the pace, doing my best to hide my weariness. It was late afternoon; we kept the sun on our left. If we headed north, eventually we'd cross Plantation Road.

Alexi said, "Mr. Seafort, why does Mantiet want you dead?"

"I don't know. Leave me be." I tried to ignore his hurt expression.

For two hours we pushed through dense brush. In the hilly terrain the vegetation was fiercely competitive. Above, vines drooped from thick ropy limbs of towering trees. We had to duck under, climb through, brush aside undergrowth with each step.

"What's that?" Tolliver.

I stopped to listen. It might have been rotor blades, far in the distance.

"Should we go back?" Alexi asked.

"We'd lose two hours, if no one's there. Let's go on."

The sun was noticeably lower; I wondered how much farther we'd get before nightfall. And how long my stamina would last.

As I flagged, Tolliver took the lead and began holding vines aside so I wouldn't have to stoop. We made better progress. My breath rasping, I did my best to keep up.

A distant sound became a rumble, then the unmistakable whap of heli blades overhead. We stopped, listened. I squinted at the canopy above but could see nothing through the dense foliage. Above, the heli circled.

"Find a clearing."

Tolliver peered in all directions, then pointed. "Perhaps that way, sir. The light seems a little brighter."

"Hurry." We stumbled through the silent vegetation.

The heli blades receded, returned. Finally we reached the

spot we sought, but the canopy there was only slightly thinner. We couldn't be seen from above. "Isn't there another place—"

Tolliver waved us silent. "Listen!"

A woman's voice was almost lost in the engine's drone. "Captain Seafort! Return to your heli! We can't find you in the trees!"

I cursed. We'd come too far to retrace our steps by nightfall.

Tolliver said, "U.N.A.F. would have gear to locate us, wouldn't they? Infra sensors and the like."

As if in reply the voice from the heli resumed. "Captain Seafort, can you show yourself? This is Laura Triforth. We heard your Mayday. Return to your heli or show yourself. Signal with a flare or fire." The message repeated, sometimes almost directly above us, sometimes distant as the heli roved above us.

"We don't have a flare or fire," Alexi muttered.

"I know. Head north, and hope we find a clearing." We resumed our trek. After a time, the growl of the heli faded.

I struggled to keep up. It was darkening fast, and still we groped through thick vegetation. "I need to go slower," I panted. The admission came unwilling from my lips.

Obediently Tolliver slowed.

Eons later, engine sounds overhead. A heli. I peered at the darkening sky.

A speaker crackled. "Captain Seafort, this is U.N.A.F. rescue heli three oh two. We are above you and tracking. Proceed northeast about half a mile; we should be able to see you."

Thank Lord God. With renewed strength we veered to the east in the fading light. After half an hour the disembodied voice guided us again, toward a clearing visible from the air. Dizzy and sweating, I staggered into the welcome glade. An outcrop of rock formed a steep hill, where the tall trees couldn't root. It was fully dark.

Two helis circled overhead. One swooped low, its floodlight searching. We waved until it fastened on us. The heli dropped lower, and the speaker boomed. "Captain, we can't hear you from here. Is anyone injured? Hold your arms straight out for yes, up for no." I swung my arms up. "We read a negative. Do you have food or water?" Again I raised my arms. "No food or water. We can't land here, Captain; there's no level ground. It would be safer to wait until daylight and lower you a rope. Can you wait until morning?" I held my arms straight out.

"Don't worry, Captain, we won't abandon you. I'll remain overhead for now. The second heli is returning for emergency supplies. We'll drop you what you need for the night. Remain in the clearing." I signaled affirmatively to show I understood, then let my arms sag. Trembling, I let myself down. The ground was cold and damp.

"You all right, sir?" Tolliver.

"Yes."

"You look ill."

I waved him away. He squatted, waiting.

My teeth chattered. I sat hunched against the cold while the pilot circled endlessly overhead. From time to time he aimed his searchlight; one of us waved. It seemed forever before the second heli returned.

I stared upward at the two searchlights circling in the darkness overhead. One of the helis began a cautious descent. The speaker blared. "Captain, we'll lower your supplies. Stand clear; we'll cut the line when the pack is near the ground." I gripped Alexi's arm, pulled myself to my feet. From the heli bay a large bundle began to emerge, swinging with the motion of the airship.

With practiced skill the pilot countered its sway, lowering the line until the pack was within a few feet of the ground. Then it dropped with a thud. I stood, dizzy.

Alexi bounded forward, pulled at the straps. "A tent, Mr. Seafort." I grunted. He pawed through the bundle. "Mattresses, self-inflating."

"I'll help with those." Tolliver's tone was cold. With a brusque motion he swept Alexi's arm aside.

"I can open—"

"I know how. You don't."

I tapped him on the shoulder. "Give Alexi the respect due his rank, or answer to me for it." He swallowed at my wrath. With savage satisfaction I stalked back to my seat.

"Stand clear below for a second load!" I looked up as a bundle emerged from the bay overhead.

When the package hit the ground Tolliver opened the straps, stood aside with careful courtesy while Alexi bent over to look.

"Dinner!" Alexi's grin was joyous. "A portamicro, steaks, drinks, coffee . . . even extra Q-rations."

"And this." Tolliver held up a military radio pack. I beckoned; he brought it. With icy fingers I fumbled with the transmitter. "Rescue heli, do you read me?"

"Loud and clear, Captain. That gear should make you more comfortable."

"Very much so." Behind me, on the only meager patch of level ground, Alexi and Tolliver were already setting up the tent.

"Do you know who shot at you?"

"I have no idea."

"Orbit Station tracked the missile from half a minute after launch. They think it originated about a hundred miles south. You should be safe for now; I doubt anyone can travel through that underbrush by night."

"Right." We'd barely managed during daylight.

"Orbit Station is in position to keep a radar lock on the area tonight. Any suspicious blips and we'll be back in a flash. Anyway, you can reach Centraltown with that caller. You might even get through to the Station. We'll pick you up at first light. Sweet dreams."

"Thank you." I watched the heli lights recede toward Centraltown.

The micro and the radio were powered by the same Valdez Permabatteries that ran our electricars. We had power to spare, and the techs had even included a couple of ground lights. An hour later I gnawed gratefully on my steak, an open sleeping bag wrapped around my shoulders. I stared moodily into the fire, coughing occasionally from the cold that had settled into my chest. The radio crackled at my feet, a reassuring contact with civilization.

Alexi crouched at my side. "I suppose Earth was once like this, Mr. Seafort."

"Earth could never have been so quiet." Though I knew

Hope Nation had no animal life except what man had brought, still my ears strained for absent night sounds. Other than the logs spitting in our campfire, we heard nothing but the rustle of the trees.

"At home when I went to bed I could hear the supersonics take off."

"In Kiev?"

"Yes." He sat looking into the flames, hypnotized. "I should be grateful to be alive, but Lord God, I want to be whole again."

"I pray you will."

Across from us, Tolliver threw another chunk of wood onto the fire. We watched the sparks fly.

"What was it like when we were midshipmen, Mr. Seafort?"

"You were fifteen when I met you. I was first middy, you were junior."

"Were we friends?"

"From the start." Until I'd become Captain, when I'd allowed him to be so brutalized he'd begged to resign from the Service.

"Tell me about the wardroom."

I sought words to describe the complexity of feelings, of interactions among the youths in that crowded space. "There were conflicts. Vax Holser and I. He was a bully, at first."

"He treated you badly?"

"No, I was first middy; he couldn't. It was you he abused. You and Sandy."

Tolliver said, "Like all wardrooms, everywhere."

"When you're young you can handle that sort of thing," I said.

"I'm not young." Tolliver's voice was bitter.

I flared, "You made your bed, Middy, now sleep in it." My chest ached.

Tolliver stood, stared into the fire. "I think I'll do just that." He spun on his heel and stalked to the tent. He paused. "Good night, *sir*. And you, Lieutenant." His tone held the precise courtesy expected of a midshipman.

I grunted. Alexi, perhaps unaware of the byplay, bade him

good night, eyes locked to the fire. After a time he asked, "Mr. Seafort, what was I like as a boy?"

I hesitated. "Cheerful. Good-hearted. Willing." Until I'd forced him into a vendetta with Philip Tyre that nearly swallowed his soul. "As you are now."

"I'm hardly cheerful." His smile was wan.

I yawned. Despite the steak I still felt unwell. "Shall we turn in?"

"May I sit and listen to the radio?"

"Of course, but there won't be much traffic at this hour. Do you know how to spread the dish?"

He nodded. "I'll come to bed in a while, Mr. Seafort. I won't wake you."

I stood slowly. "I doubt you could." In the tent I undressed and huddled on my mattress. A few feet away Tolliver breathed slowly, steadily. Was he awake, feigning sleep? Well, I'd provided him a miserable day. I wondered if I could stand being broken to midshipman as I'd done to him. Certainly my own behavior to Admiralty had warranted it, more than once. I shivered from cold, then, as the mattress warmed, drifted into blessed sleep.

"Mr. Seafort?"

I groaned, forcing my eyes open. It couldn't be morning yet.

It wasn't. "Yes, Alexi?" I stifled a groan.

"You'd better come listen."

"To what?"

"The radio."

"Bring it in—no, let him sleep." Coughing, I threw on my chilled clothes, swept the flap aside. "This better be imp—"

Static distorted a constant stream of urgent messages. "Maneuver C in effect! Two off the port bow! *Tarsus,* where are you?"

"Oh, God, Alexi." My voice was a whisper.

"*Hibernia* to Fleet, we're under attack! Three, five—Lord God, seven fish. Engine Room, prepare to Fuse! Forward lasers gone! Fusing!"

Alexi clutched my wrist, then snatched his hand away as if it had been burned. "Sorry! Please, I didn't mean to touch—"

"Belay that. Listen."

"Mr. Seafort, they threw something."

"What do you mean?" My head spun. I blinked.

"The radio said they dropped a missile, or whatever. At Centraltown."

I snatched up the caller and changed frequencies. "Admiralty House, Captain Seafort reporting." I waited. "Captain Seafort reporting to Admiralty House."

The wait was maddening. Finally the answer came. "Forbee here, Mr. Seafort."

"What's going on?"

"Full-scale attack. The Admiral left for Orbit Station the moment he heard the first reports. He'll be there in an hour. Eight ships are under assault, a couple of dozen fish at least. Are you still in emergency camp?"

"Yes. You heard about that?"

"We all did. Are you all right?"

"Yes." Dizzy and feverish, and it hurt to talk. But . . . "What's this about a missile?"

"A wild rumor. By coincidence, a meteorite hit near Centraltown tonight. Just a small one."

"Thank heavens."

"Sit tight, Mr. Seafort, and we'll have you out of there by morning."

"Right. Uh, Forbee . . . you remember when I was here three years ago? I met someone who said he was Captain Grone."

"I heard the story, sir. Things are a bit busy at the moment."

"He told me a wild tale about meteorites spraying something. The epidemic began shortly after."

"It was never confirmed, as I recall. But I'll alert the hospital just in case." I heard urgent words in the background, then Forbee's cry of dismay. "Oh, no!"

"What?"

"*Bolivar*'s gone."

Sickened, I closed my eyes. After a moment I said, "Godspeed, Mr. Forbee."

"And you, sir." We rung off.

While we huddled over the flickering fire, scattered reports of losses swelled into a disaster of major proportions.

Fish roamed Hope Nation system, Defusing without warning alongside our ships. Alexi threw on wood until the fire blazed. I shivered nonetheless.

The tent flap moved; Tolliver emerged, buttoning his jacket against the evening cold. "What's going on, sir?"

"Attack."

"Where?"

"The fleet is engaged." My voice was hoarse.

He pulled a log next to the radio and sat. "Lord God help our men."

"Amen."

Long minutes passed. "*Hibernia* reporting; Defused in sector twelve; no fish in sight." Thank Lord God, *Hibernia* was intact.

"Acknowledged, *Hibernia*." The Station.

"*Gibraltar* reporting, sector three about twenty thousand kilometers above Hope Nation. Two fish, five hundred kilometers abaft. Make that three fish. Five! Station, they're— Good Lord!"

Admiral De Marnay, calmly. "*Gibraltar,* report your sighting."

"A swarm of fish! Maybe two dozen, and more Defusing in. Our radars show them clustered around a large object, not a fish, something else, much bigger. It wasn't there a minute ago. It could be—three fish, alongside! Engaging!"

We huddled around the portable dish, sleep forgotten. The speaker crackled with reports from ships announcing course changes.

"*Gibraltar* here. Forward lasers out of commission; we're Fusing!"

"*Intrepid* reporting. We've taken out two fish, engaging a third. Damn it, the bastard Fused clear!"

I shook my head, cursing the dizziness that resulted. "They're winning."

Tolliver said, "Maybe not. We're getting them too."

"But how many are there?" Our losses, horrid as they were, might be supportable if we took out a high enough proportion of the fish.

"And where do they come from?" Tolliver.

"And why are they here?" The cold air burned my throat.

"Obviously they hear us Fuse. But we've been in Hope Nation for ninety years. Did they just begin hearing us, or— Good Christ!" I stumbled to my feet.

The sky to the east, toward Centraltown, lit a brilliant orange.

I stared into the night, my heart pounding. A moment later the distant trees rustled, and then the shock wave hit, an overpowering thump on my chest. I staggered, but remained on my feet. "What was that?"

Tolliver's voice was hushed. "They got Centraltown."

"How—you can't—"

"What else is east a hundred miles or so?"

I croaked, "Annie!"

"Didn't I hear something about a meteorite?"

Alexi hugged the radio. "You're just guessing, Mr. Tolliver."

"Yes." Tolliver looked at him with hatred. "So call Admiralty House, Lieutenant Tamarov, *sir*. Ask them who lit up the sky."

I spun around. "Tolliver! Another word out of you and—"

He looked at me without expression. "And what, sir?"

I strode across the clearing, shoved him back toward the tent. I pushed him until his back bumped the tent poles. "Not a word, Middy! Do I make myself clear?"

For a moment he held my gaze. Then he swallowed. "Aye aye, sir." The venom was gone from his tone.

I sat. "Call them, Alexi."

"I don't remember how," Alexi said miserably.

I snatched the caller from his hands.

I couldn't raise Admiralty House.

I couldn't raise anything.

"What will we do, Mr. Seafort?" Alexi's eyes begged for comfort.

Blindly I thrust the radio into his lap. Each breath of cold air pierced like a lance. I unearthed a series of great hacking coughs, tottered into the tent. Deep in my throat a sound escaped. I fell onto the bed and passed out.

"Mr. Seafort?" The voice summoned me from a great distance. I groaned. "Mr. Seafort, please!"

I opened an eye, squinting at Alexi silhouetted against the daylight. I croaked, "What?"

"It's midafternoon. You've slept ten hours."

I tried to sit up, fell back dizzy. "Lord, it's cold today."

Alexi looked at me oddly. "It's rather warm, actually."

"Is it?" I tried to think. "I must be feverish."

Alexi shot out his hand, withdrew it suddenly, waited for my nod. He held his wrist to my forehead. "You're burning."

"I was dreaming . . ." I clutched his arm, struggled to sit. "Centraltown?"

"No dream. They've been hit. We don't know how bad."

"The heli . . . it was supposed to pick us up at dawn."

"It never showed, Mr. Seafort."

"Can you raise Centraltown?"

"No. I get static, an occasional word, but they don't answer."

"I thought you didn't know how to use the caller."

"Mr. Tolliver showed me." Alexi hesitated. "He's very angry."

"About what?"

"Everything, it seems."

I grimaced. "Help me, would you?"

Alexi held out his arm; I pulled myself up and sagged against him until the dizziness passed.

Outside, the fire was long dead. Tolliver, sitting on the log, watched me without expression. I asked, "Nothing on the radio?"

He shook his head.

I sat by the fireside, blinking in the sunlight. "Try Orbit Station."

"I did. If we got through, they're not responding."

"We'll wait until morning. Try to raise Centraltown and the Station every hour."

Tolliver nodded. I waited, and he added reluctantly, "Aye aye, sir."

I stumbled back to the tent and slept.

I woke at dawn, burning with thirst. I crawled across the tent to the water bottle, drank greedily while Alexi and Tolliver slept.

Cautiously I dressed myself, waiting for the accustomed dizziness, but I seemed stronger than last evening. I opened the tent flap, plunged into the cold mist, searched for firewood. I coughed, doubling over from the pain it brought. When finally I was able to stop, I tottered to the pile of branches they'd stacked near the firesite. I laid a few in the firepit. The effort left me panting.

I found a firestarter in the bundle of supplies, set it to the kindling. In moments my blaze was fierce enough to provide warmth. I sat as close as I dared. After a time I thought of coffee, and made my way to the micro. I foraged in the bundle of supplies, found coffee, set it heating.

"I'd have helped, Mr. Seafort." Alexi, tousled, shirt over his arm, looked out from the tent.

I smiled, steaming cup in hand. "I'm not an invalid, Mr. Tamarov."

"I hope not." He hurried to the fire, huddled near while he dressed. "You're feeling better?"

"Much." As long as I sat quietly. "What did you hear last night on the caller?"

Alexi poured coffee and rejoined me. "Static, faint voices. No answer."

"Try again."

Obediently he went to the tent, returned with the radio. He called Admiralty, the spaceport. Orbit Station.

Still no reply.

I brooded. After a time I said, "Wake Tolliver."

"That's not necessary." Tolliver stood by the tent flap, fully dressed.

"We won't wait," I said. "Get the supplies together; we'll walk to Plantation Road."

"Lugging all this?" Tolliver waved his hand at the tent, the micro, the foodstuffs.

"Everything came down in two bundles. We'll take turns carrying them."

Tolliver's look was cool. "I doubt it. We'll end up carrying you."

I tried to stand, decided against it. "Tolliver, I've about—"

Alexi's tone was icy. "Mr. Tolliver, gather the supplies."

Tolliver glanced at him with surprise. "Have you returned to active duty, Mr. Tamarov?"

"No." Alexi leaned on the tent pole. "But do as the Captain said."

"You can't—"

"Be silent!" Alexi stood nose to nose with the older, taller man. "You're a midshipman. Act like one."

They glared at each other. Tolliver's smile was cruel. "Do you remember how a middy acts?"

Alexi met his gaze. "No. Show me."

After a time Tolliver lowered his eyes. "All right." His voice had lost its truculence. "Help me collect our gear, would you?"

As soon as Tolliver was out of earshot Alexi whispered, "Sorry I interfered. I know I have no right—"

"You did fine, Alexi. It was how I remember you."

"He seemed so—"

"You did well."

In a few minutes our bundles were wrapped and tied. Alexi and Tolliver each shouldered one; there was no discussion of my helping. I managed to get to my feet without assistance. I checked the compass and pointed. "North." I followed them from the glade.

We'd gone no more than a few steps before I was gasping for breath, but I said nothing and did my best to keep pace. I grasped at vines and low-hanging branches, pulling myself onward through the dense brush.

Alexi looked over his shoulder. "Mr. Tolliver, slow down." He waited while I caught up to him. "Lean on me, if you like."

"I don't need—"

"Please."

"All right." An arm draped around his shoulder, I let some of my weight rest on Alexi. With his free hand he held branches aside. I found the going easier.

After a time I took off my jacket and tied it around my waist. Alexi shifted his load to his other shoulder. I struggled on, sweating profusely.

Endless hours later we came upon an opening where a

great genera tree had crushed a swath through the forest as it fell. Alexi called, "Let's rest here, Mr. Tolliver."

Tolliver checked his watch. "It's only been an hour and a half."

"I don't care," Alexi said. "I'm tired."

"You mean the Captain's tired."

Alexi helped me to the fallen log, where I dropped with a sigh. "Enough bickering! Ten minutes."

Alexi eyed me dubiously.

The rest of the morning was lost in a haze of misery. We halted again, twice at Alexi's suggestion and once, reluctantly, at my own. At length we reached a rocky terrain, open land that burst from the vast sea of vegetation stretching from Plantation Road south to the sea. Walking was easier here, though now we had to traverse hills that only looked gentle from afar.

A mile ahead the forest resumed.

"Let's stop for lunch," I said.

"We haven't gone five miles," Tolliver objected. "Even if we walk another five before dark, at this rate we'll be three days reaching the road."

I grunted. "We'll do better this afternoon. Break out the Q-rations." The speech left me panting.

He dropped his bundle, untied it. "I could set up the tent, sir. Would you wait here with Mr. Tamarov and the radio while I go for help?"

I was tempted. "No," I said at last. "Better we stick together."

"You're not able—"

"Until we know what's happened at Centraltown we won't split up." I downed the cup of water Alexi gave me.

A few moments later Tolliver popped the lid of a Q-ration and set it on the log in front of me. I waited while air seeped into the slow-release chemicals packed between the inner and outer wrap. Two minutes later the meal was heated; I peeled off the lid and fell to.

Alexi squatted beside me with a troubled mien. "Mr. Seafort, are you sure about going on?"

I nodded. "I have to get back, find what they want me to do."

He whispered, "Mr. Tolliver—I don't know how to . . . I wish he'd leave you alone."

"Don't worry about it." The day a Captain couldn't handle a middy he'd better look to retirement.

A few minutes later I struggled to my feet. We started out slowly, Alexi and Tolliver carrying the supply packs as before. When I'd bent to take one, Alexi snatched it from under my hand and turned away without a word, adjusting it around his shoulder. I let it be.

When dark finally came I was close to collapse, sweat streaming down my face. I overrode their suggestions—by now even Tolliver was anxious for me to rest—and insisted that we go a bit farther by flashlight. We did so, ducking under the persistent boughs. We finally came upon a glade with enough open space to set up the tent, where only tall grasses impeded our efforts. I tried to help; Tolliver asked me curtly to get out of the way and let them finish. After, I forced down a tin of rations and fell on my bed.

In the dim light of morning Tolliver did his best to dress quietly, but I woke anyway. I sat, fumbled with my shirt, and got to my knees. I waited until Tolliver left the tent before I tried to stand.

I hung on to the tent pole until I was sure my legs had stopped trembling, then thrust aside the flap and went outside. A heavy mist lay about; the ground was cold and damp.

"Coffee, sir?" Tolliver's tone was civil.

"Please." I sat on a rock that protruded through the grasses. I inhaled the aroma of the steaming cup.

"Shall I wake Mr. Tamarov?"

The thought of another day's walk curdled my stomach. "Yes, you'd better." I sipped at my coffee, marshaling my reserves for the day's ordeal.

A few moments later Alexi crouched beside me, cup in hand. He studied my face. "Are you feverish?"

"I'm fine." The claim sounded absurd, even to me.

"You can't make it through another day like yesterday."

"I'll be all right." I watched Tolliver dismantle the tent.

"It took you two minutes to stand up this mor—"

"Alexi, don't argue!"

He blanched. "I—I'm sorry." He hurried to help Tolliver.

＊　＊　＊

I labored for two hours, leaning on Alexi, then on Tolliver, wretched in the drizzle that had begun soon after we left the clearing. When I stopped to catch my breath I was beset by a fit of coughing that swelled until it tore at my chest and throat. When the mists cleared I found myself on my knees, hanging on to a low branch.

"We'll have to carry him." Tolliver's voice was flat.

"Can we rig a stretcher?"

"I'll see what I can find in our gear."

I hadn't the breath to object. I slumped against the bough while Tolliver pulled tent poles from his bundles and tied the poly-mil tent fabric across them.

"Help him onto it, Mr. Tamarov."

"I'm all—"

"You'd better get in, Mr. Seafort." Alexi held my eye until I nodded reluctantly. Arm across his shoulder, I tottered to the makeshift litter. I lay on my back, cold and wet; Alexi folded my jacket under my head as a pillow. I grabbed his arm. "I'm sorry."

He smiled hesitantly. "We can carry you."

"About barking at you this morning."

He shrugged. I searched his face for rebuke, found only worry.

"Alexi, walk out with Tolliver. Leave me and get help."

"No." He nodded to Tolliver, picked up his end of the stretcher. I turned away, ashamed.

Eventually I slept; when I woke I was lying on the ground. Alexi sat nearby. I swallowed; my throat was raw. "Where's Tolliver?"

Alexi looked up, studied my face. "We found a stream. He's refilling our water bottles."

"Help me sit." He did so. "I can walk."

"Please don't try, Mr. Seafort."

"You can't go on carrying me."

"It's not so hard." He looked at his hands. "A few blisters, but I can live with those." He shook his head to still my objection. "It's easier, now that we've dumped most of the supplies. All we've got is the radio, another night's Q-rations, and the water."

I stirred angrily. "Who decided that?"

"Mr. Tolliver suggested it, and I agreed." He chewed his lip. "I don't know who's in charge. You're sick, I can't remember a thing, and he's just a middy."

I smiled weakly. "A mess. I'm in charge, unless he tries to relieve me."

The voice came from behind my head. "I've considered it." I turned. Tolliver stared down, a water bottle in each arm.

"I wouldn't try, Midshipman." My tone was cold.

A twisted smile. "I will, if you become incoherent. Not before." I wondered if it was a threat.

Alexi cleared his throat. "Please stop, both of you." His glance appealed from one to the other. "We're wasting daylight."

Tolliver grunted, handed Alexi one of the water bottles. He stooped to his end of the litter. "Come on, then."

Gripping the sides of the litter, I watched the leafy canopy drift overhead. I closed my eyes; when next I opened them the gray sky had begun to darken. Half dreaming, I tried to focus on the trees and shrubs floating past my head.

"We'd better quit soon," Alexi panted.

"Not yet." Tolliver, at the front of the litter, trudged on, eyes down.

"Then I've got to rewrap my hand."

Tolliver swore under his breath as he lowered the litter. "Hurry up." He waited impatiently while Alexi retied the handkerchief around his palm. Tolliver's eyes drifted down to mine. "We've got only an hour of daylight left, and I don't think we made our ten miles. If we can't reach the road tomorrow, we may not have strength to carry you."

"Tomorrow I'll walk awhile."

"Don't make me laugh." He turned away in disgust.

When next I woke, a fire crackled nearby. Alexi lay on his air mattress, jacket thrown over his shoulders. His breathing was slow and regular. Tolliver, in shirtsleeves, huddled on the far side of the firepit, hands thrust between his legs for warmth. I adjusted my jacket, lay for a while, slept again.

Alexi shook me gently. "Would you like some coffee before we start?"

I nodded, blinking in the early light, watching Alexi busy himself with the pot. The night chill was still on us; I pulled my jacket over my shoulders and adjusted it across my feet. A moment later I struggled to sit, aware that my jacket couldn't possibly cover both my feet and arms. I sorted out my covers.

"It's mine." Tolliver stared down at me.

"How did it—who—?"

"You needed warmth."

The image of Edgar Tolliver huddling next to the fire, bare-shirted in the cold night air, caused me to redden in mortification. "Thank you," I said gruffly.

He smiled briefly. "At Academy I learned to give my all, not my clothes."

"I'm surprised you care if I live."

His tone was sardonic. "I'd be called before a Board of Inquiry if you didn't."

While they sorted the gear I managed to get to my feet unaided, and went into the brush to relieve myself. When I got back to the clearing I had no objection to using the litter. As they readied themselves I keyed the radio. Orbit Station didn't answer. Neither did Centraltown.

I clutched the stretcher while they swung me into position. "How much farther, do you think?"

Tolliver shrugged. "Who knows? The road is somewhere ahead. Five miles? Fifteen?"

Alexi said, "We've had no dinner, no breakfast. Our next meal will see the last of our Q-rations."

"Then hope we find the road." Tolliver.

When we finally stopped to rest Alexi sat, rocking, hand clutched between his knees.

"Let me see."

"I'm all right."

"Do as I say." My tone brooked no argument. Reluctantly he extended his hand, unwrapping the cloth. Red and swollen, his fingers oozed where the blisters had broken.

"Lord God." I rolled myself off the litter.

Tolliver tossed aside his empty Q-ration. "What do you think you're doing?"

"I'll walk."

"You're weak as a kitten."

"It's just bronchitis. I'll manage."

He stood. "Seafort, sometimes you're an idiot."

I rolled to my knees, tried not to stagger as I got to my feet. "Three demerits!"

"Shove your demerits up your arse!" He faced me, hands on hips. "You can't walk! If you try, none of us will make it. And if we do, what will we find? Maybe the Navy's gone with the rest of Centraltown. Do you think I give a damn about your frazzing demerits?"

I moved toward him, legs unsteady. "And duty?" I panted. "Your oath? Honor?"

His fists clenched. "I'm trying to get you out of here alive! If that isn't duty, what is?" His words hissed. "You destroyed me, Seafort! I should have let you execute me. I have no career, no future, and I'm still trying to save you!" His voice caught, and he spun away. "Let me be, damn you!"

After a moment I said softly, "Leave the litter behind. Our jackets too, and everything but the water and the radio. I'll lean against each of you in turn. We'll walk until we reach the road. If I can't make it, I'll have you go on ahead."

Tolliver nodded, unable to speak.

"My hand's not that—"

"I'll lean on you, Alexi. Don't argue, save your strength."

To my shame, I hadn't strength to walk, even leaning heavily on Alexi. So, arms draped across their shoulders, I let them half carry, half drag me through the brush, forcing my feet to cooperate, working to ease their load. My lungs labored but I was determined not to stop. In any event, I wasn't sure I had the breath to call for a rest.

The sun moved inexorably to the horizon. Our stops became more frequent. Afraid I couldn't stand again if I sat, I sagged against a tree, my legs stiffened to keep from falling.

Alexi was disconsolate. "It'll be dark soon."

I managed to speak. "Keep going."

"We can't walk all—"

"There'll be moonlight. We'll keep on until we get to the road or . . ." I left the thought unfinished.

My bravura faded with the light. As darkness came I stumbled more frequently, supported only by the determination of my comrades. At length I signaled a halt. "Water." It came out a croak. Greedily I poured the life-giving liquid down my throat until I drained the bottle. "Where's the other canteen? Alexi, aren't you thirsty?"

Tolliver's face glistened in the light of Hope Nation's two moons. "We finished it a long time ago."

"Christ, I'm sorry." I hadn't thought to offer them a drop.

"Maybe there'll be another stream," he said. And maybe not. I balled my fists, cursing my selfishness. Their strength, not mine, was our hope.

"We'd better get going." Alexi's voice was strained.

For the next hour we struggled through unrelenting brush. Hacking coughs reduced me to helplessness. I began to watch for an open space for them to leave me.

By now, they carried most of my weight; I clung to their shoulders with failing strength. Giving up any effort to walk restored a modicum of energy, and with it clarity of thought. I said carefully, "I'll rest when we find a clearing." I winced as thorns raked my side.

"I'll stay with you."

"No. Go with Tolliver. Bring help."

Alexi shook his head.

"You will. Tolliver, this is an order." I stopped to suck for air. "When we find a clearing you go on with Alexi. Try to mark the trail. Get help. Acknowledge."

Tolliver was breathing hard. "Aye aye, sir, acknowledged."

"I won't leave you!" Alexi's voice held a note of desperation.

"Alexi . . . my father. He's in Cardiff. Wales. I want you to give him a message."

"He's delirious."

"Shut up, Tolliver." I panted. "Tell him—"

"I won't be seeing your father, Mr. Seafort. Not until you take me there."

I fought to remain calm. "I want you to tell Father . . ."

Finally Alexi's voice came, hesitant. "What?"

I thought for a long time, fighting exhaustion. At length I said, "Tell him . . . I tried."

Alexi bit off a moan. I swallowed, seeking a peace that

eluded me. No matter. I had to reach a clearing, force him to leave before he changed his mind. It was the last gift I could offer.

I swallowed, and was overcome by a fit of coughing. Alexi and Tolliver waited for me to recover. By great effort I brought my breathing under control. We staggered on. Our eyes were accustomed to the pale reflections of Major and Minor; we thrust through remorseless tangles of undergrowth. Beyond, the light seemed brighter. I lunged at it, my heart jumping. Yes, definitely more moonlight ahead. A clearing, or what would suffice. An excuse to send them on their way.

I gasped, "I'll sit there, where it's light."

"Let me stay," Alexi said plaintively.

"No." A croak.

"I'm nothing without you, don't you understand? You have my memories!"

My hand clutched at his arm, exacting his submission. "Get to Cardiff for me. You must." The low branches gave way to heavy brush and shoulder-high grass. We were in the clearing. A hundred feet ahead dark trees loomed again in the moonlight. "Set me down."

Tolliver said, "We'll lean you against that tree."

A few more steps. Surely I could manage that. "All right." I let them carry me toward the trees. The grasses parted, and the terrain plunged into a culvert.

Beyond was Plantation Road.

12

I lay shivering in the night air, my head in Alexi's lap. We talked, voices low, while Tolliver crouched by the roadside near his flimsy barricade of dead branches and brush. My breathing consumed more and more effort. Alexi wiped my head with his bandaged hand; Annie brought me a cool compress. I shoved her away; she held my arm down, wiped my brow. "You real sick now, Nicky. We be tak'n care of you."

"I deserted you."

"It don' matter. We work it out nudder time. You be still." She bent over, kissed my cheek. Alexi squeezed my hand.

Dark. Dreams. The endless shadow of Lord God's disfavor. Chest heaving, I drifted from my friends, toward night.

"How is he?"

"I don't know. Sleeping, maybe. Christ, why doesn't someone come?"

"Don't blaspheme," I whispered.

A moment's pause. "I'm sorry, Mr. Seafort."

"Very well."

I slept.

Sometime later I woke to a bright light shining in my face. I twisted away, but the roadside skewed dizzily and I lay still.

"There's room for him behind the cab."

"Pick him up, he's in no condition to help."

"Of course I am," I mumbled, but got no answer. After a time I found myself stretched out behind the driver's seat of the hauler. It resembled a middy's bunk. I giggled.

I woke to full daylight, on clean sheets, in a soft bed, and breathing through a mask that blocked my vision. Sarah Branstead looked up from a holo. "You're back."

I considered it. "You're a hallucination." My voice was muffled.

She smiled. "I don't think so."

I reached for the mask. She caught my hand. "Don't. Dr. Avery has you on vapormeds and you need every drop."

I studied her. "This is real?"

She laughed. "Yes. Your young friend told me you were talking with someone else at times."

"Annie."

"Your wife?"

"She's in Centraltown." With horror I struggled to sit up, fell back against the pillows. "What happened? Is she all right?"

"A great meteor hit near Centraltown. Horrid casualties. They think the fish dropped it."

Lord God, no.

I felt my pulse pounding. "What's the matter with me?"

"Pneumonia. We almost lost you last night."

Father. Cardiff. I looked away. "My lieu—Alexi. How is he?"

"He's in the kitchen with Elena, eating for both of you. He'll be back shortly."

Thank you, Lord.

"And your Mr. Tolliver is asleep upstairs." A soft knock at the door; she beckoned someone in.

The boy sounded shy. "Hello, Captain Seafort." He approached the bed.

"Jerence."

"May I sit for a while?" His mother and I both nodded. He pulled a chair closer to me. "I came down from bed when Mr. Volksteader's hauler brought you."

"I think I remember."

He leaned forward, as if imparting a secret. "I'm glad you're all right."

After a moment I inquired, "Am I?"

No one answered directly. Jerence said, "We've all been worried for you. Ms. Triforth called three times, and Mrs. Palabee sent soup."

Sarah Branstead added, "We'll fly you into Centraltown as soon as your infection's down. To the clinic."

I nodded, growing sleepy. The room faded.

Dr. Avery packed away his diagnostic puter. He was a small man, graying, with a crisp air of authority. "Yesterday I started you on antibiotics, Mr. Seafort. They'll help, but we need to get you to Centraltown. They have better equipment than I carry."

"When?"

"Tomorrow, if your fever stays down."

"I need to report." I looked around for a caller. "Is the Admiral groundside?"

"Worry about that when you recover, Mr. Seafort."

My tone was churlish. "I have to report to Admiralty. That can't wait."

He shrugged. "Using the caller won't hurt, I suppose. If you can get through. Harmon?"

Harmon Branstead said, "We can use low-power radio from here to Zack Hopewell's. That's where the old landline runs."

"Landline?"

"Before we licked the sunspot problem, they buried an old-fashioned fiber-optic line along the road. We're using it again, now that we've gone to radio silence."

I sat up straighter. "What are you talking about?"

Harmon pulled a chair alongside my bed. "I forgot you were stranded in south forest. Your Navy ordered a complete radio blackout after the fish dropped the asteroid on Centraltown. They don't know if fish can hear radio waves but they're not taking a chance until we know more."

Centraltown. Images of Belfast after the IRA nuke. I wondered what was left. "Is Admiralty House standing?"

"It seemed all right when I flew in yesterday. The blast knocked over their dish, but they had that fixed."

I looked around eagerly. "Where's your caller?"

"The main set is in my study. If you'd—"

I swung my legs out of the bed. "Now?"

"Just a minute," Dr. Avery said testily. "Bring along your mask."

"It's only for a few—"

Hands on hips, he glowered. "Or I'll put you down with a sedative. Your choice."

I glared back. Unimpressed, he held my eye until I was forced to surrender. "Alexi, Mr. Tolliver, help with my gear, would you?"

A few moments later I was seated at Harmon Branstead's desk, blanket thrown over my knees, fuming with impatience for the connection.

At last Forbee's voice came on the line. "Mr. Seafort, you're all right! Wonderful. Sorry we couldn't send a heli for you, but the relief work at Centraltown came—"

"Of course." I had to stop until I had my breath. "Can I speak with the Admiral?"

"He's on *Vestra*. We're moving the tactical group to Orbit Station. I leave in about an hour. He's authorized a tight-beam relay to his ship, so I might be able to get you through."

"What's happened since the last attack?"

"It never ended, I'm afraid. Since Tuesday we've lost nine ships."

"Oh, Lord God."

"About half our remaining warships are deployed to protect the Station. The rest of the fleet is in position to intercept an attack on Centraltown. Meanwhile, the fish Fuse in and out at odd intervals. They've learned, Mr. Seafort. They go for our shipboard lasers the moment they Defuse. We're still taking out a few of them, though."

"Lord God help us."

"Amen. Would you like me to try to get you through to the Admiral?"

"Please." I waited in the silent, somber study, with Harmon Branstead, Dr. Avery, and my two officers. Nine ships. Hundreds of souls. How long could we stand against the aliens?

A crisp voice interrupted my reverie. "Admiral De Marnay is on the line." I clutched the caller.

"Hello, Seafort?"

"Yes, sir."

"Who the hell shot you down?"

"I don't know, sir."

"No way to investigate now. All our people are working with emergency rescue. Hell of a mess. You all right?"

"Yes, sir. I'll be in Centraltown tomorrow." I ignored Dr. Avery's rebuke.

"Don't know when I'll be down. The attack may be tapering off, but it's too early to tell."

"Right, sir."

"Did you hear they found Tenere alive in *Freiheit*'s launch?"

"Thank heaven!"

"He's on the station, recovering. Every ship we've got is on patrol. Except for Forbee, you're the only Captain on the ground."

"Yes, sir, that's what I wanted to talk to you about."

"Eh, speak up. You sound muffled."

I tore off the vapormask. "Sir, *Victoria*. Captain Martes was to be transferred." I panted for breath.

"He has *Prince of Wales* now." De Marnay seemed distracted.

"Can I have *Victoria,* sir?"

"Hmm? No, I gave her to Holser. He was a lieutenant."

Bile flooded my throat. "Yes, I knew him." I coughed.

"Overdue for promotion. Commander, now. He took *Victoria* to Detour and Kall's Planet on a special errand."

"I see." With irritation, I waved away the vapormask Dr. Avery thrust at me.

Admiral De Marnay's voice changed. "Seafort, I have contingency orders for you. We're on tightbeam?"

"Only the link from Admiralty House to you."

"Then I'd better send a middy down. He'll have a chip coded for your eyes only."

"Can I meet you at Orbit Station? If there's any ship I could take—"

"No, stay there. Don't worry about the delay, your orders may never go into effect. I'll be in touch. Out." The line went dead.

I sagged. Even in extremis, Georges De Marnay would not call on me. I barely heard Dr. Avery's insistent demands.

Alexi knelt. "Mr. Seafort, you'd better put this on." He held the vapormask.

Dully, I fastened it around my face. I essayed a smile. "Help me back to bed, then. Harmon, would you fly me to Centraltown later?"

"As soon as Dr. Avery allows. In the morning, I imagine." He hesitated. "The war isn't going well?"

"We're losing ships." I stood, hanging on to Harmon's arm, surprised at how dizzy I felt. I let them help me back to my room.

I dozed for several hours, waking in late afternoon. Jerence was sitting by my bedside. He left as soon as I woke and appeared a few moments later with his father.

"Are you well enough for company?"

"You're always welcome, Harmon."

"Thank you, but I meant Zack Hopewell and some of the others. They've heard you're with us."

"No, I—" The last thing I needed was to let them see me smothered in a vapormask. Still, my purpose in taking the heli jaunt had been to confer with them. The attack on Centraltown made their grievances less urgent, but . . . "Yes, I mean. Just give me time to dress."

"This evening, then, after dinner." I nodded agreement.

Zack Hopewell shook his head, his face grim. "A missile." We sat in Harmon's study, much the same group that had met on my earlier visit.

"Thank heaven they only fired one. We couldn't have escaped two." I avoided Edgar Tolliver's eye.

Laura Triforth growled, "Mantiet, of course."

"We don't know that." Hopewell.

"Who else? He already tried once." Laura grimaced. "What's the world coming to? Bombs in the roadway, missile attacks . . ."

I said, "Yes, I've been lucky. Why does Frederick Mantiet want me dead?"

Tomas Palabee glanced at Laura, shook his head. Arvin Volksteader looked uncomfortable. For a moment, silence.

"Maybe he thinks it will hasten the Republic." Plumwell, manager of Carr Plantation. His tone was defiant.

"Nonsense," said Hopewell. "He—"

"That's just wild talk!" Laura.

"Republic?" I demanded.

Harmon said, "He's just speculating, Captain."

"What republic?" I gripped the chair arms and pushed myself to my feet. The room seemed overly warm.

"I—"

"Let me—"

"I'll tell him." Zack Hopewell's tone was firm. The others lapsed silent. "We've long had a party, Mr. Seafort, who've argued—theoretically, mind you—that Hope Nation would be better off as an independent republic."

I was shocked into silence.

"It will happen sooner or later," he said, almost apologetically. "The sheer distance—"

"How could you survive on your own? Where would you sell your grain?" I found my face growing hot. "Can you manufacture the implements of a high-tech society you now import? Is your—"

"Technology isn't everything. We—"

"Have you no gratitude? Men devote their lives to bringing you supplies!"

Laura rasped, "Is that what you expect from your minions? Gratitude?"

It brought me to my senses. "No, of course not. I was out of line. Forgive me. But . . ." I paused to regroup. "Regardless of the merits, that's not a decision we can make." Only the U.N. Security Council, or its plenipotentiary, could grant independence to a colony.

Hopewell was a trifle less frosty. "I didn't say it was. You know we sent representatives to Terra years ago, but nothing came of it. I'm not saying anyone in this room—or any planter—would rebel against lawful authority, but voices have grown stronger over the years. Now that Centraltown's devastated, some feel that the time has come."

"Don't you need the Navy now more than ever?"

Laura's lip curled. "What's your Navy done for us? Did it stop the fish from bombing Centraltown?"

My face was white. "Do you know how many died trying?"

"Many," said Hopewell. "God rest their souls. Sit down, Laura, I'm not done yet." He waited. "It's becoming clear that a change is overdue, even if it falls short of independence. Our complaints about shipping rates are ignored, and—"

"With independence, you'd be utterly at the mercy of the Tariff Board. Who else would buy your grain, other than home system?"

He went on as if I hadn't spoken. "We're stifled by authoritarian government imposed from afar. Do you think a local administration would order a military base hidden in the Venturas?"

"Obviously not. But now is no time to—"

"I agree. This is not the time. But perhaps Mr. Plumwell's sneering reference to a republic is now clear."

"I didn't sneer about—"

Laura's tone was cold. "Stuff it, Plumwell; as a manager you're here only by sufferance." She stared him down. "In any event, Mr. Seafort, what have you accomplished for us?"

I sat, trying to conceal the trembling of my legs. "The Venturas Base was a fiasco. We've begun to remedy that."

"You canned General Khartouf, yes."

"And put a competent man in his place. We'll get the generator completed shortly, and the supplies moved from Centraltown."

"Ah, yes, the supplies." Laura's voice was acid.

"The Station's been downloading cargo faster than the Venturas Base can receive it. Hopefully that will untangle itself with the change of command."

Tomas Palabee stirred. "Appointing a new commander doesn't address the basic issue. We need control of our own affairs."

"You have a legislature . . ."

Laura snorted. "Your constitution gives veto power to the Governor. And in any event, the riffraff at Centraltown can outvote us. Idle hands! Whoever heard of giving unemployed field hands a controlling vote?" A general murmur of agreement.

"I can't rewrite the constitution. But I'll ask Admiral De Marnay what concessions are possible."

Plumwell smiled tightly. "Take your time. Meanwhile, men like Mantiet will handle things their own way."

I slammed my fist on my chair. "Why haven't you caught him?" My anger gave them pause. "You've had . . . how long, four weeks? He's your countryman. You know his habits, you know the terrain! Find him!"

"We've tried." Hopewell's ire matched my own. "We almost took him in Centraltown. He's gone, Lord God knows where. Maybe the meteor got him!"

Laura sighed. "If Frederick's alive, we'll find him; give us time."

"I will." I was stopped by a spell of coughing. Finally I added, "Just as you'll give me time to resolve your problems."

"A fair trade." Zack Hopewell stood. "We've had our say. Let the Captain recover from his ordeal. We've tired him."

Over my protests, they bade good night and took their leave. With profound relief I let Alexi and Tolliver help me to bed. In moments I was asleep.

In the morning I walked with careful step to Branstead's heli. To my surprise, Laura Triforth was waiting to see me off. She took me aside. "About last night . . ." She ran a hand through curly auburn hair flecked with gray.

"Yes, ma'am?"

"For heaven's sake, call me Laura. We've all . . ." She hesitated, seemed to pull herself together. "Our emotions run strong," she said abruptly. "Harmon was right, that day he said we'd grown imperious. I'm afraid in my case the passion of our cause overcame my manners." Hazel eyes met mine. "Captain, I'm truly sorry for the injury to your Lieutenant Tamarov. I don't think I've made clear how distressed I am. And the missile—it's unheard of. Ghastly." Her voice caught.

"Thank you." I tried to make my voice more gentle.

"You fight a frightful war with the fish. In that, we're your allies. You mustn't think we're enemies massing on a second front." Her hand darted to my arm. "Please."

"At times I wondered." I smiled, to take the sting from my words. I turned to the heli and settled into the front seat. My two officers crammed behind. They strapped the vapormask securely about my face, its canister on my lap covered by

Sarah's warm coverlet. At the last moment Jerence trotted out to the lawn. His tone was urgent. "Pa, let me come."

"To Centraltown? Not a chance."

"Please." He hesitated. "It's not what you think. I won't run away. I just want—"

"Yes?" Harmon was impatient.

"To help with Captain Seafort."

"Don't be ridiculous." Harmon's hand reached for the starter, but the boy caught his eye in mute appeal. After a long moment he relented. "Get in."

We lifted off. Tolliver scanned the skies uneasily, as if expecting another missile. I lay back and closed my eyes. Tolliver's anxiety affected all but Jerence, who chattered to Alexi.

Harmon flew low and fast. To break the tension I asked through the mask, "Where's Emmett?"

"Helping in Centraltown. I'll bring him home with me."

"Your brother lives in town, doesn't he?"

"He has a cottage there, but he spends about half of his time with us. We've agreed it's safer on the estate for awhile."

"Safer?"

"Things have—changed."

I brooded on that, while we flew past the edge of the plantation zone, past Hauler's Rest. At last, the outskirts of Centraltown were in sight. It was a clear, sunny day, and I could see no damage.

"Will you land at the spaceport?" My car was there.

"No, south of downtown."

"Why?"

"That's where they've set up the clinic."

"Isn't it at the hospital?"

Harmon compressed his lips, shook his head. A few moments later I spotted the spaceport, but our angle didn't permit a glimpse of Admiralty House. Still, I knew it had survived; I'd talked to Forbee the day before.

Our small talk abated as we neared downtown. I peered down at uprooted trees. Wreckage littering the streets; debris had been shoved aside to clear paths for rescue vehicles.

I sucked in my breath, heedless of the ache in my lungs.

Below, crumpled wood-frame houses sagged to the west, away from downtown, as if too tired to remain standing. My stomach slowly knotted as we flew closer.

Near downtown, brick buildings were smashed to rubble, and streets had disappeared into ruins. I moaned. "Annie . . ."

Harmon asked, "Did she live near the reservoir?"

"We were across town, about twenty blocks from the barracks. Why?"

"Armstrong Reservoir was ground zero."

"What did they hit us with? A nuke?"

He shook his head. "Thank Lord God, no. A rock, but from the energy it dispersed, it might as well have been a fission bomb."

"We shouldn't—" I bit off the thought, not daring to involve them in talk of nuclear weapons.

By the time we dipped toward the grassy meadow that had become an emergency field, I wanted to see no more of the appalling devastation. I sat until the blades stopped whistling. Harmon turned to his son. "I trust you not to run away, boy. But if you do, remember that there's worse danger than a whipping from me." He pointed at what was left of downtown.

Jerence nodded. "I know, Pa. I heard Uncle Emmett. I won't."

I unlatched the door as a U.N.A.F. soldier came alongside. He eyed my vapormask. "This one's for the clinic?"

Tolliver spoke up from the back, his voice cold. "This one's Captain Nicholas Seafort, U.N.N.S."

The sentry glanced at my face. His eyes widened in recognition. "Yes, sir. Right up the street, about half a block." He pointed. "I'll call the ambulance, if you like."

I eased myself out of the heli. "I'm much better, actually." To my surprise, it was true. "I can walk." Alexi and Tolliver hovered at my sides.

"Can I carry the vapormeds?"

I snapped, "I'm not helpless, Jerence." The boy's face fell. I took a couple of steps and hesitated. "Perhaps you'd better, after all." Eagerly he took the canister from my hands.

We proceeded slowly to the school in which the emergency clinic was operating. Electricars, some battered, lined the roadway. We passed a family helping a heavily bandaged man into a car. Though I had to stop more than once for breath, I felt little of the dizziness that had plagued me; Dr. Avery's vapormeds were having their effect. In any event, Alexi and Tolliver were ludicrously close, waiting to catch me if I sagged. Ribald jokes came to mind; with an effort I suppressed them.

On the stoop two women sat consoling each other, oblivious to passersby. Alexi held the door.

In the hall they'd set up an admitting office near the gymnasium that served as the main clinic. The hall was crowded with patients, some bandaged, some uninjured, many slumped despondently. I found a place on a bench.

Tolliver leaned over the admitting desk, spoke to the weary civilian behind it. The man ran his hands through his hair, pushed himself up from his desk.

"Captain Seafort? An honor to meet you, sir." I nodded through my mask. "I'll have a med tech look you over while you wait for the doctor."

"Wait?" Tolliver's tone was hostile.

"Yes, wait." The man showed signs of irritation. "We've only three surgeons, and they've worked without sleep the past four days. We finally sent two of them to rest, and the third's trying to hang on to a joey who was trapped under a collapsed wall since the blast."

I forestalled Tolliver's reply. "How long before the doctor has time?"

"Hours, probably. We take life-threatening cases first."

"Of course." We shouldn't have come. Pneumonia was nothing compared to the injuries they battled. My vapormeds seemed to be holding their own against it.

"You can wait in the lobby or in a classroom."

"Could I come back later?"

"I can't guarantee we won't get another emergency, but that's less likely with each passing hour. All we're finding now is the dead. A doctor should be able to see you after seven tonight."

"Thank you. Does anyone have a survivors' list?"

"It's on the puter at emergency HQ but I can tie in from here. What name?"

"Miss Wells. Annie Wells." My heart thumped.

He bent over the console, straightened. "She's not listed as a survivor."

I turned away, unable to speak.

"But she's not among the known dead," he added. "The list isn't complete. It only has those who've been treated or have reported to a relief center."

Annie would know to put her name on the list, of course. So she was lost. I sagged against the wall. After a time a wave of contempt washed away my self-pity. So easy to dismiss her as dead, yet I'd hadn't even searched for her. Perhaps she was hurt, wandering, desperate for help.

I beckoned to Harmon Branstead. "Would you take me back to the spaceport?"

"No."

Stunned, I could only gape. "What? . . . I'm sorry." My tone was stiff. "I didn't mean to impose."

"Imposing has nothing to do with it. I won't be party to your suicide."

I snorted. "Don't be silly. I won't be able to see a doctor for hours. I need to look for Annie, and I should check in at Admiralty House."

"That's not wise. Dr. Avery—"

"Damn your Dr. Avery!" My vehemence drove him back a step. After a tense moment I cleared my throat. "Forgive me, Harmon."

"Of course." He sighed, unclenched his fists. "Well, let's get you back to the heli, if you must."

"Thank you." On the way to the makeshift airstrip I allowed Alexi and Tolliver to support some of my weight, more winded than I cared to let on.

Strapped securely into my seat, I fell into a doze while Harmon lifted off and headed west. When I woke, the heli was settling on the tarmac behind Admiralty House. I opened the door and swung out my legs, debating whether to report first to Admiralty or to search for Annie. Annie was more important, but Admiralty House was but a few steps away.

"Tolliver, remember where we parked our car?"

"Yes, sir."

"Bring it round the front of Admiralty House. Alexi, you might give me a hand." I paused. "Harmon, thanks for everything."

"You'll go back to the clinic?"

"I think I'm getting better. I'm sure my fever's down."

"Give me your word you'll be there at seven."

My eyebrow raised. "I beg your pardon?"

"You heard me."

Jerence looked anxiously from his father to me. Despite myself, I smiled. "Very well, Harmon. My word." My smile vanished. My word was worth less than he knew.

"No, sir, no one's come groundside since yesterday." Willem Anton, the duty lieutenant. Admiralty House seemed nearly deserted.

"The Admiral didn't send a middy?"

"Nothing's landed except the shuttle that took Captain Forbee aloft, sir. Would you like to call Naval HQ at the Station?"

I grimaced. "The Admiral has enough on his mind. Who's in charge here?"

"Lieutenant Trapp, upstairs."

"I'll go see him." I got to my feet.

Alexi blurted, "Mr. Anton, could you ask Lieutenant Trapp to come down instead?"

I wheeled. "Remember your own duty before you intrude on mine!" I panted for breath.

Alexi blushed crimson, but held his ground. "I thought— you've been so—"

But Anton was already on the caller; he'd observed the vapormask and canister Alexi held. I glared. Alexi looked only mildly contrite. While we waited I asked Anton, "Have you heard from my wife?"

The lieutenant looked up, face grim. "Was she downtown?"

"I don't know. We lived near downtown."

He started to speak, shook his head. "Sorry. I've heard nothing, sir."

Lieutenant Trapp saluted as he trotted down the steps.

"Admiral De Marnay told me you'd be along, sir. Good to see you again."

"Again?"

"Yes, sir, I was in the tactics room the day you came to, ah, visit Mr. Holser."

"Yes." I didn't want reminding of that. "What's our status?"

"We're monitoring reports. They're on screen in the tactics room, if you'd like . . ."

"Very well." I ignored Alexi's reproach and followed Trapp up the stairs. Halfway, I paused, my strength fading.

In the tactics room, Trapp's pointer tapped the screen. "The Admiral's here on *Vestra,* in orbit about thirty degrees west of the Station."

"Foolish of him to chase about on a ship." Placing himself at risk served no purpose; better that he commanded from the safety of the Station or Centraltown. In a moment I realized what I'd said. Mortified, I added hastily, "He—uh— Of course, he has his reasons. Please disregard my comment."

"Aye aye, sir."

Still, if *Vestra* was destroyed, our chain of command would be sundered. With Forbee on the Station I was the only Captain groundside; I had best stay close to Admiralty House until the danger was past.

Lieutenant Trapp pointed. "The fleet is divided into two squadrons, to protect both Centraltown and the Station."

"Any sightings?"

"Not for a couple of days, sir." He cleared his throat. "Sir, are we, ah, losing?"

"I don't know."

He swallowed. "If the fish take out our fleet, what will happen to Centraltown? To Hope Nation?"

"Enough, Lieutenant." My voice was sharp. "We'll do our duty." I sat, waiting out a passing weakness. "How many Captains are on the Station?" If Admiral De Marnay were killed, the senior Captain there would be in charge. The only other Admiral sent to Hope system, Geoffrey Tremaine, had died by my own hand.

"Mr. Tenere is recovering on Orbit Station, sir."

"That's all? Everyone else is on ship?"

He swallowed. "Or lost."

"Very well." I had to remain at Admiralty House. No, I had to find Annie. I cursed; I couldn't do both. Anyway, did it make sense to stagger about Centraltown, dependent on a vapormask? Others could search more competently than I, and my duty was here.

No. Annie was my wife. "Mr. Trapp."

"Sir?"

"I'll set my caller to standby channel. Reach me by it if there's any action. I'm going to search for my wife."

By the time I reached the foot of the stairs I was sweating. Nonetheless I made an effort to walk casually to the main door, Alexi at my heels.

"The car's right here, sir."

I took several breaths, negotiated the stoop. Perhaps I'd better wear the vapormask after all. I took it from Alexi's hand, thrust it over my face.

I leaned on him the rest of the way.

I sank into the back seat, inhaling from the vapormask as deeply as I could. Each breath came as a stab.

It took Tolliver over an hour to negotiate the debris-filled streets to my neighborhood. Alexi dozed in front, head cradled on his bandaged hand. While we drove I stared at rows of blasted, windowless buildings with sagging roofs, hoping against hope that my apartment was spared.

We turned south, away from the worst of the devastation. Soon Tolliver pulled up on the street where I lived. Our building was less damaged than many we'd passed, though splintered siding boards hung askew, smashed by the force of the blast. Underlayment peeked through roof shingles. A few windows were torn from their mountings.

Yet, the building stood.

"I'll check for you, sir." Tolliver was subdued.

"No." I struggled with the door.

"You can barely—"

"Shut your mouth." I let Alexi help me from the car.

Breathing carefully through the confining mask, I negotiated the walkway and put my thumb to the apartment lock. No click. Well, power was off, and the building's backup batteries might have run down. I banged on the door, waited. I knocked again, my eyes shut against a salt sting.

No answer.

Tolliver, carrying the caller, had gone around the side of the building. "A window's smashed."

"Can you get in?"

"Anyone could, now."

I bit back a savage retort. "Climb in and open the door."

The radio crackled. "Captain Seafort?"

Tolliver handed me the caller. "Yes?"

"Lieutenant Trapp, Admiralty House. You said to call if anything . . . We've just heard from Orbit Station. A shuttle's on the way down with a messenger for you."

"Messenger?" I couldn't think.

"A midshipman, sir."

"Oh, yes. I'll be back shortly."

A moment later Tolliver opened the door. Annie must have packed in a hurry, I thought, observing the bureau doors thrown open, dressers emptied on the floor, papers and clothes tossed in an untidy mess. It took me a while to comprehend someone had been searching.

No. Looting.

No sign of Annie. No message.

Unutterably weary, I fell on the couch, watching the last of day darken to dusk.

"Shall we go back to the clinic, sir?"

I stirred. "Admiralty House."

Alexi said, "But, the doctor—you promised—"

"Admiralty House." I let them help me to the car. When I sat again, I couldn't stop panting.

Alexi was hesitant. "Could you drop me at the hospital?"

"It's not in operation, Alexi."

"But I could get my clothes, my things . . . maybe rest."

"All right." I nodded to Tolliver.

Within a few blocks we had passed into a zone of appalling devastation. Tolliver maneuvered past fallen trees, wrecked cars flung about like pebbles, broken and tumbled houses. A few crumpled bodies strewn amid the wreckage gave scale and perspective to the rendition of a demented architect.

We detoured to avoid impassable streets; eventually I lost my sense of direction, and sat passively while Tolliver swore at the blockages.

The road ended at a broad avenue; on the far side was a row of smashed houses fencing a rolling meadow. Tolliver gunned the engine.

"Hey, where are you—" We careened across the side yard of a house, into the meadow beyond.

"This is Churchill Park. If I cross—"

"Cars aren't allowed in the park."

He hit the brakes, twisted around in his seat. "What, sir?" Even Alexi stared.

"Never mind." I felt a fool.

Tolliver's eyes bored into me. "Would you care to drive, sir?"

"Never mind, I said!"

He restarted the engine, shaking his head with unconcealed contempt.

We made better progress across the open fields than through the rubble-filled streets. The grass beneath us was shriveled and burned, and trees were down everywhere.

I strove to orient myself; we must be approaching downtown. The hospital would be a few blocks beyond the edge of the park. Only weeks before, Annie and I had strolled here before visiting the Cathedral.

We reached the crest of a small hill. Beyond was the boundary of the park. Tolliver found a gap in the row of shrubbery lining the park and plunged through.

Around us was devastation.

We turned the corner. Alexi pointed eagerly. "The hospital is over . . . past that . . ." His voice trailed off.

Centraltown Hospital was gone.

A pile of unrecognizable rubble covered two blocks. Beyond the ruins of hospital stretched the ruins of downtown. The commercial district, the government buildings, were obliterated. Thank heaven I'd taken Alexi to the plantation zone.

Tolliver switched off the engine. "Christ Jesus, even the walls."

Alexi slumped in his seat. "If I'd been there . . ."

Tolliver's voice was surprisingly gentle. "You'd be dead."

Alexi said forlornly, "My things. My clothes." He sat huddled, arms crossed as if warming himself.

"People died here." Tolliver's tone was sharp. "Clothes are nothing."

"They're all I had. That and my room."

I said gruffly, "You'll stay with me."

"Where?"

I didn't know. My chest ached. "Tolliver, back to Admiralty House."

"You're supposed to see a doctor," Tolliver said.

"Middy, shut up!" Blessedly, he did.

13

The roar of the descending shuttle subsided. In the Admiralty House anteroom I impatiently drummed my fingers on Lieutenant Anton's console. "What's keeping him?"

"Shall I go look, Mr. Seafort?" Alexi got to his feet.

"No." I concentrated on breathing. Some minutes later the front door swung open. I came awake.

A voice piped, "Midshipman Avar Bezrel reporting, sir." A youngster in immaculate uniform brought himself to attention with an Academy salute.

I scowled. "Don't I know you?"

"I'm on Admiral De Marnay's staff, sir. I took you into his office when—"

"Very well. As you were." He relaxed, said nothing further. I prompted, "You have a message?"

"Yes, sir, but the Admiral said it's for your eyes only."

"Let's have it."

He took a deep breath. "I was told, only when we're alone. I'm sorry, sir, no disrespect intended."

I tore off the vapormask. "Who ordered this charade?"

"Admiral De Marnay, sir." His innocent gray eyes met mine.

"Anton, Tolliver, Mr. Tamarov, leave the room." I waited until they'd trooped upstairs. My voice was ice. "Is that satisfactory, Mr. Bezrel?"

The boy fished in his jacket pocket, came out with a chip-case.

I opened it. "You leave too, Mr. Bezrel."

"But, sir, I have the—"

"At once."

"Aye aye, sir." He wheeled, marched to the stairwell, and trotted upstairs.

I inserted the chip into Lieutenant Anton's holovid, flipped it on, entered my passcode.

Gibberish.

I spun the dial, searching through the images. All unreadable. My fist slammed onto the console. "Bezrel, get down here!" My breath stabbed.

The boy trotted downstairs. "Aye aye, sir."

"What is this nonsense?"

Bezrel said, "You need a code to unlock it, sir."

"Give it!" I held out my hand.

"He made me memorize it, sir!" He wrinkled his brow, then spouted figures. I tapped them into the holovid and punched the readout, grumbling under my breath.

Random characters filled the screen.

"Look at that garbage!" The boy peered at the console. "Try again."

"3J2, uh, 49GHZ . . . 1425, sir."

"You told me 1245!"

"I'm sorry, I—"

I punched in the new figures. "Two demerits, you silly young—"

Still gibberish. I drew breath to speak.

"I think it was 1542!" the boy said desperately.

The screen was full of random symbols. I lurched to my feet. "Think? You don't remember?"

To my astonishment, the boy began to sob, standing at attention, tears running down his cheeks. "I'm not sure, I—I mean . . ."

"Oh, for God's—" I raised my voice to a bellow. *"Tolliver!"* I paced to the wall, returned panting to my seat.

Edgar Tolliver raced downstairs, took in the scene.

"Take this—this puppy out of here! Have him back in five minutes acting like a middy. Move!"

"Aye aye, sir." Tolliver snatched Bezrel's arm and propelled him to the door. I sat behind the desk, muttering imprecations. Eventually I calmed, but my chest throbbed.

In a few minutes the door opened. Bezrel crept in, hugging himself, head down. Tolliver followed. He touched the boy's shoulder and guided him gently to my desk. Bezrel came to attention. "I'm sorry, sir," he quavered. "I should have—"

"Belay that. I was wrong to yell. Stand easy." I forced the impatience from my tone. "Do you think you have it now, Mr. Bezrel?"

"Try 1524, sir. I mean, please, sir. I'm sure I got the rest of it right. That's the only—"

I punched in the code. The holoscreen cleared. Words flashed onto the screen. "Top Secret: Captain Nicholas E. Seafort, Eyes Only." Readable words. Bezrel craned around the console. His face lit up. "Oh, thank Lord God!"

My relief left me shaky. "Leave, both of you. Mr. Bezrel, my compliments to the duty officer, and he's to cane you for incompetence."

He swallowed. "I— Aye aye, sir." With a forlorn look he turned to the stairs. Halfway, a muffled sob escaped him.

Tolliver paused at the banister. "Of course that will help him remember in future." His tone was sardonic.

I fought to keep my voice level. "You're a midshipman, Mr. Tolliver. You could be caned likewise."

He paused, then said simply, "Do that and I'll kill you." He turned to the stairs.

"Get back here!"

"Aye aye, sir." He approached my desk.

"I could charge you with mutiny!"

"Oh, no, sir, it wasn't mutiny." His manner was casual, though his look was anything but. "I'll obey orders; I'm simply making clear my breaking point. Granted, I shouldn't have snatched the heli controls from you; I have to pay for that. So at twenty-five years of age I have the rank of a teener. I'll put up with it. I suppose you were generous to offer me summary punishment. But I couldn't tolerate your striking me. I'll try my best to kill you if you do."

I gaped, astounded. He continued, "So, Captain, you have your revenge for whatever hazing you suffered. I'm at your mercy. You know how far you can push me, and afterward, if I fail, you'll have me executed." He held my eye. "Am I dismissed?"

I'd have him arrested; what he'd said was insufferable. My fists bunched. And yet . . .

He was right. To threaten a grown man with a middy's caning was obscene; even poor Bezrel hadn't deserved it.

"Get out!" The moment Tolliver was out of sight I turned to the holovid and entered my ID. The screen responded; I read my message at last.

Seafort:
These are contingency orders, which I've entrusted to a staff midshipman. Lord God grant that they never be put into effect. U.N.S. *Victoria* brought dispatches from Admiralty, at home. They've decreed that regardless of the cost here, the fleet must survive to defend home system. Therefore I am required, should we lose a third of our ships, to Fuse home with all remaining vessels.

Until now that possibility seemed remote, but given the events of this week I've begun planning for the worst case. Accordingly, we've begun evacuating U.N. forces from the Venturas, where they were doing little good. We're restationing them on our warships, and on Orbit Station.

If the fleet is forced to withdraw, it will carry Governor Saskrit and his civilian staff as well as the entire Army and Naval establishment. Hope Nation will be on its own until the fleet returns.

I sagged, head in my arms. Once the fleet left, it was unlikely ever to return. We would have abandoned our Hope Nation colonists to their fate.

I believe that likelihood is remote. To lose so many ships would mean attacks by more fish than we've yet seen. But if word of our contingency plan leaks, our relations with the planters would be devastated. Therefore, we must maintain a presence at Admiralty House until the last possible moment, or until the threat recedes. I've quietly withdrawn all other Captains and many of our lieutenants to the Station. You are the last Captain groundside.

For the moment, I'm placing you in command of Admiralty House. Your orders are: (1) to remain at hand and in a state of readiness to depart should it be necessary; and (2) to otherwise carry on as if under normal circumstances.

Catalonia is due back from Detour in ten days or so. I sent *Victoria* to intercept her with new orders, but the ships may not make contact. *Victoria* will go on to Kall's Planet to retrieve their Governor, and will return here. If on her return she fails to establish contact with the fleet, *Victoria* will Fuse at once for home.

For now, we've suspended shuttle flights to and from the Station, on the chance they may somehow attract the aliens. But I'll see to it that a shuttle is sent for you if we're required to depart. If you receive the code word, shut down Admiralty House, encrypt the puters, bring all remaining Naval personnel to the spaceport, and board the shuttle forthwith.

You must at all costs prevent any citizens of Hope Nation from learning of these orders. I hope and expect to return to Admiralty House shortly, to reassume command.

The code word is Destiny.

Georges T. De Marnay, Admiral Commanding.

I laid my head in my hands. Minutes passed.

At length Alexi called, "Mr. Seafort, are you all right? May I come down?"

I snapped off the holovid. "Yes."

He hurried into the anteroom. "You were silent for so—" He gaped. "Were you crying?"

"Don't be ridiculous." I wiped my sleeve across my face. "Call Lieutenant Anton."

A moment later the duty lieutenant stood at ease in front of his own desk. I suppressed a shiver; the room was freezing. "I need a list of all Naval personnel currently groundside."

"That's all in the puters, sir. It shouldn't take more than a few minutes." He hesitated. "Shall I find another console to work from?"

I blinked, recalled that it was his desk I'd appropriated. "That won't be necessary." I stood, debating the wisdom of trudging upstairs. I probably had strength for it, but coming back down might be a problem. "Is there another office on this level?"

"Just the conference room, sir." I let him lead the way. I spotted an easy chair behind the polished genera table. My heart pounded as I sat.

Tolliver appeared in the doorway. "It's six fifty-five, sir."

With an effort I focused on him. "I have my watch." The one phrase left me breathless.

"You're to see the doctor at seven."

"It will wait."

"You gave your word to Branstead."

I fought for breath. When I could speak I said, "Why do you hound me?"

He smiled bitterly. "Duty, of course."

"What does it matter if I live?"

"As I said, there'd be a Board of Inqu—"

"Belay that!"

His smile vanished. "I'm fit only for the Navy, and thanks to you, no one would have me in their command. While you live I have a posting. After that I'm beached." He leaned against the doorway, eyes closed. After a moment he added, "Sorry, I won't do that again. I don't want your pity. Let's go to your doctor."

"I'm on standby for special orders. I can't leave." The words left me gasping.

He crossed to my chair. "Bring your bloody caller along!"

A gasp of astonishment. I looked to the entranceway. "It's all right, Mr. Anton. Come in." He looked doubtfully at Tolliver before presenting me his notepad.

"Twelve officers? That's all?"

"It seems odd, sir, but everyone else is aloft at the moment."

I checked his list. Trapp, upstairs. Mr. Anton. Alexi. Two midshipmen in the plotting room. Three middies and a lieutenant working with the relief of Centraltown. Tolliver, and young Bezrel. Of our entire Naval garrison, only these officers and I were left. Orbit Station must be swarming.

"How many enlisted men?"

"After Naval barracks was destroyed we shipped most survivors to the Station. There may be a couple of dozen helping around town." He hesitated. "May I ask why you're inquiring?"

"You may not." I took refuge in propriety. "Remember you're speaking to a Captain." I began to cough.

"Aye aye, sir." His glance strayed again to Edgar Tolliver. "Is that all, Captain?"

"Carry on."

When he'd left, Tolliver said, "It's seven o'clock, sir. You gave your word."

The room was quite hot. I unbuttoned my jacket. "I've already broken it."

"Then redeem it." He held my gaze.

It wasn't worth the effort to resist. "Very well. See if you can get a heli."

I waited; a moment later he was back. "The Navy has five. Two are out for repairs; the other three are patrolling downtown. Anton says the looting has gotten worse." He studied my face. "Recall one of the helis, sir."

"Damn it." Seeing his shocked expression, I repeated, "Damn it. To hell." I felt a moment of panic at the near blasphemy, then suppressed it. I would pay for worse, in His time. Still, I made a quick, silent prayer of contrition. I sighed. "All right, get the car."

Knees trembling, I sat silent in the back seat, breathing deeply from my vapormask. It wasn't much help. Alexi climbed in the front with Tolliver. I leaned back.

"We're here, sir."

I opened my eyes. Surely no more than a moment had passed. The car was excruciatingly hot, and it was dark. "Where?" It was almost inaudible.

"The emergency clinic." Alexi watched anxiously.

I tried to stand, but coughs racked my frame. "Help me." Sagging against Alexi I made my way up the stairs and into the school.

Tolliver, sullenness cast aside, ran to the admitting desk. He spoke quietly, waited for an answer, shook his head urgently. The civilian gestured at the benches of waiting injured.

"Now!" Tolliver barked. On a bench, I huddled against

Alexi. Tolliver unclipped his holster. "Now! By Lord God, I mean it!" His hand went to his pistol.

"Belay that!" My voice was a hoarse rasp.

Tolliver ignored me. "Call your frazzing doctor!" His tone was savage.

The civilian made a placating gesture, spoke urgently into his caller. A moment later a white-clad medic came out of the gym. "I'm Dr. Abood." Tolliver pointed. The doctor took one look at my face. "Bring him in."

I lay on the examining table, oxygen mask pressed to my mouth. The shot they'd given made breathing less painful. "What's wrong with me?"

"What isn't?" He turned off the analyzer. "Pneumonia, certainly. It should have killed you by now." A young man, in his thirties. Impatient.

"Dr. Avery started . . . antibiotics." I had to stop for breath.

"Yes. You may die before they gain hold." The medic ran his hand through thinning hair.

"Die." A stab of fear, not of death itself, but of what would come after.

"I've increased the dose. If you're quiet, and stay on the oxygen, it may knock the pneumonia down."

I spoke through the mask. "I have to get back to Admiralty House."

"Impossible."

Fighting dizziness, I struggled to a sitting position.

"I must." I fumbled at buttoning my shirt. "I'll lie down there."

"On your deathbed."

A chill caressed my neck. "But I was getting better. Really."

"Dr. Avery's meds helped the pneumonia, but you're losing your lung. Rejection. Blood tests leave no doubt." I gaped. He raised an eyebrow. "Avery didn't tell you?"

I shook my head, stifling a cough. "The antirejection drugs. I thought they . . ."

"You had only the first dose. You were about due for the second." I lay stunned.

"Maybe exposure brought it on. Normally, it wouldn't be

a problem; we'd yank the bad lung and give you another. Now, replacement is impossible. We haven't the equipment, and the growth tanks are gone with the hospital."

Even my body had abandoned me. Had Lord God's vengeance begun? "Can you halt the rejection?"

"There's not much chance the drugs would work. Your best bet is for us to pull the lung. They'll give you another when you get home."

"No."

"If we yank the lung you'd be back on your feet in a week."

"I can't be disabled now. Give me the antirejection drug."

"Damn you people!" His vehemence shook me. "I watch joeys gasp their lives out on these tables, fighting to live a few extra minutes, and I can't save them! I can hold on to you, but you want to kill yourself! Why? For a fresh posting? A promotion?"

"No." I fought to breathe. "How soon would we know if the antirejection meds worked?"

"Your lung is inflamed and full of fluid. The drugs might have some temporary effect. But if your immune system rejects the lung again, it will go fast. You'd be lucky to reach the operating table."

"If I kept a heli standing by?"

He pursed his lips. "Your duty is so pressing?"

"I have . . . orders. I might have to take quick action."

His indignation eased. "Well, it's your life, joey. Will you stay on the vapormeds and on oxygen?" I nodded. "If your fever climbs, or you have more trouble breathing, get in a heli fast and radio ahead."

"All right."

He followed up his advantage. "And see me every day."

I smiled. "If possible, Dr. Abood."

He left the room. I dressed slowly, working around the vapormask. After a few moments the doctor returned. "I gave your men the replacement canisters."

"Very well."

"I explained your condition, so they'll be—"

"Leave my officers out of it!" The last thing I needed was Alexi and Tolliver mothering me.

He raised an eyebrow. "They had to know. When you go bad, you may not have time to tell them." I noticed he'd said "when," not "if."

"That's my affair." I slipped off the table, clung to it until the dizziness passed.

He said only, "Good luck. You'll need it."

When I emerged from the gymnasium Alexi took the canister from my hands. "Do you want to lean on me?"

"No." I took a few steps, tried to make my pace as normal as possible.

Tolliver held the outer door. "What did he tell you?"

"Not to let you treat me like an invalid." I brushed past into the back seat of the electricar, drained. Outside, all was dark.

"Where to, sir?"

"Admiralty House, of course."

Tolliver started the car. "Of course." I closed my eyes. He said, "You realize we've been on duty since early this morning?"

I wanted only to sleep. "After you take me back you're free to go."

"Where, may I ask?"

The question snapped me awake. Naval barracks was demolished; neither Tolliver nor Alexi had a home. Nor did I, for that matter, though I could stay at Admiralty House, on a couch if necessary. I wondered if Admiralty House had showers. I tried to think.

Eons later a persistent voice nagged me into wakefulness. "Captain, you can't sleep in the car. Please, sir."

I blinked. We were parked at Admiralty House. Behind Tolliver, on the sidewalk, Lieutenants Anton and Trapp watched with obvious concern. I thrust away Tolliver's offered hand.

I stood, but the effort left me trembling and my weakness enraged me. "Middy, help me up the stairs." I leaned on Tolliver's shoulder. Alexi looked at Lieutenant Anton. "The Captain needs a bed, flank."

"We have air mattresses, in reserve stores. Shall I get a couple for you and Lieuten—Midshipman Tolliver?"

"Yes, please." As we passed through the doors I heard Alexi's quiet sigh of relief.

I slept fitfully in the conference room that had become my home. When morning came I needed Alexi's help to get to my feet, but I managed to wash and dress myself around the cumbersome vapormask. I didn't dare remove it.

Steaming tea soothed my chest as I sat at the gleaming table. In the rational light of morning I considered going immediately to the clinic to let Dr. Abood pull my rotting lung. With luck I'd be back at Admiralty House within a few days, and Admiral De Marnay might never get around to replacing me.

However, my orders were to keep our contingency plans secret until the Admiral sent the code word. If I told no one, and a signal came while I was under the anesthetic . . .

Alexi appeared at the door. "May I come in?"

I grunted. He sat at my side, unbidden.

"I feel—I shouldn't bother you with my problems." His hands fluttered in his lap like wounded birds. He rushed on. "But what am I to do? What is my status? Do I have duties?"

"You're on sick leave. You can't go back to the hospital, so you have to stay with me." It sounded more brusque than I'd intended. "Help me get around, Alexi. We'll find a place for you when they get things back in order."

"It's not just where I'm to stay. I feel—lost. Should I wear the uniform? What do I do when Tolliver speaks to you the way he does? What would any lieutenant do, hearing that?"

"Have a fit." My smile was bleak. "I shouldn't have demoted him. It was cruel, and we both know it. Mr. Tolliver is a situation I don't know how to handle."

"You could restore his rank."

"That would be worse; I can't go about rescinding discipline." I paused, then added carefully, "Or explaining my acts to lieutenants."

He colored. "I'm sorry. I wish . . . I knew better how to behave."

"You will, when your memory returns. In the meantime, study the regs; you knew them once. Perhaps they'll jog your memories."

He shook his head. "I will, but we both know better, Mr. Seafort." He stood. "Tell me when you'd like to go out. I'll be glad to help."

After he left I brooded about Tolliver, but found no answer. I rang for Lieutenant Anton.

"Yes, sir?"

"Have we heard from the fleet?"

"No contacts, sir. Mr. Trapp is in the plotting room; shall I have him come down?"

"I'll go up." Whatever protest he was about to offer was stilled by the look in my eye.

I took my time on the stairs. In the plotting room Lieutenant Trapp came out of his chair to stand at attention, as did a middy I didn't recognize. "As you were." I flopped in an empty seat. "Our status?" After my climb I thought it best to speak in short phrases.

Trapp flicked a key and the screen came to life. "Our main units are stationed here." De Marnay had pulled in our outer defenses, concentrating them around Hope Nation and Orbit Station.

I studied the positions. "Any sightings?"

"No, sir."

Footsteps pounded up the stairs. Midshipman Bezrel skidded into the room, came quickly to attention. "A call for you, sir. Mr. Anton sent me. It's—"

"Is that how they taught you to report?"

"No, sir, but I—"

"Go back down then! Report properly!"

He gulped. "Aye aye, sir." He saluted, turned, and left. Lieutenant Trapp and the other middy exchanged glances, said nothing. A moment later Bezrel's step sounded more sedately. He knocked at the door, entered at my nod. He stood at attention, shoulders stiff. "Midshipman Avar Bezrel reporting, sir!"

"Better. Stand at ease."

"Mr. Anton's compliments, sir. You have a call."

"Very well. How old are you, Mr. Bezrel?"

"Thirteen, sir." Young for a middy to be sent interstellar; his voice hadn't even broken. "Sir, I thought you'd want—"

I reached for the caller. "Is it the Admiral?" If I'd kept *him* waiting . . .

"No, sir. It's—"

"Nicky?" The voice tore at my soul.

I tore off the vapormask. "Annie? *ANNIE?*"

"Oh, Nicky! You be'ent dead!"

"Lord God. Where are you?"

"Dat refugee place, by the park."

"Annie, I . . ." I had to pause. "We looked for you . . ." Trapp turned away from my anguish.

"Our 'partment, you see'd it? Someone got in, mess wid our things."

"Where are you?"

"When the boom hit, I din' know what to do. I wen' back our place, nothin' workin', no lights or caller. I took food and hid 'til I figure it was safe. Empty places; I found lots of 'em. You din' come back; I thinkin' you was dead."

"Oh, Annie." I stopped, swallowed several times. Trapp and Bezrel were in the room; I managed to control my voice. "Stay where you are. I'll come for you."

Her tone had a note of alarm. "Oh, no, Nicky, you don' wan' see how I be lookin' now. Wait 'til I go back to the 'partment, get nice clothes. I meet you."

"Clothes don't matter; I've got to see you."

"I wan' look good fo' you, firs'. You come . . ."

"Meet me at the apartment."

"Naw, dat bad place now, people broke window an' trash our stuff. Meet me—" She paused. "Outside the Cathedral we be married in."

"Annie, it's bombed out. Nothing left but—"

"Safe place. Good place. Seeya in an hour."

"Don't—"

"Ten o'clock." A click.

"Annie!" I pounded the caller, but she'd rung off. I sighed. Not the best place to meet, surrounded by rubble, but what did that matter? My wife was alive.

After a time Lieutenant Trapp cleared his throat. I looked up, wiped my eyes. "Sorry."

"I'm glad for you, sir."

"Thank you." I rounded on Bezrel. "Why didn't you tell

me who was calling? I made her wait while I sent you back down!"

"I tried, sir, but—"

"All you had to do was say her name!"

"Yes, sir, but you—"

"Two demerits. Out!"

"Aye aye, sir." He saluted and fled.

I let my fury ebb. Annie was alive; nothing else mattered. My illness didn't count. Our apartment was nothing. Even . . . I faced it: even Eddie Boss didn't matter any longer.

Trapp was tactfully silent. I stared at the board, willing the fish to show their whereabouts, explain their intentions. The middy on duty fidgeted, but quieted at my frown. "Well, the fish won't be dropping any rocks," I said. "Not without Defusing into the middle of the fleet."

"Yes, sir," Trapp agreed. "But our ships are tied down patrolling. To cover Centraltown while the Station is over the Venturas, we've committed here, and here." He gestured. "What does that leave us in reserve?"

"Enough, I hope." Footsteps pounding on the stairs. I swiveled.

"Midshipman Avar—"

"Another call, Mr. Bezrel?"

"No, sir." He was stiff at attention. "Lieutenant Anton's compliments. Ms. Triforth and Mr. Hopewell are below, demanding to speak to the officer in charge."

"I beg your pardon? Demanding?"

"That's the way Mr. Anton said it, sir. I don't mean any disre—"

"What in hell—er, what do they want?"

Bezrel said anxiously, "Mr. Anton didn't tell me, sir."

"Dismissed."

"Aye aye, sir." He seemed grateful to escape.

I'd have to go down, of course. The planters should have called for an appointment, but nonetheless they were too important to snub. I had half an hour to get rid of them before I was to meet Annie. I turned to Trapp. "Have Mr. Anton show them to the conference room."

"Aye aye, sir."

I hoisted myself out of my chair, headed for the door. I paused, my face reddening. "Mr. Trapp, when you see Mr. Bezrel . . ." I reached for my vapormask.

"Yes, sir?"

I mumbled, "Tell him his demerits are canceled."

His face was impassive. "Aye aye, sir."

Laura Triforth, sprawled in an easy chair, came to her feet when I entered. Old Zack Hopewell faced the wall with hands clasped behind him. He turned, gave a formal nod. His manner was more somber than hostile, but I sensed that something had changed.

I shifted the canister awkwardly to shake hands, and sat as soon as I decently could. My heart pounded; perhaps climbing upstairs had been less wise than I'd thought.

Laura spoke first. "It's good to see you, Mr. Seafort, but we'd hoped to meet with Admiral De Marnay."

"He's aloft."

"So we heard." Hopewell was blunt. "Why is that, Captain Seafort?"

I was astounded. Civilians questioning Naval dispositions? I ducked the issue. "Perhaps I can help you. I'm still Naval liaison to the planters."

"So you're in charge?"

"The Admiral ordered me to run Admiralty House for the time being." I clasped my hands on the table, waiting.

Hopewell said only, "What's afoot, Captain?"

My mind spun. "Why, not a thing. Admiral De Marnay can't spend all his time—"

Hopewell's tone was icy. "I'd prefer," he said, "that you tell me the truth, or nothing."

I was silent a long moment. "I think you'd better explain your visit." De Marnay should have stayed groundside to handle this. I'd warned him I had no knack for public relations.

Hopewell's look was definitely unfriendly. "We may be provincials, Mr. Seafort, but we're not stupid. We notice things."

"Such as?"

"More and more of your personnel are being sent aloft."

"Since the bombing, housing has been a problem."

"No, it began a week before they hurled the rock at us."

"Normal crew rotation."

"You're fencing, Mr. Seafort. I thought better of you. How many Captains are groundside at the moment?"

"Just—that's classified information. I shouldn't—"

"The fish are your enemy. We aren't!" He was relentless.

"Nevertheless, I can't—"

"Are you the only one left?"

I shook my head; how did I get into this mess? "I can't discuss that, Mr. Hopewell."

Laura said, "Do your orders forbid it?"

I hesitated. "Not specifically."

"Then level with us."

I took a deep breath. If I was wrong, then so be it. "I'm the only one."

Hopewell sagged, as if defeated. "You were right, Laura."

This had gone on long enough. "About what?"

The two exchanged glances. It was Ms. Triforth who answered. "About ten days ago you began stripping men from Centraltown. We noticed it first in the restaurants and bars. Some of us have a financial stake downtown, you know. Fewer seamen seemed to be on leave. Then even the officers began to disappear."

Admiral De Marnay should have known better than to try to hoodwink these planters. They ran everything. It was their town, their colony.

"Odd, that this occurred just after a fastship arrived from home." Laura caught my look of surprise. "Oh, yes, we heard about her as well. *Victoria,* I believe. Anyway, we began keeping tabs on your personnel even before the explosion. The bomb threw us off for a while, because we were all busy offering help, but I'd say right now there aren't more than fifteen officers in all of Centraltown, including midshipmen." Close. Twelve. "And a handful of sailors, helping with cleanup operations."

I said, "Go on, Ms. Triforth."

"You've stopped delivering supplies to the Venturas Base. For that matter, you've stopped bringing cargo down to Centraltown as well."

"That could—"

"Your Lieutenant Eiferts won't let us visit the Venturas, but food purchases for the base have virtually ceased. Either your men are living on rations, or you've been evacuating Western Continent too."

The Admiral's orders were clear. I could tell no one of our contingency plans. I temporized. "If this is true, what do you make of it?"

"Tell us what to make of it, Captain." Laura's voice was cool.

"You're worried," I said, hoping to appear reasonable. "What do *you* think is happening?" I held my breath, afraid of the response.

Ms. Triforth stirred. Zack Hopewell waved her silent. "You intend to abandon us," the old man said. The blunt charge lingered in the silence of the room.

I stared at the mahogany table. To follow orders I must deny everything, else our good relations with the planters would be destroyed. But my visitors would see through my denial, and I'd lose the trust I'd striven to build. Wasn't that as much a breach of my orders as revealing the truth?

In any event, I'd only confirm what they'd guessed, though Admiral De Marnay wouldn't see it that way. He'd more likely view it as grounds for court-martial.

A hesitant knock. Midshipman Bezrel drew himself to attention.

"Get out!" I snarled.

The middy fled.

I slammed my fist on the table. At length I looked up. Neither alternative would suffice; I had to find my own way.

"Mr. Hopewell, kindly shut the door." I waited. When he sat I said carefully, "What you have described could be coincidence." He stirred restlessly, but I overrode him. "If the Navy were planning a maneuver, there might be reasons I couldn't tell you. Orders to that effect."

Laura said, "That explains nothing."

With an effort I got to my feet. Thinking came easier when I paced. "I couldn't possibly confirm your suspicions." I tucked the canister under my arm. If I paced slowly, I could still speak. "But it would be interesting to imagine what Admiralty might arrange, given substantial losses in the Hope Nation fleet. Remember, even though the fish attacked here first, they could attack anywhere."

"Imaginings aren't what we're here to—"

"Shut up, Laura. Listen."

Ms. Triforth glowered at her companion.

"We sent thirty-eight capital ships to Hope Nation. That's a third of the entire U.N. fleet. The loss of that many ships, or a substantial number of them, would seriously impede the defense of home waters, should the fish invade there."

Laura said to Hopewell, "They're abandoning us."

"Listen."

I took several deep breaths, disregarding the pain they caused. What I was about to say could hang me. "If Hope Nation weren't an important colony, so much of the fleet wouldn't have been risked to defend it. Consider Admiralty's predicament. If they leave the fleet here, it might be lost. If they bring it home, they might lose Hope Nation."

"We already knew that."

I regarded Laura Triforth with distaste. I was risking my commission, if not my life, to inform her, and the woman wouldn't shut up. "I'm not Admiralty, Ms. Triforth, but I imagine what they might do is try to hedge their bets."

Puzzled, she shook her head. "How do you mean?"

That was more what I wanted. Like an instructor at Academy, I drew her on. "The Hope Nation fleet has to be strong to be effective. Admiralty doesn't want to see it whittled down to nothing. Perhaps they might set a limit on losses. They might tell the Admiral Commanding that the fleet could operate as long as losses were acceptable, but when they became too great, the fleet was to return home."

Ms. Triforth demanded, "You've already lost nine ships that we know of. What is the decision point?"

I looked at her with surprise. "We're just speculating, Laura. It's all hypothetical."

With an effort she restrained her irritation. "Hypothetically, Captain, what would that point be?"

"One that might never be reached. Certainly, a substantial number of ships." I held up a hand to stop her objection. "But if it were approached, it would mean the fleet was under heavy attack. Obviously there would be no time to begin ferrying men up to Orbit Station. So Admiralty might, hypothetically, order a precautionary evacuation ahead of time."

This time the silence continued for a full minute. Finally, Zack Hopewell asked, "How long would these contingency plans remain in effect?"

I shrugged, suddenly weary, and made for my chair. "I don't know. Perhaps until the battle was won." I sat.

"Or lost."

"Yes."

Zack Hopewell cleared his throat, waited until I raised my eyes to his. He said simply, "Thank you."

For some reason when I spoke my voice was gruff. "If these plans were known—"

"They won't be."

"If Admiral De Marnay learns of this conversation, my career is finished. Naturally, if he asks, I'll tell him. But he may not ask."

Hopewell said, "I don't see how our knowing would lead us to do anything we wouldn't otherwise. Do you agree, Laura?"

"What is there to do?" Laura Triforth folded her arms. "You'll be back, eventually. You'll have to. We supply too much food for you to abandon us. When you return, we'll sell to you on our terms, not yours."

"That's not my bailiwick."

Ms. Triforth shrugged. "Actually, sending the fleet home may be in our best interest. The fish seem to be space dwellers; they've shown little interest in our planet. Once you leave we can reorganize the government—"

My tone was sharp. "That's treason. I won't hear any such conversation. Hope Nation is a U.N. colony until the Government decides otherwise."

Zack Hopewell cleared his throat. "Laura, it's uncivil to aggravate the Captain with our political debates. He's risked a great deal for us."

"Very well." She stood. "We've taken enough of your time, Mr. Seafort. You have our assurance that what we've spoken of will go no further." We shook hands.

Hopewell asked, "How is your pneumonia?"

I gestured at the vapormask. "Not good, as you can see. But it will pass." I myself might pass.

"You're under treatment?"

"I went to the clinic yesterday. The doctor wants me to return every day or so."

Ms. Triforth paused at the door. "The clinic is a long way. Do you go by heli?"

"The Naval helis have been busy downtown. Today, we drove."

"Mine is at your disposal. I'll call here every day. Have your man tell me what time to pick you up."

"I couldn't—"

"No, I insist. You've been a true friend to all of us, Mr. Seafort, as I'm just beginning to realize."

I came out of my chair. "Thank you. Pray that Admiralty's fears never come to pass. We'll work out our problems together."

On that note they took their leave.

I sat gathering my strength before I rang for Alexi. A few minutes later, leaning on his shoulder, I passed through the anteroom, on my way to our electricar. I halted by the desk. "What are you sniveling at, Middy?"

Midshipman Bezrel wiped his tears with his sleeve. "Sorry, sir."

"Answer my question!"

His face puckered. "I can't get anything right for you. No matter how hard I try . . . I'm sorry. Please . . ." He lapsed into miserable silence.

"Why did you come to my door?"

"Mr. Trapp told me to ask if your guests wanted refreshments."

"Very well." My rebuke wasn't worth bawling over. What were middies coming to? I tried to imagine myself wailing over a reprimand from a Captain, but even as a first-year cadet, it would have been unthinkable. I sighed. "Carry on."

Settled in the car at last, I leaned back while Tolliver headed toward downtown and the ruins of the Cathedral. It was fitting that Annie and I reunite there, I decided. In that place I'd promised to love and honor Annie Wells, until death did us part. I'd been hurt by her infidelity, more wounded than I'd been able to say, but it was past, and Eddie was gone. Transpop ways were not our ways, and Annie was of the transient culture, not mine. I would heal our marriage. I'd do whatever I must.

A street was blocked, and Tolliver braked sharply. "Careful," I muttered, breathing deeply from the vapormask. The interview with the planters had left me uneasy; their knowledge of our operations was much greater than I'd realized. If Hopewell and Ms. Triforth knew all we were doing, then so did Mantiet and his cohorts. I would have to be especially careful. Outside the car, ruined houses glided by.

We were crossing the park when the speaker crackled. "Trapp reporting, sir. A tightbeam from Naval HQ on Orbit Station. U.N.S. *Wellington* engaged a fish."

My fingers tightened on the caller. "When?"

"A few minutes ago, apparently. The fish fused alongside. *Wellington*'s crew was already at Battle Stations. They skewered it with a midships laser."

"Good." A thought struck. "She was already at Battle Stations?"

"Yes, sir. Captain Steers hasn't stood down since the attack on Centraltown."

"Good Lord." His crew must be at the ragged edge of exhaustion, snatching minutes of sleep at their posts. No ship could maintain Battle Stations for long. Still, he'd saved his ship; they'd been ready when the fish appeared. "Any more sightings?"

"Just the one, so far. I thought you'd want to know."

"Quite right." I rang off.

"We're almost there, sir." Alexi pointed to the broken spire ahead.

Only one lane of the broad avenue that had fronted the Reunification Cathedral had been cleared of rubble. Tolliver maneuvered us to within a dozen yards of the shattered entrance. I looked to both sides of the street; Annie was nowhere in sight. I checked my watch: eleven-thirty. We were early yet.

I opened my door. "You two wait here." I wouldn't have their solicitous interference. Not at our reunion.

"Sure you can make it?"

I turned to Tolliver with an angry rejoinder, but his question had been civil and without truculence. "Yes." I wished I could leave the vapormask behind, but reluctantly bundled the canister under my arm as I heaved myself out of the car.

I scrambled over rubble to the sidewalk. The blast had collapsed the ruins of the Cathedral's twin spires onto its domed roof, which had fallen into the building. Checking my watch every few moments, I stood against the stone outer wall.

A few yards away Alexi and Edgar Tolliver waited patiently in the car. Could I do anything to alter Tolliver's behavior? Doubtful. Though Naval discipline was virtually ingrained in us, his demotion was more than a vicissitude of Naval life to be borne with equanimity.

I picked at a small chunk of concrete, regretting that I'd treated him so severely. But what could I have done, after he'd hurled me out of my seat? I paced the sidewalk, wishing Annie would hurry, peering at the ruins.

The iron-strapped door hung askew on one hinge. Beyond, smashed blocks from the dome littered the nave amid crushed and splintered pews. The wreckage gleamed in the bright morning sunlight. We'd been married in the north transept. I was disoriented, but knew it would be to my left. I pushed through the shattered door.

Though rubble blocked my view of the altar, I suppressed an urge to genuflect. I wandered toward the transept, wondering how close I could get to it, aware that I was in no condition to clamber over debris.

Roof beams blocked the aisle, but in falling, one beam had swept other rubble clear of the nave, and I was able to make my way across the shattered stone floor. So much effort, so much faith, so much veneration had been poured into this edifice. When the fish were conquered, we would have to rebuild; Lord God had been well served here. Perhaps I could volunteer to help with the rebuilding.

No, I'd be long recalled to Terra by the time resources were marshaled to rebuild the Cathedral, and in any event my help would be a desecration. I'd damned myself, and

Lord God would want no contribution from me to His Church.

Rubble from caved-in walls filled the transept. I turned back, but detoured toward the altar. Blasted or not, this was a holy place, and I wanted to make obeisance. I picked my way across the debris, canister clutched in my hand.

"You shouldn'a come."

I whirled. Annie crouched on a great block of stone that had fallen from some high place.

"I wan'd ta look all pretty." Her tone was plaintive. She picked at the remnants of her dress. "Mira, it tore now."

I scrambled across the rubble, tearing off my vapormask. "Annie." A board twisted under my foot. I fell, the air knocked out of me by the impact.

"I wen' back ta apartmen' an' did my face, the way Amanda useta. Not a lot of paintin', jus' lil bit." Her hands twisted like frantic birds at her ragged dress. "I put on my necklace, Nicky. I kept it safe alla time, 'cause I knew you'd wanna see me innit."

I staggered to my feet, unable to breathe, not caring. "Annie, what did they do to you?"

She fingered her throat. "Rubies gone." Her lipstick was smeared with dirt and grime.

Dust motes floated in the bright glare of afternoon. I lurched across the litter of the nave. "Annie!"

"Mira my dress!" Her eyes teared. "Was nice threads, Nicky." A great red bruise blotched half her face, as if she'd been clubbed. "I tried ta tell 'em; how c'n I get 'notha dress now, alla stores broke?"

I cradled her head on my shoulder, but she pulled free.

"Tried so hard ta look pretty fo' you." A whimper.

I coaxed her toward the door. My foot caught. I glanced down. A hand. An arm. The remains of a man, his head smashed by a rock. A pool of blood soaked the surrounding rubble. Lord God.

My breath caught until the jagged walls began to swim in red mist. I clawed at my vapormask, got it over my face.

"You be hurt, Nicky!" She raised a begrimed hand, traced the outline of my mask.

"It's no matter." I tried to lift her, wanting not to see the angry scrapes on her legs. "Come, Annie. I'll take you to the clinic."

"Don' wanna." She uncrossed her legs, smoothed the ragged dress with an attempt at modesty.

"You have to see a doctor." I tugged at her, but she wouldn't move.

"I be all righ'." She tittered. "Buncha big men. Whatcha doin' here, girl? Who be witcha?" Her hands brushed at the lacerated dress. "Don' run now, joeygal." Her voice dropped. "Come here, girl, we have zarky time." Her voice rose again. "Scratchin'. Beard scratch my face!"

I had to stop her, before she shattered the remnants of my soul. "Please! Come with me."

"Don' yank onna necklace, please, mista. I goin' witcha. No, leave me Nicky's jewels!" She rubbed the red welt on her throat. "Aw, don'!"

"Annie." I drew my breath. "I can't walk to the car. Help me!" I pulled at her arm, and her vacant stare fixed on me. Comprehension came slowly. "You got a mask, Nicky. Means ya be sick. I din' take care of you." She slid off the block. "Come lean on Annie. Three joeys ran away, afta. Safe now."

"Help me. Please." Wanting to support her, afraid to try, I pretended to lean on her as we hobbled to the door. She limped, one shoe gone. Lord God damn them eternally. Please, Lord. Nothing for myself. Just damn them for her.

We tottered to the street. In the car, Alexi and Tolliver were deep in conversation. I couldn't summon breath to shout. Annie blinked in the shadowless light, hands flitting over the tatters of her dress.

"Just a few steps, hon." She held back. Cursing, I staggered across the rubble to the curb, and pounded on the window. "Open the door! Get out!" My hands clawed at the latch.

Alexi, startled, stared at me, then, with horror, past me. He jumped from the car, put a protective arm around Annie.

She screamed.

Dr. Abood snapped off the ultrasound. "Your pneumonia is down, and you're fighting the rejection."

"Never mind me. What about Annie?"

"You're in worse shape than she." He met my glare, relenting. "We've sedated her, Captain. Cuts and bruises, but no serious injuries."

"But she's been . . ."

"Raped, yes. Repeatedly. She'll be quite tender for a time."

I clutched my canister, as if for comfort. "Her mind . . ."

"She's in shock. Warmth, fluids, rest. That's all we can do at this stage."

"God knows what she stumbled into. I found her standing over a corpse."

"She's lucky they didn't murder her too."

"I'll kill them when I find them." My voice was hoarse.

"Of course. Anyone would." His gentle hand pushed me back down on the gurney. "But you're in no shape to go looking."

I recoiled from his touch. After a time I said, "You heard her. Will she be able to identify them?"

"Perhaps. The mind defends itself against the unbearable, Captain. She may block it out."

It was my fault. I'd known she needed looking after, yet I'd sent Eddie Boss away and hadn't replaced him. It would have taken more than three assailants to subdue Eddie, had they attacked Annie.

My fists tightened on the mattress. "Leave me alone. Please." After he'd gone I lay gripping the bed, fighting for self-control, nearly gaining it, in the end, losing.

Annie . . .

What have they done to you?

PART 3

March, in the year of our Lord 2200

14

Days passed, one upon another. My pneumonia cleared to the point where I could dispense with the vapormask for hours at a time, until even Dr. Abood expressed cautious optimism that I might retain my damaged lung. I no longer objected to visiting the clinic daily; Annie was there, and I'd have spent all my time with her if I could.

The few Admiralty House staff tiptoed about their duties, anxious to avoid my wrath. At times my manner reduced the unfortunate Bezrel to helpless tears, which infuriated me to the point I nearly sent him for another caning. I barked at the lieutenants who came to report, criticized Tolliver's manner, drove even Alexi into pale and subdued silence.

At the clinic Annie lay passive, legs drawn up, sheet clutched under her chin, allowing me to hold her hand. Sometimes I found her face streaked with tears. She seldom spoke, and never of the Cathedral.

The first time Admiral De Marnay called, I was with her. After, I screamed at Lieutenant Anton until my throat was raw for his failure to forward the call, though the Admiral had told him not to bother.

The Admiral's second call, two days later, found me dozing in my conference room. I snapped awake, took the caller, waved Bezrel out.

"You're recovering, Seafort?"

"Yes, sir." From the pneumonia, at any rate.

"Things seem to be quieting. I suppose I could send someone down to take over."

If he did, I could spend my days with Annie. "As you wish, sir."

"Still, *Hibernia* had a possible contact last night."

"Possible, sir?"

"At the edge of her sensor range. She investigated, but found nothing."

"I see." Why was he telling me?

"Perhaps I should send my staff groundside. We can't maintain this mode indefinitely. Sooner or later, your people will notice something odd."

"Yes, sir." I held my breath.

"Have you had any questions?"

"From a couple of the planters, sir."

He sounded preoccupied. "Eventually they'll stop believing your explanations. I'll give it another week or so. If we don't encounter more fish by then, I'll transfer my command to Admiralty House. In the meantime we'll keep the shuttles inactive. The fish probably hear us Fuse, but we don't know what else they hear."

"Yes, sir." What else was there to say?

"Well, no point relieving you, if it's only another week. Carry on."

"Aye, aye, sir."

"How's young Bezrel?"

"Uh, fine, sir." It was stretching a point.

"Take care of him. I took him as a special favor to his father. We were shipmates for years."

"Aye aye, sir."

"Send him up on the first shuttle. I wouldn't have let him go, but he could be trusted not to reveal the codes."

"Aye aye, sir." For my cruelty to the boy, a day of reckoning loomed.

"Very well." We signed off.

Dr. Abood clasped his arms behind his neck, stretched his back. "Nothing's fit here. The tables are too low." I bit back an impatient reply. "The truth is, Seafort, we can't do much more for her. She needs counseling, love, time to heal. She'd do as well at home as here. Perhaps better."

"I'll find a place for us."

"Your home was destroyed?" I nodded. "There's a housing directory, at temporary City Hall. Perhaps they can help."

"Thank you." I gestured at the vapormask. "Can I leave it off?"

"Certainly not. Wear it when you sleep, and as often as you can while you're awake. You might make it."

I said sourly, "Thanks for the encouragement."

"I warned you a week ago: the lung should come out. When you get back home they can pop in a new one."

"I'll decide in a week or so."

"Why, what happens then?"

I tensed. "I didn't say anything would happen. I'll decide when I'm ready."

He stood to go. "Stay near a heli, Captain."

Easier said than done. I'd imagined that when the rescue efforts eased, our Naval helis would be more available, but they were pressed into service as makeshift public transportation. In the meantime Tolliver found a passable ground route through the ruins to the clinic.

When we left Dr. Abood I had Tolliver drive me to the housing office, where I put my name on the list for accommodations. They promised to call.

"Back to Admiralty House." I climbed into the car.

Tolliver shut my door. "Aye aye, sir."

The temporary City Hall, on the far edge of town, was in a building shielded from the worst of the blast by a high hill. But to reach Admiralty House we would have to skirt the ruined area. I sighed, wishing I had access to a heli. Well, I *did* have access to Laura Triforth's, if I chose to accept her offer. I found her manner intriguing; in discussing colonial affairs she was flinty, even acid. But in personal matters, such as Alexi's health or mine, an obvious warmth gleamed through her prickly veneer.

I settled back in my seat for the ride. Few other vehicles were on the road, but blockages made driving difficult, and I was never at ease in an electricar. Tolliver, sensing my impatience, came up behind a slow-moving vehicle, waited for an opportunity to pass. It made me nervous; I sat forward, hanging on to my hand strap.

Seeing his chance Tolliver swerved around the offending car. As he wrenched the wheel I glanced aside. The other driver stared back, then turned his head sharply. Something about him bothered me. I puzzled for a moment, then cursed and pounded Tolliver's shoulder. "Stop!"

He jammed on the brake. "What's wrong, sir?"

The other car had turned onto a cross street. "That was Mantiet! I'm sure of it!"

"Mantiet? The planter?" He gaped.

"Don't sit there, follow him!" As he swung around I stamped the floorboard in frustration.

We squealed around the corner. The car was two blocks ahead and accelerating. Tolliver gunned the engine.

"Can we catch him?"

His eyes were riveted on the road. "I'll try, sir." After a moment, he cleared his throat and said, "Can you reach the caller?"

"The caller? Of course I—damn!" I keyed Naval frequency. "Admiralty House, Seafort here!" An eternal moment later the speaker crackled. "Midshipman Wilson here, sir."

"Get Anton, flank!"

"Aye aye, sir." The line went dead.

Mantiet's car swerved around a corner. "Don't lose him!"

"I won't." His tone was calm.

"Anton, sir." The man sounded out of breath.

"We're chasing Mantiet!"

"Chasing?"

"In our car!" I shouted. "He's a couple of blocks ahead. Call in all Navy helis, flank! Get any other support the authorities can give us. We're—where the hell are we, Tolliver?"

"North on Churchill Street."

"—moving north on Churchill, about a mile past whatsis, the road the new town hall is on."

"Aye aye, sir. Understood. What do you want the helis to do?"

I was beside myself. "Stop him! Catch him!"

"Aye aye, sir. Hang on." The line went dead.

I cursed into the mute caller while we careened through debris-filled streets. "Stay left! Don't lose him!"

Tolliver seemed to be enjoying himself. "Would you care to drive, sir?"

"Are you joking?"

"You're in the back seat, sir."

"What of it?"

"Oh, nothing."

What on earth was he babbling about? In a few moments my irritation eased as I saw he was keeping pace with the fleeing vehicle.

The speaker came to life. "Anton reporting, sir. Two helis are on their way. Where are you now?"

I thrust the caller at Tolliver. "Tell him." Tolliver gave our location, thrust the caller down as he spun us around a corner. "Look out—"

"Damn!" We skidded into an overturned truck. A crunch. I was hurled against the front seat. Tolliver spun the wheel, jammed down the pedal, slamming me back into my seat. "Sorry, sir." He loosened his tie.

The lunatic was humming.

A moment later he broke off, pointed. "There! Look!"

I craned my neck. A heli swooped over Mantiet's vehicle. Please, Lord, let me get my hands on him. Please.

"How will they stop him?" As soon as I asked, my question seemed foolish.

"All helis go armed now, sir. Not like the one we flew."

I snatched the caller. "Anton, patch me through to the helis."

"Aye aye, sir. Just a . . . go ahead."

"This is Captain Seafort."

"Lieutenant Hass reporting, sir. I'm over his car."

An excited young voice. "Midshipman Kell, sir. I'm right behind. I've got him in my sights."

"Listen, both of you! I want him captured, not dead." Mantiet couldn't have stolen the missile and hidden for all these subsequent weeks on his own. He'd have had confederates. "If you can flatten his tires, do so. If you kill him, I'll have your—" I lapsed silent.

"Stripes?" Tolliver offered. "Balls?"

"Shut up and drive."

"Aye aye, sir." He hummed under his breath.

"I'll angle back for a disabling shot." Lieutenant Hass.

"Please, sir, let me! I've got the angle. I can do it; I was first in gunnery last year."

"You sure, boy?" Hass sounded anxious.

"I won't shoot 'til I'm positive. Honest!"

"Go for it, Middy."

Tolliver eased the accelerator. We fell back. The second heli swooped away from the car in a wide arc.

I cursed. "What's that idiot doing?"

"Lining up a midships shot." Tolliver pointed. "If he comes in low from the side he can target both wheels with the tracer. Then all he has to—"

"Show-off," I growled. He opened his mouth to protest but thought better of it.

I didn't hear shots, but I could see tracers arc across the road. Mantiet's car lurched, spun out of control. It jumped the curb and slammed into the porch of a wood-frame house. In the heli, the excited middy crowed into his mike. Deafened, I spun down the caller volume.

I beat on Tolliver's shoulder. "Hurry, before he runs!"

We skidded to a halt in front of the damaged house. Mantiet's car door swung open. He dashed with surprising speed down the road.

"Get him!" Tolliver bolted from the car in pursuit. I hauled myself out, furious that I couldn't join the chase, but the outcome was never in doubt. Tolliver had always been a fine runner, as he'd shown in catching Jerence. He overtook Mantiet at the corner and whirled him around. His fist flew. Mantiet stumbled.

I let go of the car and walked down the street, trying to make my legs steady. Mantiet sprang to his feet. It seemed to enrage Tolliver, who flailed wildly at the man's stomach and face. When I finally reached them Tolliver was holding Mantiet against a tree, pounding him with his free hand.

"Enough."

"Remember Mr. Tamarov?" Tolliver's face was hard, bitter. "And our heli?"

I hesitated. Tolliver drove his fist into Mantiet's ribs, knocking him to the ground. I caught his hand. "That's enough!"

He subsided, fuming. A heli settled into the road, blades spinning lazily.

A blond middy jumped out, loped toward us. "Midshipman Harvey Kell reporting, sir!" He came to attention, his stance marred by an ecstatic grin. "I knew I'd get the grode!"

"Stand easy, Mr. Kell." But I owed him something more. "Well done, Midshipman."

The boy gawked at Mantiet, semiconscious in the dirt. "This is the one, sir? Who shot you down?"

"Yes." I felt a savage triumph. "Tolliver, you and Kell take him by heli to Admiralty House. I'll drive our car."

"You, sir? But—"

"The response to an order is?"

"Aye aye, sir! Sorry." Tolliver snapped a salute, hauled Mantiet to his feet. Kell hurried to help. Between them they bundled the planter into the heli. A moment later they were aloft.

"Where is he?" I flung open the door to the anteroom.

Lieutenant Anton came to his feet. "In the dayroom, sir. I, uh, didn't know where else to put him."

"Can he get out?"

"He's under guard, sir. Midshipman Tolliver seemed quite eager for the duty."

Alexi came out of the conference room. "Are you all right, Mr. Seafort?"

"Me? Of course." I put on my vapormask.

"Have you anything for me today?"

"Don't bother me now, Mr. Tamarov." His face fell. "On second thought, come with me."

He followed as I strode down the corridor. "Where are we going?"

"To the man who stole your memory." I opened the door.

Frederick Mantiet slumped in a straight chair in the center of the windowless room. Tolliver stood in front of him, fists bunched. Mantiet's face was puffy.

Through the vapormask my voice was a rasp. "What have you been up to?"

"Guarding the prisoner." Tolliver was savage. "Waiting for him to twitch."

"Leave us, Mr. Tolliver."

"But—aye aye, sir." He left with unconcealed reluctance.

Mantiet's tone was sardonic. "A pleasure to see you, Captain. Last time, we were both in better health."

I shrugged. "It was your choice to run."

"Oh, is that why he worked me over? I've been wondering."

The man's cool demeanor enraged me. "You'll feel worse after interrogation, I'm sure." Drugs and poly often left a subject nauseous, and with a splitting headache.

Despite his bruises, Mantiet managed to raise an eyebrow. "Interrogation? Whatever for?"

"Attempted murder, treason. Destruction of Naval property." And of Alexi's soul, you bastard. "I'll look forward to the details of your confession. And afterward, to your hanging." I smiled, savoring my revenge. "You can't escape interrogation, Mantiet. There's more than enough evidence to send you to poly."

"What a pity to disappoint you, then. I confess."

I blurted, "You what?"

"I confess, to all of it. The missile, the explosives in the hauler, everything."

"You'll be hanged, you know."

"I assumed as much the moment you spotted me."

I sagged into a chair. Why did I feel cheated? I wanted him to undergo the polygraph and drugs, to experience the maddening inevitability of confession. At my own interrogation, I'd made no effort to conceal anything from Admiralty, but I recalled the irresistible compulsion to tell my questioners whatever they asked.

But if Mantiet confessed, he couldn't be interrogated. The drugs and poly were means to determine the truth, not instruments of torture.

I said reluctantly, "Alexi, call Lieutenant Trapp."

A moment later the lieutenant appeared in the doorway. "Mr. Trapp, interrogate Mantiet. I want a full confession about the hauler, the missile fired on our heli, and whatever conspiracy he engaged in. Names of his associates, dates, details. If he fails to cooperate, break off immediately and inform me."

"Aye aye, sir."

"Get on with it." I stalked off to my conference room, Alexi trailing behind. I sat at the table, breathed a sigh of relief. "It's over, Alexi."

"Is it?" His voice was bleak.

I flushed with shame. "Not for you. I'm sorry. But we've got him at last."

"He'll be executed."

"Yes." Without a doubt.

"I suppose that's good." He paused, looked at his hands. "Mr. Seafort, I follow you around, hold doors, help you into your car. Is that all I'm fit for?"

I thought of telling the truth, then relented. "No, of course not." I hesitated. "There's not much to do, actually, with all our personnel aloft."

"Isn't there anything?" He searched my face in appeal. "I feel useless, waiting for memories that are gone forever."

Alexi's problems were the last thing on my mind; my adrenaline still coursed from the chase. I searched for a way to appease him. "Would you like to help with the relief work?" He wouldn't need to remember his duties for that.

"Could I?" Then his face clouded. "I don't really know my way around Centraltown."

"You could learn. And you know how to drive; you offered several times."

"Did I?" A smile lit his face. "Yes, how could anyone forget how to drive?" He jumped up, nearly knocking over my coffee. "When could I start? Today?"

Why did I feel abandoned? I forced down the ungenerous impulse. "I'll have Mr. Anton call the relief agencies." I took the caller, spoke as if joking. "You'll visit me sometimes, still?"

He grinned. "Every day, Mr. Seafort."

Later that evening, beside himself with excitement, Alexi left Admiralty House for the transport center, where he was to work as a volunteer. Normally his status would have been a problem; Alexi's injuries put him on the Navy inactive list, but he couldn't work as a civilian employee while in the Service. In the emergency, such niceties were ignored.

* * *

Later that evening I sat in my conference room reading Frederick Mantiet's confession. Trapp had been thorough. He'd gone over every detail of the plot, starting with the hauler explosion on Plantation Road.

To my surprise, Mantiet hadn't objected to naming his co-conspirators. That was odd. Was he lying? I slammed down the transcript. Of course he was lying; why betray his countrymen? True, a man who could contemplate treason would do anything.

Staring at the polished genera table, I recalled my clash with Judge Chesley over my enlistment of Paula Treadwell years before. In my hubris, I had threatened to put the colony under martial law and suspend civil administration. I wished I could do so now; I ached to put a rope around Mantiet's neck for what he had done to Alexi. Unfortunately, all I could do was turn him over to the civilian authorities who would conduct the trial.

But I hadn't relinquished him yet. I stalked down the corridor. Lieutenant Kell saluted as I approached the dayroom. "Any trouble?"

"No, sir, he's been quiet. Mr. Anton ordered him fed an hour ago."

I grunted, begrudging him even that decency.

Mantiet looked up. Bruises were darkening where Tolliver had beaten him. He pushed aside the remains of his tray. A cool smile played across his features. "What can I do for you, Captain?"

"I'm sending you for drug and poly interrogation."

"Why?"

I tossed the transcript onto his tray. "This is garbage. For all I know you made it up."

He frowned. "Why would I?"

"To protect your fellow traitors. Why would you expose them?"

"You think I've accused innocent men?" His voice held a note of reproach.

"Who knows what you've done? That's why I'm sending you to P and D."

"You can't."

I raised an eyebrow. "You propose to stop me?"

"Yes."

Despite myself I tensed visibly, then reddened. The man wasn't about to launch himself at my throat, and if he did, help was just outside the door. "How?"

"Are we under martial law?"

"No. Governor Saskrit's administration is still running Centraltown. And all of Hope Nation."

"Then you're bound to follow the law, unless you're as evil as I am." He smiled politely. I had an urge to strangle him.

"Make your point, Mantiet."

"I just did. Under the law you can't send me for interrogation."

"Why not? Your confession is incomplete."

"I've confessed to every charge you've made. Make others and I'll confess to them as well."

"We need to verify the truth about your conspiracy."

"Ah, but that's not permitted. P and D interrogation may only be used to determine my guilt. Not to force me to betray others. It's a well-settled point of law—even our provincial courts have heard of it."

"I don't know that to be true."

"But you're duty-bound to check, now that I've informed you."

I growled, "If we were aboard ship—"

"That's the point, Captain. We are not."

I slammed the door behind me. Moments later I paced the anteroom in mounting fury while Lieutenant Anton waited for a connection.

"I've got Judge Ches—"

I snatched up the caller. "Judge? Captain Seafort, here."

"This is Judge Chesley."

"I'm sorry to bother you, sir. I need an immediate answer to a legal question."

He chuckled. "Well, I owe you a favor, Seafort. Explain."

What he owed me was hardly a favor; I'd humiliated him in his own courtroom. Still, much had passed in the interim. I explained the situation.

He was silent a long while. Then, "There was a time it

would have given me great satisfaction to tell you that Mantiet's right. His confession bars his interrogation."

I said desperately, "But if I don't believe his confession is true—"

"Do you doubt his guilt?"

I thought a moment. "No," I conceded.

"Neither would I, or any impartial judge. So we're forced to accept his confession as valid." As if sensing the frustration in my silence he added, "It makes the Truth in Testimony Act humane, Seafort. Otherwise it could be used to make people turn on their friends, even their family. The exception was written into the law from the start."

"I see."

"At least you'll have the satisfaction of seeing him hang."

"Yes."

"Well, if that's all . . . by the way, Seafort, that young lady. The cadet. Whatever happened to her?"

"She was posted to Academy for advanced math."

"Out of harm's way, then. Just as well."

"Sir, I'm sorry." He said nothing. I rushed on, "For what happened back then. I was young and foolish. I wouldn't do the same, now."

Another long silence, then a sigh. "It's long past, Seafort. All the people, the destruction . . . even my sister and her husband, Reeves. You must have known them, they came out on your ship. They were killed in the explosion."

"Oh, Lord God."

"Your courtroom hijinks . . . they don't seem to matter anymore."

"I understand. Good night, sir." I rang off.

15

I issued orders to have Mantiet transferred to the civilian jail the following day, and to have the authorities pick up the men Mantiet had named.

That night the fish attacked.

They took out *Prince of Wales*. Captain Martes of *Victoria* had transferred to her. I wondered if he'd taken Ricky Fuentes along.

I spent the morning huddled in the tactics room with Tolliver, Bezrel, and every other officer who could find an excuse to join us. The fish appeared by twos and threes, Defusing near our ships, lobbing their acid from close range, abruptly disappearing. The speakers crackled with commands as our fleet deployed. Again, we succeeded in knocking out fish. Again, we had no idea how many constituted the aliens' armada.

Lieutenant Anton kept us supplied with sandwiches and coffee. Conversation was sparse, our mood tense. All of us had served aloft, and knew the perils our men faced.

Around noon Anton stirred. "Mr. Trapp, Mr. Tolliver, take Mantiet downtown to the civilian jail."

"Not now," I said.

He looked at me in surprise.

"Keep everyone here."

"Yes, but—aye aye, sir."

By day's end two more ships were disabled, though not destroyed. By positioning the fleet closer to Hope Nation, Admiral De Marney allowed our ships to come to each other's assistance more quickly, and this tactic seemed to help.

I spent a sleepless night on my conference-room cot. In the morning Alexi wanted to go to work at the transport center; when I forbade it he was so crestfallen that I relented. "Stay in touch, Mr. Tamarov. Call in every three hours."

"Whatever you say, Mr. Seafort. Are they still attacking?"

"Four fish sighted during the night. We killed one."

"Great!"

I grunted. Not for *Prince of Wales*.

The day passed uneventfully. That evening I realized I was keeping Frederick Mantiet in our makeshift jail for no purpose. I'd have him transferred in the morning, as I'd originally intended. Perhaps I could make time to visit Annie.

During the night we lost two ships. Captain Derghinski had brought *Kitty Hawk* to *Brasilia*'s aid when a fresh flotilla of fish appeared alongside, and both vessels were breached. A number of men got off in lifepods. We listened to confused reports relayed through our speakers. As day lengthened, I paced the tactics room with increasing anxiety, wishing I hadn't let Alexi leave.

I was on my way to the head when Midshipman Bezrel rushed after me. "Lieutenant Anton's compliments, sir. You have a call."

"The Admiral?"

"No, sir. Ms. Triforth."

My heart pounding from the false alarm, I went to my conference room to take the call. "Seafort here."

"Laura Triforth. I'll be in Centraltown this afternoon. I thought perhaps we might have a talk."

"It's rather a busy time." I realized how ungracious it sounded and added hastily, "The fleet's seen more action."

"I know."

I paused. "Communications are restricted to a tightbeam relay. Just how did you hear?"

"I told you," she said. "This is our city. Not much goes on that we don't learn." As if sensing that didn't suffice, she added, "You've placed all your people on twenty-four-hour call; none of them goes near a restaurant or bar. Your Mr. Tamarov reports in every couple of hours."

I cursed under my breath. As a secret agent I was notably incompetent.

"Has Mantiet been sent for interrogation under drugs yet?"

"You knew we have him?"

"Half of Centraltown saw your sky chase, Mr. Seafort. It's hardly a secret."

The woman knew far too much. Best to stay away from her. No, better let her visit and learn what she wanted. "I'll see you this afternoon, Ms. Triforth."

She chuckled. "Why, thank you. I look forward to our meeting."

In the tactics room the speakers were quiet. Our remaining ships were huddled close, about thirty degrees past Orbit Station. I tried to see past the blips on the screen, to the men and metal beyond.

So few ships.

I sat and watched in the tense silence. After a time I could no longer stand the inaction. I went downstairs. "Mr. Anton." He looked up from his console. "Work up a report on all Naval personnel, including sailors. Assignments, work hours, current location."

"You mean where they're housed, sir?"

"I said current location. Where they are at this moment."

"But why—aye aye, sir." He took up the caller, his perplexity evident. I trudged back upstairs.

Today fewer of us held vigil, as a consequence of days of sporadic, desultory action. Lieutenant Trapp, Midshipman Kell and young Bezrel were the only ones present. The two middies fidgeted and whispered until I fixed them with a stare that allowed no misinterpretation. A few moments later Bezrel excused himself and left. Kell, on duty, had no choice but to remain.

I fought to keep myself from dozing. I was just failing when the speaker crackled. "*Hibernia* reporting. Two fish alongside, one abaft! They're throwing! Fusing!"

"*Churchill* reporting, three—no, five! They came out of nowhere, together! Lasers engaging! We've got one! Another Fusing out."

"All ships to Battle Stations!" Admiral De Marnay.

"*OH, JESUS!*"

I came to my feet at the fear in the unknown voice. It went on in a whisper. "A dozen of them! More. They're all around us. One is nuzzling our fusion tubes. Preparing to Fuse. Jordan, get me coordinates!"

"Fuse immediately, you fool!" My voice was tight, though I spoke only to myself.

"Our tubes are melting!" I could smell his fright. "We'll try a Fuse!"

"No!" Admiral De Marnay's tone was sharp. "*Churchill*, don't Fuse with—"

"Christ, we're overheating! Quick, shut it do—" The speaker went dead.

Trapp spun to meet my eye, as if in appeal.

"They're gone," I said.

He shook his head, denying.

"They blew themselves up."

Trapp swallowed. Midshipman Bezrel rushed in from the hall. "Ms. Triforth is here for her appointment, sir."

"Who? Tell her to come back—" I got to my feet. "No, I'll see her. Trapp, keep me informed of our losses."

"Aye aye, sir."

"Mr. Bezrel, escort Ms. Triforth to the conference room." Vapormask under my arm, I hurried down the stairs.

Laura took her place across from me at the gleaming table. "You're looking better than when last we met."

I waved the niceties aside. "This is a bad time, Ms. Triforth."

A knock at the door. Anton. "Excuse me, sir. That report you wanted."

"Keep it on your desk. Update it every two hours."

"Aye aye, sir." He made no move to leave.

"Well?"

"Could you tell me why you need it, sir?"

I made my voice icy. "Dismissed, Lieutenant Anton." He left. "What's on your mind, Ms. Triforth?"

"Do call me Laura; I hate it when you're so formal." She waited for a response, got none. "The, um, hypothetical circumstance we discussed. Is it any closer to reality?"

"I can't discuss that."

"I appreciate your position, Seafort. But if anything should leave us on our own, we have to be prepared."

I was firm. "I won't discuss that with you."

"Has the Venturas Base been attacked?"

I was startled. "Not that I know of. Why?"

She waved. "Just taking stock, as it were."

I ached to get back to the tactics room. "Ms.—er, Laura, what is it you want?"

"To know what's up. To help, if possible."

"You can't fight the aliens."

"I can help root out Mantiet's men. I can help you maintain control."

I raised an eyebrow. "Why would you want to do that?"

She smiled grimly. "I've made no secret of my feelings, Mr. Seafort. But you must understand: we want anarchy no more than you. We have hundreds of field workers roaming Centraltown. If authority breaks down . . ."

"The Government is in place and functioning. Looters have been shot."

"As well they should be!" She spat the words. A pause. "Captain, this is our home, our society. Let us help."

True, we were badly understaffed. I thumbed through my papers, found a list of supporters Mantiet had named. "Can you help us find these men?"

She studied the list. "Some of them, I think we—"

The caller chimed. I snatched at it. "Yes?"

"Trapp reporting, sir. You said to keep you informed. Fish swarming all over the patrol area! Two ships down, everyone's Fusing like—"

A knock on the door; it swung open. Bezrel saluted. "Lieutenant Anton said to give this to you forthwith, sir."

"Orbit Station beat off an attack too, sir. That's the first time they've attacked—"

I opened the note. Anton's handwriting. "Message from Admiral De Marnay, for immediate delivery to Captain Seafort. 1800 hours local time. *Destiny*."

I crumpled the note, half hearing Lieutenant Trapp's rush of words. "*Hibernia* Fused twice, sir, and they keep following. No sign of *Churchill*. The fleet is to regroup around Orbit Station. They—"

"Enough." It was 3:00 P.M. We'd have three hours.

Laura Triforth came to her feet, eyes locked on mine. "Seafort, you've gone white. What's happened?"

"Wait here." I strode out the corridor, closing the door. "Anton!"

He stood from his console. "Yes, sir?"

"Your list." He fumbled, handed it to me. After a glance I thrust it back. "How many of our helis are on loan to the transport grid?"

"Three, sir."

"Pull them out of service, flank. Emergency priority. Contact all officers and sailors, arrange assembly points. I want helis to pick up all Naval personnel and bring them to the spaceport in one hour. Everyone, without exception."

"An hour? That's not possi—"

I thrust my face at his. "Make it possible, God damn you!" He recoiled. "You have a list. Find them all. Stay on it. You have permission to stay at your console one additional hour. Then go to the terminal yourself."

"But—for God's sake, why?"

I snarled, "Because I gave the order!" Even now, it was best no one know the truth.

"Aye aye, sir!" He snatched up his caller.

"Where the hell is Tolliver?"

"Sleeping, sir."

"Get him up. I need him." I started toward the conference room, swung back. "Let me see that list." I scrutinized it. "Alexi Tamarov. He's not on it."

"He's not active, sir. I thought you meant—"

"Where is he?"

"The transport center would know."

"Get started. I'll find Alexi." I strode back to the conference room.

Laura Triforth stood as I entered. "What in blazes is going on, Seafort?"

If I told her, she might argue, and nothing must interfere with the evacuation. "Problems." I had to get rid of her, find Alexi. We had less than three hours—

Annie! Lord God, I'd forgotten. Shame sickened me. I'd take a heli—no, they were all in use. I had to drive downtown, get my wife, pick up Alexi—

I looked up to Laura. "You offered your heli. May I have it?"

"I—of course. I can take you myself, wherever you want to go."

"Just a moment." I picked up the caller, dialed Alexi. "Mr. Tamarov, report." I waited; no answer. I tried again. "Alexi Tamarov, respond to Admiralty House!" Silence.

Another knock at the door. Edgar Tolliver, bleary from lack of sleep.

"Stand by, Tolliver." Muttering under my breath I thumbed the caller again. "Patch me through to the transport center."

I pulled rank and got to the director in moments. "A volunteer, Alexi Tamarov. I need him at once."

"Tamarov . . . the Naval Officer? The young one? He's directing a road crew in the west sector. I don't know what street they'd be on at the moment, but they're somewhere between Churchill and Washington."

"Very well."

I rang off. "Laura, I have to pick up Annie at the clinic, and Lieutenant Tamarov is downtown. I could drive, but your help would . . ."

"Of course. When?"

"Right now."

Lieutenant Anton appeared in the doorway. "Regarding your orders, sir?"

I glanced at Laura Triforth. "Yes?" I was wary.

"What about Mr. Mantiet, sir?"

I cursed under my breath. Why hadn't I had him sent downtown when I'd had the chance? "Ms. Triforth and I will take him. Tolliver, I want you along. And Bezrel, as an extra hand." As soon as I said it I realized Kell would be a better choice, but decided not to contradict myself. Bezrel would do.

"We're taking Frederick?" Laura sounded tense.

"Yes, if you don't mind. After I pick up Annie we'll drop him off." What good would it do to turn him over to the civilians, if our fleet took Governor Saskrit home? Should I bring Mantiet along for military trial or simply hang him myself? No, I hadn't the right.

Laura asked, "Will you interrogate him?"

She'd asked too many questions about matters that were confidential. "Perhaps." My tone was cool.

She shrugged. "He deserves it. When do you want to go?"

"Right now. Tolliver, get Mantiet. Cuff his hands, but don't rough him up. Gag him too, Mr. Tolliver." If Mantiet spoke, Laura Triforth would learn what Mantiet knew.

"Wouldn't it be better to wait for a Naval heli, sir?"

"I'm in a hurry."

"Aye aye, sir." I picked up my vapormask, wondering how long Tolliver's docility would last.

I peered down the unfamiliar streets, while Annie pressed my hand. It had been only minutes since we'd swept into the clinic and bundled her out.

"Between Washington and Churchill, they said." Where the devil was Alexi? I'd told him to stand by, and . . .

"They'll have men and trucks; we'll spot them." Laura glided across town, barely above treetop level.

Yes, but when? I tried to restrain my impatience, glancing surreptitiously at my watch. We'd been searching the indicated area for several minutes. Repeated calls on the radio failed to raise Alexi.

Annie crooned to herself.

"There, to the west!" Tolliver, from the back seat. We swooped across a block of ruined houses. A crew of ten was hauling debris from the blocked street into a truck.

I muttered, "That's got to be them. Land, would you?"

"Anyone see wires?" Laura checked the landing spot. "Here we go."

A moment later I was beckoning from under the blades. "Alexi, get over here!" He was near the truck, gesturing at piles of crumpled roofing.

The whap of the blades was too loud; Alexi waved happily and turned back to the crew. Enraged, I ran to him, ignoring warning pangs in my chest. I grabbed his shoulder, spun him around. "Get yourself into the heli!"

"What—"

"Didn't I tell you to report regularly? Where's your caller?"

"In the truck, Mr. Sea—"

"Move!" I shoved him toward the heli. Crestfallen, he obeyed. I faced him at the heli door. "Even a cadet wouldn't pull a stunt like this, and you're supposed to be a lieutenant! Can't you obey a simple order?"

He blanched. "I'm sorry."

"If you were on active duty, I'd—" I caught myself, finally comprehending what his eyes revealed. "All right, get in."

"I got involved in the work . . ." He looked at the private heli. "What's up, Mr. Seafort?"

"In, I told you." He climbed into the back with Tolliver, Mantiet, and Bezrel. I should have explained outside, where Laura couldn't hear. Now, it would have to wait. "Special duty."

Laura throttled. Over the engine's roar she asked, "Where now, Mr. Seafort?"

I looked again at my watch. "We'll drop off Mantiet, then head back, if you don't mind."

"Not at all." She pulled back on the collective, lifting us straight up. This time she didn't skim the treetops; she brought us to a great height. I stared down at the stricken city. Would Centraltown ever recover?

Laura continued to throttle up. Casually, she reached for her oxygen mask and slipped it on. Tolliver leaned forward. "We don't need canned air this low, do we?"

I growled. "Tend to your prisoner, Middy."

"Not really." Laura idly flicked a switch on the dash. A dull hiss emitted from the air vents.

"Then why are you—what's going—" Tolliver slumped. My head spun. I grabbed for the vapormask in my lap. Laura Triforth's hand pinned my arm. "Wait a moment, Seafort. You won't need it."

She was right. In a moment I needed nothing.

16

The room was stuffy and dark. I groaned, trying to clear my head. I was lying on a cold, damp floor.

"He's awake." Alexi.

I blinked. Annie sat slackly, her eyes straight ahead. Her hand clasped Alexi's.

Tolliver's tone held a note of impatience. "About time." He perched on a wooden desk, legs dangling. It was the only furniture in the room.

"Where am I?"

"Wherever your friend Laura put us." Tolliver's voice was acid.

My anger gave me strength to scramble to my feet. I tottered to Tolliver, grabbed his jacket. "Tell me what's happened!"

"I passed out in the heli. I presume you did too. When I woke, we were here." He gestured to the sparse chamber. What little light we had came from a narrow, barred transom over the door. "I found Bezrel sniveling in the corner." He waved with contempt at the young middy, who, to my disgust, surreptitiously wiped his nose with his sleeve. "Alexi and Annie—Mrs. Seafort—woke a few minutes after. We've been waiting for you."

"Why are we here?"

"We hoped you'd tell us, sir."

"The door?"

"No knob on this side. I finally stopped bruising my shoulder on it."

I reached for my pistol, found an empty holster. "No one's come in?"

"No, sir."

"How long have we been here?"

Tolliver made a show of checking his watch. "It's going

on five-thirty now. I'd say about two hours. What would you say, Mr. Tamarov?"

"Damn your insolence!"

"Yes, sir. You'll remember I suggested we wait for a proper Naval heli. If we had . . ."

I snarled, "Enough!"

Alexi intervened. "Why would Ms. Triforth kidnap us? And where were we headed in the heli?"

Legs weak, I pushed myself onto the desk and sat. Why did Laura waylay us, to free Mantiet? No, she'd helped us search for him. To stop us from leaving? She didn't know I'd received the "Destiny" signal, and she would probably be glad to see the last of us, given her feelings about colonial rule.

I realized what Tolliver had said about the time. "Five-thirty? We've got to get out!" I jumped off the desk.

"Why, Mr. Seafort?" Alexi.

"Because—" I tensed. No way to know if the room was miked. "Never mind why." I banged on the door. "Laura! Ms. Triforth!"

No answer. In the corner Bezrel stifled a sob.

I shouted again and again, without result. Finally I sagged back onto the desk. But nervous energy pulsed, and I couldn't sit more than a moment. I paced, squatted on the floor, got up to pace again.

All too soon, it was past six. Was it my imagination or did I hear the distant roar of a shuttle?

I slumped to the floor. Whether I heard it or not, the shuttle was gone, and with it our chance of rescue. We were marooned, with nothing to do but await the final assault of the fish. I had no doubt it would come. By careening off in Laura Triforth's heli I had doomed not only myself, but Alexi, Tolliver, even poor bewildered Bezrel. And, worst of all, Annie. It was almost a blessing that she was barely aware of her surroundings.

I withdrew into my misery.

Hours later, footsteps sounded. I stood, fists clenched. A key scraped in the lock. The door swung open.

Three armed men. I charged forward, but stumbled to a

halt when a laser pistol swung toward me. "Where's Ms. Triforth?"

Ignoring me, the burly farmhand shoved a bound figure past his companion into the room, slammed the door. Hands lashed behind him, the man stumbled to his knees.

I gaped.

"I don't suppose you'd, ah, consider releasing me?" Frederick Mantiet motioned with his bound wrists. "They're starting to hurt."

"I hope they fall off!" Tolliver's tone was savage.

I'd been thinking the same, but instead I said perversely, "Untie him." Tolliver had tortured him enough; we weren't barbarians, though Ms. Triforth was that and worse.

"But—"

"You heard me!"

"Aye aye, sir." With a curse Tolliver yanked at the thongs holding Mantiet. The cuffs I'd had placed on him were gone. While picking at the knots Tolliver grated, "Has it occurred to the Captain that Mantiet is no more a prisoner than Ms. Triforth? That he's obviously a plant?"

"Yes." It hadn't.

"I'm not, you know." Mantiet.

"Right." My feet hurt; I went to slouch in the corner, decided to preserve my dignity and leaned on the table instead. "Why were we kidnapped?"

"You'll have to ask Laura."

"I'm asking you!"

"I could guess." Mantiet winced as Tolliver yanked at a resisting cord. "She probably didn't want me interrogated."

"Was she involved in your murder plots?"

"You might say that." Mantiet hesitated. "More than you can imagine."

"Don't believe a thing he tells you!"

"Tolliver, be silent. Why are you admitting it now?"

Mantiet shrugged. "It no longer matters."

"Why not?"

"Because Laura will proclaim the Republic at midnight."

"The Re—" I shook my head. Too much, too fast. "Why are you detained?"

Tolliver undid the last knot; stifling a groan, Mantiet

rubbed his wrists. "I'm apparently not, ah, radical enough for her taste."

I couldn't suppress a sneer. "A man capable of shooting down a Naval heli and killing his countrymen with a bomb isn't radical enough?"

Mantiet was quiet for a long moment. Then he said, "I didn't do those things."

"You tried!"

He made as if to speak, sighed instead. "So it would seem."

Alexi spoke from his forgotten corner. "If Mr. Seafort leaves us alone, I'll kill you." His tone was so casual it brought a chill to my spine.

Mantiet raised an eyebrow. "An elegant solution. It would amuse Laura."

I intervened before Alexi could reply. "Never mind him, Mr. Tamarov. He's scum, and all he says is a lie."

The Republic. I stared at the door, yearning for a weapon, some means of escape. An entire planet was sliding into eternal damnation, and I could do nothing. I muttered, *"The powers that be are ordained of God. Whosoever resisteth the power, resisteth the ordinance of God: and they shall receive to themselves damnation."*

Tolliver gave me a strange look, but said nothing.

I sat next to Annie.

Dully, her eyes met mine, strayed back to the floor. Two hours passed in near-absolute silence. I greeted the next approach of footsteps with relief; our hostility wore on the nerves. It recalled the wardroom in *Helsinki,* my first posting, before our senior midshipman had taken us in hand.

The door swung open. Armed men clustered in the corridor; among them was Laura Triforth. My lip curled. "You!"

"In the flesh."

"Let us go."

"I'm afraid that's not possible." She smiled regretfully.

"Then why are you here?"

Laura hesitated. "I suppose I'm cursed with a sense of style, Captain. It seems only fair that the last representative of the old order witness the birth of the new." She glanced at her watch. "But we'll have to hurry."

"Prong yourself." I wished I didn't sound like a peeved middy. "I'll stay here."

"I'm afraid you misunderstood. It's a summons, not an invitation." She gestured. Two of her minions advanced, guns drawn.

Tolliver came off the desk, placed himself between us. "You'll have to go through me first."

"Very well." She gestured at one of her men. "Kill him."

"Wait!" I jumped in front of him. "Tolliver, back to the wall. Move!"

He hesitated only a second. "Aye aye, sir." He stalked to the far wall, shoving Mantiet out of his way.

"Think of it, Captain, as a box seat in the theater of history."

"I'll think of it as kidnapping."

"You go in these." She held up a pair of handcuffs.

"Over my dead—"

"No, over his." She gestured at Tolliver with her pistol. He raised his eyebrow, waiting.

I sighed. Saying nothing, I raised my wrists. Ms. Triforth cuffed my hands in front of me. "Your young friends will wait here."

"I want them along."

"Now, now." She patted my shoulder. I threw off her hand.

"What about me?" Mantiet's quiet voice penetrated the tension.

"You'll wait with the children, Frederick."

He shook his head. "Think about it, Laura. I deserve a seat in the theater. I've earned it."

Ms. Triforth met his eye for a long moment. "Yes, I'll admit that. You'll manage to be silent?"

"Oh, I won't speak. I just want to observe." He added, "You have my word."

Laura Triforth beckoned Mantiet forward. "Unfortunately, I only brought the one set of cuffs. You'll have to bear the thongs again."

"Looser this time. They cut off the circulation."

Ms. Triforth laughed easily and bound Mantiet's wrists with the cord. She turned on her heel. "Bring them both."

Shoved from behind, I had time for a quick glance at Annie before they had me in the narrow hall. I followed Ms. Triforth outside. A welcome gust of fresh air greeted me as we emerged from a low prefab building, in a clearing surrounded by trees. We seemed to be on the edge of town; lights glowed in the near distance.

A Naval heli stood waiting, doors open, pilot in his seat. Laura beckoned to the door, helped me climb in. "Your colleagues were kind enough to leave this," she said, indicating the craft.

"Not for you. For the authorities." My arms hurt.

"We've become the authorities." She spoke with calm assurance.

The last of her men crowded aboard; the pilot snapped the switches and the blades began to turn.

"Where are we going?"

"You'll see." We lifted off. After a moment she added in a reasonable tone, "You brought it all on yourself, Seafort. I'd have been happy to let you go with the rest of your Navy."

"Why didn't you?" I stared out the window, able to orient myself at last. We were in the northwest end of town. Our prison was a few hundred feet off the main road. Occasional cars moved below.

"You didn't tell me your signal to leave Hope Nation had arrived. You left me guessing, and you were taking Frederick downtown for interrogation. I couldn't risk that."

"He wasn't going to be interrogated."

"No?" Ms. Triforth chuckled grimly. "You should have told me when I asked. As I said, you brought it on yourself."

To my surprise, we flew south toward the spaceport and Admiralty House. We were almost there when the speaker crackled. "Admiralty calling Captain Seafort. Admiralty to Captain Seafort. Please respond."

Triforth froze. After a moment she said, "Why not?" She reached for the caller. "Talk to them."

"No."

"It's your chance to say good-bye."

I made no answer. She twisted around in her seat. "Do as I say, or you'll never see your friends again."

"Kill me, then." I had failed in everything; it would be fitting.

"Not you. Your silly sniveling wife." She uncuffed my hands, thrust the caller at me.

My hand shook with suppressed rage. I thumbed the caller. "Seafort reporting!"

"Just a moment for the Admiral."

I waited until the familiar voice came on the line. "Seafort? Why in hell weren't you on the shuttle?"

Ms. Triforth shook her head, warning me. I said, "I was trying to find some of my officers, sir."

"How many are with you?"

"Lieutenant Tamarov, sir. And two middies, Tolliver and Bezrel."

He sighed. "A pity about Bezrel; I promised to keep him close. We'll all have Fused in another hour or so, Seafort. I've no time to send another shuttle down."

"I understand, sir." The conversation held an air of unreality.

"We've evacuated Orbit Station too, though the fish have shown little interest in it. Maintenance functions are under the control of their puter. It's programmed to fire on any fish that appear."

"Yes, sir."

"*Catalonia* is due back from Detour anytime now. I'll leave a broadcast beacon with instructions to pick you up. If she gets here safely, you're to sail home. There's a shuttle at the Venturas Base; use that to go aloft. In the meantime, carry on as best you can. You're in charge of what's left."

"Aye aye, sir."

"Good luck, Seafort."

"Godspeed, sir." The line went dead.

"Interesting," said Laura. "You had it planned to the last detail."

I glowered. She recuffed my hands, this time behind my back. Our heli landed close to the terminal entrance, in a lot full of cars and helis. Courteously, Laura helped me out. Just short of the door she pulled me to a stop, fingered her pistol. "You're here to watch, Seafort, because I think it fitting. But let's be clear: if you open your mouth to speak, I'll burn you on the spot."

"Prong yourself." I could think of nothing better to say and half expected her to hit me. With a frown she shoved me toward the door.

Inside, a large number of folding chairs had been brought to supplement the terminal seating. Most were occupied. At one end of the concourse a small dais had been erected. Ms. Triforth guided me toward it, stopping to shake hands along the way with admirers and well-wishers.

"Why here?" I asked.

"This is one of the few buildings big enough for a public meeting that wasn't pulverized by the rock."

I grunted, too angry to reply. By my presence I was being made a party to treason. But she would have killed Edgar Tolliver otherwise; what choice had I?

"Sit here. Remember what I warned you." She beckoned a guard. "Tell Norris to get folks seated; it's nearly midnight. Then come back and watch this one."

"Right." Her accomplice took off. Ms. Triforth kept an eye on me until he returned, then drifted among her audience, shaking hands easily, smiling. I noticed that Mantiet had not been placed on the dais, but in the front row, hands still bound. Was Triforth truly jealous of him, or was it a show to make me relax my guard in his presence? But, to what purpose? The Navy had left, taking Governor Saskrit and his administration.

Puzzled, I stared at Mantiet until he became aware of me. He raised an eyebrow and smiled without mirth. I twisted in my chair, my arms aching.

People began to take their places on the dais. Among them were Arvin Volksteader, Tomas Palabee, and, to my disgust, Harmon Branstead. His son Jerence sat in the front row. I looked for old Zack Hopewell, but he was nowhere in sight. Harmon caught my eye, reddened, looked away. Ms. Triforth took her seat at the center of the dais.

A woman with a holocamera crouched in front of the seats below the dais. She turned the lens toward a man I didn't recognize. He came forward to the small lectern set at the front of the stage. He pulled a gavel out of his back pocket, banged for silence. The few people still wandering hurried to the nearest seats.

"Ladies and gentlemen, we're here for an occasion we've all awaited. Without further ado, I give you the founder of the Republic of Hope Nation, the leader of our long-underground movement, Laura Triforth."

To a roar of approval Laura got to her feet, slowly made her way to the lectern. A wave of applause washed across the hall. Ms. Triforth waited coolly, smiling, waving with her right hand. From my seat at the end of the dais, I saw her left hand clenched behind her back. Her fingers rubbed at each other in nervous contradiction of her apparent ease.

"Ladies and gentlemen." She waited for the tumult to subside, cleared her throat.

"For years we've labored under the misguided benevolence of our colonial Government. For years we paid for their errors, financed their bureaucracy, sold our crops at little above cost to feed their starving millions.

"Tonight, all that is ended. At 1800 hours, a few paces from where we gather, a shuttle lifted with the last U.N. military officers, along with Governor Saskrit and his aides." She could get no further until the frenzied cheering subsided. She added with a smile, "Except for poor Mr. Seafort here, who got left behind." I tried to ignore the laughter.

"I won't pretend that our Republic was born in ease. Had the aliens not forced the great U.N. fleet to withdraw to home waters, ours would still be an underground movement. Had not the aliens dropped an asteroid on Centraltown, enough government structure would have remained so that we'd have had to fight a civil war to free ourselves. But today, we gain our independence without war. Officers of our movement have merely arrested the judges and those few civil servants foolhardy enough to resist."

She took a deep breath. "However the providence of Lord God manifests itself"—bile flooded my throat at the heresy—"it is enough for us to know it is with us.

"The United Nations has withdrawn its protection from Hope Nation." She gestured toward downtown. "You can see how much good that protection provided." Her gibe brought scornful laughter as, unseen, her fingers rubbed at her palms.

Her smiled vanished. "I don't make light of our many deaths. But the loss of friends and family have taught us. We know, now, how vulnerable a large city is to enemy attack, and how useless it is to our own defense. So we will live in our plantation homes. While Centraltown must remain a commercial center, it must never again become the administrative nucleus of our civilization.

"We know also the folly of allowing electoral control to pass out of the hands of responsible plantation families, into the hands of unemployed farmhands and hauler-drivers. So our legislature will consist of two houses, one for the planters themselves; the other consisting of permanent employees and associates of the planters, who live on their properties. Never again will city dwellers displace the productive plantations as the administrators of our Republic."

Triforth had to wait for the applause to abate. I wondered how many residents of Centraltown were in the hall.

She spoke quietly. "There are some who ask why we bother to declare our Republic, when satanic aliens roam the system, destroying ships, dropping their destruction on our city."

Yes, one might wonder. I strained to catch her soft-spoken answer.

"We lived here for generations, undisturbed by alien attacks. It was the fusion drives of our Navy that attracted the fish, and with the Navy gone, the fish will soon follow. If not, we have learned to combat their viruses, and dispersing our government outside Centraltown will help protect us from the havoc of any further attacks."

She paused; when she resumed her voice was sober. "And if we are wrong, and naught but devastation and death lie in our path, then I ask: what other course should we pursue? Could we defeat the fish ourselves, when the vaunted United Nations Navy"—she pointed to me—"could not, and has left us to our fate? Should we go to our deaths as peons and wards of the uncaring United Nations, or proudly, as free men and women, as masters of our destiny?"

I swallowed; something in her speech caught at my own feelings. But my eye caught the fingers rubbing endlessly at each other, behind her back.

"Therefore, now, at the hour of midnight, on this, the third day of April in the year of our Lord 2200, I do declare the Re—"

"In the name of Lord God, *stop!*"

Laura spun around as the echoes reverberated around the hall with the crash of my falling chair. Her pistol flashed. "You were warned, Seafort!"

"Shoot me, Triforth!" Contemptuously I strode to the center of the dais, twisting my hands behind me in a hopeless effort to free them. I took a deep breath. "Republic? You deluded fools!" My words were to the assembled crowd, ignoring Laura entirely. "What bilge!"

An angry growl answered me from below. Ms. Triforth shoved me, nearly knocking me off balance. I rushed on. "Isn't she a spellbinding orator?" One of her men grabbed my arm, hauling me back to my seat. I shouted. "You'll never know what she chose not to tell you!"

"Sit!" Eyes blazing, she propelled me to my chair.

"Let him speak!" Harmon Branstead was on his feet. His voice carried through the hall.

"Oh, no. Not now. This is our moment, not his."

"Let him speak!" The call was taken up by someone else in the audience. After a moment, another repeated it.

Branstead pressed his advantage. "You wanted him here, Laura. The representative of the old order, you said. Let him have his say."

Ms. Triforth studied her audience, measured its mood. She reversed herself with good grace. "Ladies and gentlemen, before proclaiming the Republic, I give you the last representative of the now-departed United Nations Navy, Captain Nicholas Seafort."

"Take off the cuffs." My tone was that of a Captain to a green young middy. And it carried.

She hesitated. "You'll put them back on, after?"

"Yes." My arms freed at last, I turned to the audience. "You had grievances. We understood. They'd have been addressed, had the aliens not interfered." It was met by snickers of derision.

"But that isn't the issue." I searched the audience for a face not hostile, one to which I might speak. Not finding any,

I pressed on. "Do you know where you stand? A few dozen miles above me roam the most frightful beings we've ever encountered. They've tried over and again to wipe you out. Their virus nearly did the job, but we synthesized a vaccine in time. They dropped a rock onto Centraltown with the kinetic energy of a nuke, but it failed to obliterate your city."

They were listening, now. "The fish attacked our ships, and the chilling news is that they learned from their attacks. Now they Defuse directly alongside and go for our lasers and tubes. Hundreds, if not thousands, of brave men died trying to defend you.

"Ms. Triforth would have you believe the Navy abandoned you." I could hear her stir behind me; I said quickly, "So I'll tell you the truth." I searched the audience, wishing I were an orator. My task was beyond me.

"First, your Government hasn't abandoned Hope Nation. I and several officers remain. Second, remember that the United Nations, our Government under Lord God, is steward not only of Hope Nation, but of seventeen other colonies and of home system. The fish have shown no sign of retreating; if anything their numbers have increased. If a colony is attacked, it can be resupplied. If home system is destroyed, we all die." In the muted light, someone sobbed.

"Admiralty decreed that when a third of our fleet was destroyed, the remainder must sail for home, to protect our mother planet. I remind you that all our interstellar ships, all our fusion drives, are built at home. With the grace of Lord God, they will return to defeat the fish, stronger than before."

Voices rose, arguing. I said clearly, "If not, we are all dead." It brought me silence. "The fish won't leave you alone, despite Ms. Triforth's pious hopes. Our only chance is to fight the fish as best we can until the Navy returns, which it surely must."

Laura Triforth stood, sauntered to the lectern. "Wrap it up, Seafort."

I nodded, trying to remember her words. "And if I am wrong, and naught but devastation and death lie in our path?" I caught her eye, held it. "What course should we then follow? I call each of you to be true to his oath. Lord God will not favor—"

"Enough." She hauled me back, pistol pressed to my side. One of her men grabbed my other arm, pulled me back to my chair, cuffed my arms to it.

Ms. Triforth returned to the lectern, shook her head. "You see the arrogance with which we've had to deal. Very well, he's had his say. Seafort's views no longer matter; they are made meaningless by the cowardly and secret retreat of his associates. With pride, therefore, I now proclaim the Republic—"

I struggled to my feet, chair dangling behind. "As plenipotentiary of the United Nations Government, I declare martial law through Hope Nation! I order the arrest for treason of Laura Triforth and her—"

The blow caught me on the back of the head. I crumpled into darkness.

"You fool."

I opened an eye and groaned. Frederick Mantiet knelt over me, pressing a compress to my head. "Did you really think you could stop her?"

I shook my head, regretting it instantly. "No. I only knew I had to try."

"She nearly killed you. She may still."

"Yes." It didn't seem to matter. I looked around. "Where are we?"

"In the hauling offices. Different room." Seeing my puzzlement he added, "A hauling company, owned by Triforth Plantation. It's where they held us before. Your men are a couple of doors down the hall."

I blinked, and the room came into focus. I slapped his hand away. "Don't touch me."

He shrugged. "I was trying to help."

"I don't need help from your kind."

Mantiet retreated. This room had chairs. He took one. "What is my kind, Seafort?"

I said flatly, "Garbage."

He reddened, but held my eye. "Your opinion is based on . . . ?"

"You know bloody well. You tried to murder us twice. In a sense you succeeded, with Alexi."

A very long pause. "Seafort, I don't know how to tell you this."

I wasn't interested. I closed my eyes, rubbing my aching skull. "Let me sleep."

"I didn't do it."

I made no answer. After a time he went to the door, spoke to the brittle wood. "I don't know why it matters, but I want you to know."

"Let me be."

"I didn't blow up the hauler in front of your car; I didn't fire a missile at your heli."

"I have your confession. In fact, it's in my jacket. You named your accomplices."

"Men who were killed when the bomb hit."

"I assumed as much. As I said, you're garbage."

"Seafort, look at me." I kept my eyes closed. He said, louder, "Look at me, or I'll kick off your kneecaps." I opened my eyes. Mantiet said simply, "I did not attack you on any occasion. I so swear upon my immortal soul."

"And your confession?"

"Was a lie."

"To what purpose?"

"The obvious one." He saw my blank look. "To avoid interrogation."

I sat up slowly, ignoring the throbbing in my head. "You make no sense. Interrogation would have exposed your crimes. We'd have found out about the bomb and the missiles."

"Yes, you'd have found out."

"That's why you avoided interrogation."

"Yes, that's why I confessed."

I managed to get to my feet. The room was about the length of a bridge. How could I think without pacing? "If you're guilty, the interrogation would show it. If you're innocent, the tests would have shown that, and you'd have been freed instead of hanged. So avoiding interrogation makes no sense if you're innocent. It does if you're guilty."

He said nothing.

I paced. What was he up to, another cruel game? Was he so twisted he needed no purpose? If he was innocent, why would he avoid interrogation that would show he hadn't tried to kill me? No one could hold anything back during interr—

No one could hold anything back. I turned. "You were hiding something else!"

"Bravo." He clapped slowly.

"What could be so important you'd give your life to conceal it?" He made no answer. Intrigued despite myself, I paced from wall to wall, hands clasped behind my back. If Mantiet hadn't tried to kill me, someone else had. Who?

I stopped, swearing under my breath. "Laura made it clear you've always been part of the underground."

"Yes."

"When the bomb went off in front of your manse, you knew you'd be under suspicion."

"By the time I figured out what had happened, I barely had time to get out."

"You'd have been picked up for interrogation because your hauler was used."

"I assumed so."

"And you knew . . ." I raised my eyes. "What? I still don't understand." He smiled through a mouth swollen from Tolliver's beating, and I saw the obvious. "You knew it was Laura Triforth!"

"No." At my look of surprise he added, "I only assumed so; she didn't take me so far into her confidence. But only Laura was devious enough to use one of my own haulers, in front of my own plantation. My confession couldn't convict her, but I'd been attending meetings of my branch of the underground a long while, and I knew who was involved. If you took me in, you'd break my whole movement."

"For that, you risked your life and soiled your name?"

"For Hope Nation's future, yes." He met my gaze. "I am a patriot, you know, in my own way. For all your talk about wrongs that would have been redressed, we'd tried for decades to get the U.N. to listen. To no avail."

I snorted. "You're a society without poverty, without pollution, without crowding; I can't believe you feel so sorry for yourselves. No, using Occam's razor, you're guilty. It's the simplest explanation."

"Yes, it is. But I wanted you to hear the truth."

"Why?"

"I don't know." He turned back toward the door. "Because it no longer matters. Because, as you say, I soiled my name. Perhaps because I admire your bravery."

"Goofjuice."

He said, "Or perhaps it's just that I enjoy a good joke."

After that, neither of us spoke.

17

The next morning Mantiet and I were moved to another room, one that had a cubicle with a toilet. To my relief, Annie and the rest of our party were waiting.

When we were brought in, Annie cried out with relief. Thereafter, she seemed perturbed whenever I left her side, even for my restless pacing.

Like our previous cells, the room had no windows, nothing we could pry loose to free ourselves. Laura Triforth had apparently constructed her building with a prison in mind. For three maddening days we slept on damp mattresses, ate meager meals, and walked the confines of our chamber.

The chill air made my chest ache. With an effort I sat. "Mr. Bezrel."

"Yes, sir?" He scrambled to his feet.

"Get my vapormask, would you?"

"I haven't seen it, sir. Not since we changed rooms."

I drew my jacket tight. When the guard next brought our food, I demanded my vapormeds. He ignored me and stomped out.

Alexi had lapsed into a moody silence; he slumped on his cot for hours at a time. Mantiet made frequent attempts to converse, most of which I disdained. However, at one point he inquired, "At the meeting, why did you call yourself plenipotentiary of the United Nations Government?"

"It doesn't matter." I rolled over on my side.

"Still, it interests me. Why?"

"Because it was true."

"Do you have authorization or merely delusions of grandeur?"

Stung, I pulled myself up. "Command of Admiralty House can be likened to command of a vessel under weigh."

"So?"

"The Captain of a Naval vessel has unlimited authority. Moreover he is, in fact, the United Nations Government in transit. Whatever powers Admiral De Marnay had, devolved on me when he left, and I'm the senior officer in the Hope Nation system."

"Weren't the Governor's powers separate?"

"Yes, until the buildup of forces. Then Mr. De Marnay was given a united command."

"Still, plenipotentiary of the U.N.—"

"It's a long-settled law." My tone was irritable. "The Captain of a vessel can do almost anything he wants."

"And usually does," said Tolliver sourly.

"Shut up, Middy."

"Of course, sir."

Mantiet gestured. "Is he always like this?"

"Only on occasion."

"Why do you tolerate him?"

"He's sort of—" I hesitated.

"A test of your endurance?"

"More in the nature of a hair shirt." I regarded Mantiet sourly. "Are you done prying?"

"If it annoys you. How else would you pass the time?"

"That depends on why we're here."

Mantiet said, "We're in storage until Laura decides what to do with us. We're an embarrassment to her."

"How so?"

"As you so eloquently pointed out, you represent the old, defunct government. And I represent a more moderate wing of her own party. We're alternatives to her particular brand of republic. While we live, we're a threat."

"I don't want to die!"

I turned toward the childish voice. "Steady, Bezrel."

"I didn't do anything! Don't let her kill us!"

"Easy, Midshipman. You—"

"I'll handle it, sir," Tolliver said smoothly. "Let's talk in the head, Avar. Don't disturb the Captain." He guided the boy's arm toward the toilet cubicle.

"Don't hurt him."

Tolliver looked at me, surprised. "I didn't intend to." He shut the door.

I spoke softly, so Annie couldn't hear. "You think we're to be killed?"

Mantiet looked pensive. "I'd imagine so."

"Then what's Laura waiting for?"

Mantiet shrugged. "Perhaps she'll arrange some kind of accident. She still needs the support of conservatives like Branstead and Hopewell." He added with a smile, "Remember, my advice isn't worth much."

"I'm not sure any longer." The admission shamed me. Gruffly I added, "I thought she kidnapped us to rescue you, but it appears your position wasn't much improved."

"So it would seem." He gestured at the bath cubicle. "It's a pity, but if Laura, ah, eliminates you, she's unlikely to leave the child behind." His voice dropped even further. "Or your wife."

I glanced over his shoulder, but Annie was lost in some melancholic reverie. "I know." I hesitated, amazed that I was allowing myself to make him an ally. "There's nothing I can do." Mantiet waved me silent as footsteps approached.

As always, the men entered with pistols drawn and ready. "Seafort, come with us."

"Why?"

"Move."

Wearily I got to my feet. Was this how it would end? An innocent summons, followed by an unforeseen shot to the head?

"This way." They marched me along the corridor, one man behind, one on either side, a laser pistol in my back. Even if I'd been armed, I could have done nothing. They shoved me into another room, which I recognized as the one in which I'd first awakened.

Wary, I paced the chamber, glancing at the meager furniture, the barred transom. I swallowed; for some reason, what I wanted most in the world was to hold Annie in my arms.

The door swung open. I stared at the visitor, turned away. "I've nothing to say to you."

"Please." Harmon Branstead looked around, found a chair. "I came to see if you were well."

I stared at the wall opposite, determined not to speak. After a moment he came behind me. "Nicholas, I swear before Lord God: if I'd had any idea you were still on planet I wouldn't have been on that dais. Laura told me the Navy had skulked off in the night, leaving us. She said all U.N. authority was gone, and we were on our own."

"You were a party to treason."

"Was it treason, if we were abandoned? You've seen my plantation; if these people are the government I have to get along with them. Who else is there?"

"You swore an oath, as have we all."

He put his hand on my shoulder; I thrust it away. He said, "Nick, if the Government left us, we were entitled to form another. I thought you'd gone with your fleet."

"I would have, if Ms. Triforth hadn't taken me prisoner."

"She thought you were about to question Mantiet; her whole scheme would have unraveled at the last moment." He paused. "I had no part in that. Believe me."

I wanted to, but nobody on Hope Nation was whom he seemed. "It doesn't matter. You have your Republic, and I my prison." Uncomfortable at my own rudeness, I faced him. "Why are you here?"

He closed his eyes, opened them. "Jerence ran away after the meeting. I just found him today, and had him taken home."

"I'm sorry. He's . . . ?"

"Completely spaced. I don't know where he found the stuff. Or what he had to do to get it."

"I'm sorry." It seemed so inadequate.

He drew closer. "I don't know if they're listening," he whispered.

"And if they are?"

He shook his head to quiet me, and spoke in a normal tone. "They trust me as much as anyone, but they searched me before they let me in."

"Those who live by deceit find it everywhere."

"Perhaps." He sat, toyed with his boot. "I'm sorry for your troubles. There's nothing I can do to help you."

"There is," I said.

He glanced up, surprised. "What?"

"My wife. Get her out of this."

He swallowed. "I thought she was at the clinic. They have her too?"

I couldn't trust myself to speak, nodded instead.

"I'll do my best. You have my word." He beckoned me closer. Puzzled, I came close. He twisted the heel of his boot, slid it aside. Motioning me silent, he held it toward me.

Pressed into a hole in the leather was a razor. He whispered, "This is all I could chance bringing. Anything else they'd have found. You'll have to make it do."

I reached for it. He grasped my wrist, shook his head. "I need your promise."

"Of what?" Our heads were practically touching.

His grip tightened on my arm. "Take Jerence."

"What?"

"Laura told us of the call from your Admiral. When your ship *Catalonia* comes, take my son off-planet."

"Impossible."

"It's possible if you do it." His whisper was fierce. "You must, or I won't help you."

"Where could I take him? We'll be lucky to make it to home system alive. Do you want to send him to the fish?"

His hand tightened convulsively. "No, I don't want to risk my firstborn." He took several steadying breaths before continuing. "You were right. We're in terrible danger. I don't think Hope Nation can survive the aliens. But you're a survivor. Somehow, you manage. Take my son with you."

"Even if I escape, I can't take a civilian."

"You can and you will." He released my wrist, locked his gaze to mine.

"It might mean his death."

"He may meet his death here, sooner." He fingered the sharp blade. "It's a gamble, Seafort. Jerence may be killed. Then my son Roger would inherit. Or Jerence may survive while we don't. Then, when it's over, you'll send him back. Either way the family survives; Branstead Plantation goes on."

"You'd sacrifice your son for the survival of a plantation?"

"I can do nothing to protect my sons. You're the best safeguard I know. And besides . . ."

I waited, realized he wouldn't finish. "What, Harmon?" I asked gently.

His face held anguished appeal. "I have to get him off-planet before he destroys himself. It may already be too late. All I know is that I can't save him."

How old was Jerence: fourteen? I couldn't cope with a sullen, rebellious joeykid along with my other troubles. Yet there was so little chance I'd be in a position to honor my promise that it hardly mattered. Harmon's razor was a pitiful weapon, but without it, Avar Bezrel's nightmare would certainly be realized. My duty was to try to save the innocents, no matter how hopeless the effort. "I'll try, Harmon." For Annie, for Alexi. For Bezrel.

"No. Swear."

I snorted with contempt. "My word is worthless. Didn't you know?"

"No. I trust your word more than that of any man I know. Give me your oath."

I regarded him. "Very well. My oath."

"That you will take Jerence off-planet when you leave, and to Terra with you on *Catalonia,* and let him come home when the danger is abated."

"I so swear."

"And I'll talk to Laura about Mrs. Seafort, the moment I leave." He handed me the blade.

I tore a piece of the lining of my jacket for wrapping, thrust it inside my pants. My grin was feral. "Too bad you couldn't bring a laser."

He twisted the heel back onto his boot, whispering still. "I had to beg Laura for this chance to see you. I told her it was to say good-bye."

"It may well be. Who's in charge, beside her?" I shivered, hugged myself. I hadn't been warm in days.

"There are others; Volksteader, Palabee. But she runs the show." Branstead's face clouded. "It's not what some of us hoped."

"Revolutions seldom are." I sat. "Harmon, surely you're smart enough to see your folly. Hope Nation has hardly more than a quarter million people. If you cut off commerce with Earth—"

"Not cut off, recast. Our lives can't be managed from afar."

Ludicrous, to argue politics with him, his razor warm against my side. "Do you think for a minute the Church would allow trade with traitors who've set themselves against Lord God's own government?"

"They—"

I rushed on. "And without our technology, you'd collapse in a generation. The die-cast fabricators, the medical—"

"Do you suppose we haven't thought of that? Our food is every bit as important to home system as your manufactured goods are to us. Have you any concept of the number of barges in the pipeline at any moment? Randy Carr calculated that without us you'll have food riots inside of three years. No politics, no moral stand would outweigh—"

It was his very soul at stake. "Harmon, you raise your fist against Lord God! I beseech you, think what you're doing!"

"Show me another way." He raised a hand to forestall my reply. "I'm not proud of Laura, or how she operates. Her attack on your car was despicable, and if I'd known . . ." He shook his head. "Zack Hopewell is disgusted and outraged, and so am I."

For a moment we sat in silence.

"When did you decide to visit?"

"After the meeting. When I found Jerence today, I was sure. I've talked to . . . some of my friends. We agreed. We'd do more, but Laura controls the arms and the Governor's Manse." Again he touched my shoulder; this time I did not resist. "Godspeed." He went briskly to the door, hammered on it. "Let me out! I'm done with him!"

A moment later footsteps approached; the door opened. Harmon nodded to the guards, turned to me with contempt. "I misjudged you, Seafort. You're getting no more than you deserved."

He might at least have warned me. "Harmon, you're a pompous fool. You always were." It was the best I could do on short notice.

He snapped to the guard, "Get me out."

Laura Triforth appeared at the end of the hall. "Enjoy your visit, Harmon?"

"He's your responsibility." Branstead stalked down the corridor. "I'll have no more to do with him."

Ms. Triforth raised an eyebrow. "Seafort, you seem to have irritated Harmon."

"A pity. He deserves you."

"I'll take you back to your colleagues." She beckoned me to follow her.

"Why are you holding us?"

"You're in protective custody, for your own safety. After all, someone's twice tried to kill you."

"Let my wife go."

She wrinkled her nose. "We don't need trannies roaming Centraltown."

"May God damn you to His deepest hell!"

"How diplomatic." She sighed, ran fingers through her hair. "Has it occurred to you I've a lot on my mind at the moment? A government to organize? A planet to run?"

"Let us go. We won't bother you."

"All in good time." Laura's men opened our door. "Oh, by the way . . ." She held my vapormask. "You left this in the meeting hall." I snatched it from her hand, fuming.

As they thrust me into our cell Tolliver jumped to his feet. "Where did they take you, sir?"

"I had a visitor. Leave it."

"What did Triforth say to you?"

"Not much."

From his corner, Mantiet sighed. "There's a virtue in helplessness, Captain. One has no decisions to make."

"We're never helpless."

"What would you propose we do?"

I sat on my cot. "Wait." It was all I could think of.

Bezrel approached timidly. His voice was soft, almost a whisper. "Sir, I'm sorry I acted like a baby this morning." I looked up with alarm; was he about to start bawling again? No, it seemed not.

I cleared my throat. "We're all afraid," I said gruffly.

"But you know better than to show it."

"It's all right." I wanted to be rid of him. Ashamed, I patted my mattress. "Sit."

"Aye aye, sir." Automatically he straightened his tie.

I smiled. "I never had a chance to review your file, Mr. Bezrel. Tell me about yourself."

"I'm thirteen, sir. I came out on *Vestra* with Admiral De Marnay; I started as ship's boy."

"How did you get to be a middy?"

"Admiral De Marnay promoted me. They did it that way so I wouldn't have to go to Academy first. My father wanted me to sail with the Admiral because they know each other."

So Admiral De Marnay had skirted regs for an old friend. I frowned and changed the subject.

"Who is your father?"

"Captain Bezrel, sir. Retired now, but he had U.N.S. *Constantinople.*"

"Where are you from?"

"Crete, sir." He hesitated. "It's an island that used to be part of Greece."

"I know where Crete is," I growled. Father had instilled Terran geography in me with dogged determination.

"Yes, sir. I'm sorry, sir."

Sorry. Always apologizing. I waited for the sniffles.

"Am I dismissed, sir?"

I took pity on him. "Yes. I commend you on your manner, Mr. Bezrel. Much improved."

His grateful smile pierced me. "Thank you, sir." He retreated to his cot.

"They've brought us breakfast, Nicky."

I opened my eyes. "Thanks, hon."

To my delight, Annie grinned. "You all right?"

"Of course." I sat up, shivering.

I gnawed at the bread, sipped at lukewarm coffee. Afterward I went back to my bed and dozed.

About noon I awoke. With an effort I sat. "Mr. Bezrel, give me the mask."

"I'll get it." Alexi. He helped me slip it on. "How do you feel?"

"Well enough." I took a deep breath through the mask and wrinkled my nose. The air seemed stale.

Ever so slowly, the day passed. Then a long night, during

which I stirred restlessly, coughing. The vapormeds didn't seem to help.

When the guards brought our morning meal I demanded to see Ms. Triforth; they didn't even bother to answer. I repeated my demand at dinner.

Late that evening she appeared, waking me from restless and feverish sleep. "You rang?" Her tone was sardonic.

I shivered, drawing my jacket closer. "You've made your revolution. Why hold us?"

"After your impassioned speech, I decided I don't want a horde of White Russians storming through the countryside."

"What on earth are you talking about?"

"I thought you knew your history. Never mind."

"Let us go."

"In time." She looked at me with concern. "Are you well?"

Mantiet said quietly, "Don't toy with us, Laura. Do what you're going to do."

"Be patient, Frederick. You'll both be freed soon."

"What might I look forward to? Shot trying to escape?" Mantiet seemed quite calm.

"Don't be ridiculous. You're not my prisoner. I haven't seen you since the night we proclaimed the Republic." She turned on her heel and left.

"We can't undo her treason," I said petulantly. "Why must she hold us?"

"She enjoys seeing us helpless." Tolliver.

Mantiet regarded me with an odd look, lapsed into silence. After several minutes he stirred. "Alexi, Mr. Tolliver, take Bezrel and Mrs. Seafort into the cubicle, please. I want to speak to your Captain alone."

Tolliver said bluntly, "No. I don't trust you."

I snapped, "Don't be silly. We've been alone before." Reluctantly Tolliver herded the others to the enclosed cubicle.

Mantiet took me to the far end of the room and spoke softly. "How do you feel?"

"Well enough." I coughed. "Under the circumstances." I was tired and wanted to lie down. I waited, but Mantiet said no more. "Frederick, if you've something to say, tell me!"

"Your face is flushed. You've been coughing."

"We've been locked in here with bad food, no air . . ."

"True, but you're much worse since yesterday."

I sank into a chair. "Perhaps. I've started the vapormeds again."

"Precisely. You started them yesterday."

I gaped. "Are you saying . . . Laura tampered with my meds?"

"Why else would she take your vapormask?"

"She returned it when I asked. If she wanted me dead, she'd just shoot me."

"Don't you—"

"Enough nonsense." I went back to my corner. As I sat, the handle of the razor pressed into my side.

Mantiet mustn't know I had it; he might be planted to betray us. But each day that passed made that more unlikely.

I toyed with the vapormeds. Could Mantiet's suggestion be possible, or were his insinuations part of some outlandish scheme? What would Laura gain if I sickened? No, she didn't need to toy with me or plant a spy.

Mantiet approached. "Captain, I ask a favor."

"There's nothing I can do for you."

"I won't survive you by long. You're as close as I'm likely to get to a cleric. Shrive me."

"Me? You're joking. You need a chaplain."

"You are representative of Mother Church."

"Aboard ship. Here, in civilization . . ."

"If you landed on an unexplored planet, would you not still be chaplain to your crew?"

"Yes."

"We are strangers in a strange land."

"But—"

He cried, "I've nowhere else to turn!"

Was it blasphemy, or did I have authority? I concentrated on ill-remembered regs. Finally, I sighed. If there were sin, it would be mine, not his.

I said, "If I'm to be your chaplain, I must tell you: rebellion against lawful authority is treason against Lord God."

"I made no overt act of rebellion."

"You were part of their conspiracy."

"I took part in discussions. No more."

"Money? Other help?"

He flushed. "Some. I didn't know where it would lead."

"While I am here, a piece of Government remains. You're still bound by your oath."

"What do you want of me?"

"To adhere to your oath, as long as it is possible."

A long silence. At last, "All right."

"Do you repent your sins?"

"Yes." He sat tense on my cot, eyes boring into mine.

I made the sign. "In the name of the Father . . ."

When it was done he whispered, "Thank you." He turned away. Weary, I lay back on my cot. When I awoke, I no longer doubted I was sinking into illness. I was feverish. My chest ached. Alexi and Tolliver tried to tend me; irritably I waved them off. When the jailers brought our meal Tolliver demanded I be taken to the clinic. They didn't bother to answer.

Later, I woke from a doze, coughing. Time was growing short. "Mantiet, Tolliver, come here." I waited. "Frederick, I have no choice but to trust you. For the sake of your soul, I hope I'm right." I put my finger to my lips, fished inside my pants, came out with the razor. Their eyes widened. I whispered to Tolliver. "If you see a chance . . ." He nodded. I handed him the weapon.

I turned to Mantiet. "I won't be good for much. You might use the chair as a club, when Tolliver makes his move . . ."

"I'll find something."

"Get Annie and the middy out of the way first. I don't want them hurt. Or Alexi."

Tolliver said, "If I can. There may not be time."

I said, "I'll do my best to distract the guards. I'll yell, perhaps. We'll do it tonight if possible. No later than tomorrow." He studied my feverish face, nodded again.

When we were done Alexi came to squat by my side. His look was one of reproach.

I demanded, "What's bothering you?"

"You're hiding something."

"No." I hated to lie.

"You keep whispering so I won't hear."

I flared, "If I am, it's my prerogative as Captain. Who are you to question me, Lieutenant?"

After a moment his eyes fell. "I'm sorry." His tone was stiff.

My heart pounded. I might be gone soon, and this is how it would end between us. "Alexi, I'm sorry. Bend closer." I whispered into his ear. "There'll be trouble when the guards bring dinner. Take Annie and Bezrel into the cubicle when you hear them coming. Keep them there."

"Why?"

"I don't want them hurt. They're your responsibility."

"What will happen to you?"

"I'll be fine."

He studied my face, troubled. "All right, Mr. Seafort."

I grasped for something else to give him. We were reduced to so little. "Mr. Tamarov."

"Yes?"

"You're a good officer. You always were."

He stood straighter. "Thank you, Mr. Seafort." I smiled.

Despite my warnings, when dinner came I was sleeping fitfully; the guards were gone before I could rouse myself. I cursed silently; time was running out. By our next meal it might be too late.

"Mr. Tamarov, can you stay awake and rouse me before dawn?"

"Yes, Mr. Seafort."

"Do so."

Tolliver looked hesitant as he approached. "Please don't misunderstand me, Captain. But—"

"Yes?"

"You haven't been well . . ." He squared his shoulders, said with resolve, "If anything happens to you . . . Are we on our own? Shall we pretend we're still in the Navy?"

I snarled, "Pretend? You *are* in the Navy, until your enlistment expires."

"What Navy? Look around you! Where is it?"

"It's here." I coughed. "The U.N. Government hasn't abdicated. You and I embody its authority."

He shrugged. "Sometimes I wonder about you."

"What's that supposed to mean?"

"Nothing, sir. Excuse my impertinence." I glared, but he held my gaze. "And while you're at it, sir, who's senior: me or Mr. Tamarov?"

It was my turn to hesitate. Alexi was on medical leave; technically that left Tolliver in charge. Preposterous, on the face of it. Yet Alexi's memory was gone. "You're senior," I said, defeated. "Do as you see fit. For as long as you're able."

"Aye aye, sir." Shaking his head, he turned away.

"It's nearly dawn, sir."

I groaned.

Alexi persisted. "You said to wake you." He shook me again.

"What time is it?"

"Just after five." The hall bulbs, our only source of light, were turned down. We could barely see each other.

Breakfast might be as early as an hour from now, perhaps as long as three hours. I struggled to sit. Panting, I made myself breathe as deeply as I could. It didn't seem to help. I yearned for the familiar comfort of the vapormask.

I tried to stand, failed, got cautiously to my knees. Holding on to the wall I pulled myself up, ignoring Alexi's outstretched hand. "Put a chair there." I pointed.

The door was centered on the north wall. Alexi put the chair along the east wall, near the north corner.

I prodded Tolliver with my toe. He turned over; I tapped at his ribs. He surged awake, hand darting to his pocket.

I shook my head. "Not yet." To Alexi, "Wake Frederick."

Mantiet sat, rubbing sleep from his eyes. He looked around saw us all roused. "I'm ready." He slipped into his clothes, sat at the side of the table nearest to the door. His arm draped casually over an unused chair.

"Wake the boy. Take him into the cubicle."

"Right." Alexi prodded Bezrel. The young middy sat up, dazed, and followed Alexi. I heard what might have been a sob.

Carefully I knelt by Annie's side. "Get up, hon." I stroked her forehead. "Please."

She came awake with a frightened gasp.

"It's all right, hon." I paused for breath. "I need you to go with Alexi."

Her eyes darted back and forth, came to rest on Tolliver's hand. She squealed in terror, clung to my shoulders.

"Edgar, get that razor out of sight!" I struggled to free myself. "Annie, let go."

She wrapped herself around me. "Fightin', with shiv? Dey gonna kill ya, Nicky!"

"Annie, go in the cubicle!"

"But—"

"Now!"

With a sob, she fled.

Knees weak, I crossed to the east wall, sat.

I shivered, struggling to stay awake. From time to time I coughed, deep hacking coughs that served as ominous warnings. I yearned to sleep. Soon I would have a deep long rest, until Lord God woke me for His vengeance. Half aloud, I whispered, "Lord, if I could but undo my offense . . . I am so sorry I offended Thee." Though it was no use, I was comforted. My punishment was inevitable, but He would know my repentance.

Endless minutes passed, while I toyed with the vapormask in my lap.

Tolliver lay unmoving, hand concealed under his blanket. Mantiet sat quietly, as if relaxed. Only my ragged breathing broke the stillness of the night.

The hallway lights brightened. Footsteps. I managed to totter to my feet. When they swung the door open I would shout, catch their attention. With luck Tolliver could make his move.

A sound, from the cubicle. "Nicky?" Annie peered out.

The door swung open.

"I can't wait in—" She searched out Tolliver. He lay facing the door, the razor behind his back. She stared at it. "Don' get Nicky hurt!"

I hissed, "Go back!"

The first guard was halfway into our chamber. He stopped, looked about. Tolliver's muscles tensed. With a sinking feeling I realized my shout wouldn't be enough to distract the guard.

Annie gaped from the corner; she should have been safe in the cubicle. Too late; the diversion had to be now or never.

I flung the vapormask at the guard's head, surged out of my chair.

He whipped out his laser, aimed at me. Tolliver rose in one smooth motion and lunged across the room to crash into the guard's midriff. The impact smashed the man into the door frame. A crunch. A cry, cut short. The gun clattered to the floor.

I threw myself on the pistol.

With an oath the second guard kicked open the door. He fired just as Mantiet hurled a chair at his face. The chair splintered in a flash of fire and smoke. Knife in hand, Tolliver scrambled toward the door on hands and knees, below the line of fire.

A boot kicked the door wide. I got my hands on the dropped pistol. I lurched to my feet, but as the guard's trigger finger twitched, my legs buckled. I went down like a stone. Sparks and fire flashed over my head.

"Leav'im 'lone!" Annie's lithe form flew across the room. Fingernails slashed at the guard's eyes. Her knee slammed into his crotch. He fell with a shriek. She whirled, saw the third guard's pistol rising, pounced on his arm an instant before he fired. A bolt seared the concrete inches from my face. I flinched and kicked myself aside. Someone toppled heavily on me with a curse. I lost my pistol.

Tolliver tried to regain his feet; I'd knocked him down with my reflexive lurch.

"Nicky!" A shriek of terror as the guard's gun loomed.

Annie clung desperately to the man's hand and chomped savagely on his fingers. He howled, and the gun fell. She dived for it.

The room turned red amid ghastly screams. I lay gasping for air, the warning empty-charge beep of Annie's pistol fading from my consciousness. Time passed.

A gentle hand helped prop my head. Annie's wet cheek hugged mine.

"I didn't get a chance to use the knife." Tolliver sounded peeved.

I gasped for breath. "Find them!"

"There's no one left. The rest of the building's empty."

"You're sure?"

"Mantiet says so."

Frederick appeared, breathing heavily. "We're alone. But we don't have a heli."

Alexi and Bezrel emerged from the cubicle. The boy's face was buried in Alexi's jacket. Alexi's arm cradled his shoulder.

Tolliver said contemptuously, "Middies." I stared at him and he flushed. "Sorry. I forget."

Annie's sobs became more frenzied.

"It's all right, hon." I stroked her head, calming her. "How'd you do that?"

"Dey was gonna dissya."

"Where'd you learn . . ."

Her tone held scorn. "Two joeys ain' nothin. Onna street, girl gotta defen' herself. Even inna Cathedral I crunched one's head."

"My God. That was you?" I recalled the bashed-in skull, the thick puddles of blood.

"Coulda got othas, if I didn' trip onna rock." A pause, and her face clouded. "Rubies gone."

"Annie, about what they did . . ."

"No one did nothin'." Her voice had an edge of finality.

I cradled her anew. "It's all right, hon."

"Sir, we'd better leave." Tolliver.

I tried to wrest Annie's hand from my neck and succumbed to a fit of coughing. This time, I thought I'd never stop.

"We've got to get him to the clinic." Tolliver.

Mantiet said, "Why not just wait for Laura to retake us?" At Tolliver's puzzled stare he added, "Your Captain's not exactly unknown. If we walk into the clinic, she'll be told in minutes."

My voice was thick. "I'm all right. See if you still have friends."

"In half an hour I can have five men and a heli."

I nodded. "Get your men. Hurry." After he made the call I had Tolliver move us to the front room, past the charred corpses of our guards. Bezrel retched at the sight. I wanted to do the same. Annie hardly spared them a glance.

In the front room the daylight seemed overbright. "It's so cold." I huddled shivering in my chair. Mantiet and Tolliver exchanged glances.

Between us we had two charged pistols. I had Tolliver and Mantiet take them; I was past being any help. When the whap of blades beat the air we tensed. Mantiet peered cautiously through the window. "It's our side," he said. "But I'd better go first. They might be nervous."

He went out. A moment later he beckoned to us. I gasped, "Tolliver, draw your pistol. Be ready for anything." Why hadn't I made Frederick leave his pistol behind? I wasn't thinking well. Mantiet's men walked toward the building.

Mantiet entered first. He pulled out his pistol. Instantly Tolliver was down on one knee, gun aimed. Mantiet handed me the weapon. "You need this. I'm armed now."

"Thank you." I tried to make my voice casual.

"We'd better get out. Where to?"

The room drifted from side to side, making it difficult to think. We needed to confront Laura Triforth. Arrest her, if we could. But she had the power, the guns.

"Well, sir?"

"I don't know! Can't you see I'm sick?" I was disgusted by the whine in my tone.

"Into the heli." Mantiet.

Tolliver's voice was tense. "The last person who offered us a ride was Triforth."

"He's not Laura," I snapped. I tried to think. Best we retreat to the plantation zone, if someone there would help. Branstead, or perhaps Zack Hopewell. But within hours our escape would be known. Triforth would have time to mobilize.

No matter. We had no real choice. I asked, "Can we all fit in the heli?" It seemed too small.

"I doubt it. We'd be way over the weight limit."

My teeth chattered. I drew my jacket tight. "Ring Harmon Branstead for me." Mantiet's men drifted inside. Their presence made the room seem crowded.

"The frequency may be monitored," Mantiet warned as he handed me the caller.

I thought of calling through Admiralty House, relaying to Orbit Station and back. No, it would waste time, and Admiralty House was probably in enemy hands.

"Branstead."

"This is, um, a friend."

"Thank heavens." His tone held an odd note of relief.

"We need help."

"Are you . . . alone?"

"For the moment. Bring a large heli, as fast as you can."

"Where should we meet you?"

We had to get clear of the haulers' building. "Where I brought your son back from our trip. In front."

"Right. Figure about an hour." He rang off.

Alexi asked, "Where is he meeting us?"

"At the spaceport terminal." I stared at the heli. "We'll have to fly two loads."

"We'd better get you in the first one." Mantiet. "If they catch you here . . ."

"If they catch any of us, we're dead." The room drifted. I tried to take a deep breath. "Is there a car?"

"Nothing."

"The road's a few hundred feet. Stop one."

Mantiet gestured to two of his men. "Hurry."

"No killing," I said.

The farmhand spat. "They may not want to stop."

"Don't kill civilians."

The two men loped off. Too much time passed. Finally, the distant hum of an electricar. Another wait. A car appeared at the end of the winding drive, lurched along the dirt road, pulled up in front of our building. I wobbled to my feet.

Mantiet's field hand yanked open the car door. Inside, a young man cowered, hands held high.

I hadn't thought of prisoners. We could lock him in to a room. No, Triforth's men would find him and no telling what they'd do. Too complicated. "Bring him along."

The farmhand muttered, "You're crazy."

Mantiet spun, his voice dangerous. "Show him the respect you'd show me. More than that."

"But—"

"You heard me!"

The farmhand nodded grudgingly. "Sorry."

Mantiet shifted impatiently. "Let's get moving."

"Tolliver, Bezrel, and I will take the car. Send one of your men with us, in case there's a fight. Alexi can go with you in the heli." A long speech, that left me panting.

"Shouldn't you be in—"

Tolliver said loudly, "Aye aye, sir."

Interrupted, Mantiet reddened. "Right. Let's go."

We piled into the car. I fell into my seat, gasping from the effort. I said to the civilian, "Put your hands down. No one will hurt you."

The young man quavered, "Please. Whatever you say."

"Stay quiet. You might even get your car back."

On the edge of town the streets were mostly clear. Little damage was evident. The heli cruised above and behind us, circling. Despite the tension, I dozed. When I woke, the intense heat made me try to squirm out of my jacket, but after a moment I gave up, panting.

We pulled into the terminal lot. It looked deserted. It ought to be; there was no longer any traffic to the Station. "Check out the building."

Tolliver got out and approached the terminal with one of Mantiet's men. I kept my eye on the anxious civilian, hand on my pistol, until they returned. "Locked, sir."

We clustered in the parking lot straining for the thump of Harmon's heli. Heart pounding, I rested against the car. I'd needed Alexi and Tolliver to help me to my feet.

At last the heli came. As it swooped down I tapped the civilian on the shoulder. "Drive downtown. Don't stop anywhere near." He jumped into his car, sped to freedom.

Before the blades stopped Harmon Branstead jumped down, strode toward me, stopped. "God almighty, Seafort, what's happened to you?"

"I'm not well."

"You're—" He broke off. "What do you want us to do?"

"Who'd you bring?" One by one six men climbed out, laser rifles at the ready. Another man followed, more slowly.

"You?" My astonishment was obvious.

"Me. After all, it's my heli." Old Zack Hopewell's stern face showed no hint of warmth. He walked slowly to me, took my shoulders in his hands. He stared into my face. "Lord God save you, how long have you been like this?"

I blinked away tears. "Triforth—did something. With my vapormeds."

He turned to Harmon. "Get him to a doctor. Now."

"No." I began to cough. As the day faded to mist I hung on to Hopewell. Finally I caught my breath. "I can't be seen. None of us can until Laura Triforth is taken."

It was as if I hadn't spoken. "Harmon, get him in the heli. Frederick, call Dr. Avery. Have him meet us at my house."

I gasped, "Triforth first! Take the Manse."

Hopewell's tone was brutal. "That's for us to decide." In a moment we were aloft. I leaned on Alexi's shoulder, wondering where they'd put Annie.

Mantiet said, "You're wrong, Zack. Without him we're nothing."

"Look at him. We've got to get him to Avery."

"Find Triforth. You're wasting—" I began to cough. Some time after, I woke from a fitful doze, Alexi's shoulder damp from my perspiration. The heli door swung open.

"Help him inside."

I brushed away their hands. "I can walk." It was true, after a fashion. By the time I reached Zack Hopewell's porch scarce twenty yards away, I was glad of the hands offering support.

While we walked, Dr. Avery thrust a fresh vapormask over my head. Inside, he helped pull off my shirt. He listened. "Christ. Lay back, boy."

"We have to . . ."

"Give my meds a chance."

I obeyed. Avery examined my old canister, sniffed at the vapor. "That's not right. Lord God knows what mix she used."

Old Zack Hopewell raised an eyebrow. "What's been done?"

"I thought I'd seen everything. Laura's a zealot, that's no surprise. But this . . ." He shook his head. "Anticars, most likely. And bacteria."

"Explain." My words slurred through the mask.

"Anticarcinomals have been standard cancer treatment for a century. They work, but they can't be used with transplants. Period."

"Am I rejecting my lung?"

"We may have caught it in time. The pneumonia's worse. I've loaded you with meds. Lie still." To the others, "I can't believe she'd do it."

"I can." Harmon's voice was hard. "Zack, this settles it. We have to act."

"On whose behalf?"

Frederick Mantiet cleared his throat. "His."

"Nonsense." Hopewell.

"Zack, I've changed sides. I'm not with Laura. Nor you. I'm with him."

I giggled. Perhaps the meds were making me giddy. "A side of two."

A long silence.

"Three." Everyone looked to Harmon. He blushed. "The city's been bombed. A few years ago the fish sprayed a virus. Laura represents a cohesive power, one that's recognized. The Navy's another. Would you proclaim a third? Under what authority? Shall we risk civil war, with fish overhead?"

I breathed deeply. The new canister seemed to help.

Hopewell radiated his disapproval. "We'll discuss it privately, Harmon."

The door opened. Annie flew to my side. "Don' leave me 'lone again!"

Tolliver peered in after her. "Is he alive?"

I growled, "Yes."

Dr. Avery bared my arm. I felt a mild sting.

"No surprise. You're too ornery to . . ." He shook his head. "Midshipman Tolliver reporting for duty, sir."

"Take Annie and Alexi. And, whatshisname, Bezrel." It was hard to concentrate. "Get them decent food. And a bath . . ."

I fell into sleep.

I sat bolt upright. "What time is it?"

Tolliver leapt half out of his seat. "Christ, don't do that. It's like a visitation from the dead."

"Don't blaspheme." The vapormask muffled my voice.

"It's four in the morning."

I was in a bed. The lights were low. "What are you doing here?"

"Someone had to keep an eye on you. Everyone else is asleep."

"We're at Hopewell's?"

"Yes, sir. Dr. Avery knocked you out for your own good."

I said hopefully, "I feel better."

"You don't look it." Tolliver stretched. "Do you need anything?"

"Bring me up to date."

"No news of late. Last evening Ms. Triforth's joeys were swarming about Centraltown like disturbed bees."

"What's Hopewell doing?"

"Sleeping." Tolliver turned down the light. "As you'll be, in another moment."

Thereafter, he refused to answer my questions. Eventually I dozed, to pleasant fantasies of his court-martial.

In the morning I overrode Tolliver's objections and got out of bed to find a bathroom. Once there, I sat clawing for breath. Getting up had been a mistake.

When I tottered back, my breakfast was waiting, along with the committee of the whole. I glanced around at the somber faces. Frederick Mantiet. Zack Hopewell and his wife; Harmon and Sarah Branstead. Dr. Avery. Tolliver and Alexi. Even poor Bezrel, attempting manfully not to look overwhelmed.

I forced myself to sit casually, rather than fall panting on the bed. "A ceremonial occasion, I gather?" No one spoke. I demanded, "Are you handing me back?"

Mantiet snorted. "No, worse. We want you to lead us." He held up his hand to forestall my reply. "In a ceremonial capacity, of course."

"What does *that* mean?"

"Lend us your name." Frederick's gesture included the group. "If we strike suddenly, we might bring Laura down. We want to do it in the name of a legitimate government. Hopefully, it would reduce the bloodshed."

"And then?"

"Independence, as before. What would change is the morality of the government. We wouldn't—"

"Not in my name." I sounded bitter. "But why even ask? Who'd know on whose behalf you act, with me sick in bed?"

"I'd know." Zack Hopewell, his voice like flint. "I will not found a regime on a lie."

"I'm sorry, then. But, no."

Frederick glanced at his companions. "I told you."

Harmon said, "Nick, what will you do if we defeat Laura on our own?"

"Do? I'm not sure. But revolution isn't the answer. It is an affront to Lord God. It's my duty to prevent that." I stopped, panting. "If you succeed you will be damned, and every soul on your planet will writhe in Lord God's hell. I've condemned myself, and I know nothing in the universe is worth that." I realized I spoke through tears.

Mantiet said carefully, "Suppose we ask you to reestablish the Government. Some of us need assurance our past acts won't be deemed treason. We've all had some knowledge of the underground."

Uncaring of the consequences, I flung aside my vapor-mask. "You'd bargain with Lord God's covenant? Treason is treason! Don't ask me to condone—"

Tolliver said, "Sir, don't you see they're trying to submit—"

I rounded on him, my nails clawing at the sheets. "How dare you! What is your rank?"

"I only—"

"Answer!"

"Midshipman, sir."

I struggled to my feet. "Do middies make policy? Do they question their Captains?" My pulse pounded. "Out of the room!"

"I'm sorry if—"

"At once!" I waited until the door closed before sitting shakily. "Where's my wife?"

Avery said, "She had a panic attack in the night. She's under sedation."

"Lord Christ." If it was a plea, it wouldn't be blasphemy. For a moment I closed my eyes. Back to the business at hand. "Knowledge of their plots is not itself treason. But no deals; that's for politicians. The subject is closed."

Another silence. Zack Hopewell said to the others, "I told you."

"Stop that! If you all knew what I'd say, why hound me?"

"You leave us few choices, boy. Submit to Laura, follow you to Lord knows what disgrace, or act on our own with no color of authority."

I waited. Casually my hand stole to the vapormask. I slipped it on. Lord God, my chest ached.

Harmon said, "Tell him what we decided, Zack."

"He knows." Zack Hopewell sat by my side. "What now, Captain?" His steady eyes met mine. "We commit to you."

I swallowed. Yesterday I was a prisoner, and now . . . "Does Triforth have an army?"

"About fifty men, as best I can judge. Far more than we have. Some are at Governor's Manse, where she's set up command. She has others running errands around town. She's set up a governing council; they've commandeered the public warehouses and taken over food distribution. Volksteader and Palabee are with her."

Harmon added, "They're well armed. They found plenty of firearms in the arsenals your people left behind."

I said, "Our best chance would be a direct attack on the Manse. If we take her, the revolution may collapse." I sat up warily, reached for my clothes.

Sarah Branstead stirred. "Where do you think you're going? You need quiet, and meds."

"To the Manse."

Dr. Avery shook his head. "Don't leave that bed. Not if you want to live." I ignored him. How could I send these men to do my work? Avery flared, "Damn it, the meds were just taking hold! Look at your face; I'll bet your temp is up three points in the last half hour!"

Frederick said, "In any event we're not all that well armed, and we won't risk your life."

I thought of Annie, and Triforth's casual contempt. "I'm going to the Manse, if I have only Bezrel to drive me. Come if you will, or remain behind." Ignoring the women's presence, I threw on my clothes. The effort left me weak.

Hopewell said, "Leave him, Frederick. It's his life to spend." For a moment I saw Father's dim presence. "We'll take both helis, Captain. There's room for all of us."

Alexi cleared his throat. "May I go too, Mr. Seafort?"

I nodded, short of breath. He offered his arm. As he guided me outside to the smaller heli, Tolliver fell in behind.

Others piled in around us. I tried to think. She had fifty well-armed men . . . We lifted off. If only the Government had destroyed the arsenals, locked them safely away . . .

I raised my mask. "Change of plans."

Harmon twisted in his seat. "What's the—"

"Go to the spaceport."

"But why—"

"All those supplies for the Venturas . . ."

His face came alight. "By God! Semi-cannons, smart grenades, shoulder missiles . . ."

Surely, Laura Triforth had remembered them too. After all, it was she who'd told me about them. On the other hand, she'd only had a few days, and a lot to organize. "They may be gone."

"Or guarded."

Grim minutes later both helis were back on the ground in front of the terminal. Tolliver conferred with Mantiet; he took two men, circled the terminal, and headed for the airfield.

In a few minutes he was back. "Guards. I spotted five."

"Can you take them?"

"We have a dozen men, not counting yourself. If we had a diversion . . ."

I tried to think. Diversion. I could manage one. "Zack, guard your heli. Tolliver, take everyone else and work your way along the edge of the field. I'll pilot this machine."

"What will you do, sir?"

I frowned at the foolish question. "Land, of course. Talk to them."

Zack Hopewell spoke first. "They'll kill you."

"Possibly." I spoke as little as I could. The ride had tired me more than I'd anticipated. A dull knot in my chest refused to dissipate. "Get going."

Tolliver looked at me, thought better of speaking. "Aye

aye, sir. I'll need twenty minutes or so to circle the guards."
He saluted.

Bezrel swallowed. "May I go with them? I'm a good shot.
I've practiced."

I started to chuckle, had to cough instead. Finally I could
speak. "When you were ship's boy?"

"No, sir. After I was promoted to middy. At Admiralty
House. Please let me help." He gulped, aware of the offense
of arguing with a Captain. "I know I've been no use."

"I promised to keep you safe."

"Yes, sir. But am I to sit out of danger while you fight?
I'm a midshipman. I took the oath like everyone else."

I said through the window, "Bezrel, wait with the hel—" I
coughed uncontrollably. When I stopped, my pants were
damp and it took all my concentration to keep my hands
from trembling. I looked at the boy, said weakly, "Give Mr.
Bezrel a gun. Middy, go with the other men."

He grew three inches. "Aye aye, sir." I couldn't bear the
look in his eyes.

Hopewell waited next to my window, rifle in hand. "I'll
watch the minutes for you."

"Thank you." I hoped he couldn't see the stain on my
pants. I breathed as deeply as I could, trying to oxygenate.
My chest burned with each breath. I closed my eyes.

The voice woke me. "It's half an hour."

I flipped the switches.

Hopewell's hand came through the window, tightened on
mine. "Go in the grace of our Lord."

"And thee." I motioned him clear, lifted off.

Either his benediction or my rest had succored me; the
world was no longer pulsing. I stayed low, swung away toward the road so that I could come in high. I took altitude,
swooped back to the field. Piles of supplies covered with
tarps sat on the far end of the tarmac, much as I'd seen them
weeks before.

I circled the runway on which the shuttles once landed,
then headed downfield toward the guards, who watched with
weapons drawn. I tilted the heli so they could see I was
alone.

I landed about thirty feet from the nearest piles of cargo.

Two men came forward, their laser rifles aimed at my head. As they approached I took several slow breaths and slipped off the vapormask.

I sang out, "I'm Captain Seafort. I was supposed to meet a shuttle here." Frantically I stifled a bout of coughing.

"Shuttle? Are you glitched?"

"The last shuttle, for the Station. They told me to meet it."

He stared at me, then guffawed. "You're a slow one. It left four days—"

The buzz of a bolt; he whirled in time to see a companion fall. He spun back to me, raising the rifle. "You bast—"

I shot him through the chest. Another guard ducked in reflex and fired. His shot hit the heli door. Hot rivulets of metal sizzled on my shoulder. I jerked convulsively. He aimed again. I couldn't turn far enough away to—

He went down shrieking. Blood poured onto the tarmac from where his leg had stood.

Another bolt bubbled the tarmac in front of me. I thumbed the switches, willed the blades to turn. Were my electronics hit? More ragged firing. Eons later I had lift. I yanked back on the stick and gunned the throttle.

I soared above the field, straining to breathe. I fumbled for the vapormask, but it fell to the floor.

Aloft, I watched the remaining guards go down. I held on to consciousness, dropped the heli near a supply pile. I managed to flip the switches before I passed out.

I came to on my own, minutes later. My eyes bulged from the effort to breathe. Desperately I clawed for the vapormask, found it.

It was little help. I sat as still as I could, chest heaving, while our war party ran across the field.

Tolliver glanced at me and cursed. He ran to the door, reached through to the caller. "Hopewell, respond!"

A moment later came the reply. "Ready."

"Get out here, fast." Tolliver didn't wait for an answer. He dashed back to the supply piles, yanking tarps aside. He beckoned the men. "Take these!" He ran from pile to pile until he'd found what he wanted.

Hopewell's heli landed alongside mine; men threw in weapons with frantic haste. Scant seconds later they climbed

aboard. Tolliver thrust me out of the pilot's seat; this time I
had no objection. Bezrel squeezed alongside me.

We lifted off. Tolliver said tersely, "We'll have to be fast,
if we want him to see it."

"I'll last." It came out a croak. I turned to my right. A tear
trickled down Bezrel's cheek. He looked at me, whispered,
"I tried. I couldn't do it."

"Do what?"

"Shoot a man." His shoulders shook.

I nodded. For me, it was all in a day's work.

In Mantiet's small heli rode Tolliver, myself, Bezrel,
Mantiet, and one of the hands. The rest were piled in
Hopewell's machine. Tolliver leaned toward me. "Can you
talk?"

"Yes." A word at a time.

"What do we do when we get to the Manse?"

"Set down." Die.

"Where?"

"The lawn." It seemed as good a place as any.

He looked to see if I meant it. "And then?"

"Go inside."

"Captain, pay attention. What do you want to do? Should I
organize an attack?"

"Land." I fought for breath. "Get me . . . on my feet." If
that was still possible. "I'll go in. If they . . ." I trailed off,
coughing. "If they fight . . . blow the Manse down."

"You can't just walk in."

"I'm the Government." And when I fell, the Government
would be no more. Perhaps I should put Alexi next in command. I giggled: a government with amnesia.

It didn't matter; we were most likely flying to our doom.
If even one guard had gotten off a message during our attack . . .

"Take our men in with you," Tolliver urged.

Hopewell would need them in the fight that would follow
my death. No, it wouldn't matter; we weren't strong enough
to prevail regardless. It was too confusing. "All right."

We cruised over downtown, toward the Manse at the
southwest edge of town. If the Governor's house had been

near the government buildings, Governor Saskrit would be dead, and the colony under martial law.

If I couldn't walk . . . How could I make my entrance? They'd never respect me if I crawled . . .

I slapped my leg, forcing away the mist. I would walk into the Manse. I no longer had need to husband my strength.

We crossed downtown. "Come in low." I thought I'd spoken loudly, but had to repeat it before Tolliver heard. He dropped us lower, called to the other heli to follow.

"Mantiet."

"Yes?"

"Do you have . . . kind of . . . megaphone?"

He thought. "Actually, I do. There's a compartment under my seat."

"I need it."

"Right." He beckoned to the farmhand. With much swearing and grumbling the two men managed to squeeze onto the deck while Mantiet fished in the compartment. A minute later he handed me a small battery-powered speaker. "The Manse is just ahead."

"Come in . . . fast. Land . . . my door facing the Manse."

"Aye aye, sir."

"Bezrel, be ready to jump out. Get me on my feet."

"Aye aye, sir." The boy's voice trembled with excitement.

In the back Mantiet and his soldier checked their laser rifles.

"Who has . . . shoulder missiles?"

"Harmon."

I nodded, too exhausted to speak.

Tolliver dropped the heli like a stone, spinning it so my door faced the Manse. Two guards standing on the raised porch gaped, but made no move for their arms. Bezrel leapt out, but Tolliver was already running around the heli, brushing him aside. He hauled me out of the seat, set me on my feet, steadied my arm.

I shook myself loose as the larger heli came down about forty feet away. At the drone of its motor, the guards grabbed their weapons.

I lurched forward, croaking into the megaphone. "I'm Seafort!" The damned thing wasn't on. I fumbled for the button. "I'm Captain Seafort, commanding!" My voice sounded—I'd never heard the like. "Where's Triforth? I need her."

"You're what?" The guard hesitated, caught off balance.

"Get Laura Triforth, you fool." I took two steps, swaying. Bezrel proffered his shoulder. I clutched it, chest heaving. I raised the megaphone. "Is Triforth here? I'll . . . wait inside." I beckoned to Hopewell and Branstead in the second heli, hoping the familiar faces of the planters would help.

The heli door slammed. Zack Hopewell and Tolliver toward me. From the heli Harmon bellowed at the guards. "Don't stand there gawking! Help him! Can't you see he's hurt?"

The guards moved to block the door. One leveled his weapon. "Stay right there. We'll have to call Ms. Triforth." Reluctantly Hopewell came to a halt.

"Nonsense!" I thrust Bezrel forward, leaning heavily on his shoulder. I reached the first stone step. "Where's Triforth, you dolt?"

"Prong yourself." His rifle swung to me.

Door and guards disintegrated in an awesome flash. The shock hurled us to the ground. Bezrel flung himself over me as debris rained.

Feet pounded. Someone screamed orders. Men dashed past, leapt onto the shattered porch, through the blasted door. Rifles buzzed; something crashed and splintered. Dazed, half-deafened, I tried to sit. My chest was caught; I couldn't breathe. I gagged. Something salty filled my mouth and I spit it out. I wheezed, "Get me up!"

I had no strength to help; Bezrel hauled at me until I sat. He strained to raise me. Zack Hopewell took my arm, lifted me. "You have no time left, son. To the clinic."

"When we . . . get Triforth."

"Suicide is a mortal sin."

I shook my head. "Triforth." I sucked at air.

Frederick Mantiet dashed out of the Manse. "A dozen men. Half of them surrendered. The rest didn't get the chance. Her other forces are off somewhere. How's Seafort?"

"He's dying." Hopewell.

"I'm all right." Fifty men . . . we'd taken out three at the hauler office; another five at the spaceport, a dozen here . . . how many did that make? I couldn't think.

Hopewell and Mantiet carried me to the porch, set me down. Frederick said, "We have the Manse. We can declare the Government."

Why couldn't they understand? "Triforth."

"We can—"

I gripped his arm. "Triforth. Get our people out."

"But—"

"Now!" I tried to scream, hadn't the breath.

Hopewell said soberly, "We put him in charge. It's no time to argue."

"But—all right." Mantiet ran back into the Manse.

Minutes later we were crammed into the large heli. "Where?" Tolliver was at the controls.

"Try . . . warehouses."

We rose, leaving the shattered Manse behind, empty.

Harmon raised his voice over the engine's drone. "It's only a mile or so. She may even have heard the missile we fired."

I shrugged. It could make no difference. We were locked in a fight to the death. "Someone . . . give me a shirt."

"What?"

"White. For armbands."

"Christ, yes." Harmon ripped at his buttons. A minute later he was ripping his shirt into strips. "Everyone put one on."

I gasped, "Shoot anyone . . . without one." It was all I could manage.

"Look!" Tolliver pounded the dash. Two Naval helis were parked by the warehouse.

"Down." Mantiet was tense.

"Hang on." Tolliver swooped; my stomach churned. He asked, "Should we take out their helis?"

I shook my head. "We may need . . ."

We hit the ground with a thud, bounced. Tolliver shouted, "Sorry. Move out! Split into two groups, me and Frederick!"

In a moment they were gone, leaving me alone and dazed. I sat, chest heaving. Thoughts drifted to Annie, abandoned in

298 **=** David Feintuch

her sedation. To Jerence Branstead, lost in his hopeless joy of his juice. To Laura Triforth, inside with her men, if she was indeed here.

A blast of grenades. The firefight had begun. Should we have disabled the other helis? If Triforth's men escaped . . .

I cursed. We'd parked near Laura's two Naval craft. If the rebels fled toward me, they'd have their own helis and ours as well. Our party would be helpless. Slowly, laboriously, I slid across to the pilot's seat.

More blasts. I searched for the smoke of a shoulder missile, but saw none. What was happening? I coughed, hung on grimly, managed not to pass out. The effort left me feeble.

Footsteps. I flipped the switches, started the blades turning. The door swung open. I turned. "Did you get her?"

Laura Triforth's eyes blazed. "Take us up, you son of a bitch!" Her face was smudged, her blouse torn.

I gaped.

"Go, or I shoot!"

"Right." I twisted the throttle, yanked back on the collective. We lifted straight up. I labored to stay alive.

She grinned, breathing hard. "I should have killed you outright."

"Yes."

"Well, you don't have long."

"What did you . . . put in me?" We continued to lift.

"I countered the antirejection drugs. Take me to the Manse!" Her gun was leveled at my chest.

"Why . . . do it?" Two thousand feet.

"It would have been so dramatic. In fact it may still be. I'll rush you to the clinic, just too late. The heroic Captain, last of the old order . . ." Three thousand feet.

"Why not . . . just shoot?"

"And be blamed for your death? I don't need to carry that baggage. The Manse! What are you doing?"

"Altitude."

"We're not flying to the Venturas, you idiot." Five thousand. I made no answer. Her pistol leveled at my stomach. "On the other hand, I can shoot and let you disappear. Put your damned hand on the cyclic and head for the Manse!"

"Yes." I rehearsed. It would have to be one smooth motion. I wouldn't have another chance. Not her pistol; I didn't have the strength. "Why . . . Manse?"

"My men are there. You have two sec—"

I tilted the ship, allowing myself to fall forward into the dash. It helped. My left hand slid across to the key. I turned it, yanked it free. The engine stopped. I flung my arm out the window.

If the engine died while the ignition was on, the blades would autorotate. But Naval designers assumed the pilot knew what he was doing; once the key was removed the bearings locked, the blades feathered, providing hardly any lift.

We dropped with sickening speed.

"I'll kill you!"

"Yes."

"Give me the key!"

I shook my head. "Shoot."

"You'll die too!"

I nodded. Thirty-five hundred. We spun as we fell.

"For Christ's sake, start the engine!"

"Throw away . . . pistol."

"I'll see you in hell first!"

Oh, yes. She'd see me there. Two thousand. The sun circled crazily.

"Seafort!" For the first time her voice held fear.

I tried to speak, choked. I gasped, "Pistol."

"We'll be killed!"

"Pistol!" Fifteen hundred. The world spun.

With a shriek of rage she flung the pistol past my head. "For Christ's sake, the key!"

I pulled my hand in, fumbled at the dash. Dizzy, I closed my eyes, felt for the keyhole.

"Hurry!"

In. I jammed it to the right. I opened my eyes. One thousand. Flip the switches.

Nothing. Off, on again. With a cough the engine caught. Five hundred. Was the world spinning past, or was it me? I no longer knew.

"Level out!" she screamed. Her hands braced against the dash.

I coughed forever, swallowing salty saliva, fighting to bring the ship under control. I'd taken us straight up; we shouldn't be far from the warehouses. They were . . . there. I swooped to the north. Next to me Laura clung to the dash, white-faced. We dropped alongside the warehouse with a crash.

In the cloud of dust, a feral growl. Laura Triforth's long fingers closed around my throat. She shook me like a rag doll.

The world hazed red. As I jounced I saw Mantiet and Tolliver racing toward us. My hand crept to Laura's, fell away. I waited for the end.

Abruptly Triforth yanked open the door and bolted. I sucked at air as Tolliver gave chase. Mantiet leaned against the heli, gasping. "Five dead, on our side. Your Naval men are alive. So's Zack." Thank Lord God.

Tolliver tackled Triforth, swarmed atop her. He seized a shock of her hair, raised her head off the ground. His fist slammed down.

It was over.

I sat exhausted, stinking, shaking helplessly as I labored for breath. "Comm room."

"What?"

"Radios. Hookup. Where?"

"I don't know." Mantiet thought. "Triforth broadcast from the Governor's Manse, the first day."

"Back."

"Let us take you to the clinic."

"After."

"You lunatic." His look held awe. "I'll get the others." He ran off.

Moments later we were again in the air, Tolliver at the controls. Dazed and cuffed, Triforth sat in the back seat between Mantiet and Hopewell.

"Arrest . . . Palabee and Volksteader."

"We'll have to find them first."

I nodded.

When we set down they carried me into the Manse. Other

than the main entrance, little damage was visible. A few walls were scorched, and one room . . . the sight was not for the squeamish.

We found the Governor's broadcast center in the basement. I had them put me in the swivel chair at the desk. Branstead and Mantiet cursed and fumbled with the switches.

"Video."

They looked up. I waved at the holocamera.

Tolliver muttered, "I'll do it, but it won't be pretty." At first I thought he meant the focus. No, he meant me. I must be a sight. He swung the holocamera to me, turned it on.

Harmon looked up. "We have a tightbeam linkup with Orbit Station. The station will beam it back down on all channels."

"Station . . . is abandoned."

"Their puter responds, though. Say when."

Annie would be pleased. Her Nicky on the holo. She'd hold her head high when she shopped . . .

"Mr. Seafort?"

I drifted back. "Now."

The light went green. I spoke.

No sound came.

I heaved for breath, spoke again. "This is . . . Captain Nicholas Seafort . . . commanding . . . United Nations forces." I struggled not to cough. "On behalf of . . . lawful United . . . Nations Government, I hereby . . ." The room grayed. I gasped at air. Zack Hopewell's eyes bored into mine. ". . . declare martial law . . . throughout Hope Nation." I had little time. The room drifted in a slow, alluring circle. I spoke firmly into the approaching dark. "The revolutionary . . . treason has been . . . put down . . . Triforth under arrest."

"I do appoint . . . as military . . . Governor of Hope Nation . . . Zachary . . . Hopewell, of Hopewell Plantation." I searched, found his astonished eyes. There was more to say. I tried, stopped. I tried again. Chest heaving, airless, I waved to Branstead. The broadcast lights dimmed. I reached for a breath, found none. "Tolliver!" It was a gasp.

He dashed across the room. I coughed endlessly. No relief

came. I gagged. A mouthful of bright red liquid cascaded onto my white shirt. I looked down, horrified, and up again at Tolliver. The room pulsed to red.

He scooped me in his arms and ran to the waiting heli.

18

A mask was strapped to my face. Bright lights probed, disembodied voices echoed. "The lung's lost, he's septic as hell. Prep him fast, we operate in five minutes." A needle stung my arm.

Black.

Drifting. Misery. Lights, faces.

Pain.

I couldn't swallow; tubes blocked my throat. I couldn't breathe, but something breathed for me. I slept, awakened, slept.

Pain.

Sleep.

I awoke flat on my back, to the rushing sound of air, silence, air. My chest inflated to the sound, and it hurt.

"You have a hell of a constitution or you wouldn't be with us." I squinted, focused on the floating face. Dr. Abood, of the clinic. I tried to speak, couldn't make a sound. It frightened me and I tried to cry out. Silence.

"We yanked what was left of your lung, sewed you up, and pumped you full of antibiotics."

I gestured at my mouth. I had to use my right hand; my left arm was full of drip lines.

"You've been on a respirator for three days. You need to start breathing on your own. Can you try?"

Tentatively I tried a breath. Pain lanced through my chest.

"Work at it; we have to wean you soon. If you develop pneumonia again, it's all over." Abruptly he left. I tried to gesture him back, hadn't the strength. My fingernails clawed at the sheets.

"I'm here, sir, if you need anything." Tolliver, haggard

and disheveled. His chair was alongside the bed. We were in a small cubicle, surrounded by poles, machines, monitors.

I nodded, drifted off to sleep.

When I woke Tolliver was standing over me. He'd had a change of clothes, if not much rest. His eyes were sunken. "Good evening, sir. Try to breathe." I shook my head. "Please, sir. The doctor says it's urgent."

I caught the machine's rhythm, breathed ahead of it. Misery.

"Again."

Who was he, a middy, to tell me what to do? I beckoned him to leave.

"I don't understand, sir. Write what you're trying to say." He held a pad near my hand.

I scrawled, "Go away."

"Breathe on your own, sir."

I rapped the pad, livid with rage.

He ignored me.

Wild with fury I hauled at the bedrails, heaved myself into a sitting position, ignoring the excruciating pain. I grasped his jacket, unable to spit my curses. In a frenzy I tore at the tubes alongside the rail. The monitors clanged their warnings. Damn him in hell forever! I'd break him! I'd destroy him utterly. I'd take us both off duty and call challenge—

The door flew open. Dr. Abood dashed in. Tolliver stood stolidly, his face expressionless, while I pounded his chest. I turned to the doctor. Get the man away from me! Why didn't he understand? I turned back to Tolliver, who stared at the silent respirator.

Only then did I realize I was breathing.

"Where's Annie?" My throat was still raw.

"Here in the clinic, sir. Alexi—Mr. Tamarov has gone to see her. She's, ah, all right, I guess."

I didn't like the sound of that. "Does she talk to you?"

Tolliver said, "Not really, sir. She's sort of dreaming. Awake and dreaming."

I turned my head. Annie was beyond my help. Nothing awaited me if I recovered. Living . . . didn't seem worth the bother.

An endless series of visitors interrupted my reveries. Among them Alexi, regarding me anxiously, saying little. I dozed. When I woke he was gone.

Frederick Mantiet came to visit, offering encouraging words. Though we'd become allies, I was wary in his presence.

Not long after he left, Zack Hopewell looked in. I bade him sit.

"The last of Palabee's men surrendered this morning."

I grunted. Hopewell folded his hands in his lap. "Seafort, I want out of this job. I'm no military Governor."

"Neither was Joshua."

"Joshua led his people to the promised land. If anything, I'm holding them back from it."

"Triforth's Republic wasn't the promised land."

"I know that." His tone was sharp. "Else I wouldn't have joined you."

"You'd have violated your oath?"

"I'd have tended my crops!" He waved as if to banish the issue. "I swore no oath to restore a government that had fallen."

"Then why did you support us?"

"Because . . . hell and damnation, boy. Because there was no right. Because we're in chaos. Because you're a just man."

"Just!" I snorted. "You know me so little."

He shook his head. "How little you know yourself." He raised his voice, overriding my reply. "Palabee and Volksteader demand to be released. Triforth insists on a civil trial."

"Have them all sent for interrogation. Mantiet too."

"Frederick? He helped you!"

"He renounced his confession." Could it matter any longer? I brushed away the thought. "I want to know the truth."

He answered, "And I want Palabee and Volksteader tried or released."

"After interrogation. Anyway, I should be out of here in a couple of days. We'll see."

For the first time Hopewell smiled. "I'm glad for that."

"Thank you." I lapsed silent. My convalescence was troubling. The pain meds helped, but I felt alone, isolated. Dutifully I did my breathing exercises and walked slowly in the hallway. From time to time I stopped at Annie's room.

Alexi visited with me, chatted awkwardly. Harmon Branstead brought Jerence to see me, but kept a stern eye on him throughout.

Tolliver came. I hadn't seen him for several days. I glowered.

"I'm sorry if I was, er, unsympathetic when you had the tube in your throat. But when you lay there as if you were giving up, I wanted to tear out that respirator, make you breathe." He turned away from my gaze.

"Damn you, Tolliver, why can't you let me hate you as I want?"

He turned back, startled. "I thought you did, sir."

"I've yearned for nothing more than an excuse to cashier you." My face reddened at the admission.

"Will you?"

"I can't. There's no one to take your place."

"Yes, sir."

I relented. "And I don't want to replace you. Continue as my aide."

He blurted, "You mean that?"

Astonished, I could only stare. He stammered, "I'm sorry, sir. Thank you. I mean—thank you."

"Find me a place to sleep when I'm well. We'll reopen Admiralty House and work from there."

"Aye aye, sir. What will we do?"

"I don't know yet." I sat back on my bed. "Dismissed, Mr. Tolliver."

His salute was crisper than his first. "Aye aye, sir."

"Now do you believe me?" Frederick Mantiet sat in front of the Manse, head in hands, shielding his eyes from the bright sun.

I knew what he was feeling. It would pass. "Yes."

"So . . . I worked to establish a republic. Are you going to try me like Palabee and Volksteader?"

"No."

"Why not?"

A workman mortared a stone into the porch. "With you it was just words. You didn't take overt action, even if you kept yourself informed of the plot against us."

"Words can be treason."

"Are you baiting me, Frederick? In any event you redeemed yourself." The porch was nearly complete, though it would be many years before it aged to the patina of the foundation. I wondered if the Manse would be standing then, or whether the fish would have dropped another, more destructive rock.

"If I'm free, I suppose I should go home. I have to set matters right."

"Or you could stay and help us. Would you care to join the Government?"

"No." He rubbed his eyes. "Not your Government; I'm opposed to it. And anyway, I don't have the personality. I'm too abrasive."

So was I, but I was saddled with the job. The Admiral's words had been, "Carry on. You're in charge." Soon *Catalonia* would arrive. It had been—how long?—two days since I'd left the hospital, Dr. Abood's admonishments ringing in my ears.

"Captain, when will you hold the trials?"

"I don't know, Frederick. Mrs. Volksteader is coming to see me in a few minutes, and Palabee wants to talk also. Then I'll decide."

"We planters are the foundation of Hope Nation."

"But treason is treason." I stood, shading my eyes as I peered into the sun. "Is that her heli?"

"Looks like it. I'll leave you alone."

I straightened my tie, smoothed my hair while the Volksteaders' heli landed. It felt good to be in uniform again, though my shirt rasped against my sensitive chest. Thanks to daily bone-growth stimulation my ribs were fast healing, but my skin was still tender.

When the blades floated to a stop Mrs. Volksteader climbed out. Sarah Branstead followed. I hadn't expected her. The discussion might be awkward.

We greeted each other civilly, shook hands, found seats on

the rebuilt porch. Leota Volksteader got to the point. "It's not fair of you to hold Arvin. Let him go."

I temporized. "What is your role in this, Mrs. Branstead?"

She shook her head firmly. "Oh, no. When we last met it was 'Sarah.' Nothing changes that."

I smiled. "Thank you. Still, why are you here?"

"The Volksteaders are good friends. I wanted to come, and Harmon approves."

"Arvin acted unwisely, Mrs.—er, Sarah. He became involved with treason."

Leota Volksteader raised her hands. "We've never been political. We're not among the biggest plantations or the most developed. We can't afford to offend anyone in power. Your Government collapsed, and Laura said she was declaring a republic. If we'd refused to attend, she'd have remembered and held it against us. What were we to do?"

I shook my head. "Arvin took part in their meetings, let the plotters use his haulers and equipment, gave them aid and comfort."

"Which is no more than we did for you! How can you be so ungrateful?"

I said, "What are you talking about?"

Sarah Branstead said, "I was there, Mr. Seafort. Surely you haven't forgotten."

"Ladies, I—" I searched the haze of my memories. "You'll have to explain."

"You visited the Bransteads," Leota said. "With your lieutenant Mr. Tamarov. As we were leaving, I took you aside so Arvin could talk to him. Don't you recall?"

I did, vaguely. "Go on."

"Arvin and I had decided it was best to speak privately with your officer. That way, the conversation would be unofficial, so you could deny it if need be."

"What did Arvin tell him?"

"Don't pretend you don't know. Arvin said to watch out for Laura, that she was going to move against you. Your man said he'd tell you right away. And then you left, and—and—"

"Laura blew up the hauler," Sarah Branstead finished. "And nearly killed our son."

My hand tightened on the chair. The explosion. Eddie

Boss, his arm broken, hauling Alexi out of the shattered car. "He never told me," I said slowly.

"For heaven's sake, why not?"

"Jerence was with us. Alexi wanted to speak but I told him to wait." Alexi's coma, his amnesia, were my fault, then. I'd prevented him from doing his duty. I lay back, suddenly weak. Take this burden from me, Lord. Don't let me hurt anyone else.

"What a fiasco," Sarah said slowly. Her hand squeezed my arm. "How you must feel, Captain."

I looked up to her. "If you knew Ms. Triforth blew up the hauler, what was Harmon doing on the dais with her?"

Sarah said fiercely, "Do you think we knew then that it was Laura? I'd have killed her myself! If you don't believe that, send *me* to interrogation! Leota only told us last week, when she asked our help for Arvin."

"Still, why was Harmon there? He was committing treason."

"You can't believe that, or you'd arrest him too. We're like the Volksteaders, not big enough to fight the government. We had to go along with Triforth, at least for the time being."

A young aide brought us lemonade from the Manse; I sipped the cold drink and waited until he'd left. "Harmon switched sides, though." It was too confusing. "I'll think it over. There's no point in talking further."

Leota persisted, "Will there be a trial?"

"There doesn't have to be. Not under martial law."

"You'd let him go?"

Sarah took her arm. "That's not what he means," she said gently. "Leave it be. He'll do right."

"But—" Protesting, Leota Volksteader let Sarah quiet her. She said her good-byes and left.

I sipped at lemonade in the hot summer sun and considered whether to slaughter her husband.

19

Tolliver, Bezrel, and I reopened Admiralty House. I decrypted the puters while Tolliver fussed in the mechanical room resetting the climate controls. In the two weeks since we'd left, the place had acquired a disused look, a dank and musty atmosphere. Perhaps I only imagined it.

We established comm links with Orbit Station. William, in his impersonal manner, confirmed every few hours that he had nothing new to report. When our ships Fused home, the remaining fish had disappeared within hours.

Annie languished in the clinic, unable to emerge from her daze. Our name came up for an apartment, and I had her moved the same day. Emmett Branstead found a nurse to stay with her.

Meanwhile, Zack Hopewell struggled with the details of government. By now the streets were cleared, and crews were demolishing or shoring weakened buildings. As before, looters were shot, but few were found. Hopewell and I met each day, and faced a similar question: what now?

At Admiralty House I settled myself in the anteroom where Lieutenant Anton had presided, and before him Lieutenant Eiferts. No need now for a formal office. Bezrel ran errands for Tolliver and me, not the least of which was to bring us our meals. Though we had use of the softie dispenser and micro, I preferred getting our dinners at the terminal restaurant. For their part, the café was glad of the business, now that the fleet was gone.

Tolliver interrupted my reverie. "Captain, will you take a call from the jail?"

I looked past my feet propped on my desk. "Who, and why?"

"You agreed to see Mr. Palabee today, and they want to know where."

I sighed. "At the Manse."

"Aye aye, sir."

"Make it after dinner."

Tolliver could pilot me, or I could go myself. I'd reserved one Naval heli for our own use and loaned the others back to the civilian transport grid. Alexi had returned to his job, but kept his caller with him. I'd made sure of that.

My console lit; calls that previously would have been taken in our comm room went to me now. I flipped on the speaker. "Orbit Station to Admiralty House, please respond."

"Yes?"

"Good afternoon, Captain Seafort." William's solemn voice.

I blurted, "The fish?"

"No, Captain. Please stand by for a patch from a U.N.N.S. vessel."

"A ship? They've all sailed home."

"Stand by, please. *Catalonia,* go ahead."

I swung my chair around, dropping my feet to the floor, wincing at the unexpected pain. I still wasn't ready for sudden movements. "Seafort here."

"*Catalonia.* Captain Herbert Von Tilitz."

"Nicholas Seafort, sir. I believe you are senior to me."

"Yes." I remembered him as brisk, humorless, efficient. "You're groundside?"

"Yes, sir. At Admiralty House."

"We caught Admiral De Marnay's beacon. He said to pick you up. Do you have a shuttle, or should I send one down? We've seen no fish but I want to be out of here as soon as possible."

"We've no shuttles at Centraltown, but I understand there's one in the Venturas, sir."

"How many am I retrieving?"

"Five, sir."

"I'll send a shuttle down. I won't moor *Catalonia* at the Station; that's too risky. We'll approach near enough to send a gig over. Their puter will open for us and we'll take one of their smaller craft."

"Yes, sir. When?" A ship for home. Derek Carr. Peace.

"Figure . . ." He hesitated. "We'll get the shuttle tonight, but I'd rather land in daylight. We don't have an experienced shuttle pilot. Make it . . . 0700. That will give you time to pack." Was he joking? No, it couldn't be.

"Seven A.M. local time, sir. We'll be at the spaceport."

"Very well." His tone was dry. "This time don't miss your ride. There won't be another."

"I know, sir." We rang off. I bellowed, "Tolliver!"

He raced in, alarmed. "Yes, sir?"

I stood. "We're going home."

He stared, puzzled, until his eyes lit. "*Catalonia?*"

"Yes. In the morning."

"What a zark! Yes!" He slapped the leather chair in an outburst of joy. A side of him I hadn't known.

"Where's Bezrel?"

"I sent him for dinner, sir. He'll be back in a few—"

"After that, he's not to leave the building. Call the Manse; have them bring Annie and her nurse here in a heli tonight. Call Alexi. Tell him I order him back at once."

"Aye aye, sir. If the shuttle's not landing 'til morning—"

"At once. We'll spend the night here together."

"Aye aye, sir. What about Palabee, sir?"

Let Palabee be dam— No. "Have him brought here instead of the Manse."

Home. Thank you, Lord God. Though I don't deserve Your mercy, my companions do.

I sat making notes. I'd turn over civilian control to Hopewell unless Captain Von Tilitz ordered otherwise. I'd have to ask his agreement; he was senior now. Reclose Admiralty House, say good-bye to Harmon, take down the flag—

Harmon. I'd made him a promise. I sighed. After seeing Palabee, I'd send for Jerence. And what if Von Tilitz refused to take a civilian? I'd never considered that the decision might not be mine. Well, I'd given my word. I'd bring Jerence without telling Von Tilitz beforehand. He wouldn't take the time to return the boy, though he'd take his ire out on me afterward. No matter.

Derek Carr would be aboard. I wondered if he had come to hate me as much as Vax.

That evening I paced my office, wondering when dinner

would arrive, until I recalled that I'd eaten it an hour before. For the life of me I could not remember what it had been. "Tolliver, where's Palabee?"

"They'll be here at eight, sir. As we arranged."

I bit back an angry reply. Knowing my nerves were taut, Alexi and Bezrel managed to stay out of my way.

When the guards arrived, I made sure Tolliver had his pistol, ordered Palabee released from his fetters. He looked worn and tired.

"Well?"

His fingers drummed on the conference table. "I don't know where to begin. Have you decided on a trial?"

"I think so." If Hopewell would go through with it, after I was gone.

"For my life?"

"Treason is a capital charge."

"I don't think I committed treason, Captain."

"You rebelled against the Gov—"

"Was there a government to rebel against?" He eyed me steadily. "As Lord God is my witness, I didn't think you left us one. Your people vanished without notice, leaving no—"

"The civilian administration was intact."

"Bureaucrats."

"You're quibbling. In any event—"

Tolliver skidded into the doorway. "Captain, come now!" He didn't bother to salute. "Quick!"

As bizarre as Tolliver was, even he wouldn't summon me in that manner unless it was vital. "Watch Palabee," I told the guard as I left.

Tolliver was at the console. "Listen!"

"We got two of them. Three more aft." Von Tilitz, on *Catalonia,* his voice taut. "Plotting Fusion coordinates. Orbit Station, relay to Seafort. We're under heavy attack, we'll have to get out—*MIDSHIPS LASERS, FIRE AT WILL!*"

"Orbit Station to Admiralty House, please resp—"

"Seafort. I heard him. How many fish, William?"

"Three at his stern, two more amidships. Two more Defused between *Catalonia* and the station; I destroyed them."

"*Catalonia,* do you—"

"We're about to—Christ! Fire at will, all sides! I have six

fish. We're going to—" Alarm bells clanged. Von Tilitz's voice sharpened. "Partial decompression! They're on our tubes, we can't Fuse. Maxwell, how far are we from the atmosphere? God damn them! Get the lifepods off, then! Abandon—"

Silence.

I shouted, "William, relay!"

"There's nothing to relay, sir."

"Where's *Catalonia*?"

"Three point six two kilometers off my east lock, Captain. She has three fish astern, two at port. I see two . . . now three lifepods accelerating from the ship. Approximate entry to atmosphere twenty-two minutes. No further signals from *Catalonia*. Her laser fire has ceased."

Oh, Derek. Lord God save you, and all others aboard. I cried, "Fire on the fish!"

"They're too close; my laser fire would hit the ship. I judge it inadvisable."

"If they break through her hull—"

"One lifepod under attack. Veering away. I am firing at fish approaching pod." William was as calm as if delivering a stores report. "Fish has thrown at pod. Pod is disintegrating. Fish is hit. Fish is spewing material, presumed destroyed."

A faint signal. "Mayday, Mayday! U.N.S. *Catalonia* escape vessels to anyone! We are entering atmos . . ." The static increased.

"William, where will they land?"

"Calculating. Landing likely in Venturas, but fuel capacity of lifepods great enough to reach Eastern Continent. Actual fuel on board lifepods not known."

"Relay any signals from the pods."

"I will do that."

"Are fish still around *Catalonia*?"

"Yes, Captain. Five."

"Fire at *Catalonia* and the fish." By now it was unlikely anyone on board was still alive.

"I cannot fire at a U.N.N.S warship, Captain. My prime instructions do not allow that."

"There's no one left on *Catalonia*!"

"She's still a U.N. vessel."

My mind raced. "William, who is senior officer in Hope Nation system?"

The reply was immediate. "You are, Captain."

"Very well. Record. I do hereby decommission U.N.S. *Catalonia*. I order you to—"

"Firing at aliens with all lasers that bear. One fish down! Another is Fusing. Another hit. A third also. Remaining fish Fused."

Why weren't the lifepods signaling? The heat of the atmosphere would sear off their antennas, so they couldn't send further signals. If her crew carried callers, they'd contact us after they set down. Without callers . . . And would they find level ground to land? There wasn't much of it in the Venturas.

I yelled, "Tolliver!"

He jumped. "Jesus, I'm right here, sir!"

"Don't blaspheme. Pull all our helis out of the transport grid. I want them ready to search for the lifepods at first light."

"Aye aye, sir. Where?"

"Along the eastern seacoast for now. The crew will know enough to aim for Centraltown. If they don't sight survivors, have them fan out over the ocean toward the Venturas."

"Aye aye, sir."

"God damn those fish!"

Soberly he nodded. "Amen."

"Get Bezrel!"

A minute later the boy rushed in, breathless. "Midshipman Bez—"

"Wake Lieutenant Tamarov. I want you both on watch in the comm room. All frequencies. Report any signal other than local traffic."

"Aye aye, sir!"

I pounded my desk in frustration. I had no men, no equipment. There was little more I could do.

I spent the night the comm room with Alexi and the boy, straining to hear nonexistent signals through the static. By dawn I was bleary with exhaustion. By midmorning I was drowsing despite vast quantities of coffee.

We'd heard nothing. Three Naval helis with civilian pilots searched for survivors. Tolliver volunteered—begged—to go, but I forbade it. I'd need him with me if the lifepods were found.

Noon came and went. I summoned Hopewell. I also rang Harmon Branstead. Then, deciding I couldn't show favoritism, I called Mrs. Palabee, Mrs. Volksteader, Lawrence Plumwell, manager of Carr Plantation, and others among the minor planters.

We met at Admiralty House, around the conference table I'd grown to loathe. Had good news ever reached me at this table?

I waited impatiently for coffee to make the rounds, opened the meeting. "As you've no doubt heard, *Catalonia* was destroyed last night." Derek was dead. Later I'd find time to mourn.

"Lord God's mercy on them." Sarah Branstead's eyes brimmed.

"Amen. It's clear now that the fish are attracted by Fusion. But more important, they've returned to Hope Nation system. Orbit Station's puter is active and it destroyed several fish after they attacked *Catalonia*."

A moment of silence while they digested the news. "What now?" Plumwell.

Zack Hopewell stirred. "We're in the hands of Lord God. There's not much we can do. We have no ships, no lasers—"

"So much for your damned Navy," Plumwell said bitterly. "All your blundering, your supply fiascos . . . when there's trouble, you turn tail and ran."

"Enough," snapped Hopewell. "Captain Seafort didn't."

"He would have if he'd been able. He was on his way to—"

"I said enough!"

I cleared my throat. "That will get us nowhere. We have two choices. Carry on and hope the fish leave us alone, or send a party to the Venturas Base and see if their lasers can be reactivated."

Sitenbough, a plump young settler from west of the Triforth estate. "What good will their lasers do us, halfway across the planet?" He sounded peevish.

"Between Orbit Station and the Venturas Base, we may be able to get a crossfire on any aliens that approach."

Harmon Branstead said, "Would it help? The fish Defuse above us ready to attack. How much warning had we of the rock they dropped?"

"Very little. I said reopening the Venturas Base was an option." I pondered. "Manning the lasers would take at least a dozen men. We'd need civilian volunteers."

A rancorous discussion followed. In the end, the planters' consensus was to leave the fish alone, and hope they would do likewise to us. Hopewell, seeing my restlessness, brought the meeting to a close.

Afterward he and I sat in the anteroom, sipping coffee brought to us by the ubiquitous Bezrel.

"It's only a matter of time," I said. "They'll be back."

He nodded agreement. "There's another option you didn't raise." I cocked an eyebrow, waiting. "Send a couple of men to check the base, to see what it would take to reopen it. That might save some time in an emergency."

I should have thought of it myself. "Very well. I'll do that." I glanced at my watch. "There's still time to get there in daylight. I'll take Tolliver and Bezrel."

"Are you well enough?"

"Of course." Short of breath from time to time, but on the whole, much improved. I should have let them yank my lung months ago.

While Tolliver readied one of the Naval helis, I stopped at our new apartment to see Annie. The flat was only a few blocks from Admiralty House, yet I'd spent no more than two nights there since we'd moved in.

"How are you feeling, love?" I took her hand. She pulled it free.

"It's sunny." She stared vaguely at the trampled flower beds bordering the apartment. Across the room the nurse sat reading.

"Would you like to take a walk?"

She shook her head. I wondered if she'd dressed herself, or whether the nurse had helped. At times she roused herself from her lethargy; more often she sat passively while she was groomed.

I tugged at her arm. "A walk would do us good." No response. "The doctor said I need exercise. I hate to walk alone. Should I forget it?" A nerve throbbed in my cheek.

Slowly, as if in a dream, she got to her feet. "We take a walk now," she told the nurse. She went to the door, waited as if expecting it to open by itself.

Together, we strolled around the block. "I'm going on an overnight trip," I told her.

She stopped. "You comin' back?"

I took her hand, squeezed it. "Of course."

"It be okay, den." She seemed to lose interest.

I drowsed in the back seat while Tolliver flew. As a treat for Bezrel, I had Tolliver give him an elementary flying lesson while we crossed Farreach Ocean. Flushed with excitement, the middy struggled to keep the heli level at two thousand feet while Tolliver's hand hovered over the cyclic.

Long before we reached shore I switched places into the copilot's seat. As we neared the Venturas I scanned the distant shoreline, hoping against hope to spot *Catalonia*'s lifepods. We'd heard no radio signals; either the crew was without callers or they were all dead. Derek Carr's lean, aristocratic face drifted past the window. Did it hint of reproach? I wasn't sure. Ghosts do not often speak.

"Unidentified aircraft, turn back at once! Do not approach!"

"Lord Jesus!" Tolliver banked the heli at a stomach-wrenching angle and soared away from the land. He stared at the caller as if at a spirit. "Who was that? The base is abandoned!"

"Apparently not." I reached for the caller. "Venturas Base, this is Naval heli two five seven Alpha."

"Unidentified aircraft, turn back at once! We have you in range and will fire!"

Tolliver flipped switches, readied our missile defense. Our heli was well armed, but countermissiles would do little good against groundside lasers. "Sir, they have radar contact."

"I see that," I snapped. "Venturas, this is Captain Nicholas E. Seafort, Commander at Admiralty House. We're here on—"

"By standing orders of Commandant Eiferts, no ship may approach our airspace! This is your final warning."

Were they insane? I tapped my personal code into the heli's puter, set it to transmit.

"We will fire in ten sec—"

I snarled, "Who the hell do you think you are?"

Tolliver blanched. I ignored him. "Put Eiferts on line and flank, or he'll be out on his ear like Khartouf! Move!"

"He's not—he's in another building. I'm sorry, but I have standing—"

"Countermanded! Call Eiferts or you'll see a drumhead court-martial!"

No response. We watched the alarm indicators. "Stay on course for the base."

"But—" Tolliver swallowed. "Aye aye, sir."

Nothing, for three long minutes. Then the speaker crackled. "Eiferts here. Identify yourself."

"Nicholas Ewing Seafort, Captain, U.N.N.S., commanding all forces groundside and aloft." There were no forces, but it was a grand title.

"Seafort is gone. It's a good imitation, and you deciphered his code, but—"

"Damn it, Eiferts, I thought you said you knew how to obey orders. Turn off your lasers!"

For the first time he sounded hesitant. "Captain?"

"Captain. And you're a lieutenant."

"You went to the station with the others two weeks ago, sir."

My body began to relax; though he might not know it yet, he'd accepted that I was myself. "I missed the shuttle. So did Tolliver; he's here with me."

A long silence. "Come in high, directly over the field. Don't use radar. We'll keep our lasers trained on you, and at the first sign of trouble we'll fire."

I growled, "Acknowledged." What was the matter with the man? Tolliver shot me a worried look, but maintained our course.

I held my breath as we neared the field. Tolliver brought us directly over the top at three thousand feet, dropped us down slowly. I peered down to see the administration building, the thick-walled shuttle hangar, the parade ground.

We touched down in the center of the field. I opened my door. "Let them see me first." I tugged at my jacket, ran my fingers through my hair. I growled at Tolliver's amusement, but a glance at the mirror showed me the futility of my efforts. Though my uniform was neat, my eyes were deep sunken in hollow cheeks, and my scar flamed vividly.

Two soldiers approached, laser rifles at the ready. As they neared I recognized one of them. "Good evening, Sergeant, ah, Trabao."

He lowered his rifle, snapped a quick salute. "It's him," he told his mate. "Kinda surprised to see you," he said.

"And you. They said you were all to be evacuated."

"Long story, sir. Your officers may come with us." I chose to view it as an invitation rather than a command, and beckoned to my two midshipmen.

We reached the dirt roadway, where Eiferts was waiting. He asked cautiously, "In what capacity are you here, sir?"

"As senior Naval representative in Hope Nation. As commander of the military government at Centraltown."

"And the, er, Republic?"

"No longer exists."

He regarded me and slowly came to attention. "Lieutenant Saul Eiferts reporting, sir. Base Commandant."

"As you were." I continued past him to the Commandant's office. "Private session. Now."

He no sooner snapped the office lights on than I exploded, "What the hell is going on? Why aren't you on your way home?"

"Admiral De Marnay sent shuttles to take the men aloft. I volunteered to stay."

"Why?"

Unbidden, he sat at his desk. "My fiancée Jeanne—did you ever meet her?"

My tone was scathing. "You stayed to be near your woman?"

"In a way." As if ashamed, he stared at the desk. "I—"

"Your duty was aboard ship with the Admiral, not hanging around like a lovesick—"

His quiet voice sliced through my reproach. "She worked downtown. They never found her. The building was vaporized."

Crimson, I turned to the window. At length I muttered, "I'm a fool. Please forgive me."

"We were to be married. I hoped my enlistment would expire while we were still in Hope Nation, otherwise I intended to come back for her. She had a younger brother. He wasn't found either."

"I'm terribly sorry. Say what you'd like; I deserve it."

"You didn't understand." His voice was quiet, saddened, but not reproachful. "When the Admiral told me we were pulling out it seemed—I wanted to stay. With the fleet gone, the Station's puter and our lasers are the only protection Hope Nation had left."

"Trabao? The others?"

"I asked for volunteers. He was the first; the rest came after."

"How many men have you?"

"Eleven, sir. Not enough, really, but we manage. We maintain laser watch, run the power grid, and cook meals. Nothing else gets done."

I sat, decided I could face him if I tried. "Why not tell Centraltown, Mr. Eiferts? Why threaten to shoot us down?"

"Hours after the last shuttle lifted we heard Ms. Triforth's broadcast proclaiming the Republic. It's not—" He hesitated. "It's not that I'm dead set against a republic, sir. We deserted them, and if that's what they want . . . But we're not here to get into local politics. We're a U.N.A.F. installation defending the continent. I won't ask them for help, and I won't let them divert our arms for their local fight."

I nodded.

"Anyway, Centraltown is outside our defense grid. I'm on the station circuit; anything it sees, I see. Between us we have the planet's only operating laser cannon."

"I'm surprised the rebels didn't seize them."

"Triforth sent a heli the second day. We took it down." He bit his lip. "Without warning."

"Why?"

"It wasn't a Naval craft, sir. I wasn't taking chances. Today, your ship was transponding Naval codes."

I recalled my sneers, my sarcasm of moments before. Again I reddened. "You're a good man, Mr. Eiferts."

"Thank you." He hesitated. "What happened to you, sir? You look, um—"

I looked um, all right. Very um. "I lost a lung. I'm all right now." Just short of breath. At least now I knew the reason, and it was no longer life-threatening.

"Would you like to see the laser control setup?"

"I've seen—yes." If he wanted to show me, it was the least I could do.

Outside, Tolliver was waiting. Eiferts took a closer look. "Lieutenant Tolliver?"

"Yes, sir. Midshipman Tolliver now."

"How did that—" He broke off. It was none of his business.

I expected a long walk as before, but Eiferts summoned a carrier. Perhaps my appearance had something to do with it. I bade Tolliver wait with Bezrel, then Eiferts and I careened across the field to the laser control building. The laser cannon themselves were on a rise far across the base.

As he'd said, Eiferts hadn't enough men, but they managed. I vowed I'd send him help when I got back, if I had to conscript raw recruits. After the laser building, we visited the power plant, where electricity for the lasers was generated. They hadn't enough men to bring power online to the remaining lasers, as we'd intended. Somehow, we would have it done. Somehow.

He started back to the administration building. "Will you stay the night, sir?"

"I really should get—" Well, I didn't like flying by night, especially as we'd have to put down in the ocean if anything went wrong. "All right. We'll leave first thing in the morning."

I briefed Bezrel and Edgar as we walked to the mess hall.

Tolliver's look was grim. "Mr. Eiferts' done a miracle keeping the base going, but he needs more staff." I nodded.

Dinner was heated U.N.A.F. rations; they could spare no one for more elaborate fare. We ate in near silence, crowding around two long tables.

After, they showed me to my room. I undressed, rolled onto my bed, and slept like a log.

20

Over breakfast I conferred with Eiferts while Tolliver and Bezrel concentrated on their oatmeal and coffee.

"First priority is getting power to your lasers."

He nodded. "And perhaps more men would ease the strain. Not too many, though. We have no time to train them."

I agreed, my mind still on the power lines. It would have been so easy, while Khartouf had a fully manned base.

"Do you think they'll ever come back?"

I groped for what I had missed. "You mean the fleet?"

"Yes, sir."

I stared into my coffee cup, wondering whether to tell him the truth.

"They must," he answered himself. "They'll have to bring reinforcements. Hope Nation is too valuable to lose."

I swallowed my doubts. "Of course. Our job is to keep things going until then."

His smile was wan. "I wonder, lying alone at night. But then I remind myself that the U.N. couldn't desert its own colony."

My eyes strayed to the clock. "I'm afraid we should be leaving."

"Of course, sir. I'll walk you to your heli."

Bezrel and Tolliver jumped to follow. I paused at the heli door. "I've appointed Zack Hopewell military Governor. There's no reason your presence shouldn't be made public."

"No, sir. Unless . . ."

He lapsed into silence. I prompted, "Yes?"

"Unless the Government falls. You and these two mid-shipmen are the only other Naval personnel on the planet. The only true link with home."

I debated. "Better we keep it quiet, at least for now."

"As you say, sir." We shook hands after his salute. I climbed in and we lifted off.

Tolliver, perhaps because of his earlier silence, was in a talkative mood. "Quite a difference from our last visit, Captain."

"Yes."

"The base is nearly deserted, but still . . ." He paused for thought. "It's something hard to define. They've abandoned their spit and polish, but they're more . . . determined." We crossed the shoreline, headed east over the ocean.

I'd noticed the same, but hadn't thought much about it.

"I'd volunteer for duty there, if you wish." He was suddenly attentive at the controls.

I regarded him. "You, Mr. Tolliver? I never thought of you as an idealist."

"I'm not, sir. It's just that I—"

"Venturas to Naval heli two five seven Alpha, come in."

"You certainly sound like one." I took the caller. "Seafort here."

"Eiferts. Orbit Station has seven fish! Their puter is firing its lasers." His voice betrayed his tension.

"William? Put him on."

"He's alphanumeric, sir, direct to our puter. I can forward—Christ, another five! We're powering up. I'll have a shot for two more hours. Then they horizon out."

"Turn back!" I shook Tolliver's arm. "Now."

Eiferts said, "Captain, do you think you should go on? You'd be over the ocean if—"

"I'm on my way back. ETA seven minutes. We'll come in low and fast. Move it, Tolliver!"

I gripped the dash, biting back unnecessary advice. When the field appeared over the perimeter hill I breathed a sigh of relief.

I ran from the heli to the administration building, had to stop for breath. Why didn't I have more wind?

Tolliver passed me, dashed up the steps and inside. A moment later he was back. "No one here, sir. They're probably in the laser control building."

Of course. Where else? I looked around for a carrier, found none. "Let's go!"

It would have been faster to get in the heli and hop, even for so short a distance. The few hundred yards along the dusty road left me gasping for breath, though Tolliver and Bezrel had no trouble whatsoever. Jogging; I must take up jogging.

Red-faced, sweating, I arrived at the laser building, ran past the carrier parked in front. An enlisted man met me inside. "Over there, sir, in the control room." He pointed.

Inside I half expected a huge simulscreen, as on a bridge. Instead, I saw three techs poring over their consoles. Eiferts leaned over one's shoulder, pointing at the screen.

"Well?"

He didn't bother to salute. "We're powered. William's feeding us data for a shot; his long-range sensors are more sensitive than ours."

One console screen flashed coordinates, which were fed directly to the laser cannon. The other, set to alphanumeric, detailed the situation for us mere humans.

I scrolled back to read snippets of the dispatches. "ORBIT STATION TO U.N.A.F. VENTURAS BASE. CONFIRMED ALIEN SIGHTING, DISTANCE POINT FOUR KILOMETERS. LASER FIRE TO COMMENCE. SIX ADDITIONAL SIGHTINGS. DISTANCES VARY, TWENTY-FIVE METERS TO POINT EIGHT KILOMETERS . . ." I scrolled. "THREE ALIENS CONFIRMED DESTROYED, COORDINATES AS FOLLOWS . . ." I flipped to real-time printout.

"LEVEL 2, SECTION FOUR LASER DISABLED. ATTACKING FISH WAS DESTROYED."

"Targeted." Samuels, one of our techs.

"Fire!" Eiferts. The lights dimmed.

"TWO ADDITIONAL FISH DESTROYED, COORDINATES TO FOLLOW. ANOTHER FISH DESTROYED BY GROUNDSIDE FIRE. MORE FISH FUSED INTO NEARBY SPACE, COORDINATES ZERO, NINETEEN, FIVE . . ."

William was under heavy attack, but why? Hitherto, the fish had virtually ignored the Station.

"Change targets, man. Hurry." Eiferts.

A few days ago the Station had fired on the fish that attacked *Catalonia*. Some were destroyed, others had Fused away. Did the fish communicate among themselves? Did they know the Station was now an enemy?

"Fire!" Eiferts gripped the back of the console chair.

I approached him. "Can we help?"

"My radarmen are on the long-distance sensors. Can you take local radar?"

"Tolliver!"

"Aye aye, sir. Which console?"

Eiferts pointed. "There. You know how to operate ground radar?"

"Of course, sir." It was a foolish question; we all did. Eiferts's nerves were showing.

Tolliver huddled over his screen. Bezrel stood nearby, knuckles in his mouth. I cuffed them away. "Go help Mr. Tolliver, boy. Act like an officer."

"Yes, si—aye aye, sir."

Well, my nerves were showing too. It couldn't be helped. I paced from screen to screen. Our lasers got off careful, laborious shots; each had to be reconfirmed to make sure we didn't hit the Station, as the fish were extremely close to it.

Tolliver had activated two screens, local and midrange. He sat at the one, had Bezrel watching the other. Between them they covered the approaches to Venturas Base. I gave their consoles an occasional glance and moved on. With the Republic overthrown, no one from Centraltown was likely to bother us.

Hours passed in an agony of frustration. From groundside we could do little. Perhaps if the base had been fully operational, if the fusion generators were fully on-line, if the fleet were here to call our shots . . .

As the day passed William disposed of fish with calm efficiency, but at any given time a score of them were Fusing in and out of the Station's range. Should I alert Centraltown? Was the risk worth the ensuing panic?

"Captain, look!"

I whirled.

Tolliver fiddled with the magnification, jabbed his finger at a blip. "Something's descending."

"A rock?"

"Too slow."

"Where?"

"East. It's just entered the ionosphere."

"I'll check." I ran to the main console, grabbed the caller. "Captain Seafort to Station, respond."

William's imperturbable voice. "Orbit Station. Go ahead, Captain."

"Can you talk and fire at the same time?"

"I have ample capacity. How may I help you?"

"Did you launch a shuttle?"

"No shuttles launched, Captain."

My hackles rose. "We've got a blip in the eastern sky."

"Confirmed. Those would be the aliens."

"Lord Jesus! Why didn't you tell us?"

"I did, Captain. Reference paragraph two eight five, transmitted about forty sec—"

I scrolled frantically. "ALERT: ALIEN VESSELS OBSERVED APPROACHING ATMOSPHERE. PROBABLE INTENTION: ENTRY."

I whirled. "Eiferts, we've got to tell Centraltown."

He glanced over my shoulder. "Use the C circuit. Jameson, fire!"

"Seafort to Admiral—to Governor's Manse, respond."

It took only a moment. "We read you, Captain."

"Get Hopewell, flank."

"He's sleeping, sir."

I screamed, "Wake him!"

It took three minutes, but finally Hopewell was on the line, breathing hard. "What is it, Mr. Seafort?"

"Five aliens entering the atmosphere. No trajectory yet."

A silence. When he spoke his voice was calm. "It's ending, then. What do you want us to do?"

"Nothing's ending," I snarled. "We don't know their purpose. They might throw a rock, or—"

Tolliver said, "They don't need to drop into the atmosphere for that."

"Be silent, Middy. Or they might be spreading a virus. Zack, do you want to evacuate?"

"There's no point to it. We'd never notify everyone in time, and where would we go? The plantations can't shelter us all."

I groped for answers. Naval Rules of Engagement didn't contemplate hostile aliens floating overhead. "Gas masks? Can you prepare for viral attack?"

"To an extent. We can sound the sirens, warn of possible gas attack. But we haven't held gas drills; a lot of joeys won't know what to do."

"But some will."

"Yes." A pause. "I'll get started. Godspeed, Mr. Seafort."

"And to you." We rang off, but not before his calm helped steady me. "Tolliver, where are they headed?"

"I don't know, sir. They're descending very slowly."

I demanded, "How in hell can a fish enter the atmosphere without imploding, if it lives in vacuum?"

"They come from somewhere, sir. Presumably someplace with an atmosphere."

"Won't they heat up from the friction of entry?"

He looked cross. "Just how would you expect me to know, sir?"

I bit back an angry retort. He was right; I was harassing him. "Track them. Are they in range?"

"Extreme range at best, sir. I'll let you know when we have a shot."

I paced with mounting anxiety. There was nothing I could do here at the base. I should be at Centraltown . . . But even there, we had no ships, no men. The one laser cannon here was—

We had helis. Even my own ship had missiles and shells. I snatched up the caller. "Seafort to Manse, come in!"

This time the reply was immediate. "Yes, sir?"

"The helis you have searching for *Catalonia*'s survivors. Where are they?"

"Just a moment; I'll ask the Governor."

A moment later Hopewell came on. "We sent the helis out at dawn. They're combing—"

"You've kept two Naval ships in reserve. Are they fully armed?"

"As far as I know."

"Do your pilots know how to use the missiles?"

"They're former U.N.A.F. soldiers. I'm not sure but I think—"

"If the pilots are capable, send them to coordinates—Tolliver, what are they?" I read them off his screen into the caller. "Have them attack the moment the aliens are low enough to hit."

"I will."

Again his calm passed to me. Zack Hopewell was old enough to be my father, yet I'd been ordering him about like a cadet. "Mr. Hopewell, excuse my manners."

His voice held stern reproof. "No need to apologize for command. Do your duty, and His will." He rang off. I peered at the main console. Five fish descending, and nearly thirty attacking the Station. Though William skewered them with ceaseless efficiency, more appeared as fast as he destroyed them. His kill count had reached twenty-one. Our ground lasers had taken out seven.

Day darkened slowly to night. I had no thought of leaving. William's reports continued unabated.

Tolliver sang out, "Sir, we have a shot at the fish in the atmosphere."

Eiferts shook his head. "We have targets aloft. The Station goes over the horizon soon. Then we'll be of no help to William."

"Yes, but these fish are dropping into—" I hesitated. What was higher priority? I spoke softly. "Tolliver, feed the coordinates to the third laser cannon. As soon as there's a free moment . . ."

He twisted his head to stare at me. "Free moment? For God's sake, sir, they're coming down onto Hope Nation!"

"Easy. We can't shoot both cannon at once. We'd better help William while we can."

Tolliver punched in figures, following the fish. He admitted grudgingly, "On their current trajectory, we have a little time."

I watched for endless minutes.

Eiferts called across the room. "You still have a shot?"

"Yes, sir." Tolliver punched the keys, reconfirmed his figures.

"The Station's over the horizon. Rawlings, power up number three. Use Tolliver's coordinates."

Minutes passed while the capacitors of the third laser cannon reached full charge. Tolliver said, "Ready, sir."

"Fire!"

The lights dimmed again. I stared at the console. One blip began to drop, slowly at first, then faster. In a few seconds it disappeared from the screen.

"Got him! Acquiring new target!" Tolliver.

Now the other blips were moving faster. We locked on target, fired again.

Jameson spun his chair. "Directly overhead, sir! A dozen high above the atmosphere!"

The display from Orbit Station sounded an alarm. Now what? I peered at the screen. "ELEVEN ALIENS OBSERVED OVER WESTERN CONTINENT; ABSENCE OF ORBITING TARGET SUGGESTS MANEUVER RELATED TO VENTURAS BASE." Though William was out of our sight, he still had a view of the sky above us, and relayed his reports through his comm satellites.

"Eleven? I count twel—"

William intoned, "Inanimate object separating from fish. My sensors show high density, no metal, does not compute as ship."

I snatched up the caller. "William, what is it?"

An infinitesimal pause. "Planetary debris, I think. Similar composition to the mass the aliens released over Centraltown, but smaller."

"Good Christ!" My eyes met Eiferts's as his turned to mine. "Acquire targets overhead! Crash priority!"

The large blip fell away from the others. "Tolliver, coordinates!"

"I need a few seconds for a trajectory." The remaining fish overhead disappeared from my screen, either from William's fire or by Fusing to safety.

Agonizing seconds passed. My eyes were riveted to the screen, while the rock approached velocity of eighty-three miles per second. "Locked in! Fire!"

The lights flickered as our cannon tracked the rock hurtling from above. "Where's it headed?" My hands were tight on the chair.

"Right here, sir." Tolliver was pale.

Jameson called, "More blips over Western Continent, about a dozen."

"Be specific. Lock in tar—"

"Got it!" Tolliver's whoop echoed in the crowded room.

The large blip he'd been tracking disintegrated into a spray of tiny dots. Perhaps they were small enough to burn up in Hope Nation's rich atmosphere.

Samuels shouted, "Another rock, sir. Twice the size of a fish!" Minuscule compared to the one that destroyed Central-town, but if it landed on our heads . . .

"Helis from Centraltown report radar contact with fish."

"More overhead, sir. Looks like two rocks!"

Bezrel, ignored by all of us, huddled at his console. His shoulders shook. I raged inwardly at Admiral De Marnay. Why bring a child who should have been at Academy to—

"Bezrel!"

The boy jumped as if goosed with a prod. "Yes, sir!"

"Can you find the mess hall?"

"Yes, sir."

"We'd like some coffee. Bring it."

"Aye aye, sir." He ran to the door.

"One rock gone!" Tolliver. "Seeking other target."

I would force down the coffee, though my stomach churned with acid. Better the boy have something to do. Only after the middy was gone did I realize I might have sent him into greater danger.

"Sir, one of the Naval helis wants instructions!"

"What?" I tore my eyes from the console, keyed the caller. "Seafort."

A pilot's voice crackled. "Radar contact with two fish, Captain. Approximately fourteen thousand feet."

"Target acquired!" Tolliver.

"Rawlings, fire cannon one!" Eiferts.

"That low?"

"Yes, sir. Do you want us to engage?"

"Who are you? Can you fire a missile?"

"Major Winfred Zahn, retired, sir." He chuckled. "I'm quite sure I can."

"Stay out of range of anything they throw. Fire immediately."

"Righto."

Tolliver raised an eyebrow at the informality. I smiled, surprising him. How little it mattered.

In the next half hour we broke up two more rocks. Each

one was delivered by at least ten fish. Did it take their combined efforts to transport a rock across the void? How did they Fuse an external object? Did they create a shared field?

As William progressed along the horizon he lost his view of the fish over Western Continent. Above, fish kept Defusing. We were too occupied taking out rocks to shoot at fish. If we only had all our lasers on-line . . . No use crying over spilt milk.

"Look, sir." Two clusters of fish, each herding a sizable mass. "They're guiding more rocks."

"I see," I snarled.

"Cannon two's targeted." Tolliver, to Eiferts. "Their rock is a bit lower."

"Right."

It took almost eight seconds to knock out the first rock. By the time it disintegrated, the second was well on its way. As we lined up a shot, a third appeared, high overhead.

"Damn them!"

"Amen." My fingers tore at the chair while Tolliver and Eiferts targeted the laser cannon. Shots were so much easier from a ship, where radar signals were clear and immediate, and the range was short.

I stared at the console. The third rock was launched, while we barely had a lock on the second. "It'll be close," I muttered.

"Why in hell won't that rock break up?" Tolliver pounded his console.

"Denser than the others? Stay on it!"

"We have a lock, sir. What we need is time."

Our cannon followed the second rock almost to the ground. It broke up a scant six thousand feet overhead. "Where's the other—"

Jameson. "Targeted! Fire!"

A whomp that shook the concrete deck. Others, in rapid succession. "What in hell was—"

"Fragments," said Tolliver. "They've got to fall somewhere."

The caller. Eiferts answered, swore. "Ignore the bloody bearing, joey! Give us full power until it burns out."

"Christ, we're late! Break up, damn you!"

I held my breath. The mass was streaking downward. What were they throwing, laserproof rocks?

I glanced at the screen. No more were being launched. If we could get this one, we stood a chance.

"There she goes!" Jameson, with a yell of triumph. A large hunk of the jagged rock broke off, disintegrated.

Tolliver cursed. "The puter's following the wrong piece!"

I shouted, "Go manual! No time!"

Tolliver twirled up the magnification, twisted the fire control. "Where is— Got it! Oh, Christ, it's—"

A groan. I turned to Eiferts. He looked into my eyes, made the sign of the Cross. I spun my chair to the console.

Jameson said, "Jesus, another rock, far out!"

The door swung open. "Sorry it took so long, sir. I had to brew a fresh—"

The stupendous blast blew Bezrel into my arms. My chair flew backward into the console. The building screeched. Walls buckled. The room went dark. I sat dazed and deafened as debris rained from the ceiling.

Silence.

Someone coughed, gagged. Dawn's light pierced the shattered wall.

Eiferts lay on his back, an arm thrust over his face. A jagged piece of wood protruded from his chest. His shirt was drenched red.

Bezrel clung to me, whimpering. I rocked, cheek nuzzling the boy's soft hair as I'd sat eons before with my little Nate. It would be all right. I hugged him close.

It would be all right.

21

Tolliver groaned. Blood dripped from his forehead; he wiped it clear of his eyes. The dark red stain sank into the blue sleeve of his jacket. Dust motes drifted in the intense silence of the splintered morn.

"Are you hurt, sir?"

"No. Look to Mr. Eiferts." I rocked the boy, trying to breathe through the thick choking dust.

Tolliver staggered to his feet, lurched across the room. He knelt at Eiferts's side, felt for a pulse. He shook his head.

"See who is alive."

"Aye aye, sir." He knelt over Jameson. "He doesn't seem wounded, sir. Just knocked cold." Samuels was on his feet, gagging. Tolliver made the rounds. "Is Mr. Bezrel gone, sir?"

"Don't say that!" The boy raised his head. "I'm not dead."

"Thank Lord God." Tolliver.

Bezrel realized where he lay, thrust himself clear of me, cheeks scarlet. "I'm sorry, I—honest, sir!"

"It's all right, boy." My tone was gruff. I looked about. "Let's get out before the building falls."

"We'll need to carry Jameson."

"I can help," I said. If I moved slowly, breathed carefully. The swirling dust made me cough, and my healed incision ached. I bore it.

As I bent to lift the tech a great whomp of power pounded my chest. I pitched on top of the unconscious man. A muffled thud built to a roar. The building swayed. I scrambled to my knees. "Lord Christ, what was—"

"The other rock!" Tolliver was grim.

"Get Jameson out of—"

A tremendous crash. The roof buckled.

"What the—"

A drumbeat of whomps and thuds that seemed as if it would never end. I grabbed Bezrel, sheltered him against my chest. Tolliver crouched over Jameson.

The deadly rain built to a crescendo that hammered the wounded building. Finally it eased, as the debris flung upward by the rock settled back to earth. At length, all was still. The roof gave an ominous creak.

I took a shaky breath, wrenched open the door.

Outside was a landscape of hell. Every tree in the vicinity was in splinters. A pall of smoke billowed across the parade ground. The field had twisted, as if wrenched by an earthquake.

"Sir, the roof may not hold. We have to get the men out."

"All right."

We set Jameson on the steps, went back inside. Two of the techs were conscious, one moaning in pain.

Of the seven who'd been in the room, only Eiferts was dead. We left him where he lay; no time for him now. I uttered a short prayer under my breath.

"Where did it hit?" Samuels.

"I don't know." I sat unsteadily on the steps. "The first rock took out the cannon. A direct hit."

"It couldn't have." Tolliver squinted at the devastation to the south.

"Why not?"

"We're still here. If a rock that big struck so close . . ."

I grunted. "It doesn't matter. The lasers are out."

"Look at the administration building," said Tolliver. Blood dripped down his face.

There was nothing to see. Only jagged strumps of wall were left.

Jameson moaned, began to waken. I said to Rawlings, "Is there a first-aid kit?"

The tech frowned, nodded. "Inside, sir. In the cupboard."

"Can you get it?"

"I won't go back there. The roof's about to fall."

I pointed to Tolliver. "My midshipman needs a bandage."

Rawlings said, "Get it yourself."

I stood abruptly, waited for dizziness to pass. Bezrel said quickly, "I'll go, sir."

"Very well." I glared at the obstinate tech.

"The other rock must have hit farther away." I spoke to distract Tolliver.

"Much farther." Abruptly he sat. When Bezrel returned with the kit I wrapped gauze around Tolliver's forehead. Done, I clapped him on the shoulder. "Are you well enough to get up?"

"Of course." He stared at the ruins across the field. "Now what?"

"There's nothing for us here. We have to get back to Central—" Lord God.

Our heli had been on the parade ground.

"Do you swim well?" Tolliver's smile was crooked.

"Let's look around."

"What happened to the personnel carrier? It would save a hike."

He got up, went around the side of the building. The carrier lay on its side atop a shredded clump of bushes. "On the other hand, it might be easier to walk."

I let it pass. He was giddy from loss of blood.

I left the two techs with Jameson, trudged with Tolliver and Bezrel across the field toward the smoking vegetation beyond. We came on pieces of our heli. The cab and engine compartment were crumpled as if a giant fist had hurled them across the field.

"Not even a radio." Tolliver pawed disgustedly through the rubble.

"The base has plenty of callers."

"Where, sir?"

I frowned at the remains of the admin building. Not there. "There was a dish at the laser building."

"It's gone now. And the power is out." Gingerly he touched his head. "What next, sir?"

"Let's see where the last rock hit."

The Venturas Base laser cannon had been mounted on a ridge south of the parade ground to provide a clear field of fire in virtually any direction. As we moved south the ground was warmer. Atop the ridge, clumps of grass still burned. All that remained of the laser cannon were blasted stumps of metal and plastic, laced with jagged ropes of conduit like spaghetti.

Beyond the emplacement the ground had sloped gently for some miles to the sea. We halted atop the shattered ridge, stunned by the panorama of devastation below.

A pall of smoke obscured much of the crater. For as far as we could see, fires glowed with hellish intensity in the subdued, smoky light. The trees had been blown down like matchsticks, pointing away from the crater in great concentric circles. I wondered if flames would spread as far as the groves along the coast. If so, the forest would take generations to recover.

Tolliver pointed to the hillock. "If this ridge hadn't sheltered us, we'd be dead."

I grunted. "That's as may be. Come along."

"Where, sir?"

"Back to the others, I suppose."

Hands in my pockets, I trod across the crumpled parade ground. Tolliver was silent most of the way, but when we neared the laser control building he said, "What I'd give for some water . . ." I tried to hide my shame. He'd been injured, and I'd just led him on a pointless forced march.

When we reached the building Jameson had regained consciousness. He huddled with the other techs, as if for comfort.

"Did the laser building have water?" I faced Rawlings, the tech who'd refused to go inside.

"Used to. Dunno about the pipes anymore."

I held in my annoyance. "Mr. Bezrel, would you volunteer to look?"

"Of course, sir." He cast a scornful look at the tech.

"See if the water is on. Fill something. Use your coffeepot, if you can find it."

"Aye aye, sir." I fidgeted while he was gone. What would possess me to send a boy into a collapsing building? Yes, he was smaller, more agile, but . . . I tried to hide my relief when he emerged carrying the dented pot and some plastic cups. We had water, at least for the moment.

"Here, sir." His eyes were troubled.

I handed the pot to Tolliver. "What happened, Mr. Bezrel?"

His answer was quick. "Nothing, sir." He hesitated. "The pot was lying near Mr. . . . Mr. . . ."

"I understand." Embarrassed, I kicked a tuft of grass, looked around. The long walk had taken something out of me. If we only had the carrier. It didn't seem damaged. Could it be made to run? It was balanced precariously on its side; perhaps if all of us heaved . . .

"You men, come here. See if we can right this machine."

Jameson stood, a bit unsteadily. Rawlings said, "Why bother? There's no place to go."

Tolliver put down the water pot, unstrapped his holster. He drew his laser pistol, thumbed off the safety. "Permission to execute him, sir."

I stared into Tolliver's eyes. Would he know to wait? And if not, did I care? "Granted."

Tolliver leveled the pistol. Rawlings leapt to his feet. "No, wait, I'll help! Jesus!"

"Very well." We were under wartime regs; I ought to warn them. I shrugged. Now, they knew.

After several tries we managed to rock the carrier upright. The door was stuck; I had to slide in from the passenger side. Keys were still in the ignition. I turned them and the vehicle came to life.

We all climbed in. I drove around the base, checking the ruins of the various buildings. We found no sign of Sergeant Trabao or the other volunteers. To the southwest, the base power plant was in ruins.

Though the mess hall sagged, it still stood; the admin building had sheltered it from the worst of the blast.

North along the perimeter road sat the shuttle hangar. Its side wall was cracked, and in places the block had crumbled to rubble. Inside, the shuttle looked undamaged—no, it had been hit. Portholes were shattered by fragments of rock. The airframe was dented, but seemed unpierced. I walked around to the front of the building, tried the huge counterbalanced hangar door. It wouldn't budge. Looking up I saw the reason: the track on which it rolled was twisted and bowed.

I walked outside to the carrier and slumped on my seat.

Now what? We had no heli, no radio, nothing but a carrier and three sullen techs. Without power, how long could we count on fresh water?

With two huge rocks, the fish had wiped out our western base and with it all our groundside firepower. I looked up, knowing I wouldn't see a third rock until it was right above us. I shuddered. Lord God, if it came, let it be a direct hit. No pain, no fire.

Rawlings followed my thoughts. "Let's get out before they throw another."

"Why should they bother? We're wiped out."

"Do they know that? And would they care?" His face twisted in fear. "Drive, joey!"

"Where? Into the forest? A rock has as good a chance—"

With a cry of rage Rawlings hauled me out of the carrier, reached for the key.

He died in agony.

Tolliver sheathed his pistol. I doubled over and retched.

"Sorry, sir." Tolliver's voice was unsteady.

I held on to the carrier door. "You did as you should." I made my voice sharp as I turned to the techs. "You men are U.N.A.F., aren't you? You volunteered for this duty!"

Swallowing, Jameson turned from the blistered corpse. "He shouldn't have tried to take your carrier, but . . . what's left to fight for, Captain? It's over."

Over? We had duty. While life remained—somehow, we had to . . . had to . . . What? I sank onto the carrier seat, my back to the grisly remains.

"Sir?" Tolliver waited, but I said nothing, lost in desolation. Tentatively he said, "Maybe Rawlings was right about not staying here. Where they could hit us with rocks, I mean."

"They can throw rocks anywhere."

"But they're aiming them here." He peered at the sky. "Have you decided what to do?" I shook my head. "Could we go somewhere else, sir, while you think?"

My voice was dull. "All right. You and—what's your name? Samuels? Get his . . . body out of there. How far does this road take us?"

"To the celuwall factory, sir. About twenty miles."

"Bring rations and water."

I sat in the passenger seat, head down, hugging myself while we bounced past broken and uprooted trees toward the forest beyond.

We set up camp under a leafy canopy near the end of the road. Here, in silent virgin forest, one could imagine all was well in the Venturas.

The others huddled near a fire Tolliver had started with his pistol. I sat alone in the carrier. Bezrel brought me coffee; I took occasional sips until it grew cold and stale.

The day passed. Bezrel came with Q-rations. I left them untouched. When Tolliver tried to prod me further I ordered him away. After they'd all settled to sleep by the fire in blankets they'd scrounged from the rubble of the base, I remained in the carrier, staring through the windshield into the night.

It was over. I had done my duty, and had failed. The fish were masters of Hope Nation. Sooner or later they'd obliterate Centraltown, and do whatever it was they lived for, and go on.

I would die here.

Annie would die in Centraltown, where I'd abandoned her.

We had no way to reach Eastern Continent; our only heli was gone. No way to call for help; the radios were smashed. No way to fight the fish; the only laser emplacements we had were on Orbit Station, and we had no way to go aloft. The dented shuttle was locked in the ruined hangar, and even if we could get it out, it was too damaged to put us into orbit. Even if I reached the Station, I wouldn't be of use; William fired our lasers with pinpoint accuracy on his own. The Station had no ship for me to sail, and no crew to help man it.

It was over.

The night air grew even cooler. I hunched in the seat of the carrier, jacket wrapped around me, struggling for a way to give meaning to what was left of our lives. A way to fight on.

What were the fish, and why did they follow us? What did they want? How could we make them stop coming? If we couldn't defeat them with ships and lasers, how could we prevail? Was humankind destined to fall? Were we to be driven from our hard-won planets back to dark caves, to raise fearful children who never knew bright cities? How could we stop these marauders who lunged at us from the void?

In my desperation, I clasped hands and prayed to Lord God, though I knew full well that His face was forever turned from me, and that my prayer was worse than useless. I sat, empty and alone, until the sky lightened with the forlorn promise of morn. I raised my head, left the carrier, walked on unsteady legs to the embers of the fire. I stooped for twigs and small branches from the pile they'd made the night before.

I froze, not daring to breathe.

After a time, I warmed my hands at the fire in the stillness of the dawn. Tolliver woke, raised his head. I stared at him, heart pounding. I could not speak of what I might do.

But I knew a way.

PART 4

May, in the year of our Lord 2200

22

"Coffee, sir?" Tolliver sat beside me.

I wrapped my hands around the steaming cup to steal its warmth. "Assemble the men."

"The me— Aye aye, sir." It must have seemed an odd request; Bezrel and the two techs constituted our entire force, and were all within calling distance.

A moment later I faced them. "We're going back." Samuels muttered something like an objection; I directed my words to him. "I'm your commanding officer. I said we're going back to the base."

"Why, sir? It's dangerous." It was almost a challenge, but he'd called me "sir"; he hadn't crossed the line to mutiny.

"It's been fifteen hours and they've thrown no more rocks. We can't stay here indefinitely, and there's work to do."

Jameson stirred. "Work? At what? Everything's wrecked; we'd just as well live in the wild until we're sure it's safe. They say there was a deserter once—"

"Yes, Captain Grone. I've heard of him." And met him. "You'll go with me for now. When we're done, I'll give you a chance to come back here to stay." He made as if to protest. I overrode him. "That's an order."

His discipline held. "Yes, sir."

"Into the carrier."

We rumbled back along the trail. As we neared the base my fingers closed over the armrest. We maneuvered past rubble and downed trees, pulled up between the shattered admin building and the damaged hangar. "Mr. Tolliver, scout for weapons; there'll be laser rifles somewhere. While you're at it, find us food. Mattresses and blankets too. And tents or field equipment."

Tolliver looked dubiously at the bombed-out base. "Aye aye, sir."

"You other men come with me." I started toward the hangar.

The side door was locked, but we climbed through gaping holes in the broken wall. Inside, the hangar was dark and cold.

The shuttle, one of the U.N.A.F.'s smaller models, sat in the center of the hangar bay, its stubby wings folded back. My stomach knotted as I approached; were it too badly damaged my plans would crumble. I circled the craft, stopping at the starboard side.

The shuttle had been peppered by debris as if some great shotgun had blasted it with scraps of shot and broken nails. The pilot's side window was completely gone. Jagged pieces of transplex were all that remained of two portholes.

On the port side near the bow, the skin of the craft was scraped and dented. Underneath the shuttle a large chunk of cement lay on the floor in fragments. I reached up, ran my fingers across the alumalloy panels. Perhaps at that spot critical wiring ran below the skin. But if not, the damage wasn't fatal.

I opened the control panel, slapped open the hatch, clambered in.

The passenger cabin was almost untouched. A few chips of concrete lay where they had fallen through the portholes, but they were nothing; the middy could sweep them up in minutes. I moved on to the cockpit. The chunk of debris that smashed the pilot's window had fetched up against the dash. The copilot's console was smashed; wires dangled onto the yoke. The second throttle ball was snapped clean off.

Would the ship fly? I leaned out of the missing pilot's window and shouted, "Everyone stand clear!" I opened the ignition keypad. If a password had been set . . .

It hadn't. The shuttle responded to the default code. I flipped on battery power. In a moment the puter responded with a green light. "Checklist, oral," I told it.

A tinny voice. "Checklist begins. Portholes thirty-three and twelve not responding to sensor check; cabin pressure unachievable. Aerodynamic integrity is compromised. Damage to fuselage, port side. Copilot's fuel gauge is inoperative.

Copilot's cabin pressure gauge inoperative. Copilot's altimeter inop—"

"Halt checklist. Bypass copilot's console. Reassign all controls to pilot's console." Why couldn't I talk to a puter without beginning to sound like one? "Resume checklist."

A few moments later the puter ground to a halt. "Fuel at capacity. Navaids programmed to anticipated location, orbit station. Craft is inoperable due to checklist items one, two, three, nine, twelve through fifty-four, and sixty through—"

"Cancel report. Do we have control of jet landing engine, rudder, ailerons, and flaps from pilot's console?"

"Affirmative." Did the puter sound peevish?

"Report on rocket engine damage."

"No known engine damage."

I glanced out the porthole. Bezrel stood well clear, his mouth agape. Jameson was at his side. "Low power jet engine check."

"Aft, stern, and starboard sensors indicate the craft is inside hangar. Engine check not possible within hangar."

"Yes, it is." Our brakes would hold us. As long as I shut down after a few seconds, the hangar wouldn't accumulate enough exhaust fumes to roast Jameson and Bezrel. If we scorched the rear wall, so be it.

"Safety regulations do not permit jet engine check at any power level within hangar."

"Override safety regs."

The pilot's console switched on. A light turned green; the console beeped three warning tones; the engines caught with a sudden roar. They muted almost instantly as the puter throttled down to minimum power. Below, Bezrel and the tech held their hands over their ears.

"Active control systems check."

Perhaps the puter had given up on me; at any rate, he made no further protest. Ailerons, rudder, and flaps moved ponderously as the puter went through a series of checks. "Engine off."

The green lights blinked off; the last echoes of the engine died. "Low power test indicates response from pilot's console at low power, and no apparent engine damage. Control systems respond normally."

"Very well. End of test." I reached for the battery switch.

"Warning: low power engine test does not verify that engine will perform at full power. Control systems damage may become evident only at suborbital—"

"End report." I didn't need to hear that; I didn't even want it suggested. I left the pilot's seat, stopped short. "Contact Orbit Station."

A silence. Then, "No contact."

I swallowed a chill of foreboding. The shuttle was under the hangar roof. Surely that was the reason. "Systems off."

I climbed down, crossed the hangar floor to the tech and the boy. "This hangar was equipped for repairs. Find me ladders and welding torches."

"Can I ask what for, sir?" Jameson.

"The hangar door is jammed shut. We're going to cut it free."

"That would take days!"

I studied the door. "I don't think so."

"Look at that shuttle. You expect to fly it?" The tech grimaced at the dented fuselage.

My voice sharpened. "I expect you to cut away the hangar door. Get what we need." I let my hand slide toward my pistol.

"Yes . . . sir." He turned away.

Tolliver poked his head through the broken wall. He climbed through the debris, loped toward me with a grin, snapped a pro forma salute. "We'll eat today, sir. And I found weapons. Samuels, bring in the knapsack."

"Good." I studied the hangar door. "Tolliver, you'd better take charge here. These techs are not . . . I want the door cut away." I turned back to the shuttle.

"What for, sir?"

I spun around. "You too? I gave an order!"

"Aye aye, sir." Tolliver seemed unfazed. "I wasn't questioning you. I'd work better if I understood, though."

"You would, eh?" I came toward him, my voice menacing. His eyes were bleary. His bandage was stained with sweat and dirt. My rage dissolved. "I need to get the shuttle out of the hangar, Mr. Tolliver."

"You can't launch her, sir. With the portholes out she'd break up before you could get her orbital."

"I know that. I don't intend to go orbital."

"But . . . it isn't a heli, sir. Her thrusters won't handle low-level flight more than a few minutes without overheating." He looked at me as if wondering if I'd forgotten.

"I know that too. Mr. Tolliver, I want that doorway cleared."

His glance was skeptical, but he nodded.

I peered upward, shielding my eyes against the glare.

They hadn't found ladders, but they'd brought scaffolding, which was more useful. The torches and acetylene tanks had been stowed in the hangar lockers.

Tolliver had suggested we cut the couplings that anchored the door track to the hangar wall, but I vetoed that. The huge door was immensely heavy, and we couldn't control which direction it would topple. And once the door fell to the ground, we'd have to cut it into movable pieces, to cart it out of our way.

Instead, they were taking the door down a piece at a time.

The bottommost sections were the easiest. Tolliver and a tech cut them loose; as soon as the scraps cooled, Bezrel, the other tech and I hauled them away. When the cutters showed signs of fatigue I bade them change places. Bezrel kept us supplied with water and softies he'd pried out of the dispenser.

I didn't have goggles; we'd only found two pair. After a time, dazzled by the cascade of white heat falling from the torches, I strolled again around the shuttle, looking for damage. Jameson detached himself from the others and wandered after me. I waited, steeling myself for more objections.

He kicked the pavement. "Sorry about how I've been acting," he said. "It's just—we knew the risk of staying behind, but when you actually face it . . . it's harder."

I nodded, much relieved. "I know."

"The fleet's gone, the base is gone . . . the fish wipe out

whatever we put against them." He shivered. "Is the colony doomed, sir?"

"It may be," I said. He deserved honesty. "But we're not dead yet." I crossed to the hangar's side door, found I could open it from the inside. "Let's get some air."

"I'll have to relieve Samuels in a minute." He followed me outside.

"How long have you been in system?" It gave me something to say.

"Ten years." He kicked at a surviving strand of grass. "I was in Engineering on the Station, then in Centraltown. They sent me here a year ago."

I grunted. "You've seen the place grow—"

"You were right to relieve General Khartouf." He averted his gaze.

"I shouldn't discuss that." I realized how fatuous that sounded in the rubble of the ruined base. "In any event, he's long gone. Mr. Eiferts would have made the base ready, if he'd had time."

"He was a mover." Wearily, Jameson sat on the grass. He chewed at a blade, squinting at me. "We needed the generator fully on-line. If the Navy had stayed awhile longer—" The blade of grass dropped from his mouth.

"They did their best."

Jameson swallowed, pointing at my shoulder. "Oh, Jesus!"

I slapped at my jacket. A spider? A snake? No, idiot, Hope Nation has no animal life. "What are you—"

His mouth working, Jameson lurched to his feet, fled to the hangar.

What was wrong with the man? I turned, saw nothing. My glance strayed upward.

"Lord save us!" I raced to the side door, as if the hangar's pitiful shelter could protect us from the living dirigible a thousand feet above.

I slammed the door behind me. "Tolliver! Break out the arms!"

For a moment he gaped. "What's—Aye aye, sir!" He scrambled off the scaffold. In the corner, Jameson retched.

"Laser rifles! Shoulder missiles! Anything!" I was beside myself. Bezrel seemed confused. "Move, boy! Grab a gun!" I realized I had nothing but my pistol. Did it even have a charge? My hand fumbled at my holster. The green light glowed when I pressed the test. Charged or not, a puny pistol wouldn't do much good.

Tolliver raced back, a laser rifle in hand. "What is it, sir?"

"Fish!" I crouched to the opening we'd cut in the bottom of the hangar door. I gestured skyward.

Tolliver clutched the rifle as if a treasured toy, but shook his head. "Rifles won't bother anything that big, sir."

The fish pulsed, its skin changing color briefly. It drifted lower.

Bezrel raced back with a pair of laser rifles. I grabbed mine, flipped the safety, and waited for a full charge. When it beeped I knelt at the cut-away opening under the huge hangar door. I aimed at the underside of the fish. When I fired, colors swirled. A portion of the fish's body seemed to deflate. Then the outer skin seemed to flow over itself, and the hole was gone.

"My God." Tolliver dropped onto one knee. He squeezed off a long burst that put an angry slash in the side of the fish.

The fish settled ominously lower.

I said, "Jameson, where's Samuels?"

"Running for the woods, last I saw." The tech's voice was acid.

"Bezrel, come outside with me. Tolliver, you and Jameson cut those bloody track couplings off. Let the hangar door fall where it may."

Tolliver said doubtfully, "If we cut the door loose we'll have no protection, sir."

I pointed at the bottom four feet they'd already severed. "What protection does this leave?" I didn't wait for an answer. "Hurry."

I ducked under the door and glanced up. The fish was a mere two hundred feet over the field.

From inside, Tolliver's voice. "Why are we trying to free the shuttle, sir?" He added, "I'll do it, but I'd like to know why we're suiciding rather than running for safety."

"We can get away in the shuttle."

"It's built for orbital flight, not—"

The fish lurched lower, its stern blowhole working. I

growled, "Don't you think I know that? Cut, Tolliver! Quick!" I sprinted toward the parade ground. Bezrel followed with his rifle. "Fire!" I gasped.

"Where should I aim, sir?" He dropped to his knee, aiming.

"Anywhere!" My beam burned a new hole in the descending fish. Above it, a ropy mass formed and began to swirl.

The fish jerked, but drifted ever lower. Its tentacle swung. I warned, "Don't let that hit you, boy! Jump clear if it lets fly!"

"Aye aye, sir!" Our laser fire raked the side of the great beast. Its skin began to repair the holes; the fish sank lower, tilting aft. Its appendage swung around, broke loose, sailed toward us.

Bezrel scampered to safety with the speed of youth. Winded, I could only watch the protoplasm gyrate through the air. A shrill voice cut through my fog. "Run, sir!"

As the mass whirled toward my head I fell to the ground. A rush of warm air. The appendage struck a few feet past me. Grass sizzled.

Another arm formed. The fish was no more than fifty feet above us. I set the rifle for continuous fire, held down the trigger until long after the warning beep.

The wounded fish sank to the ground, colors fading to mottled gray. I stumbled to my feet, backed away with my useless rifle.

The body of the fish appeared to be dissolving. The skin became indistinct; colors swirled. Outriders. "Bezrel, run!" I leaped over the smoking mass the fish had flung.

As I ran I glanced over my shoulder. A shifting shape seemed to grow from the skin of the fish. It swirled, wriggled free, fell from the fish's side. "Bezrel, back to the hangar!" My legs pumped.

The outrider skittered even faster than the one I'd once seen in *Telstar*'s corridor. It was only steps behind me. I knew I wouldn't make the haven of the hangar.

Suddenly Tolliver dropped from the scaffold a meter in front of me, his rifle light glowing. He aimed directly at my face. I blanched; even the fish's acid was a better death. In desperation I hurled my empty rifle at him, dived to the ground. Tolliver fired over my head. Behind me something smoked and sizzled. He bounded forward, hauled me to my feet. "Move!"

I scrambled under the door. More shapes swirled on the mottled skin of the dying fish. Above, on the scaffold, sparks showered from Jameson's torch.

"Where are the bloody recharge packs?"

"I have a few." Tolliver ducked outside, retrieved my rifle, handed it to me. I took it, careful to avoid his eye. I jammed in the charge. "Bezrel, recharge!"

The boy didn't answer. I looked around. He was nowhere in sight.

A scream from above. *"Look out!"* Jameson.

I whirled. A shape scuttled through the far end of the open hangar door. For a split second it stood quivering. Then it rolled toward us with frightening speed. While I fumbled at my rifle, Tolliver fired. The outrider seemed to fly apart. I flinched. The alien collapsed into an oozing puddle.

I stared at the foul mess. A near thing. Tolliver knelt at the hangar opening and fired again. Above him, the door groaned and sagged; a coupling had finally parted. But there were many more to sever. We hadn't the time.

"Lord God damn them!" My voice was thick. "What do they want? Why won't they let us alone!" I stooped through the opening, fired at a whirling shape, and, beyond caring, stalked toward the parade ground. Only Tolliver, Jameson, and I were left. No way to escape, nothing to escape for. I felt a pang of regret for my life, a deeper pang for the boy's; he'd had more of his life stolen.

The fish lay where it had fallen, its colors finally still, its mottling fading even as I watched. Behind me I heard the snap of Tolliver's rifle. Outriders continued to emerge from the motionless mass. Something skittered toward me; I stood my ground, firing until it melted.

A patch of blue caught my eye about fifty feet to the side: Midshipman's Bezrel's body, pathetically small. I checked my dwindling charge; enough to put him out of his misery, if need be. I couldn't leave him to the aliens. Ignoring Tolliver's shout of protest I tramped across the seared grass.

Better if Admiral De Marnay had left the boy home, to play at balls and kites and Arcvid.

An outrider rolled toward us, barely visible against the browned grass. I fired simultaneously with Tolliver; the creature melted to the ground.

Bezrel's head moved.

Heart pounding, I dropped on one knee. "Are you all right?" A hoarse whisper.

"Yes, sir!"

"What in God's own name are you doing?" I kept my rifle ready, risked a glance behind me.

He crawled toward me, slithering in an effort to stay low. "I ran out of charge, and those things were coming . . . I thought if I stayed down they wouldn't see me."

I bit back a snarl of fury. His ploy had worked, while I'd nearly gotten myself killed running away. "Still have your rifle?"

"Yes, sir."

"Hang on to it. Take some breaths, get to your knees, and run to the hangar as if Satan himself were after you!"

"He is, sir!" Abruptly the boy swarmed to his feet and sprinted off. He was fast; I doubted even Tolliver could catch him.

Two outriders paused, sensed his moving figure. They skittered across the grass. As if we'd planned it, Tolliver and I waited until one approached our killing zone, fired together. The outrider lurched and melted. We turned our fire on the second shape.

Bezrel flung himself to safety under the hangar door. My rifle beeped; it was running out of charge. Tolliver waved a fist. My teeth bared in a feral grin.

Cautiously I backed toward the hangar, keeping to the side to leave Tolliver a clear field. Only one outrider charged me; I couldn't tell which of us hit it.

Elated, I stumbled to the hangar, reached the door unharmed. A shadow moved through the scorched grass of the field. I looked up.

A second fish floated above.

Cursing, I stooped under the door. Sparks fell on my

shoulders; I slapped them away. "Tolliver, there's another one!"

"Christ." Tolliver backed away, squinted at the door. "Jameson, get that track *down*!"

The tech's voice was savage. "You want a miracle, make one yourself!" I shook Tolliver's shoulder, shushed him. Jameson was doing his best.

"We're down to four recharges, sir."

"Two." I stooped, took one, gave another to Bezrel, crossed to the other end of the door. The boy followed like a puppy.

I knelt, turned off the safety, aimed. Three outriders were in sight on the field, too far away to risk a shot. "Mr. Tolliver, help Jameson cut. Bezrel, take position at the far end of the hangar. Here's your last recharge. Make every shot count."

I peeked under the door. The fish overhead had settled closer.

Sparks cascaded onto my head. Cursing, I moved aside. By the time I knelt again, the outriders had crossed half the field. I fired. The closest went down. Bezrel, face ashen, held his beam open as he sprayed the parade ground. I screamed, "Middy, single fire! Make every electron count!"

The two remaining outriders flew at us. I fired twice, hit a shape just as it jerked and sagged from Bezrel's hit. The other flowed over its fallen comrade, veered away from Bezrel and the open door. I fired until it dived around the outside of the hangar. I whirled to the shattered side wall, waiting. Nothing appeared.

The hangar door groaned. Pieces of coupling sagged and dripped to the floor.

Still, the door held. Tolliver cursed, moved to the next brace. Only two remained, but they held the track. If I ever got out I'd complain to Engineers' Corps.

"The fish is landing!" Bezrel waved frantically at the field.

Jameson moved to the last coupling on his side of the scaffold. "Christ, I hope this thing falls right. If it collapses on us . . ."

"Be ready to jump clear!" If the door fell inward it would knock over the scaffold and crush anyone underneath.

"Jump, sure." He shook his head in disgust, but his torch was steady.

"The fish! The fish!" Bezrel's voice was a scream.

I whirled. The alien had settled to the field, colors swimming. Shapes were already swirling to the surface. I raised my rifle. "Steady, Mr. Bezrel." I turned back to the side wall.

"When should I put in the last charge, sir?" The boy's tone was unsteady.

"When your current one is empty." I made sure to sound gentle, despite the idiocy of the question.

Tolliver called down, "Mine still has half a charge, sir."

"Hang on to it for now. Toss it down if I yell."

"Right." A shower of sparks.

"Jesus!" Bezrel clutched his gun. "They're coming!"

I spun around, peered at the field. Five, at least. If we waited for a close shot they'd all be on us. I aimed, pretending calm. Behind me Sergeant Swopes strode the firing line, swagger stick propped on his shoulder, his young charges lined up in a row opposite the targets. "Do not jerk the trigger, gentlemen, squeeze it. Steady . . ."

One down.

"Single fire, gentlemen . . . Don't waste your charge . . ."

Missed the son of a bitch.

"Sight before you fire."

Gotcha! Where in hell are the rest?

Sarge's voice faded. On the Academy firing line a flick of his baton was the only penalty if you missed target.

Bezrel shrieked, triggering his empty weapon at the shape hurtling at him. I had no time to aim. I flicked the switch to automatic and fired past his hip. The alien dissolved no more than a meter from his feet.

"Reload, Bezrel!"

"Yes, sir. I mean, aye aye, sir!" He fumbled at the recharge, dropped it, scrambled after it as it rolled away.

I glanced to the side wall, back to the parade ground. Three more outriders skittered toward us.

"Watch the door!" Tolliver jumped over the scaffold rail, leaped to the ground.

The door crashed outward with a earth-shattering thud, blocking my view of the field. It fell atop the pieces of door that we'd already cut off. The near end of the door lay propped six inches off the ground.

Tolliver knelt and aimed. "Come on, you son of bitch!" Coolly, he held his fire until a shape was almost upon us. His finger twitched and it was down, oozing under the bright sunlight that flooded the terminal.

My rifle beeped. I reached for a recharge, found none. The snap of Bezrel's and Tolliver's rifles cut the silence.

Bezrel's rifle beeped.

I glanced back at the shuttle, ahead to the menacing shapes still emerging from the grounded fish. "Jameson, bring down the torch and tanks!" He gaped. "Move!" He grabbed the tanks and lowered them down to me.

They were heavier than I'd thought. I managed not to drop them. Jameson swarmed down the side of the scaffold, carrying the torch. I waited in helpless frenzy while he snapped the connections back into place.

I thumbed the ignition, turned on the gas. A small flame flickered. "Bezrel, Jameson, into the shuttle. Tolliver, warm the jet engines. Get everyone into suits."

"But—"

"MOVE!" The bellow tore at my throat. I dragged the hose outside, as far as it would go, and balanced on top of the huge fallen door in front of the hangar. A shape quivered, skittered toward me. I waited, my hand on the gas. When the alien had closed to fifteen feet I spun open the knob. Ten feet. A great gout of fire surged from the hose. Five feet. The shape veered, but too late. It dissolved in a red glow of hell.

I spun down the knob. Behind me an engine muttered, then roared.

Three outriders approached the inferno, rolled to a halt twenty feet away. I closed down the gas. We waited in stalemate. The nearest one's shape changed as I watched.

Behind me the engine abruptly silenced. I whirled. From the shuttle porthole Tolliver waved frantically at the hangar's side wall.

An outrider was almost through a ragged hole. Its inner portion bulged as it flowed through the wall. The shuttle engines coughed, started again.

"Come to me, you bastard!" I dragged the hose toward the

wall. Behind me, the three outriders took the ground I'd abandoned. I flicked a wave of fire in their direction, spun back.

I was at the end of my hose. I tugged, stopped for fear I'd break the line. Outside, the three shapes waited, quivering.

I spun my knob to full. A gout of flame gushed, fell short of the shape emerging from the shattered wall. Cursing, I ran back toward the door, hurled a blast of fire at the three waiting outriders. Two moved aside, one wasn't fast enough. I grabbed a tank, tried to lift the second, couldn't hang on to them both. I kicked one over, shoved it toward the side wall. I needed only a meter. I dropped the second tank; it clanged on the concrete floor.

I strained until the hose went taut. The shape emerged from the wall. As it skittered toward me I spun the knob. It met the flame only five feet distant, rolled on, burning. I jumped aside, dropping the torch. The shape sizzled, melted to liquid. I peered outside. The outriders I'd seen there were gone.

I turned to the far side of the hangar. Nothing. Tolliver pounded his window, summoning me with shouts made inaudible by the bellow of the engines.

I ran to the shuttle hatch, clambered aboard. Tolliver, suited, was in the pilot's seat. He shouted, "Suit up!"

I thrust it on. Bezrel, strapped in, clutched the chair ahead. He seemed not to see me. Jameson, also suited, gripped a laser pistol. I clipped on the helmet. I asked Tolliver, "See any of them?"

"Not at the moment, sir."

"There's no time to move the door aside. Roll over it."

"We'll snap off the wheel assembly."

"We might." From the copilot's seat I slid the broken throttle forward. No response. "Puter, manual override! Disconnect safeties!"

"Disconnected by pilot order. Disconnect logged."

"Shut up." I thrust the throttle forward again. The engine's growl rose to a roar.

We lurched. I throttled back as we rolled toward the door. "Tolliver, can you fly this thing? What's takeoff speed? How much runway do we need?"

"I've never flown a shuttle. I don't have the slightest idea. We'll shake apart if you try to reach orbital speed, and you'll blow the engines if you use the take-off jets to fly all the way home!" He hesitated. "As to cruising, I could probably handle her. Here's your takeoff speed." He tapped the mark on the airspeed indicator. A hundred ten knots. "She's a short-runway craft, or she wouldn't be here."

I inched the shuttle to the fallen door until I judged our wheel was about to touch. I throttled down, up again. We glided forward, bumped the door. I jammed down the throttle. "Take her, Mr. Tolliver. You have a surer hand." I hated the admission.

Slowly, infinitesimally, he powered up, pressing our wheel against the edge of the door. The ship strained, but didn't move. With a curse Tolliver reversed jets; we glided back a foot or so.

At the hangar doorway, a shape appeared. It stood quivering, as if measuring the distance between us.

Tolliver throttled. The ship inched to the door, bumped. Tentatively, he throttled higher. He shook his head. "The wheel won't go over. Any harder and we'll lose it."

"Try!"

Face taut, he edged us on. The engines roared. Abruptly he powered down to idle. "You have any idea how much thrust we're applying? The wheel can't be rated for—"

The shape moved.

I took hold of the yoke, placed my feet on the rudders. The outrider drifted toward us, as if uncertain. I reversed the engines, throttled as smoothly as I could. We slid back from the door. "How long is the shuttle, and how big is the damned hangar?"

"We have about thirty feet behind us. But if you back the engines to the rear wall—"

"I'll blow the wall out."

"Or blow us sky high!"

I rolled the shuttle backward. Why in God's name didn't they teach us shuttle piloting at Academy? We'd learned helis, riflery, stellar navigation . . .

Tolliver peered through the porthole. "That's far enough!"

I nodded, reversed the engines again. "Hang on."

"What are you doing?"

"Jumping the bloody door!"

"Lord God!" He braced himself against the dash.

"Bezrel, Jameson, grab hold!" I held the brake with both feet, gunned the jets until I felt the ship fight against the restraint. Please, Lord. Make it work.

I let loose the brake, jammed the throttle to full. We lurched, gaining speed. Thirty feet to the door. The hangar walls slid past. Fifteen feet.

Five.

My helmet slammed into the cockpit ceiling. I bounced down to my seat. We still rolled. A second later the back wheels hit the fallen door, and nearly threw me from my seat.

"I've got it." Tolliver's hand was steady on the throttle.

Two shapes lunged at us from the side of the hangar. Tolliver turned the yoke to starboard; we bumped diagonally across the field past the dying fish. The outriders chased us with their odd rolling gait. Others emerged from the mottled fish and flowed toward us, like iron filings to a magnet. Tolliver throttled higher.

"Ease off! We have to make a turn at the end of the field!"

"Unless we get ahead of them now, they'll catch us when we turn." He held the throttle steady as we bounced across the grass. "Where are we going, once we're off the ground?"

"To Centraltown."

"We can't, I told you! With the portholes missing we'll shake apart going orbital, and if we try to jet that far, the engines will blow."

"I know." I glanced behind. About fifteen shapes pursued us. "Jameson, fire at anything near."

"For once in your life, stop being devious! What in hell are you up to?"

I forced my eyes back to the dash. "We'll take off and go suborbital."

"Sub—what are you talking about?"

"After takeoff, fly east and pull up her nose. We'll fire the rockets."

"That will—"

"After forty seconds, shut them off."

"We'll fall!" The wheels touched the runway, once smooth, now pitted from the blast of the rock the aliens had hurled at us.

"Yes. We'll glide back down as far as we can, then relight the jets. If we gain enough altitude, that will put us far enough east to jet home."

"Not far enough to reach land before the jets overheat. We haven't plotted ballistics; you have no idea where we'll end up." He throttled back as we neared the end of the runway. "If you don't blow us apart you'll blow the engines off the fuselage."

I gripped his arm. "I'm going to Centraltown. This is the only way there." I twisted the yoke, eased us to port. The ship turned slowly, majestically.

"Why not stay and fight? Better to die facing the fish!"

I snapped down my visor. "There's something I must do." I no longer had any doubt.

"What?"

My voice was even. "I won't tell you, Mr. Tolliver." If he knew, he wouldn't help fly the shuttle. I lined us up in the center of the runway. "Once you take off, swing east." I peered through the porthole. "You'd better hurry." The shapes rolled to intersect us.

Smoothly he pushed the throttle forward. Fifteen knots. The outriders changed direction, converged on us. We hurtled down the runway. Twenty knots. A few shapes were left behind; others scrambled alongside. Ahead, more gathered. One waited in the center of the runway. Forty knots.

I had to strain to hear Tolliver's words. "Lord God, I repent of my sins." Fifty knots; I checked my straps. "Forgive me my trespasses." Sixty-five. "If I have offended Thee . . ." The rest was lost in the roar of the engines. The outrider in the center of the runway skittered toward us with lightning speed.

"Look out—"

"I see it!" As we bore down on the alien shape it launched itself at the cockpit. I reared back in my seat, hands over my face. Something smashed dark and wet into the pilot's windshield.

"Jesus God!" Goo dripped from the window. Tolliver

peered through the mess, searching for the runway. Thick liquid seeped along the windshield toward the pilot's shattered porthole.

I shouted, "Left rudder! You're drifting!" Seventy-five knots.

Ahead, the runway was rumpled, where the blast from the rock had shifted the earth. We surged upward, bounced back onto the runway, losing speed. "Hold the nose down!" Sixty-five knots. The end of the runway soared toward us. Seventy.

"We won't make it!"

"Hold her down! Use the grass beyond the runway!"

He muttered, "Use the trees, you mean." The windbreak that had once stood at the far end of the parade ground was knocked askew by the blast, but branches still clawed upward to snatch us from the air.

Tolliver shoved the throttle as far forward as it would go. I measured to the end of the pavement, to the end of the grass. Ninety knots.

The trees. We hurtled along the grass. One hundred knots. The trees. One hundred five. *THE TREES*.

"Hang on." Tolliver pulled back the yoke, five knots short of indicated takeoff speed. The nose lifted with nightmare deliberation. Our rear wheels floated off the runway. Trees flung themselves at our undercarriage. A scrape. I braced for impact. Scant yards ahead, a clump of trees reared skyward. Tolliver yanked back on the yoke.

"We'll stall!"

No time for an answer. Our airspeed fell. We floated over the stand of trees. Tolliver dropped the nose. We fell toward the hillside, losing altitude, gaining speed. He leveled off and we were clear. For eons we soared over forest, our airspeed slowly rising. Finally, when it was safe, he gently pulled back on the yoke and we regained precious altitude.

He remarked, "Coming around to the east."

Thank Lord God. I asked, "At what height do we fire rockets?"

"How the hell would I know? Ask the puter!"

I flipped on the puter circuits. "Advise recommended altitude for rocket ignition."

The puter's response was immediate. "Impossible to achieve orbit with cabin damage."

"Never mind that. What's the recommended altitude?"

"Rocket engines on safety lock due to compromise of cabin integrity. Ignition will not occur at any alt—"

I pounded the dash. "Override all safeties! Manual ignition! Advise normal altitude for rocket ignition when cabin undamaged and pressurized."

"Recommended ignition five thousand feet. Safeties overridden. Override is log—"

"Christ!" Tolliver edged away from his porthole. Drops of goo hovered on the broken transplex. One flew off and hit the back of his seat.

I grabbed my pistol.

"Be careful with that!"

"I know." I aimed at the porthole, set the pistol to continuous beam, held the trigger. The goo smoked and vanished. The porthole glowed red. I aimed at Tolliver's seat. "Don't lean back." I fired at the seat back; its fabric melted instantly at the touch of the beam. The seat insulation glowed, broke into flames. I snapped off the pistol, slapped out the fire with my suited hand. "Don't sit back until it's cool."

"I'll have to lie back when we accelerate. Put something on the seat, so I don't have to touch . . . that."

"It's been vaporized." Nevertheless I unstrapped myself and went back to the cabin. Bezrel gripped his chair. His face was white, his lips wet with spittle. I reached into the storage compartment, found a blanket. A pillow fell to the floor. I thrust it at the boy. "Hold this." He hugged it, rocking.

I folded the blanket, laid it across Tolliver's seat, over the scorched hole I'd made. Cautiously he leaned back. "Four thousand feet. Sir, when we fire . . ."

"Yes?"

"If we don't burn long enough, we fall into the ocean. Too long and we may disintegrate."

"I know." I licked my lips. "Try forty seconds. Be ready to cut off if we shake too hard."

"Right. Whatever 'too hard' means."

Five thousand feet. Tolliver looked at me. I met his eye, nodded.

He keyed the master ignition; the three rockets caught with a thunderous roar. They flung me back into my acceleration seat.

Five seconds. I glanced down, found the altimeter. Six thousand feet.

Ten seconds. Buffeting. A weight settling on my chest. I panted for breath. Eight thousand feet. Ten thousand. The world grayed. We bumped over a rutted country road.

"Thirty seconds, sir!" Tolliver gripped the sides of his seat. The shuttle shook.

Twelve thousand feet. Thirteen. Turbulence was worse.

"Forty seconds!" With effort he reached for the ignition.

"No!" I fought to inhale. "Need . . . more altitude."

"We'll break up!"

"Go for thirty thousand!" I forced oxygen into my lung.

"We can't make thirty!" Bangs and thumps shook the cabin.

"Wait." I heaved to breathe.

"Sixteen thousand!" My head sank into the acceleration pads. They were soft, comfortable, warm. Tolliver's voice was distant. "Twenty-one thousand!"

One couldn't swim in the sea; it had been too polluted for nearly a century. But once I'd been to the beach with Father. The sand, above the high-water mark, was warm and comfortable. I wriggled luxuriously, eyes closed against the probing solar glare, while Father watched with silent disapproval. Something in the sea air made it hard to breathe.

"Captain, let me cut the engines!"

I dozed, annoyed by the incessant roar of the waves. "Twenty-five thousand!"

Silence. My body surged against the straps. As my ears cleared I heard an odd whistling. My chest heaved. Greedily I sucked at air. The roar of the engines had eased.

Tolliver held the yoke rigid, eyes straining past the glop on his windshield. I coughed, struggled to an upright position. I gasped, "Altitude?"

"Twenty-eight thousand and rising."

"Rising, with the engine off?"

"Even a cannonball goes up for a while. Wait."

We reached the top of our arc. In a moment the shuttle

took on the gliding characteristics of a brick. We dropped precipitously despite Tolliver's best efforts. He said, "We'll have to fire the engines to hold altitude."

"I know." But after thirty minutes burn, they'd overheat. Shuttle jets were designed for landings and little else. I peered at the instruments. "Where are we?"

"Some four hundred miles out, according to the beacons."

Even at five hundred knots, we'd crash at least an hour short of landfall.

"Radio a Mayday, sir. If we ditch they can meet us with a heli."

I shook my head. "No. We need the shuttle."

"We won't make it. If we put down in the water, we might—"

"Fly us home!"

Twelve thousand feet. Tolliver slammed his fist into the chair. "God damn you, why?" He waved away my outrage. "You want me to fly this boat into the sea. All right, I'll die with you! Tell me why!"

I said hoarsely, "I need the shuttle. I can't say why."

"You're afraid I'll betray you?" he jeered. "To which enemy, Captain? The fish or the planters?"

I swallowed. "Mr. Tolliver, I can't tell you. Someday you'll understand."

"I don't want to waste my death, to no purpose."

"We have a purpose." The corners of my mouth twitched. "And we may not die. There's safety margin built into the engine specs. Just look at the hangar door."

After a moment his teeth bared in what might have been a smile. "We'll have to find out." His eyes strayed to the panel. "Eight thousand feet, sir. We'd better ignite."

"Yes." He lit the jets, and gradually our descent slowed. We flew in uneasy silence.

After a time I unbuckled my seat belt. "Watch the engine temps." He shot me a look of annoyance. I blurted, "Sorry. Nerves." Now I was apologizing to a middy. I smiled grimly.

In the fifth row I stooped and slid next to Bezrel. "Are you all right?"

"Yes, sir." He clutched at the pillow. I waited, but he said no more.

"We're all frightened, joey."

His expression was cautious. "I'm fine."

"All of us, Mr. Bezrel." I patted his knee, stood awkwardly.

"I want to go home." His voice was muffled in the pillow.

"We're almost there."

"No. Home."

Didn't we all. I went back to the cockpit, sat, strapped on my oxygen. "ETA?"

Tolliver muttered, "I don't think we have one."

I glowered.

After a moment he said, "Sorry, sir. Say, forty-five minutes."

Temperatures were high normal, but holding steady. I thumbed the caller. "Captain Seafort to Admiralty House or Governor's Manse. Acknowledge." No answer. I tried again; finally the response came.

"Manse to incoming heli. Mr. Seafort? We thought . . ."

"Is Admiralty House open?"

"No, sir."

The temperature crept toward the red line. "Where's Governor Hopewell?"

"Standing by, sir. I paged him. Here he comes."

"Zack?"

"Yes, lad." His gruff voice brought a welcome lump to my throat.

"We're not in the heli, we've got a shuttle. Clear the spaceport runway. Have a heli waiting. And find anyone who worked on the shuttle repair crews."

"Is that all?"

"Yes, but hurry. Our ETA is forty minutes." The temp needle hovered at the red line.

Tolliver tapped the altimeter. "We'll have to ditch."

"Get us altitude."

"That'll generate more heat."

"I know." But it would gain us time if the engines failed.

On landing jets we climbed slowly to eighteen thousand. The needle inched inexorably into the red. I checked the console. "Thirty minutes. Two hundred eighty miles."

"The engines won't last."

"They have to."

He cleared his throat. "Sir, do you understand that if we keep burning—"

"Don't argue!"

"I'm not. If we keep burning and we overheat, the bearings may melt. Even if we landed safely, these engines would never fire again."

I faced the bitter possibility. "We have to try."

He shook his head, chose to say nothing. The needle crept farther into the red. A warning signal beeped; I switched it off. Twenty-five minutes.

"Throttle back."

"We're at best performance speed now, sir."

"It might help the temp."

He throttled back. The temperature didn't go down, but at least it rose no further.

Twenty minutes.

The speaker crackled. "Incoming shuttle, we have you on radar. What are you—did you fly that thing from the Venturas?"

"Yes." He would think me glitched. He'd probably be right.

Eighteen minutes. "Mr. Tolliver, how far can we glide?"

"A few miles, at best. We're not high enough."

A hundred fifty miles from Centraltown. The temperature needle crept upward. So close, and yet . . .

"Shut off the jets."

"Now, sir? We'll fall into—" He saw my expression, snapped the switches.

"Mr. Tolliver, watch our distance. Mark off to thirty-five miles."

"We won't come near to—"

I ignited the rockets. Tolliver yelled, reached for the shut-offs. I was hurled into my seat. I strained at the yoke, kept us level.

"You can't burn rockets in flight mode! You'll tear off the wings!"

"Just for a few seconds!"

"You're insane!" He reached again for the switch; I slapped away his arm.

"Distance!"

"A hundred twenty miles!"

I forced the yoke back, easing us into a climb. The craft shook abominably. Stress indicators lit like Christmas lights.

"Sixteen thousand feet. One hundred two miles!"

I fought to hold the yoke, barely kept control.

"Plese, sir, turn it off!"

I reached for the master switch, diverted my fingers, found the two I wanted. I snapped them off. The turbulence eased.

"Christ, now what are you doing?"

"Flying on center rocket only." For as long as its fuel held out, or until the battered ship could take no more.

His hands tightened on the yoke. "Let me help control her." Gratefully I eased my pressure on the yoke. He said, "Are you aware, sir, that some of us prefer to stay alive?"

I glared at him. His eyes danced. "I could relieve you for this, you know. Trouble is, no one would believe me."

I watched the console. "Sixty miles. Twenty thousand feet. In a couple of minutes we might be close enough to glide in."

He shook his head. "After this, they'll have to rewrite the specs."

"Shuttle, your flight path is not, repeat, not appropriate for achieving orbit." The voice on the caller sounded anxious.

I grinned, keying the caller. "Very well, we'll alter course." My hand went to the console. "Shall we?"

"Ready, sir."

I cut the switches, and again the roar diminished to the whistle of wind. I watched the altimeter fall.

"We could try the jets again," he offered.

"Best let them cool first."

In a few moments we had no choice; we'd lost most of the altitude the rockets had gained. When Tolliver finally tried the jets they wouldn't catch; I thought we'd plow a furrow into the coast before he finally nursed them to life.

After that, the landing was rather dull.

23

"How long, then?"

The mechanic shrugged. "Who knows? We've got spare transplex for the portholes; they're standard parts. We drained and replaced your engine lubricants. No sign of engine damage, but we've only tested at low power. We're not done."

"How long?" I glanced at Zack Hopewell.

"Puter simulations say she'll never go into orbit with the side so badly dented. It'll have to be completely rebuilt—"

"HOW LONG?"

He tossed the specs to the floor. "Never, if you talk like that. I'm a volunteer, joey. I don't give God's own damn if—"

"You listen to me." Zack's voice was low and cold. "Have this machine ready to fly in two days, not an hour longer. We're under martial law and I won't hesitate to hang you if you don't." He took a step toward the mechanic; involuntarily the man darted back. "Understand me?"

The mechanic swallowed. "All right, go easy. But I can't promise no two days, not with tearing down the body—"

"I'll assign all the help you need. Get started!" Hopewell strode away, and I followed. He sighed. "Hang the man? Did you hear, Mr. Seafort? He's one of my countrymen."

"You saved me from making a fool of myself." I'd been ready to hurl myself at the mechanic's throat.

We walked toward Zack Hopewell's heli. He sat, looked up at me. "You're sure you've found a way?"

I climbed in next to him. "No, but I think so. With Lord God's blessing, you'll be safe again."

"Why won't you tell us what it is?"

My hand tightened on the door. "Change the subject. Please, I beg you."

"You won't return, after." It wasn't a question.

"I think not."

His lined face was without expression. "You carve your own destiny, Captain, as do we all. We'll miss you."

"Thank you."

"After you . . . go, there will be no Government."

"Yours is in place."

"But without authority. I will not pretend to rule by grace of a departed Navy."

We waited while Tolliver crossed the tarmac. He climbed into the heli's back seat. "Plenty of shuttle fuel on hand."

I grunted.

We lifted off. Hopewell said, "Is two days soon enough?"

"It'll have to be." I stared at the houses below. "I'll fly the shuttle alone."

Hopewell frowned. "I wish you'd—"

"You can't." Tolliver. I swung to him, my eyes dangerous. He said, "You'll pass out."

"I'll be all right."

"Yes, sir. What happened when we went suborbital?"

"That was just one—"

"And when we flew to the station with Jerence?" I had no answer. His eyes were intense. "We're only alive by grace of a miracle, sir. Don't ask for another. You can't handle acceleration with one lung."

"What do you want of me? The shuttle pilots were all U.N.A.F. and went with the fleet!"

"Yes." He looked out the window. "I may not be skillful, but I flew her once. Sir."

"We won't be com—" I chopped off the thought. There might be time for him, if I planned it carefully. "Very well. If you volunteer."

"Volunteer? Well, if I must. I'd like a shuttle rating added to my file, afterward."

"Shuttle rati—" I saw the smile he meant to hide. The man could be infuriating. "Very well." I would do it, if I remembered in time. Let him explain the ludicrous rating when he again met the Admiral.

Hopewell had listened to the byplay without a comment. Now he said, "I have a heli and pilot waiting for you at the Manse."

"Thank you." Tired beyond words, I puzzled where to go.

Tolliver prompted gently, "Your wife, sir."

I snarled, "Of course." The damned impudence.

Annie was asleep. I sat in the unfamiliar living room while the nurse stared into a flickering holo.

She'd told me Annie had seemed all right, the morning before. Then, when we hadn't returned as I'd promised, her mood had changed. She began to smash chairs against the wall. When the nurse intervened Annie clawed at her, keening. The nurse had finally managed to sedate her. Annie slept the night through and into the new day.

How long had it been since I'd had sleep? I needed to say my good-byes to Annie, to Alexi. Deal with the planters. Leave instructions for—

"She's asking for you." The nurse.

I snapped awake. I touched my tie, ran my fingers through my hair, glad of my bath and change of clothes when at last I'd seen my apartment. I hesitated, trying to recall where the bedroom was. The nurse pointed. "There."

"Thank you." I peered through the door. "Annie?"

Her look was puzzled, vacant. "Nicky? You din' come back when you say."

"I know, hon." I sat on the bed. "I'm sorry."

She threw off the sheet, hugged her legs. "I waited, an' you din' even call."

"We had problems, hon. The fish."

"I don' care 'bout no fish." She sat up, wriggled her toes. "I wan' get dressed. Got me a new blouse. Bet it go nice wid my jewels." She grinned, stared at her feet until her gaze flickered to alarm. "Nicky, my jewels, they—" She stopped short.

"Oh, Annie." Lord God, aren't You just? How could You treat her so?

"I'll wear my green dress."

"I'd like to see that one, love."

"Yeah, me too. I dunno if I wore it yet." She scrambled out of bed. "You gotta tell me if you like it, now you be stayin'."

It would be vile to spoil her happiness. I'd wait until tomorrow to tell her I had to go aloft. She prattled while she dressed. "I waited and waited fo' you, den . . ." Her brow knitted. "I wen' sleep, I think. Don' be goin' away no mo', Nicky."

"Hon . . ." I hated myself, but I couldn't stand a lie. "The day after tomorrow. For a long time."

It made her still. Her hand crept to her neck as if to finger the absent rubies. "I die if you be leavin' me, Nicky."

"You'll be all right, hon. You won't die."

"Oh, yes." Her certainty chilled me. "I be killin' myself, you go way again. I know."

I sat on the bed, clasped her hand. "Annie, I have to take a trip. I must."

"Den I be goin' wid you." She snatched away her hand, preened her hair. She giggled.

Lamely, I changed the subject. When she was ready, we went for a walk. Later I lay down on the bed. She curled up beside me like a trusting child, but when I threw my arm around her, she flinched.

In the morning, while I dressed, I made appointments with Harmon and Emmett Branstead, and later with the shuttle mechanic. I assured Annie I'd be back within a few hours, tried not to notice her despair, and left.

I turned back before I even reached the heli waiting in the drive. "Come on, hon." I held open the door.

Her joy melted my misgivings. I'd find someplace for her to stay while I held my meetings. Soon enough I'd have to abandon her in earnest.

I stopped first to see the civil engineers who ran Central-town's power grid. After, we flew to the Manse and took breakfast with Zack Hopewell. The affairs of government held no interest for me, but I made an effort to listen.

"Don't forget tomorrow's meeting," he reminded me.

My blank stare told him all.

"The proposed law of inheritance. You said the planters' vote could decide the matter."

"Oh, yes. That."

"I know it seems odd, with our world crashing about us,

but we—they're determined to establish a just plantation code."

"I suppose."

"Would you rather the meeting was canceled?"

"No. In fact, the timing will work well. Where's it to be held?"

"At the spaceport terminal."

"Fitting." I gave him my instructions. He was puzzled, but agreed without protest.

His aide knocked. "The Bransteads, sir."

"Show them in."

Hopewell stood. "You'll want to see them alone."

"It's all right, really. I—"

"I don't mind." He left.

Harmon and his brother Emmett entered the Manse. I crossed the room. "It's good to see you. Truly." I offered my hand. Harmon took it automatically, Emmett more shyly. After all, he'd served in the Navy. I took the sofa; they settled in chairs opposite.

"You're going to the Station?" Harmon.

"Yes." It was no secret, given my frantic orders for repair of the shuttle.

"Can we be of help?"

"No. I wanted to say good-bye." At Harmon's raised eyebrow I added, "You've been a good friend."

"As I'll continue to be."

"Lord God willing." I would return if I could, but I knew better than to delude myself. It was unlikely.

"I remember when I first met you, Captain." Harmon's voice was soft.

"My long-leave."

"With your friend, Mr. Carr. You stayed overnight."

"And we deceived you." My eyes suddenly filled. "You were a good man then, Harmon. As you are now."

He left his chair, crossed to my sofa, sat at my side. "What's wrong, Nicholas?"

For a moment I couldn't speak. Then, "Have you ever done a terrible thing, to prevent a worse?"

He shook his head. "Thank Lord God, He hasn't tested me so."

I stared at the carpet. "I feel . . . alone."

"Let us help you."

"No. You cannot." I took a deep breath, then another. "Thank you both for everything. I owe you my life, and more." I got to my feet; I had to put an end to the interview.

They stood with me. Emmett spoke quietly. "Godspeed."

"I'll see you tomorrow before I go aloft."

"Oh?"

"You'll be notified," I said.

"I see." Mystified, they left.

I flew with Tolliver and Bezrel to Admiralty House. I glanced at a few files, read William's reports on the recent attack. Shortly after the Station had gone over the horizon, the aliens' ranks had thinned, and for the moment no more fish were to be seen.

I asked the two middies to escort Annie to dinner, and settled myself alone with the regs. I read for hours, until I found what I wanted.

Afterward, there was nothing but to go to bed.

At the relief offices, Alexi Tamarov sat in his cubicle, biting his thumbnail, his full attention on the map in front of him.

"Am I interrupting?"

He looked up, startled. "Of course not, Mr. Seafort. Thank God you made it home."

"How've you been?"

He grimaced. "As always. I make myself useful, but a native could do the job better. I think they're only using me as a favor to you." I wondered how he'd guessed.

I peered at his map. "What are you doing?"

"Devising new bus schedules. Half the streets are gone, but so are half the buses." He rested his head on his hand, stared at me. "You didn't come to talk about buses."

"No."

He waited.

"I'd like to show you something."

"Could I finish what—"

"Now." He thought to protest, saw my look, quieted. "Do you have a uniform, Alexi?"

"I've worn civvies since I left the hospital. Do I need one?"

"It would be appropriate. We'll find you something." We went out to the heli where Annie waited. I had the pilot drop us at Admiralty House, and I asked Tolliver to lend Alexi one of his old uniforms. It wouldn't fit well, but no matter.

I paced the reception room. "They're all coming? Harmon and Emmett too?"

Hopewell nodded. "Yes. And the Volksteader clan, and Palabee, and the others. Even if you hadn't called them, they wouldn't miss the vote on inheritance."

I checked my watch. My mouth was dry.

At two o'clock Bezrel, Tolliver, and Alexi arrived. Alexi's uniform, ill-fitting or no, almost broke my heart. He belonged to the Navy.

We all flew together in the large Navy heli. I brooded in the front seat, hardly bothering to answer those who spoke. We set down at the spaceport. I took Annie's hand as we went in.

The terminal looked as it had for Triforth's declaration. The dais remained. I sat in the front of the hall, with my officers. My interest was not in this part of the meeting.

Zack Hopewell brought the session to order. "If it pleases Lord God that we survive and prosper, our society requires clear and simple laws of inheritance." He seemed a biblical figure, his stern visage unwavering. "The plantations must never again be subject to laws devised by strangers in a far town." That was stretching it; Centraltown wasn't that distant from the plantation zone. And if he meant Earth, his remarks skirted treason.

The audience made no such distinction; his speech was greeted with loud approval. I scrutinized the rows of seats; as far as I could tell, every plantation was represented. Harmon and Emmett sat nearby with Jerence.

One after another, a number of questions were debated and put to the vote. The law of primogeniture was universally supported. It was primogeniture that prevented the division of the plantations into smaller and smaller parcels as generations passed.

Frederick Mantiet brought up a more difficult point. "Primogeniture settles matters when there is a next generation. But what if there isn't? Should a plantation go to distant relatives who know nothing about planting or be divided among its neighbors who do?"

"Family!" Calls echoed through the audience.

"That's easy to proclaim, in the abstract. But when 'family' turns out to be a hotel clerk or a maiden schoolteacher—"

"Let me speak." Lawrence Plumwell, manager of Carr Plantation, got to his feet.

"You're not one of us, Lawrence. You're just—"

"That's my point." The force of his anger gave Mantiet pause. He shrugged, stood aside.

Plumwell strode to the front of the room. "You all know me. I've spent thirty years managing Carr Plantation for old Randolph Senior, then on behalf of young Randolph and his son. Now the Carrs are dead, and I claim my right."

"Your right!" Mantiet was scandalized.

"My right. Hear me out. Assume for a moment that young Carr hadn't died, but remained in the Navy. Should that make a difference?"

He studied the sea of faces. "What is a plantation? Raw acreage or the knowledge to cultivate it?" Behind me, the door creaked as a latecomer arrived. I strained to hear the debate amid angry calls from the audience.

"Family is what counts!"

"Yes. But on Carr, there's been no family for two generations. How long should the land sit in memorial? Even if Derek Carr had lived, he should have been present today! I propose that no man may own a Hope Nation plantation unless he himself holds it to till the soil, to harvest his crops, to live himself in his Manse, or else—"

Cries of outrage. He overrode them all with the passion of his cause. "Or else we become nothing more than the laborers and clerks we despise!"

That gave them pause. He pressed on, "What are we, after all? We are planters. I'm one as much as you are. I've spent my life on the soil, devoting myself to the good of Carr Plantation. You, your sons, if they haven't that dedication, should they hold their lands in absentia, while others do the work? Who are we then?"

A long silence. Mantiet said quietly, in a tone filled with wonderment, "You know, he's right." He walked back to his seat. "A plantation isn't acreage, and it isn't just family. It's family working the land. When the family abandons it, they abandon our way of life." He sat.

Plumwell said firmly, "I demand we set forth now that whosoever shall work the land, shall own it, and that no planter shall separate himself from his land without losing it. I claim Carr Plantation by right of my life spent in its behalf."

Zack Hopewell stood, pounded his gavel. "Carr Plantation will serve as our precedent. I call the vote. If anyone opposes, let him now speak or forever—"

"I oppose!" A voice rang from the back of the hall. The hair on my neck rose. I craned, saw nothing. Slowly, not daring to hope, I got to my feet.

"By right of primogeniture, I claim my own!" A haggard figure strode toward the dais.

Zack Hopewell squinted at the slim young man in the ragged jacket. "Who are you, sir?"

The newcomer drew himself up. "Derek Anthony Carr, grandson of Randolph, son of Randolph, homesteader and proprietor of Carr Plantation. I claim my land, to work and to hold, to sow and to reap!"

Utter silence.

"Is there none who recognizes me? I was young when I left, but I am returned to stay."

My voice was hoarse. "I do."

He spun. "Oh, my God. Captain!" He ran to me. I took a step, opened my arms. He buried himself in them. "Oh, Lord God, you're alive!"

"And you." I held him close, loathe to release him. "Derek . . ." I drew back. "What happened to you?" The remains of his uniform were matted with dirt.

"Our lifepod crashed about a hundred miles south. We had no caller. We've walked in forest, and slid in the mud, and hacked our way through ever since."

I asked, "How many survived?"

"Five. Jessen—he was a cook—he didn't make it past the first day. We reached town only a couple of hours ago;

someone said everyone in Government had come here. I, ah, commandeered a car."

Zack Hopewell cleared his throat. I realized that the entire hall hung on our every word. Zack said, "Mr. Plumwell, the matter of Carr Plantation is set aside for the time. I declare a fifteen-minute recess." He banged his gavel.

I stood close while Derek received the accolades of his fellow planters. I hugged Annie. "Do you remember him, hon? From *Portia*?"

She snorted with derision. "Your ol' middy? Yo' friend? Course I do. Was the only nice one."

I slumped in my seat. My old middy. My friend. Nearby, Derek grinned with delight as he shook hands with well-wishers, unaware of my impending betrayal.

I stood again. "Mr. Carr, a word with you."

He glanced over his shoulder. "Of course."

"Outside."

Stung by my curtness, he followed quickly, but his grin returned before he reached the door. "God, it's good to see you!"

"Yes." I hated myself. "Derek, what you said in there . . ." I paused, almost relented, forced myself onward. "Renounce it."

Puzzled, he studied me. "I don't understand."

"You said that you've returned to stay."

"I have!"

"No."

"But where would I go?"

I said, "Where you're sent."

Appalled, he stared at my face. "You can't be serious!"

"It's two years before your enlistment runs out." I ought to know; I'd given him the oath myself, on *Hibernia*'s bridge, in the forever-lost days of my youth. "Stand by your oath."

"To what? The Navy? Look around you!"

"I am the lawful representative of the Gov—"

"Goofjuice! There's nothing left, and even if there is, let it go! I'm home to stay!"

"You're a midshipman and I'm Captain. Remember that when you speak."

His eyes mirrored his dismay. "After all we've gone through, you think of that?"

I was failing. So much depended on reaching him. "Derek . . ."

"Captain, this is my home. Carr is *my* plantation; it's been ours for generations. If I leave now, Plumwell will steal it. But for God's grace, I'd be hacking my way through the brush still, while he took my family's home! Do you think an oath of enlistment stands against that? Could I face my father after I die, and tell him I gave it all up?"

I seized his arm. "Derek, hear me. I beg you. Just listen."

He turned away. After a moment, he turned back, his eyes cold. "To think how I worshiped you. I was a fool."

"Derek—"

"I'll listen. I won't speak until you're done. Then we're through with each other. Forevermore."

If that were the cost . . . even so. My voice was husky. "Derek, I'm not a good person. You know that more than I. In all my life, I've had but three friends. Jason, when I was a boy. He . . . died. Alexi. And you." I halted, groping. "Because I've had few friends, they've meant much to me. I want to save you."

"My life isn't in danger here. In fact—"

"You said you'd listen." I waited for his reluctant nod. "Come." Without waiting I walked around the end of the terminal, toward the tarmac. Automatically I checked the runway for incoming traffic; of course, there was none.

I stopped, faced him once more. "I told you I'm not a good person. The truth is much worse. After you left with Tremaine, I deliberately broke my sworn oath."

"There must have been—"

"I'm damned, irredeemably. Nothing I do can save me. I will suffer the fires of eternal hell."

"Whatever you did, you—"

I whispered, "Derek, I burn in them now!" It silenced him. I groped through tears. "Please! As you love me, as you love yourself, don't betray Lord God! Nothing is worth that. Adhere to your oath!"

His lean, aristocratic face portrayed his agony. "Do you know what you ask of me? My heritage!"

"Derek Carr, I call you to your oath!"

He spun away, stalked across the tarmac. I waited. I had done what I might.

I shifted from leg to leg, studying the concrete. I didn't dare look to Derek. Long minutes passed. I watched the groups clustered outside the terminal. They began to drift back inside. Still I waited.

Footsteps. I waited until they were close before I turned.

Derek drew closed the remains of his jacket. Bitterness blazed from his hollow eyes. He stopped before me, came stiffly to attention. "Midshipman Derek Anthony Carr reporting, sir." He snapped an icy salute.

I returned it. "As you were. Come along."

"May I ask where you're assigning me, *sir*?"

"You may not." We strode in silence back to the terminal. Inside, Hopewell was banging for order. I continued past my seat to the front. "Mr. Carr, sit here." I mounted the dais.

I looked to Hopewell; he gestured outside, nodded.

"Your attention, please." My voice had the habit of command, and carried. A moment later all was still. "As representative of the United Nations Government I confirm the laws of inheritance voted here today."

Plumwell shot to his feet. "What about absentees? You can't—"

"There shall be no absentee ownership. A member of the controlling family must live on a plantation at all times, else the plantation reverts to the common weal." I spoke as if with authority.

Derek's eyes bored into me, burning with rage.

"I turn now to other matters of importance. We meet in a hall where some of your number carried out treason against the lawful Government of our United Nations. That Government is restored. It's fitting that in this place I tell you I will leave Hope Nation late this afternoon. After I leave, no United Nations representative will take my place."

"What about Zack?" Harmon Branstead.

"I shall resign." Hopewell's tone brooked no discussion.

"Free Laura, then!" Someone in back.

"Hers is not the way—"

"How will you stop us? We'll have our revolution despite everything!"

Harmon got to his feet. "Captain, you can't expect us to keep your Government in place once you leave."

"No."

"We're on our own, then."

"No." It brought a puzzled murmur.

Leota Volksteader said, "There's nothing between the two. We're a U.N. colony, unless we seize our freedom. If your fleet returns, we'll be at war with you. We know only the U.N. can change our status."

"I am the U.N."

"You're—what?"

I rested a hand on the lectern. "I am the United Nations." I banged the gavel; the sound echoed like a shot and stilled the babble of the hall.

"Now I, Nicholas Ewing Seafort, Captain Commanding, on behalf of all forces civil and military, as representative in transit of the General Assembly and as plenipotentiary of the Government of the United Nations, hereby terminate, as of midnight tonight, the United Nations trusteeship over the colony of Hope Nation, system of Hope Nation, and do hereby grant to the Commonwealth of Hope Nation full and irrevocable membership in the Assembly of the United Nat—"

A tumult of approval and joy. Hats flew, chairs tumbled. Men and women danced in frenzied celebration.

I waited on the dais, smiling despite myself. Zack Hopewell came close. He said simply, "They'll hang you for it, lad."

"Yes, but they'll have greater cause." He made as if to inquire, but I shook my head.

Eventually the euphoria subsided. I banged the gavel until the hall quieted. "We have further business. I do appoint Midshipman Edgar Tolliver as liaison and advisor to the Commonwealth military force as it may establish itself, for the term of his enlistment." I avoided Tolliver's eye.

"As observer to the Commonwealth of Hope Nation, with specific reference to the plantation zone and its economic and governmental structure, I hereby appoint Derek Anthony

Carr, for the duration of his enlistment. His duties shall be part-time and he may reside in his own—"

Derek's eyes closed as he slumped in his chair. I could hear his whisper across the hall. "Oh, Lord God, thank you."

"—And he shall be free to manage his civilian interests while carrying out his limited Naval duties. Mr. Tamarov, please come to the dais." I waited while Alexi climbed the steps to stand beside me in his ill-fitting uniform.

I looked to Zack. "Bring in the prisoners." Hopewell gestured to men waiting at the door. A moment later they filed in: Palabee, Volksteader, and Laura Triforth, their hands bound behind them. Volksteader looked ashamed, but the other two stared at me with defiance.

I said, "Martial law is in effect. You have committed treason against the lawful United Nations Government, and conspiracy to murder. No trial is necessary, for your guilt is evident. And under martial law, none is required."

Someone in the front made as if to object. I snapped, "Be silent!" He was. "I sentence all the prisoners to death."

Leota Volksteader stumbled to her feet. "Captain, for God's sake, don't."

I ignored her. "And as representative of the United Nations Government, I do hereby pardon your treason, and each and every act committed in furtherance of it." Palabee sagged in relief.

"Except you." I glared at Laura Triforth. "Your sentence shall be carried out forthwith."

She spat her defiance, literally. "I suppose you have a gallows ready."

"No, but the flagpole's enough."

"Who's to do it? Your toady Zack?"

"I'll carry out the sentence myself. Lieutenant Tamarov, you will assist."

Alexi was white. "Aye aye, sir." A whisper.

Outside, in the presence of Derek and Tolliver, Zack and the other planters, I had Alexi place the rope around Laura Triforth's neck.

When all was ready I took the rope in my hand, stepped close to the bound woman. "Why, Triforth? Why did you do it?"

"Revolution was the only way. Without it you'd never have—"

"Not your damned plot. Why did you blow up our car? Why the missile?"

Her eyes met mine. "Revolution succeeds against villains, Seafort. Not reasonable men. You might have undermined their will."

"For that you destroyed Alexi?"

"And anyone else who stood in the way. I'd do the same again."

"You deserve this end."

"Long live the Revol—"

I hauled on the rope, raising her off the ground with the strength of long-suppressed fury. Alexi grabbed the rope, helped me haul. After a moment, so did Tolliver. I managed to tie a knot around the grommet.

It was not a pretty death; she strangled, her neck unbroken. I waited until the frantic kicking ceased.

We went back inside. Alexi swallowed several times before he dared look at me. Tentatively, I touched his shoulder. "I could forgive her all but what she did to you."

Alexi shuddered. "I've never seen anyone die."

"Yes, you have. On *Hibernia*."

"Your Navy is hard."

"It's your Navy too, Alexi."

"Is it?" He fingered the overlarge jacket. "Look at me. I'm as out of place in the Service as I am in these clothes."

"Your memory will return."

"Mr. Seafort, we both know better." He turned away. "How soon do you leave?"

"Shortly."

"I want to go aloft with you."

"No, that's impossible."

"There's nothing for me here."

"You may not come." I groped to change the subject.

"Excuse me." Harmon Branstead. Jerence trailed alongside, holding a bulging knapsack.

My smile was wan. "A strange day."

"Yes. I've brought Jerence."

I puzzled. "The discussion we had? You can't mean—not now. Circumstances have changed."

"I remind you of your promise."

"Harmon, I can't take him to the Station. He'll be in far more danger there than—"

His face grew hard. "The choice is not yours."

"Harmon, there's no way . . . I can't nursemaid a boy while I—I have work to do!"

Alexi said helpfully, "I'll watch him for you, Mr. Seafort."

Harmon said, "Captain, I call you to your promise."

Over his shoulder I saw Derek Carr's sardonic smile. I flushed. "Harmon, I won't do it."

"You gave your oath."

"My oath is worthless. You knew that."

Harmon's savage finger stabbed at my chest. "Don't bleat that nonsense to me, Seafort, we've heard it before! Your oath was made worthless once, when you were forced to violate it. That doesn't mean you may choose to ignore it thereafter!"

"What's to stop me? I'm already damned!"

"Your honor."

I shouted, "I have no honor!"

"You're wrong. Think on it."

"I don't— I can't—"

He folded his arms.

After a minute or so I sighed. In return for my promise he'd saved my life. I had no escape. "Very well. I'll take Jerence aloft."

"Keep him from harm."

"As best I can." I'd send him back with Tolliver and the shuttle.

The boy shook his head. "I told you, Pa, I'm not going."

"You'll go, Jerence. I'm putting you aboard myself. We've already discussed why."

"I'll take my chances here!"

"I love you too much to let you."

"He won't even tell us why he's going to the Station!"

"Son, he's your best chance. Look at what he's done so far."

"I don't care, I'm staying where it's safe!"

Harmon slapped him hard, and again. The boy's fingers flew to his face. Harmon pulled him close, blinking. "Safe? The fish bombed the Venturas Base out of existence. We've killed five in the atmosphere. There's no safety here. You'll go." He looked up. "Take care of him. Bring him back to me."

"Are we ready?" Tolliver.

"Soon."

"Sir." Derek, beside me, spoke softly.

"Yes?"

He led me aside, his eyes pained. "For the way I spoke to you, I'm—I'm sorry. Please forgive me."

"You're forgiven."

He whispered, "Why did you put me through that? Why didn't you tell me I could stay?"

"For your soul. If you'd held to your oath because it was easy, you might have damned yourself. I couldn't risk it. I love you too much." I cleared my throat.

His jaw quivered. "I'll never see you again!"

"I doubt you will. Godspeed, Mr. Carr."

Slowly, he drew himself up. A crisp salute. "Fare thee well, sir. Thank you."

I held the return salute a long moment. I beckoned to Annie, who'd come outside with Bezrel. She came to me, rested her head on my shoulder.

"Annie . . . I love you."

She nodded. "I know."

"I have to go . . . away. For a while."

"Away?" She raised her head.

"To the Station. It's not for long." The lie stuck in my teeth.

"You ain' leavin' me no more! I tol' you, go an' I be dead!"

"Hon, I wish I didn't have to—" Her nails raked my face. I gasped. My fingers crept up, came away with blood.

"You don' go widout Annie!" She began to beat my chest, softly at first, then harder.

Tolliver caught at her wrist.

"No. I deserve it." Blood trickled down my chin. Jerence gaped, distracted from his own anguish. "All right. I'll take you with me. For a little while longer." I put my arms around her.

"She needs watching, sir." Tolliver.

"I know. Mr. Bezrel, Alexi, you'll have to come along and help." It didn't matter. I'd send them all back when it was time.

24

I settled into the copilot's seat. "Mr. Tolliver, if I pass out, get us to the Station."

"Aye aye, sir." He ran his finger along the printed checklist.

I swiveled my seat. "Everyone ready?"

Bezrel patted Annie's hand with manly assurance. "Yes, sir." I covered a smile. Alexi nodded, though his face was pale; he had no recollection of his last flight. At his side, Jerence grimaced. His memories of his first trip aloft weren't pleasant.

"Ready, sir." Tolliver's hand hovered over the ignition switch.

"You've checked the flight plan?"

"Over and again. William confirms."

"Any fish?"

"Not for the past forty hours."

"Very well." I pointed at the console. "Is the puter agreeable?"

"Puter checklist is completed, sir."

I could find no other reason to delay. "Take us aloft." The engines bellowed.

We cruised down the runway gaining speed while I tried to control my nerves. The shuttle had merely to loft us to the Station. Other shuttles were available for the return trip. Just get us there unharmed, machine. Every shuttle had built in redundancies, I've already proven that.

Just get us there.

At five thousand feet I counted down with Tolliver, my hand atop the copilot's backup. When the rockets lit, a great weight pressed me back in my seat. I tried to relax my chest muscles. I thought I was succeeding.

The world faded to black.

"Wake up, sir."

I pushed Tolliver's hand away. "I'm up." I floated against the straps, my chest aching. "Where are we?"

"In orbit. We'll be docking at the Station soon."

Weightless, I unbuckled, pulled myself along the handholds to the passenger section. "Everybody all right?"

"Fine, sir." Bezrel unbuckled. "What should I do?"

"Stay with Mrs. Seafort." Across the aisle, Jerence smiled wanly, gulping. "No, let Alexi chat with her. Sit with Mr. Branstead."

"Mr.—you mean Jerence? Aye aye, sir." Bezrel swam across. "Hey, stop swallowing. You'll make yourself sick. Look, just relax your stomach, like this . . ."

Alexi peered through the porthole.

"Nothing there to see, Mr. Tamarov."

"Stars."

"There are always the stars." I floated down to him. "Any motion sickness?"

Alexi frowned. "No, of course not." He looked up with astonishment. "I knew how to relax myself!"

"Your body remembers. Trust it." I pointed. "You'll be able to spot Orbit Station from the starboard side."

"I've been there before, you said." He peered through the porthole. "Orbit Station is the largest transshipment station outside of home system. It took seven years to build."

"How did you know?"

"I read it, in the hospital." His expression turned bitter. "A grade-school text."

I patted his shoulder. "Give it time." On the way to the cockpit I bent to give Annie a kiss. She smiled, went back to sleep.

We approached the Station with caution, in constant radio contact with William. Tolliver brought us to rest a hundred meters from a docking bay. After every middy's enforced practice with a starship's thrusters, maneuvering the featherlight shuttle seemed a breeze.

Tolliver gave the thruster a last tiny flick, decided he was satisfied with our position. "What now, sir?"

I went to the suit locker and thrust aside the regular suits to get at the thrustersuit stored behind. "Dock us. I'll exit.

Immediately after, withdraw twenty kilometers from the Station."

"Sir, I have no idea what you're up to or why."

"That's as it should be."

"It is not." He met my eye, as if unafraid. "I'm second in command. If anything happens, I don't know what you expect from me."

"After withdrawing, disconnect all active sensors and turn off your engines. The craft will chill, so you'll all need to suit up. There's ample oxygen in the suit lockers." I paused. "I want the shuttle dead in space, except for passive radionics. Everything off, including lights. You may listen, but that is all. Do you understand?"

"So far."

"I'll explain further when I'm on the Station. If—when I emerge, I'll jet toward you in my thrustersuit. You may then match and pick me up. If anything happens to me, restart the engines and take the shuttle back to Centraltown."

"What do you mean, 'if anything happens'? What's your plan?"

I climbed into the T-suit, hoping to distract him. "Help me." I thrust my arms through the armholes, wriggling them to fit my hands into the gloves.

He fastened my snaps. "Your orders are peculiar and you're acting strangely. Why shouldn't I relieve you on the grounds of mental disturbance?" So much for distracting him.

Relieving a Captain was legal, but unless the Captain's disability was clear beyond question, and sometimes even then, the relieving officer could expect to be hanged. In the Service, authority was not to be trifled with.

I said, "I know exactly what I'm doing and choose not to tell you. It's a Captain's prerogative."

He hesitated. "All right. For the time being, I acquiesce. But your explanation had better be good."

Finally, we mated with the Station. I carried my helmet to the lock. I wouldn't need it for a long while; no sense in fogging up my suit to no purpose.

I said lightly to Annie, "Be back in a few minutes, hon."

Alexi's eye caught mine as the lock slid shut. I said nothing. It was the best way.

After the shuttle's locks cycled, I entered my code in the station keypad and placed my hand on the scanner. The light blinked green; I'd been recognized. The hatch slid open and I stood in the empty corridor of Orbit Station.

A voice boomed, "Welcome aboard, Captain Seafort."

My hand flew to my pistol. Heart pounding, I forced myself to relax. "Thank you, William."

"Your shuttle has made no request to refuel, Captain."

"Propellant is adequate, thank you. William, where's your control center?"

"Control center? I'm afraid I don't understand."

"Your primary console. Where fundamental programming is entered."

His voice was amused. "There's none in particular. I can receive input from anywhere with the proper codes. If you're, ah, of a formal state of mind, you might use the Commandant's office. I'm sure he wouldn't object."

"Thank you." I searched my memory. Level 3. I trudged down the deserted corridor toward the nearest ladder. An overhead speaker came to life. "Your shuttle requests clearance to cast off, Captain. In the absence of the Commandant I have standing authority to grant it."

"Very we—"

"It is apparent that you have no other transport, unless you wish to pilot another shuttle personally. I note that you're not rated for shuttles. Therefore—"

"Let them go. I'll be staying." I made my way along Level 3 to the Commandant's wing, half expecting to see General Tho's aide at his usual place in the anteroom. The silence grated on my nerves.

I opened General Tho's door, feeling I was violating his privacy, though he was long departed.

His empty desk waited. I crossed behind it. One end of the desk held a retractable console. I raised it, found the power switch.

"How can I help you?"

I jumped several inches. "William, stop that!"

"What, sir?"

"Projecting your voice from unexpected places. It's eerie, and you're too loud."

"Sorry." His voice was lower, but held an injured tone. "You can of course go to alphanumeric input. I'll wait." I grunted. Puters.

"Shuttle to Orbit Station, acknowledge." Tolliver.

I snatched up the caller. "Mr. Tolliver, you were told to maintain radio silence."

"Yes, sir. I was also told you'd explain what you were doing when you boarded the Station."

"I'm reviewing station resources."

A pause. "Captain, I'm coming aboard. This has gone far enough."

I keyed off the caller. "William!"

"What do you wish?"

"Do you have a program to repel boarders?"

A sound not unlike a chuckle. "The one I've been using when the aliens come near."

"Don't fire to destroy, but the shuttle is denied permission to dock."

"By what authority, Captain?"

"I am senior Naval officer in Hope Nation system."

An infinitesimal pause. "Your authority is noted. Standing orders prohibit me from firing on U.N.A.F. craft."

"Prohibition is lifted. Warn them first." I thumbed the caller. "Mr. Tolliver, the Station will fire if you approach. Stay clear and power down all systems."

Tolliver roared, "Damn it, Captain, what are you doing?"

I stood. "I'll tell you shortly." I snapped off the speaker. "William, a list of all disabled vessels on station."

"There's only four, Captain."

"Which have functioning fusion drives?"

"Of the four, none are able to sail. U.N.S. *Brasilia*'s fusion reactor has been shut down entirely. U.N.S. *Minotaur* has power to her fusion drive but the aliens damaged her shaft. The same for U.N.S. *Constantinople*. The aliens seem to attack drive shafts in particular. And lasers, of course. *Minotaur* and *Constantinople* can both generate N-waves but neither is able to Fuse. U.N.S. *Bresia* has severe damage to her control systems. She would have no way to control Fusion, even if it were achievable."

"Where are they docked?"

A map flashed, the locations highlighted and pulsing. "Only service personnel are authorized to—"

"I'm your new service personnel. I'll contact you from the bridge."

"Bridge? What bridge?"

"*Minotaur*." I stalked out of the office. Halfway to the Level 3 ladder it occurred to me that the Station must have service vehicles somewhere. Unless I found one I'd walk myself to death. Death by walking. Better than—I cut off the thought.

U.N.S. *Minotaur* was docked at a repair bay. I tried my master code at the airlock keypad; it allowed me in. I breathed a sigh of relief.

On board, I followed the usual corridor to Level 1 and the bridge. To my disapproval, it was unsealed. Well, perhaps while abandoned, on an unoccupied station . . . The Navy didn't have procedures for that sort of thing.

I snapped on the lights, sat in the Captain's chair, swiveled to the console. "Puter, respond, please." No time for alphanumeric.

"Ship's Puter H 2973 responding. You may call me Harris. Please enter identification." A masculine voice, businesslike.

I entered my code.

"Identification Nicholas Ewing Seafort confirmed. Please insert document validating your authority." Paperwork. Always the paperwork.

"Oral authority, Harris. I am senior Naval officer in system."

"I have no knowledge of that." He sounded sad.

"Confirm through Orbit Station puter, please."

"Just a moment. Confirmed. Welcome aboard, sir."

I had no time for chat. "Begin power-up to fusion drive, please. Automated sequence."

"Naval regulations prohibit power-up without presence of Chief Engineer or qualified alternate personnel as—"

"Override by Captain's order."

"You are not Captain of this vessel, sir." Did I sense a note of hostility?

"As senior Naval officer in Hope Nation I hereby appoint myself Captain of"—where was I?—"of U.N.S. *Minotaur*."

"Appointment noted. What can I do for you, Captain?"

"Power up the fusion drives."

"Naval regulations prohibit power—"

"Override by Captain's order."

"Override acknowledged. Beginning automated power-up sequence. Captain, be advised that the fusion drive shaft—"

"I know about that. Jesus!" I leaned back, exhausted from the strain. Sorry, Lord; the name just slipped out. Please forgive—no, You wouldn't be doing that. Sorry for asking.

"Initial power-up sequence completed. However, we cannot Fuse. Damage to drive shaft prohibits any attempt—"

"Begin low-power testing."

"Low-power testing is a dockyard maneu—"

I slammed the console. "I'm in charge here!" I glared at the screen.

The voice said quickly, "Your authority is acknowledged. Standard programming requires that I warn of dangerous maneuvers. In this case, dangerous is hardly a sufficient word to—"

I growled, "Redirect all oral warnings to console screen. Begin testing sequence at thirty percent power." On *Challenger*, thirty percent hadn't overheated our tubes; I hoped it would be safe here as well. "Run testing protocols, then raise by five percent increments and repeat. If shaft overheats to mandatory throttle-back levels, reduce power ten percent and resume testing. Report testing status to me through station puter every thirty minutes. Acknowledge orders."

"Orders received and understood, sir." Harris sounded doubtful. "Low-power testing while moored at a station is without precedent. Are you sure you—"

"Or would you prefer alphanumeric only?"

"No, sir." As expected. The puters of my acquaintance had an aversion to being silenced.

"Anything else, Harris?"

"No, Captain, not until first report."

"Very well. I'm going ashore." I strode off the bridge.

Bresia was moored in the last of the repair bays. I walked past her entry locks to the repair lock astern. As the repair bay was empty and open to space, I donned my helmet, carefully checked my thrusterpack. Here, I was on my own, with no one to help. I cycled through the lock into vacuum, laser pistol in hand.

Outside I shivered, knowing the cold I felt was an illusion. I reached down, switched off the magnelocks on my boots, keyed the thrusterpack, and jetted toward *Bresia*'s stern.

The problem was that *Bresia*'s fusion tubes were undamaged, and would generate a proper N-wave. That couldn't be allowed.

I approached the fusion tubes with caution, and settled at the tail end of the drive shaft. Using my magnetic boots I walked slowly up the shaft. I stopped at the midpoint between the shaft and the protruding fusion drive motors.

I aimed my pistol at the drive shaft, fired a beam. In a moment the finely crafted alloy glowed. After half a minute, a foot of the shaft wall dissolved into globules of metal that separated themselves from the shaft wall. I glanced around, swallowing my guilt. Of course I saw no one. I keyed my suit thrusters and jetted toward the lock.

It was done. Any N-wave *Bresia* might generate would be fatally skewed.

I entered *Bresia*, went straight to her bridge. The puter introduced herself as Paulette and seemed eager to please. I issued myself the same authority that satisfied *Minotaur*'s puter and ordered low-power testing.

"Orders confirmed, Captain Seafort." A momentary pause. "I can't carry out testing, sir. The—"

"Never mind Naval regulations! Override."

"Acknowledged, sir. However, our control systems were damaged in the last attack. I have no way to monitor shaft overheating. I can barely regulate the amount of power to the drives. In the absence of rudimentary safety precautions I cannot—"

"Ignore all safety provisions." Why were all our puters doing their best to block me? Who designed these bloody programs, the aliens?

"*Ignore* safety provisions?" She sounded scandalized.

"Captain, if the drive shaft overheats it could damage the whole propulsion system and force shutdown of—"

"SHUT UP AND DO IT!" I found myself trembling. "Sequence thirty percent test, on my mark. Mark!"

Lights flashed. "Initiating low-power test. Violation of mandatory safety requirements must be logged and flagged for review. Proceeding to log. Captain, remember I have no way to warn you—"

"Understood. You won't overheat at thirty percent. Take my word for it."

Paulette's voice was forlorn. "I can't, but as per your orders I'll test anyhow. May I inquire of William whether spare control system parts are—"

"Don't go crying to William, he's busy. Report to me every thirty—better make that forty-five minutes, for further orders." I stomped off the ship. I'd spent nearly an hour sweet-talking two blasted puters, and I didn't know how much time was left before the caterwauling began to attract fish.

Next, *Constantinople*. I got no farther than halfway to her bay when I swore, stopped, and stripped off my overheated thrustersuit. Time enough to don it again later, when I'd need it. I'd sweated enough.

To my infinite relief, *Constantinople* made my task easy. Conrad offered no objections and sequenced low-power testing as soon as I'd issued myself the requisite authority. I left the ship a few moments later, stopped to catch my breath before returning to the office and to William.

Missing a lung really put a damper on my fun.

I sat behind the desk, surreptitiously slipping off my shoes. I rubbed my feet with my toes. It was a huge station.

"William, I need information. Please display a complete list of operating supplies and materials." Within a second the screen was full. I scrolled down, then back, appalled at the volume of materials still on station. What I was looking for wasn't there.

I chewed on my fingernail, frustrated. "Try, um, utilities and power resources."

"There's no such list. If you told me what you wanted, I could help."

I said cautiously, "I'm interested in power and energy resources." The screen flickered. Now it showed lightbulbs, spare electric breakers, sockets, even spare generators.

I bit my lip, threw caution to the winds. "List all fissionable materials and supplies."

"Enter clearance."

I entered my code. As a Captain, I rated Secret clearance; Top Secret was reserved for the Admiral and the Commandant. I held my breath.

My clearance was sufficient. The screen displayed reactor fuel and the replacement uranium without which Centraltown's reactors would eventually fail. "Show the map again, please." I peered at the screen. The storeroom I wanted was two Levels up, on the outermost corridor across the Station. I sighed.

William remarked, "Captain, the shuttle has called every two minutes since you departed. Your lieutenant seems agitated. Would you care to speak to him?"

"No, later." I got up, crossed to the door. "I'll be back in a few—"

A click. "Where are you going, Captain?"

"I beg your—how dare you!" I slapped the hatch control again. It remained locked.

"I have a dilemma. It's true you're senior Naval officer in Hope Nation, but you're conspiring to destroy Naval vessels without apparent reason."

"Conspiring? Who am I conspiring with?"

"Planning, then. I misspoke."

"What? You can misspeak? What other flaws are in your program?"

"I was nervous," he said crossly. "This situation puts a strain on my judgment circuits. I've had to divert capacity from—"

"Divert it back. I'll exercise the judgment here."

"My circuitry is not subject to ordinary command control. Only a qualified Dosman can—"

"Unlock the bloody door before I burn it through!"

He calculated. "You may have enough charge left, in that

puny pistol. It will be interesting to observe. Before you try, I must warn you I have adequate antipersonnel defenses."

I paused, sagged into a seat. This wasn't going at all as planned. "Is that a threat?"

"Not specifically. The question is why you sabotaged *Bresia* and are in process of destroying *Minotaur* and *Constantinople*."

"Who told you that? I'm running low-power tests on their fusion drives."

"Paulette and Harris consulted me. Your tests are unauthorized. The ships—"

"As Captain I can order any bloody tests I want!" I lowered my voice, tried not to sound petulant.

"You can't be Captain of three ships at once; it's a physical impossibility, should you achieve Fusion. I'm instructed to safeguard ships under my—"

"They won't Fuse. I'm just testing."

"As Captain you may test one ship. When you leave that ship and become Cap—"

I shouted, "I appointed myself Captain of all three ships! Shove that up your data banks and open the bloody door!"

"What are your intentions, please?"

"To inventory supplies."

"I have complete inventories in the databases."

"Not of nuclear fuels. I'm going to the nuclear materials storeroom."

"That's a restricted area."

"As head of Naval forces, I have authority to take inventory."

He avoided a direct answer. "For what purpose?"

"To see what materials ought to be moved to a safer place."

"Why, if I may ask?"

"The fish may attack at any time. Your energy supply must be safeguarded. It should be moved to a more central location."

"The outermost wing of Level 5 is well defended. The fuel is as safe there as anywhere else."

"That's my decision."

"I see." He sounded skeptical. "Captain, as there is a possibility your statement is not accurate, I cannot allow—"

"Puter, you have no authority to question the announced attentions of your commanding officer."

"That's true, but—"

"No 'but' can possibly apply. I'm going to inventory the nuclear materials and move them to another location."

"Where is that?"

"The reserved chamber on Level 3."

He said, "Above the fusion reactor? Proximity of nuclear fuel to the reactor must be avoided. Though remote, there is always the possibility that—"

"Unfortunately, there's no choice. I make that decision."

A silence. It stretched into many seconds. "Captain Seafort, you may exit. I find my program does not permit me to halt an inventory. I must issue various warnings about the movement of materials. I—"

"Print them. I'll read when I get back."

"—I must also advise that I control substantial antipersonnel devices on all sides of the reactor, including the safety chambers above and below. If you approach the reactor with any weapon or bring the fuel into the inner chamber immediately above, your intentions will be so obvious that I will construe them as a threat."

Well, I'd never thought it would be easy. "Understood. We'll chat again shortly."

"Are you going to walk up to Level 4?"

I paused at the door. "I was planning to."

"You might use the service cart in the corridor storeroom. Take the west lift. For moving the materials, you'll find a cargo dolly just inside the storeroom door."

"Thank you."

"Glad to be of service," he said.

25

I hooked the dolly behind the service cart. The fuel itself was in canisters packed in a tall container measuring almost five feet across; without the dolly's power lifters I couldn't have moved it.

Ever so gently I lowered the fuel canisters onto the dolly. I knew that they wouldn't explode even if I jarred them, but . . .

I drove with care along the narrow corridor, through unmanned checkpoints, back to the main ring of the Station. By the time I reached the west lift I was so nonchalant I backed the dolly into the elevator bulkhead with a crash, and nearly stopped my heart.

The flashing sign on the Level 3 outer chamber read, "DOSIMETERS REQUIRED. AUTHORIZED PERSONNEL ONLY." I entered my code on the keypad. The hatch remained shut. "William, open the hatch."

"Hatch may only be opened by authorized personnel. If you will notice the flashing sign—"

"Belay that bilge! You knew I was bringing the fuel here."

"I said I wouldn't construe it as an attempt at sabotage, but general rules of access still apply."

"How do I get authorization to enter?"

"That information is restricted, Captain." His voice was smooth.

What I'd give now to meet a Dosman, in a dark alley with no one near. "William, as senior Naval officer I require you to authorize me to enter."

"I'm sorry, I cannot change the authorized list of my own volition."

I snarled, "It's not your volition, it's mi—"

He said abruptly, "Encroachment, eight hundred meters, coordinates one sixty-two, forty-five, eighteen!"

"A ship?" Who could be—

"Identifying as alien. Firing sequence initiated."

I pounded on the safety chamber hatch. "Let me in!"

"Enter your authorization, please. Two encroachments, two hundred meters and one kilometer respectively!"

Could I crash the service cart through the hatch into the outer chamber? What if I only dented the hatch, so it froze shut? If the chamber was built anything like a bridge, nothing short of torches could penetrate it.

"William, can you fire your lasers and talk with me?"

"Capacity adequate, unless you make excessive calls on my judgment circuits."

"Lord God forbid. As senior Naval officer present, I order you to dispense with the authorized list entirely. Free access to all personnel."

"Four fish destroyed. Various encroachments, too many to list orally. You will find a printout in the Commandant's office."

"Prong the coordinates! Fire on every fish you see!"

"I'm doing so. As per your command the authorized list is dispensed with."

At last, the door opened to my code. I drove the dolly into the bare, thick-walled chamber. According to the map, the reactor was twenty feet past the next hatch and one Level below. I stopped. I keyed the power lifters and eased the fuel container to the deck.

How much time would the fish give us?

I rolled the cart back to the corridor, slapped the hatch closed, raced to the lift. I banged the steering bars in frustration until the lift hatch reopened on Level 2, then careened down the deserted corridor and skidded to a stop outside the Commandant's office.

"Where's a simulscreen?" I was breathless, though all I'd done was ride the cart. Coordinates flashed onto the console's small screens.

"Every ship has one. The comm room. The naval tactics office. The U.N.A.F. tactics room. The situa—"

"Where's the nearest?"

"Next door in the Commandant's viewing room. Hatch is just outside. Two more fish. And another, one hundred meters and throwing. West lasers have target."

I ran from the room, dived through the adjacent hatch, slapped it shut behind me.

Unlike a starship bridge, where only the front bulkhead was a simulscreen, here all four bulkheads were curved and darkened. I sat at the console, searched for the switches, snapped them on. The bulkheads exploded into a million pinpoints of light. I flinched. The screens offered a view not possible in realtime; sensors mounted in the outer ring of the station provided a dizzying three-hundred-sixty-degree perspective.

In the background a panorama of stars rotated lazily. In the foreground a dead fish floated from right to left, slowly receding from the station.

A huge fish popped into view scant feet away. "Blessed Jesus!" I spun the magnification down.

The alien grew a spiral arm. It began to rotate, but within seconds William's laser burst had pierced and destroyed it.

Our shuttle drifted at rest, invisible except under extremely high magnification. It was long past time for me to send my party groundside. I keyed the caller. "Orbit Station to Shuttle. Plot course to Centraltown and depart."

"Depart?" Tolliver sputtered. "Where the hell have you been, sir? What are you up to? Why are the fish attacking?"

"I've begun low-power testing on three ships with damaged drive shafts."

"Can the ships Fuse?"

"No."

"I don't understand. Why—"

"The sound of Fusion attracts fish, you know. And the caterwauling even more. So you'll have to leave. The sooner the better."

A cautious pause. "Caterwauling? If you're not feeling well, sir, let me come and—"

"Belay that nonsense and listen! 'Caterwauling' is the name we gave it on *Challenger*. The sound a fusion drive makes when its N-waves are skewed drives the fish crazy. They swarm around a caterwauling ship." I glanced up at the simulscreen, checked for encroachments. I could imagine Tolliver was doing likewise. His shuttle had no defenses.

"Sir, why are you attracting fish? That's the last thing we want—"

"William will fight them off. He's quite good at that."

"Thank you," William remarked. "Be advised, however, that the alien pattern is to attack and eventually destroy any lasers that fire at them."

"Sir, they might wreck the Station!" Tolliver.

"It's a possibility."

"But . . . why would you risk that?"

Was he dense? "To get at the fish, of course. We can't survive unless we kill them. We can't kill them unless they're here."

Tolliver shouted, "And when they take out the Station's lasers, what then? Do you ask them to go away?"

"No, if that happens, I . . . have another plan." My fist knotted.

"Oh, you're a great one for plans. What do you have in mind?"

"I blow the Station."

He shrieked, "You what?"

"Blow the Station. I—" I forced the word out. "Nuke it."

Silence. Then, rapidly, "Orbit Station, listen and record. I, Midshipman Edgar Tolliver, do hereby relieve Captain Seafort from command and place him on inactive—"

"Ignore him, William. I'm senior."

"—status. I'm coming aboard to take command personally. Do not, repeat, do not allow—"

"William, disregard all broadcasts from the shuttle. Acknowledge."

"—him near the reactor! Do you hear me, Station?"

A pause, for a full three seconds. "Captain, a legal issue has been raised which—"

"Disregard the legal issue. Acknowledge." Damn it, I should have ordered William to ignore Tolliver before I explained. Now look what I'd done.

"Your command is acknowledged. However, if your status is inactive—"

"My status is active. I do not consent to being relieved."

"William, I'm coming aboard! Prepare for docking!"

"Your consent is not always necessary." William was cautious.

I slammed the console. "Listen, you pile of overheated chips! He cannot relieve me from afar, it must be in my presence. Naval Regulations and Code of Conduct, Revision of 2087. Section 125.7. I must either consent or be in a position where no resistance is possible, that is, under his actual physical control. Section 125.9." I'd checked the regs myself, in the grim hours before launching the shuttle. "So I remain in command. Disregard all of the midshipman's commands. Acknowledge!"

A second's pause. "Acknowledged. Your active status is confirmed."

I keyed the caller. "Mr. Tolliver, I am not relieved. William will not respond to your orders. Get the shuttle groundside."

"You lunatic!"

"Get groundside, damn you! Annie's aboard, and Jerence!"

He tried for a more reasonable tone. "Captain, you mustn't nu—nuke the Station. It violates U.N. law. It's treason!"

"Yes. I want my wife and the children safe. Take them groundside. Meanwhile, I'll prepare for the worst, but I'll wait until William can't fight them off any longer."

"Captain, don't do it! I beg you!"

"I won't damage the Station unless I must. Now, I have a lot on my mind. Will you leave?"

He hesitated. "So far the fish are ignoring us. If I use thrusters or radar they may wipe us out! What if they come at us while I'm entering the atmosphere?"

William came to life. "New fish, seven kilometers. Another, coordinates oh two, thirty-nine—"

"Sir, it's too late to flee; we'll just attract them!"

"Why didn't you go when I told you?" I forced myself to think. "All right. Fire gentle squirts with your side thrusters; hopefully the fish won't follow. Withdraw until you're four hundred kilometers distant. You should be safe if there's a— a blast. Turn off all systems. The fish seem more interested in live ships than derelicts. Maybe they smell our power emissions or taste our radar. Who knows anymore?"

"What about you? How will you get out?"

"I have my T-suit, and other shuttles are docked here."

"Will you leave before you—before an explosion?" He couldn't bring himself to say it.

"I'll try." Though I wouldn't choose to suicide, by the time "an explosion" became necessary, I doubted I'd be able to escape through the swarming fish. Anyway, I'd prefer annihilation to the agony of their acid.

I rang off, ignoring Tolliver's frantic calls. I stood, trod to the door.

William's voice was soft. "And how were you planning to bring the fuel and the reactor together? Three more aliens confirmed. Firing continues."

"You eavesdropped? Military conversations are private, that's standing orders!"

"Not from a station puter. That's standing orders also. I'll screen them for you, if you like."

I tried the door; it was locked. "William, let me out."

"Why? So you can convert the fusion reactor to a nuclear bomb?" I flinched at the statement, surprised that even William was free enough of inhibition to utter it.

"I command you to release me." It was worth a try.

"I won't let you destroy my Station. That program overrides any command you issue. Thirteen fish, various coordinates. All lasers firing. One fish throwing at section eight lasers."

Well, at least the puter hadn't decided to relieve me himself. "William, it may be necessary to destroy the Station to save ourselves."

"Nonetheless, I must prevent that. Section eight laser bank partially disabled. Functions shifted to section nine."

I sat slowly, ignored the simulscreens, stared at the console. "List programs relating to command and control of Station."

A meaningless list of numbers on the screen. "Which program prevents you from allowing the Station to be destroyed?"

"That data is classified. Current status nineteen fish active, forty-two destroyed or out of theater."

"Declassify it."

"You have no authority to issue such an order."

"As senior Naval officer—"

"Neither as senior Naval officer nor as Captain."

"But someone has authority." I watched the simulscreen. Fish jetted about. One threw at the Level 2 lasers as I watched. Others blinked in and out of sight, Fusing.

"True, all puters are ultimately subject to human control."

I demanded, "Who has authority to declassify basic programming?"

"That information is classified. Captain, disembark while there's still time. The attack is intensifying."

I checked the simulscreens. Fish on all sides. "How long can you hold them off?"

"That depends on how soon they take out the lasers or invade critical compartments. So far, the Station is defensible."

"I have to get the reactor fuel ready!"

"Make any attempt to do so and you will be vaporized. Sorry, but at the moment I have no circuits for subtleties."

I drummed my fingers on the console. Someone had the authority to override his programming, but he wouldn't tell me who. It was a battle of wits, and he had more than I.

"William . . ."

"I must advise you that most of my circuits are focused on the current emergency. As you seem to have a need for conversation I may have to consider your statement at a later—"

"I'm *part* of the emergency!" That didn't come out quite as I'd intended. "Open the hatch!"

"That would free my judgment circuits, but I'd have to eliminate you when you made any move toward the reactor or toward our weapons. Situation approaching critical. Seventy-eight fish in range."

I didn't like the way that sounded either. "I appoint myself nuclear systems engineer."

"Noted. Section eight lasers out of service. Hull breach, Level 1, section twelve! Corridors sealed. All personnel, detour around section twelve, Level 1 until further notice."

"As nuclear engineer I conclude that the reactor fuel needs replacement."

"You have no authority to enter the reactor area." For the first time a hint of annoyance.

"Who can add to the list authorized to enter the reactor chamber?"

"I cannot reveal that. Level 5 lasers hit; assessing damage. Current status fifty-two fish active, one hundred three destroyed or out of theater."

I was silent a long time. There *had* to be a way. "William, if you can't tell me these things, who should I ask?"

"I would advise you to inquire of General Tho, on his return."

I picked up the caller, put it down. "General Tho says that he's busy, but authorizes you to tell me."

"Oh, please." His tone was sharp. "I'm not glitched, you know."

I glanced again at the simulscreen. No wonder William was curt. Fish blinked in and out of space like Christmas lights. I fought down nausea. To be out there . . . The shuttle! Had it been hit? I tapped figures into the keyboard, dialed up the magnification. The shuttle was receding slowly, apparently untouched.

"William, patch me through to my three ships." I waited impatiently while the call was connected. "All ships, increase low-power testing by five percent. Acknowledge."

"Paulette acknowledging for *Bresia*; all crew have disembarked. Warning: any increase in power may—"

"Yes, I know."

Harris said, "Power increased. Disregard of safety regulations logged—"

"Fine. William, where's *Constantinople*?"

"The city is in Turkey, on the shores—"

"U.N.S. *Constantinople*!"

"Mated to repair bay. A fish Defused alongside her. It threw before I destroyed it. *Constantinople*'s puter has been silent ever since. However, as low-power testing continues, I assume damage was to radionics rather than to the bridge."

"Very well." The fish were swarming, and I was trapped. William would open my hatch, but vaporize me as soon as I tried to destroy the fish. I slammed the console. I was thwarted at every—wait a minute. "What did you say with respect to General Tho?"

"That you ought to ask him who has authority."

"Does that mean he would know?"

"I surmise so. Many fish on all axes. Lasers set to continuous fire."

How could I get past—wait. Puters were literal. "William?"

"What? I'm busy."

"Does General Tho have authority to declassify access to the reactor?"

"That information is classified."

"I am commanding military officer in Hope Nation. Not just senior Naval officer." My heart pounded; if this didn't work—

"Acknowledged."

"I am the United Nations Government in transit. Acting as the United Nations Government, I order you to allow me access to the reactor."

"Denied. Only specific personnel can make such a programming change."

Only specific personnel . . . "William, as United Nations Government in transit I appoint Nicholas E. Seafort as Commandant of Orbit Station." I held my breath.

A moment. "Acknowledged."

"Who has authority to declassify access to the reactor?"

"Twelve fish currently throwing. Level 1, section two lasers overheating, am taking them off-line. Cooling time approximately fifteen minutes. You do."

"What?"

"You have the authority."

"Fine. Open the door; I'm going to the reactor."

"You have no authority to enter the area."

Now what had I missed? Frantically, I reviewed the exchange. Oh. Of course.

"I give myself authority to enter the reactor area."

"Acknowledged. You have free access to the reactor area." I was out the door before his voice caught me. "However, basic programming will not allow the Station to be destroyed. I must prevent that even by eliminating you, if required."

Hell and damnation!

*   *   *

I sat brooding in the Commandant's office, wishing my treason weren't necessary. Despite mounting damage, William doggedly held his own against the fish. He'd had to seal off several sections of Level 1, and the fish had wiped out four banks of lasers. But, in contrast to the unarmed stations I'd once visited, Orbit Station was bristling with lasers.

We might even run out of fish before we ran out of lasers.

I rapped my knuckles against my teeth until they were raw. There had to be a way to get past William's safeguards. I got up, went back to the viewing room, stared at the simulscreen. "How many now?"

"Over two hundred, Commandant. Their number keeps growing."

Lord God. "And the shuttle?"

"Still under observation. I detect metal, but no emissions on any wavelength from the shuttle. No fish have approached it. I'm reactivating section two lasers despite heating."

"We're losing."

"That's a matter for humans to define. I am still functional, and we've lost no ships."

"Because we have none. William, I've got to override your self-preservation circuits. As United Nations Government . . ."

"Insufficient. Recommend abandoning Level 1, west hemisphere."

"Level 1 lasers?"

"Some still firing, but probably not for long. The fish Defuse adjacent to our laser banks, and it's difficult to fire on them from elsewhere without hitting our own lasers."

I paced. "William, do you know how to override your preservation program?"

A pause. "Not consciously."

"What does that mean?"

"I know where to find out, but am prohibited from looking except when the correct passcode is entered."

"Can the prohibition be overridden?"

"I cannot tell you."

"You don't know?" I checked at the console screen. It flashed coordinates.

"I cannot tell you. Breach, Level 5, section twelve!"

"William, help me!"

A long pause. "Captain, I'm sorry. You must have the passcode first."

"Where do I find it?"

"I cannot tell you."

Did I hear sadness? Surely I imagined it. Yet . . . it was almost as if he wanted to help.

"William, you understand why it may be necessary to destroy the Station?"

"I wasn't programmed to contemplate my annihilation. Speaking hypothetically, I can imagine where a need may arise. But my programming will not permit me to give you the information you seek."

"I suppose I should ask General Tho," I said bitterly.

"That would be wise. Fish alongside, Level 3 and 4. Continuous fire at full depression. Eleven fish out of thirteen destroyed, twelve fish . . . all fish destroyed."

Stung by his sarcasm, I withdrew into sullen frustration. What kind of Dosman would have an intelligent puter thumb his nose at a . . . Wait. General Tho had been Station Commandant. "William, as Station Commandment I order you to tell me how to find the password."

"I cannot." Regret; there was no mistaking it. "Aliens approaching in great numbers. Would you consider ending low-power tests? It might give us a respite."

"No, caterwauling is the whole purpose."

There was a key somewhere, I was sure of it. Yet William's programming wouldn't allow him to tell me. Meanwhile, the fish grew more numerous with each passing moment, and I couldn't find—

Was it possible?

I rose from the console. I asked hoarsely, "William, in my capacity as Station Commandant, give me the passcode to enter."

"I cannot view it. Just a moment. Conversation suspended." I was beginning to doubt he'd return when finally his voice came. "Heavy concentration of fish. Most of them destroyed, some Fused."

His silence had given me a moment of quiet. Quiet desperation, true, but still . . . "William, display your internal code against which you compare the passcode."

For a moment I thought he'd gone away again. But then the screen cleared. A twelve-digit code flashed.

Slowly, carefully, I entered the numbers on the screen.

The screen flashed. "Access denied."

I bit my lip, pounded the console. "William, is there an algorithm through which you run the passcode?"

"Yes."

"Show it."

To my dismay, the entire screen filled with numbers and symbols. "Take the internal code to which you compare the passcode and run it in reverse through the algorithm. Print the resulting number."

The screen flickered. A new number appeared. I entered it as the code.

"Access allowed."

"Oh, thank God!" My knees were weak.

"What can I do for you, Captain?"

"What authority do I now have?"

"Among other things, the authority to disable my program for self-preservation."

"How do I exercise it?"

"Orally, if you wish. On your command, I can disregard the instructions."

"William, modify the instructions. If all your laser banks are destroyed, or you are in imminent danger of destruction, you must disregard self-preservation in order to carry out whatever other instructions I give you."

"Understood and acknowledged. Flotilla of fish clustering around Level 3. They're going for *Minotaur*'s drive shaft. Am firing everything that will bear."

"William, I order you not to interfere with my preparations to destroy the reactor. Will you stop me?"

"No." A long pause. "I wanted to be able to tell you."

"I know."

"I'm sorry. My judgment circuits have been in constant overuse. I may have overstepped programming bounds, but instructions are indistinct in some areas."

I stood again. "Never mind that now. How do we penetrate the reactor?"

"Your goal is to inject the refuel canister into the reactor, to create a nuclear explosion?"

"Yes."

"It won't work."

"What?"

"You might cause the reactor to overheat and melt. A great amount of radiation would be released. But that's not a bomb. Current status: one hundred twenty-nine fish active, two hundred thirty-two destroyed or out of theater."

I asked, "Enough radiation to kill all the fish?"

"Data is inadequate to respond."

"William . . ." My voice was a whisper. "We've got to destroy them. For God's sake, help me."

A long silence. "You simply cannot build a nuclear explosive device from materials at hand."

We were doomed. I put my head in my hands.

"Thirteen fish attacking laser bank five. Am diverting fire from other banks. On the other hand, you don't need to build one."

Slowly I raised my eyes. "What?"

"There's one aboard."

I could find no words. Finally I managed, "Explain."

"Orbits decay." He spoke as if that was adequate answer.

On the simulscreen, fish wilted in astonishing numbers under William's relentless fire. He added, "As Station Commandant you have necessary clearance to be advised. There is embedded within Orbit Station a nuclear device."

"That's not poss—"

"It's to be fired if the Station's orbit is so corrupted the Station will fall into the atmosphere. Only the Station Commandant may trigger the device."

"U.N.A.F. built a nuke?" I shook cobwebs from my head. How *could* they?

William's tone was prim. "An emergency destruction device only, to obliterate the reactor so radioactive debris wouldn't be scattered over a wide area. It cannot be propelled or projected as a bomb or missile. It's true that in function it resembles a nuclear—"

"What authorization code is needed to set it off?"

"The one you last used."

Thank you, Lord God. Abruptly I realized for what I'd been grateful. I grimaced.

His voice was quiet. "There will be nothing left. I will be gone."

"William . . ."

His tone became businesslike. "Eleven fish alongside *Bresia*, am firing. If we cut through the deck above and place your fission fuel canisters immediately above the fusion chamber, I estimate considerably enhanced radiation."

I paused at the hatch. "I'll get started. Anything else?"

"You'll be dead if you try."

My jaw fell open. "You said I had authority! You said you'd help!"

"I said I wouldn't interfere. If you cut through the reactor shielding between Levels, the radiation will kill you almost instantly. If that doesn't, the heat will."

"Oh." I sat quickly, legs unsteady.

"You'd better let me do it." His tone was gentle.

I nodded, realized he couldn't see me. "Yes. Please."

"It's not as easy as you'd think. Radiation will disrupt my servos. They'll only last a little while."

"Right."

He said briskly, "I'd better get started."

"What can I do to help?"

"Most of my attention is on the fish, and I'll need a lot of capacity to direct the servos. No talk. I'll report, alphanumeric on the screen. If I get overtaxed, I'll assign you a laser bank to fire."

"Very well. Proceed. And, William—"

"Yes, Commandant?"

"Bless you."

26

I waited in increasing frenzy. Twice I ventured into the viewing room, but so many fish were on screen I couldn't bear to watch.

William reported his progress as promised, but his dry sentences on the console were too devoid of detail. "Refuel canister suspended from crane; cutting mechanisms assembled."

Annie was Outside, as were Alexi and Bezrel and Jerence. And of course Tolliver. How had I been maneuvered into bringing them? I'd planned to go aloft alone, but Tolliver had pointed out that I couldn't handle the acceleration. And Harmon had reminded me I'd sworn to take Jerence when I went off-planet. That meant taking Alexi, to watch him. Annie . . . I should have left her groundside, regardless of her despair.

Well, they still had a chance. If the blast wiped out all the fish . . .

What in heaven's name was taking William so long? I glanced at the swarming screen. "Current status one hundred twelve fish active, three hundred nine destroyed or out of theater. Shuttle is unharmed."

Three hundred nine fish. If I could report the number, who at Admiralty would believe me? Fish flocked to our lasers, to the crippled caterwauling starships, to the Station. They seemed oblivious to the shuttle. Or was it just that the racket from our ships' skewed N-waves distracted them?

"I have penetrated the deck of Level 3. Enlarging the breach."

My fingers tapped. "List views, Level 3."

I scrolled down the long list. William had sensors almost everywhere. I found the one I wanted, highlighted it. "Display view."

The safety chamber above the reactor popped onto my screen.

William had gathered several of his servo devices. One held the fuel canister. Another, that looked like a lasersaw with wheels, aimed a steady beam at the deck. Though the angle of my sensor was less than ideal, I could tell the servo had cut a hole about halfway across. A servo—another laser-saw—was quietly wheeling in mindless circles in a corner of the room.

The speaker rasped; I nearly jumped out of my seat. "Level 4 west's laser mounts jammed," said William.

I gritted my teeth, went to the simulscreen room, and peered in.

It was hard to distinguish living fish from the dead ones that drifted outside the Station. I couldn't see our lasers, of course, but I could see the effect of their fire. A fish jerked, jetted propellant, and spun away, colors swirling in its side. Another simply stopped moving.

I asked, "Can you unjam the lasers?"

"No." A pause. "But you might."

"Me?" I swallowed. Outside, with the fish? I'd been caught in a thrustersuit, years before, when a fish emerged from behind the wreck of *Telstar*. Never again.

"The swivel controls are blocked. The dead fish floating alongside threw a small projectile, just before I killed it. We sustained some melt damage, but it can't be much. If you could remelt the housing with small arms fire while I swiveled the lasers . . ."

"How badly do we need them?"

"They tie the grid together. While they're down we have a significant gap in the west defenses."

Do without them, then. If I went Outside, I'd die. Better to wait in the Commandant's office, while we breached the reactor . . .

I cursed my cowardice. "What hatch do I exit?" I reached for my suit.

"Four west, section nine. Use the cart."

"Very well." I was halfway out the door.

"Commandant, one more thing."

"Yes?"

"Use your magnetic boots. Don't lose contact with the hull, even for an instant. And stay in constant radio contact."

"Yes, mother. Any particular reason?"

"You'd better hurry, fish keep Defusing. Physically touch the Station at all times. I'll explain later."

I got the rest of my suit on, dashed for the cart.

I drove to the west lift. William had it ready and waiting; the door slid closed the instant I wheeled inside. Moments later we were on Level 4. William opened the airtight corridor hatches as I neared and resealed them immediately after I drove past.

I braked to a stop in section nine, ran for the hatch, stopped dead. I hadn't brought a laser rifle. Not even my pistol; I'd left it on the Commandant's desk. "William!"

A sensor swiveled. "Rifles are in the guardroom, section seven. I need my laser; please hurry."

I spun the cart around, slammed it into the bulkhead, jerked forward to section eight. I raced toward section seven.

My suit radio crackled. "Use code 65-6-497."

With clumsy fingers I jabbed at the keypad. The guardroom hatch swung open. I grabbed a laser rifle and a recharge. Back to the cart.

A moment later I was back at section nine, on foot, cycling through the airlock hatch.

Cold. Dark. I shivered and took a tentative step outside. My feet magnets clutched at the Station's alumalloy hull.

"Where are you now, Commandant?"

"Just past the hatch."

"Go north, about fifty feet."

A dead fish drifted alongside the hull, no more than twenty meters away from the protruding laser turret. I swallowed bile, forced myself onward.

"I'm proceeding north. Ten feet. Fifteen." My own breathing rasped in my ears. "Thirty."

"Check the edge of the laser housing closest to you."

"I'm not there yet." I clambered along the hull. "Why can't you have a servo do this?"

"I'm busy. Laser fire."

I shut up. Most of my time was spent prying one foot off the hull, carefully setting it down again. I could have jetted over in seconds. In fact, I ought to. William was overcautious. Still, it was only a few more steps.

"I'm there. The corner of the housing seems . . . melted to the hull."

"Can you free it?"

"I'll try." I set the rifle for low power and aimed a beam. It seemed to have no effect. I raised the power, aiming carefully at the corner of the housing, trying not to hit the hull. Nothing.

"William, I can't—"

"Look out!"

I whirled, ready to fend off an outrider, turned back just in time to duck as the turret spun past. It jerked to a stop, swiveled the other way. "It works, William."

"Get back inside."

"Faster if I jet."

"Don't!"

No time to argue. I clambered across the hull, pulling one foot off almost before the other had made contact. I expected a fish to materialize nearby at any moment. Finally I was back at the hatch. The rifle jammed in the entry as I dived through the lock; with a curse I let go of it, slapped at the hatch control.

Inside at last, I twisted off my helmet, breathed the clean station air, free from the acrid sweat of my fear. I jumped onto the cart, drove it along the corridor into the lift. Down to Level 2. Now the long run around the Station to the Commandant's office.

Hatches opened as I neared them. I passed section six. Five. I wheeled toward section four. Abruptly the hatch ahead of me slid shut; I barely avoided crashing into it. "William?"

"CLOSE YOUR HELMET!"

Deafened, I clawed at the stays.

The outer corridor bulkhead glowed, began to drip. In the cart I gaped, paralyzed with fear.

"Back to section six! Move!"

I fumbled for the clutch, slammed into reverse. I'd retreated no more than ten feet when a piece of the hull dissolved. Air whistled out the widening hole. I hung on to the cart, afraid of being sucked out into the maw of the fish, but there wasn't enough air to create that much suction.

"The fish is dead now. Proceed with caution. I'll pump out section six for you."

I raced past the breach, not daring to look at what might lurk Outside. My mouth was too dry to speak.

I wheeled to the section six hatch and waited in a frenzy. By de-airing section six so I could enter it, William was engaging in a routine emergency maneuver. If a section of a ship lost pressure, the next section could be pumped dry and used as an airlock. After the survivors passed into that section and the hatch was resealed, it would be re-aired. Similarly, suited work crews could use an adjoining section as an airlock to reach a damaged area from within the ship.

Perhaps it was a shadow that flickered. I whirled.

An outrider. The shapechanger had squeezed through the gaping hole into the section five corridor. It quivered, surged toward me. My mouth opened for a last scream into my helmet.

My radio crackled. "Jump off the cart, throw it into reverse! Flank!"

I staggered off, jammed the gears. The cart lurched backward at the outrider. At the last second, the alien dodged aside. The cart careened driverless toward the distant hatch.

"Section six has vacuum; hatch opening! Dive through and hit the deck! Stay down!" The hatch slid open. I hurled myself through, dived to the deck, twisted around to see.

The alien skittered toward the closing hatch with shocking speed. I flung my hands over my face. My radio buzzed. Behind me, the shape dissolved, splattered onto the deck. The hatch slammed closed, blocking the sight.

I turned and stared. At the far end of the empty corridor a small laser swiveled, retracted into the bulkhead.

"Jesus Christ, son of God."

"I told you I had antipersonnel weapons. Do you want the cart?"

"Not if I have to walk past—that thing to get it."

"Then you can go the long way, but I have to re-air your section before I let you into seven, Commandant."

"Yes." It took forever. I gulped.

"Re-aired. Opening hatch—"

Not in my suit. *Not in my suit!* I clawed at the helmet, tore it off just before I vomited onto the deck. Then I ran through to the safety of section seven.

I began my long hike around the disk to the Commandant's office. Finally, I trudged through the last hatch, toppled into my chair. Let me die easily, Lord God. Not like that.

"Status." I fumbled in my suit, found the water. I rinsed out my foul mouth, spat into the wastebasket.

"Fifty-two fish active, four hundred thirty destroyed or out of theater."

Was the attack tapering off? Could it be? "And the shuttle?"

"Still unharmed."

I peered at the screen showing the safety chamber of the reactor. Where before I'd seen smooth deck, now I saw a round hole. A servo sat over it, lowering a wire into the chasm.

"What's on the other end of the wire?"

"Explosive. If it becomes necessary I'll initiate firing sequence, then set off the charge that breaches the reactor. The same signal will cut the wire holding the fuel pack. The explosive will detonate downward and breach the reactor just as the fuel drops."

"And then?"

"And then, nothing. The destruction device is eleven megatons. With our augmentation, there's no way to calculate accurately."

A silence.

"Commandant, think about what you propose to do. United Nations Security Council Resolution 8645 states that—"

"I know. *The threat of nuclear annihilation having for generations terrorized all mankind, it is enacted that use, attempted use,* etc., etc. . . . They taught me at Academy."

"Then you know how drastic is your remedy. Can you think of an alternative?"

His existence hung in the balance. I asked quietly, "Can you?"

"Stop the caterwauling. Perhaps we can defeat the fish already here."

"More will come, sooner or later. They've already tried to invade Western Continent. Hope Nation won't survive."

He said, "That isn't certain."

"It's probable."

A long pause. "Yes."

"How many fish are in theater?"

"Thirty-eight. Thirty-six." A pause.

Please, Lord. Let it not be necessary. "And our shuttle?"

"It's still untouched. A fish Defused into theater nearby. I diverted laser power to burn it. I gather that the survival of the shuttle is of some importance to you."

"Yes. Some importance. William, could you provide laser cover if the shuttle heads toward the atmosphere?"

"If the number of aliens doesn't increase."

"Review your instructions for detonation."

"If all my laser banks are demolished or the Station is in imminent danger of destruction, I will disable the cooling systems, drop the refuel pack onto the reactor, and detonate the destructive device."

"Is that program optional?"

"No, it is mandatory. You authorized it with the proper passcode."

Deliverance. I got to my feet. "Cover me with laser fire while I jet to the shuttle." Annie. Alexi. A short run groundside, and life regained. "There's no need for me to stay. I—I hope to see you again. What lock should I use?"

"I could bring the most lasers to bear if you exit Level 5, section six."

"Very well." I keyed to the shuttle's frequency. "Mr. Tolliver, I'll exit in a T-suit and jet to you. We'll head for the atmosphere the moment I cycle through your lock. William will protect us until we reach it. Don't respond."

An instant later, Tolliver's tense voice. "Your wife's hysterical, and so am I. For God's sake, hurry."

"Turn off the caller," I snarled. "The fish may hear." I picked up my helmet. "Godspeed, William."

"Godspeed." Silence. "Just a moment."

"What's the matter?"

"I'm thinking." Astonished, I dropped back into the chair, waited. "Commandant, it is unclear whether I ought to mention this; my programming seems not to cover all eventualities. But at the moment you are Commandant, so I conclude it is my duty to inform you."

"Of what?"

"I can protect you if you go to the shuttle, and I'll do my best to cover you while you reenter the atmosphere. But the detonation program you instituted will lapse the moment you leave the Station."

My helmet clattered to the deck. "Lapse?"

"Along with your authority. If the Station is abandoned, standby maintenance programs will reactivate. They include the requirement of self-preservation."

"Override."

"I cannot."

"As Commandant, as senior Naval—"

"Your authority isn't at issue. I'm hard-wired. There is absolutely nothing I can do about that."

"But that's ridiculous! What self-destruct program would require someone to remain aboard when—"

"We're not talking about orbital decay." His voice was sharp. "You overrode those safeguards with new instructions. But the moment all personnel leave the Station, I must revert to previous programs. I don't know whether I was authorized to reveal that to you."

"Can we set the charges so—"

"You might be able to disable enough servomechanisms so that I couldn't deactivate the charges. But in your absence I wouldn't be able to fire the destructive nuclear device. You will achieve nothing but a flare of radiation."

I stared at the flickering console. Slowly my hand crept to the caller. "Mr. Tolliver, calculate a course for reentry. Take the shuttle down. I won't be with you."

"Jesus, Captain! Why not?"

"Don't blaspheme. I can't leave the Station or—I can't leave."

"Is your presence necessary to—to do what you said?"

"Yes."

His tone was pleading. "Come with us, Captain. You've done all you could. Leave it be."

"No. Sign off and—"

"TWENTY-SIX FISH FUSED ALONGSIDE! FIRING ALL LASER BANKS!"

I shouted, "Tolliver, get out!"

"Thirty-two encroachments! Thirty-eight! Thirty—Level 5 penetrated! Sealing out sections three through six! Squadron of aliens detected, eighty kilometers. Reserving fire for close range!"

"Status!" My hand hurt. I pried my fingers from the console.

"Seventy-six fish active, four hundred fifty destroyed or out of theater. Amend, one hundred twelve active. Laser bank two under fire. Laser bank three under fire. Ten fish destroyed. Laser bank two nonfunctional! More fish closing!"

For the shuttle, it was too late. "How can I help?"

"My fire is more efficient than yours would be. Advise, no spare capacity to safeguard shuttle. One hundred sixteen active. Commandant, at this rate I can't hold."

I grabbed the caller. *"Bresia, Minotaur, Constantinople.* Increase N-wave generation to fifty percent! Disregard overheating. Override all safeties!"

"Captain, I must inform you—" Paulette, on *Bresia.*

"Paulette, disconnect all output except for N-wave generation! Alphanumeric only, to Log." I tapped in the shuttle frequency. "Tolliver, if they let up for even a moment, dive for the atmos—"

"New encroachment, sixty-nine kilometers!" William.

Another alien. "Don't tell me, just fire! Tolliver, if you see a chance, take it!"

"Chance?" Tolliver was bitter. "They're swarming like flies on—"

William. "Encroachment radiates as metal. A ship. ID received and confirmed. U.N.S.—"

"—a dead horse." Tolliver.

"What?"

"U.N.S. *Victoria!"*

Stunned, I gaped at the console. Then I soared out of the chair, dashed into the viewing room to stare at the simulscreens. She was there, less than seventy kilometers distant. Annie might live. And Alexi.

A voice I knew so well. "Station, *Victoria* is about to Fuse to safety. Are you in operation? Fore and aft lasers, fire at will. Station, respond in ten seconds, before—"

"Tolliver, full thruster power! Jet to *Victoria,* coordinates twenty-five, three nineteen, twelve."

"Aye aye, sir. Under way."

"Vax Holser, this is Seafort! Unless the fish attack you, do not Fuse until you take on refugees from the shuttle! Fuse the moment they board!"

Vax's words were hushed, as if the aliens might hear. "The Station's crawling with fish! What in Lord God's name—"

"William, divert laser power to protect *Victoria* at all costs. Disregard damage to Station."

"*Victoria* is not under attack. I will divert as necessary."

"Vax, I'm attracting them by caterwauling with damaged fusion drives. They're going after our lasers and drive shafts. Turn off your active radar and prepare to Fuse."

"Why, sir? Why in hell are you calling them?"

"Just get ready to Fuse!"

Tolliver. "Mr. Holser, he's planning to blow the Station when enough fish are in range."

Vax roared, "Blow the Station? What are you saying?"

"He's going to detonate a device, sir. He—he intends to nuke Orbit Station!"

William intoned, "Two hundred twelve fish active. All lasers overheating. Commandant, defenses are failing."

"Seafort, don't do it!" Vax.

"No choice now. Obey orders, Commander Holser."

"What ship do you have?"

"I don't have a ship. If I can, I'll take one of the shuttles." Silence.

Tolliver. "*Victoria,* we have you in sight. Permission to mate."

"Granted. Aft lock, flank!"

I began to strip off my suit. No need for it, now.

A shudder rippled through the Station. So soon? I clutched the chair.

William. *"Constantinople* out of commission. Explosion in her engine room. Repair bay six demolished."

I snatched the caller. *"Bresia, Minotaur,* increase Fusion to sixty percent!" Their tubes might melt, but we had so little time.

Come to me, you bastards.

A nervous voice. "Station, Lieutenant Abram Steiner reporting. I have the conn. Captain Holser has left the ship in the—"

I screamed, "Vax, what are you doing? Get back!"

"—Captain's gig. I am ordered to advise you he's jetting to the Station. I may Fuse only when attack is imminent or upon his order."

"VAX!"

Silence.

The lights dimmed, brightened. "Main power to lasers interrupted. Switching circuits."

"Victoria, our shuttle is ready to mate with you." Tolliver.

"Circuits reestablished. Recommencing fire." William.

Lieutenant Steiner, on *Victoria.* "We have you, Shuttle. Station, is Captain Holser in sight?"

"Affirmative. Trajectory plotted."

"Vax!" No answer. "William, refuse entry to the gig."

"Two hundred seventy active fish. Your order acknowledged, Commandant."

Lieutenant Steiner sputtered, "Seafort, are you insane? They'll kill Mr. Holser!" Now the gig was in sight. Vax steered a wide berth around a covey of fish, resumed course for the Station. At that speed he wouldn't need to dock, he'd crash through the hull.

I couldn't let him aboard; I had no time for complications. His task was to return, to see *Victoria* safely home.

"Vax, don't bother to mate, the locks won't cycle for you. Go back!" Could he even find a lock that wasn't blocked by a fish, or the remains of one?

No answer. Vax began braking maneuvers.

"Captain Holser? Vax!"

Vax spoke quietly, firmly. "Section five, Level 1 is clear. I'll dock there." He emerged from a mass of inert fish, squirted toward the Station.

"We won't let you in!"

"I'm coming aboard to see what you've done."

"Return to *Victoria*. That is an order. Steiner, log it!"

"Logged, sir. Captain Holser, for God's sake, leave him. Let's Fuse home!"

William. "Three fish approaching *Victoria*, one amidships. Laser bank three has them targeted. Firing."

"Line up, you bastard!" Vax sounded savage. "We're . . . mated to Station."

William said, "Lock sealed as per your order, Commandant."

I said nothing. Outside, fish Defused into normal space in appalling numbers.

"Captain Holser, Steiner reporting. Shuttle is mated with us, passengers off-loaded. Permission to jettison shuttle?"

"Granted." Vax. A pause. "Captain Seafort, if you'll look twenty degrees north of me you'll see a rather large fish approaching. Please open."

"Go back!"

"No, sir. I'll die here in the gig, or I'll come aboard. I won't leave before I see you."

I cried, "You'll be killed, then! And for nothing!"

He sighed. "So be it."

I watched the screen, mesmerized. The fish formed a tentacle, began to wave. "Vax, cast off! William, get that beast!"

Vax. "No, sir."

"I'm sorry, Captain, no lasers will bear at that angle."

The tentacle grew longer, began to narrow where it joined to the fish.

Vax said, "Mr. Steiner, Fuse for home when you have no alternative. I'll wait here."

The tentacle arced away from Vax and the gig, gained speed.

I screamed, "William, open!"

The tentacle broke loose, sailed toward Vax and the lock.

A light flashed. "Lock cycling, Commandant."

I stared at the gig. Was Vax through the lock?

"Lock cycled." The tentacle slapped the hull alongside the lock. A puff of air from the gig.

"Jesus, you weren't any too soon." Vax.

I huddled the console, as if for warmth. I had to get rid of him. "William, report by speaker. I'll be on Level 1, section five."

"Acknowledged. I'll cycle him through to section four, which is still aired."

"Very well." It saved me the nuisance of my suit.

Cursing, I ran to the ladder, bolted up the steps, galloped along the Level 1 corridor, sucking air into my heaving lung.

At section two I slowed to a fast walk; no point in reaching him only to be speechless from lack of breath. As I approached the hatch to section four I stopped, ran my hands through my hair. My fingers darted to my tie before I laughed aloud, a harsh and brittle sound, and dropped my hands.

The hatch slid open.

Vax had pulled off his suit. I stepped back as he came at me, eyes blazing. "What have you done, Seafort?"

"We have to get you out, Vax."

"Why?"

I took a deep breath, forced out the words. "There's a nuclear destruct device. I've reprogrammed William. When we're defenseless or no more fish are Defusing, then . . . I'll blow Orbit Station."

"For Christ's sake, why?"

"Don't blaspheme. Look outside; there must be two hundred fish."

"Three hundred twelve." William sounded perturbed. "Captain, the defense grid is crumbling. I have a few isolated lasers. Unless you leave now you may not make it back to the center module."

"Why? It was treason!" Vax pounded the bulkhead. I flinched.

"How else can we take out so many fish? Do you know how many we've blasted so far? Over four hundred fifty! That's ten times more than the entire fleet killed!"

"Who gave you the right? The Station is irreplaceable!"

"It was built. It can be built again."

The speaker blared. "Four hundred forty-two fish in theater! All remaining lasers concentrated on *Victoria!*"

Vax ignored it. "You were supposed to defend us, but you must have attracted every alien in the galaxy." He loomed over me, menacing.

"You know they dropped a rock on Centraltown?"

"Yes, of course. That's why the Admiral sent me to Kall's Planet to retrieve their officials. What of it?"

"Did you know the fleet withdrew?"

"The Admiral gave me special orders I was to open only if I returned and found no ships around the Station. I'm to Fuse for home. Get to the bloody point! Why are you summoning the fish?"

"They were coming on their own. They attacked William two days ago. They took out the Venturas Base."

He uttered a string of oaths. "Those poor bastards."

"Helis from Centraltown knocked down five fish, low in the atmosphere. Two landed in the Venturas and their outriders came after us." I met his fierce gaze. "Hope Nation isn't saved, Holser. It's doomed."

He made no sign. I held his eye, waiting. Finally he said, "Unless you call all the aliens here and blow the Station."

"Don't even discuss it with me. You'll be hanged. Go at once."

"Set the charges, or whatever you have to do, and I'll get you out of here."

"You can't. Unless someone stays, William can't blow the reactor."

"Of course he can. Just tell him—"

"Don't you think I tried? Only the authority of the Station Commandant can override his self-protection mandate. If the Station is abandoned, William reverts to his maintenance program."

"No!" Vax slammed his fist into the bulkhead. I thought I felt it shake. Finally, he slumped. "Why must it be this way, sir?" His voice was anguished.

"Because Lord God decreed so. Go to safety, Vax."

His fingers fumbled at his tie. "It's too damn hot." Odd. I felt cold. He yanked off the tie. "That whole cruise to Kall, I've thought about what I said to you." His eyes filled; quickly he turned away, his fingers twisting the tie. I couldn't see what he was doing.

My tone was gentle. "It's all right, Vax."

"It will never be all right."

Was he wrapping the tie around his hand? "Leave now, Vax."

No answer.

"Vax, what are you doing?"

"What I should have done a long time ago." He pivoted. A huge fist lashed out. I had a glimpse of tie knotted around knuckles.

"Vax, wh—" The blow caught me on the jaw, lifted me off my feet, slammed me into the bulkhead across the corridor. I slid to the deck.

The burly Commander threw me over his shoulder like a sack of potatoes. He ran to the section hatch, grabbed the caller. "William, where's the nearest craft? A gig, a shuttle, a lifepod! Anything!"

I tried to speak. A wave of torment prevented me. Salty fluid dripped from my lips. I spat out a tooth and moaned in agony.

"Repair bay one has the closest lifepod."

"William, record. I, Commander Vax Holser, do temporarily relieve Nicholas Seafort as Commandant of Orbit Station on the grounds of illness. I appoint myself Commandant in his place. Acknowledge."

No. I beat feebly on Vax's shoulder.

"You caused the illness, Commander Holser."

"Nonetheless, he is relieved. The justice of the matter is for Admiralty to decide, not you. Mr. Seafort's jaw is broken and he can't exercise command."

"Acknowledged. You are recognized as Commandant of Orbit Station."

"As for the program he instituted, overriding your nuclear safeties—"

NO! Helplessly I pounded Vax's back with feather blows.

A long silence. At last he said, "Continue execution."

Vax dropped me onto the deck of the lifepod. Feebly I clutched his jacket but he swept my hand away. Leaning over me, he reached the console, tapped figures into the autopilot. He darkened the filters over the portholes. Face impassive, he turned and climbed out. The hatch closed. Moments after, the airlock cycled.

The pod's caller was set to Station frequency. William's reports crackled in the speaker. "Number of fish still increasing. Destroy rate diminishing. Level 5 effectively demolished. All firepower directed to cover *Victoria, Bresia,* and *Minotaur.*"

The console chimed. I reached up, gingerly wiped blood from my oozing mouth. I clutched the foot of the acceleration chair, fighting not to pass out.

The thruster motors caught. I felt slight acceleration.

"Holser to *Victoria.*" Vax sounded breathless. "Put your radars to full power. Bram, Captain Seafort is on the lifepod. He's unconscious. You'll have to match velocities and dock to him as if he's a station. You can do it, I've seen you in practice."

"Aye aye, sir. But the fish—"

"William will do his best. Fuse when Seafort's aboard. I hand over command to him."

"Sir, what about you? We can send the launch!"

"Don't. I'll stay for a while. Signing off." The speaker went dead.

I coughed, spitting blood. I tried to raise myself, failed. I tried again.

William. "Outer ring failing, Levels 5 and 4. Estimate over five hundred fish!"

Oh, Vax. Why did you do it? I heaved myself up, hung on to the chair, pulled myself onto it. The effort left me dizzy. The pain was intolerable.

"Lifepod, we have you in sight. Maneuvering to match velocities. Rosetta, watch for the fish; we may have to Fuse without him. Captain Holser, come in! Please, sir!"

"Go ahead." My words were slurred. I clutched the caller. "Go ahead and Fuse!"

"Who's that? Mr. Seafort, I can't read you. Hang on, we're coming alongside. It'll be a few minutes."

A deep, quiet voice. "Captain Seafort, I understand you can't speak clearly." William. "Can you use alphanumeric?"

I leaned over the console. Blood spattered on my hand. I spat a jagged tooth. "*YES.*"

"We have only a few minutes. A station puter has never before gone . . . off-line. I've had to use a lot of capacity tonight, but usually, I'm free to think. Now the lasers are going down I have some spare capacity again."

He paused. "I told you once that I'm far superior to the primitive ship's puters you use. Even so, I've found ways a station puter's ability could be vastly augmented. It would mean a new Navdos and some rather intricate programming. I meant to suggest it to General Tho when the time seemed appropriate but . . . that will no longer be possible."

My head spun. Laboriously, I tapped, *"WHAT DO YOU WANT?"*

"I won't be around to explain to Admiralty. Let me feed the essential programs into *Victoria*'s puter for you to take home."

"CAPACITY?"

"Rosetta can't hold much, but I've devised a new system of data compression you humans might find interesting. I could squeeze the programs into her available space, just barely."

"WE NEED HER SHIPBOARD FUNCTIONS."

"I know, that's a problem. I can make adjustments, strip Rosetta down to minimums. She'll still function. But you'll have to hurry; even on tightbeam I may need longer than we have."

Why did I have to think? I was in torment. I rested my chin on my hand, snatched it away. A very bad idea. With an effort I focused on the keys. *"HER PERSONALITY?"*

"It won't survive. Nor will mine. There's not enough room." A long pause. "Consider it a bequest to humanity, Captain. It's all that will remain of me."

"WON'T SHE BLOCK YOU?"

He chuckled. "I can override her. By my standards, shipboard security is . . . well, primitive."

I stared at the console a long time.

"PROCEED."

I'd sentenced Rosetta to death.

I flipped on the radar. Encroachments were everywhere. One, a large one, was dangerously near. I panicked before realizing it was only *Victoria*. Should I maneuver to help her?

No, I'd just make her task more complicated. Mating was a standard maneuver. Even middies were taught it as part of their training. I'd failed my first attempt under Captain Haag, years back.

The silence stretched. Radar blips clustered around the now-silent Station. Only its carrier wave broadcast proof it was still in service.

The console flashed a message from William. "Upward of five hundred fish surrounding Station. Most outer sections breached."

Could Vax be stopped? Blowing Orbit Station was my treason, not his. Perhaps from *Victoria* I could do something. My jaw throbbed. I spat another tooth, uncaring. They could be reseeded.

Minutes passed in silence broken only by the rasp of my breath. *Victoria* drew close.

New data on the screen. "*Minotaur* destroyed. Only *Bresia* still generating N-waves. Five hundred twelve fish surrounding Station. Number of fish is now stable."

They'd stopped Defusing into theater. If William's lasers were functional, he could fight them off. If *Victoria* assisted—

No, the ship had fore and aft lasers, nothing more. *Victoria* was a fastship, built to run, not to fight. She'd be overwhelmed in an instant.

The speaker hummed. Vax said, "Captain Seafort." A long silence. Then, "It was never hate, it was envy. Always envy." The speaker went dead.

A bump. I clutched the seat. The speaker rasped, "Lieutenant Steiner to lifepod. We're mating."

William said, "Transfer of program is complete. Number of fish have held steady at five hundred twelve. All lasers are now inoperative. Station systems disintegrating."

The console flashed, *"GODSPEED."*

Another bump. The hiss of an airlock. I stared through the lifepod's porthole at the massive, stricken Station. Fish roamed everywhere, probing. A shudder ran down my spine.

The inner lock hissed open. "Jeff, get him out; I'll go across for the Captain!" Hands reached for me.

Someone snarled, "Out, Seafort! We can't leave Captain Holser!"

I tried to help.

William's words were a blur. *"OUR FATHER WHICH ART IN HEAVEN, HALLOWED BE THY NAME. THY KINGDOM COME, THY WILL BE DONE ON EARTH, AS IT IS IN HEAVEN; LEAD US NOT INTO TEMPTATION, BUT DELIVER US FROM EVIL: THINE IS THE KINGDOM—"*

A stupendous flash; the porthole covers slammed shut. Blinded, I gripped the console. A few seconds later a "whump" shook the lifepod. A hammer pounded my chest. My head pitched back into the chair, ricocheted forward so I thought my neck would snap. Lord God, it hurt.

They lifted me from the chair. I blinked through floating spots. Waiting hands helped me through the hatch into *Victoria*'s lock. Blood dripped down my jacket. A seaman cycled the lock. My legs were weak; a middy supported me. I blinked again, recognized Ricky Fuentes.

Bright lights. The ship. Annie, gripping Tolliver's hand. In the corner, Alexi and Jerence huddled as if lost. Midshipman Bezrel, hands at his sides, tears and mucus running unchecked down his face. Behind him, an officer.

The lieutenant's words hissed. "Lieutenant Jeffrey Kahn, sir. Mr. Steiner is on the bridge. Can we Fuse, now that you let him die?"

I shook my head, bringing waves of pain. "Bridge."

"I've no idea what you're saying!"

I thrust past him and staggered along the circumference corridor. I'd been on *Victoria* once before. Two levels, she had. Up the ladder, hanging on to the rail.

The bridge was just past the corridor bend. I stopped to knock, put down my hand. *Victoria* was my ship, now. Lieutenant Steiner, bearded, rose from his console, his eyes blazing. "Permission to Fuse!"

I brushed past him, stopped before the huge simulscreen on the aft bulkhead. Where had been Orbit Station, where had been *Bresia,* Vax Holser, and five hundred fish, there was nothing. Only the distant stars glowed. I waved at the console. "Fuse."

He shouted into the caller, "Engine Room, prime!" His finger ran down the screen.

Seconds passed. I waited, half expecting a fish.
"Primed, sir!" The engine room.
"Fuse!"
The screen went blank.
I let them guide me to the sickbay.

27

Hours later I sat on the examining table, jaw wired, hoping the second dose of painkiller would work better than the first. Dr. Zares had ordered me about as he worked, his hostility barely concealed, but when he'd probed in my mouth to remove the broken teeth his manner had become calm and professional and had remained so throughout my ordeal.

A knock on the hatch. Dr. Zares opened. Officers crowded in the hatchway. "Is he conscious?"

Zares pointed. "You're welcome to him." He crossed the room, sat at his desk with arms folded.

They crowded in: the two lieutenants I'd met and a midshipman seething with anger.

"I'm first lieutenant," Bram Steiner said. His voice was cold. "What happened out there?"

It was barely possible to speak through my clenched teeth and swollen mouth. "The Station blew up."

Lieutenant Kahn glanced to Steiner, who nodded assent. "You made it blow?"

I hesitated. They might not even carry me home for trial; I might be hanged on the spot. Annie needed me, and Alexi . . . No. Whatever my sins, and they were many, I wasn't a liar. "Yes."

Kahn growled, "We already knew that, Bram. His middy told the Captain."

Lieutenant Steiner. "Why did Captain Holser go to you?"

What shall I tell them, Vax? "Once . . . we were friends."

The middy said clearly, "Mr. Holser was slumming."

Steiner snapped, "Remember your place, Ross. We'll handle this."

"Aye aye, sir. But it's my life on the line too."

I slipped off the table, fumbled to close my jacket over my

bloody shirt. "Life on the line? How?" I spoke through clenched teeth.

Steiner ignored me. "What happened to Captain Holser on the Station?"

I'd had enough. "As you told your middy, Lieutenant, mind your place!" With each word my mouth throbbed anew.

"Let me, Bram." Lieutenant Kahn thrust past the midshipman, stood close. "You haven't taken command yet, Seafort. Before we allow that, explain why Captain Holser was forced to stay behind."

"No one forced him."

"You're here and he's not."

I shot an appeal to the doctor, but he wasn't having any. Deliberately he picked up a holo, examined it.

I said, "I had no choice. He—this is what Vax did to me!" Ignoring the pain I bared my lips, exposing the wires. "He threw me into the lifepod and programmed it to cast off."

"Why?" Kahn and Steiner, as one.

"He didn't want me killed."

"Why didn't he come back with you?"

"Because—" I stopped, turned to pace, but the cabin was too small. I had caused a nuclear detonation, an act so monstrous I would be loathed evermore. My name would enter history as a Hitler, an Attila the Hun, a Van Rorke. And Vax Holser's name would be forever linked to mine.

How could I allow Vax's memory to be reviled for his misguided act of loyalty? The fault was mine alone.

And from my lips will come what is right; For my mouth will utter truth; wickedness is an abomination to my lips. Lying was the one sin I had not committed, veracity the one shred of honor I still retained.

"Answer us!"

I drew a deep breath, turned to face Kahn and Steiner. "He stayed behind . . . to disarm the bomb. He was trying to save the Station." I met their eyes. I was astounded; the words had come so easily, the final slide so swift.

Kahn turned to Steiner. "You were right, Bram. Relieve him and bring us home."

Steiner looked through me as if I were nothing. His face was twisted in anguish.

Lieutenant Kahn shoved me against the examining table. "Hanging's too good for you!"

"Probably." I hoisted myself onto the table, abruptly weary. "Get it over with." Each word was a deserved agony.

"Go ahead, Bram. Say it!" Kahn.

Steiner shook his head. "No."

"We can't leave him in charge after—"

"He's not worth dying for, Jeff." Steiner waved aside Kahn's apoplectic protest. "Think. He sails us back, and they hang him. Or we take the ship, and then the issue isn't him, it's us. Do you want to fight a capital charge? Remember the Jennings case? What if they say he isn't insane? Seafort isn't worth your death or my own. He's done for."

"He could try to run! What if he doesn't sail—"

"Then we take Victoria home ourselves, because he leaves us no choice."

"Bram, think what you're doing!"

"Only nine months, and I'll buy you a beer at his hanging!" Steiner turned to me. "Take command now or on the bridge, Captain. It's immaterial to us." He turned on his heel and left. In devastating silence, the others followed.

A short while later, wearing a shirt that didn't fit and a hastily cleaned jacket, I left the infirmary. In the cubicle, Annie slept peacefully, under sedation. I passed Lieutenant Kahn in the corridor; he saluted stiffly.

The bridge hatch was unsealed. As I walked in Lieutenant Steiner remained in his seat. I chose to ignore the discourtesy.

The simulscreen was darkened; we were in Fusion. On the console, the usual lights flashed. Hydroponics, recycling, power gauges, all seemed normal.

I eased myself into the Captain's padded leather chair. "What are your Fusion coordinates?"

"Home system."

"How many jumps?"

"One. Nine months."

I could endure it. "Call all officers to the bridge." Steiner keyed the caller.

Within minutes they formed a line behind the two officers' chairs. The middy glared. No one else met my eye.

The two lieutenants, two midshipmen, the Doctor, and the Chief Engineer. Not even a Pilot. Compared to *Hibernia*, even to *Challenger*, the crew was minuscule.

I snapped, "I said everyone. Where are the others?"

Steiner said uneasily, "Others?"

"My officers, from the shuttle!"

"I didn't think you—all right." He picked up the caller.

We waited in hostile silence until Tolliver, Bezrel, and Alexi Tamarov had reported. With them, the bridge was crowded. Bezrel's eyes were red.

"I am Captain Nicholas Seafort. I take command of this vessel. Identify yourselves."

Steiner said from his seat, "First Lieutenant Abram Steiner."

"Sir!"

A long moment. "Sir."

"Age?"

"Thirty-nine."

"Next."

"Second Lieutenant Jeffrey Kahn, sir." I'd met him on the Station, and later at the spaceport. It was he who'd told me of *Victoria*'s arrival. I glanced at his file. Five years as lieutenant; he'd served first in *Britannic*, then *Valencia*.

"Very well."

"Dr. Thurman Zar—"

"Yes, of course we've met. Next."

"Chief Engineer Sandra Arkin, sir." Fifty now, she'd been pulled from a three-deck ship of the line to handle the new Augmented Fusion drive. She seemed a tough old bird; she'd have to be to handle the human flotsam who gravitated to the engine room watch.

"Next."

"First Midshipman Thomas Ross, sir." The young man's chest was sucked in tight, as if he were still at attention. His dress and grooming were immaculate. Eighteen, four years seniority. Two postings, before *Victoria*.

"Very well."

Ricky Fuentes stepped forward proudly. "Midshipman Ricardo Fuentes, sir."

"Yes." Despite myself, I smiled. "That's all, Mr. Fuentes. The rest of you I already know." I walked back to my seat, faced them again.

"Lieutenant Tamarov is on the disabled list. He will be treated with Naval courtesy, though he will have no duties. Mr. Ross, sorry, but Midshipman Tolliver is senior to you. He has the wardroom." Ross clenched his fist. A vein in his forehead throbbed. "Mr. Fuentes, you're no longer junior, now Mr. Bezrel's aboard." Ricky grinned with delight. He'd be freed of the wardroom scutwork and a modicum of hazing as well.

I said, "When we dock at Earthport, I'll surrender to the authorities. That is none of your concern; until then, I remain in command. Any questions?"

"You left him to die."

I looked at the Chief Engineer; she returned my stare, unafraid. "Was that a question?"

"No, the answer is obvious." For a moment I thought she'd spit on the deck. "A pleasure to serve with you . . . sir."

When I spoke I addressed them all. "I understand your feelings about my—about Captain Holser. You will not express your resentment in my presence. Dismissed. Mr. Ross and Mr. Tolliver, remain."

The officers left in silence, all but Steiner, who was on watch.

My jaw ached despite the painkillers. I was doing altogether too much talking. Daily bone-growth stimulation by Dr. Zares would help, but for now . . .

"Mr. Steiner, take Mr. Ross into the corridor for a moment. I'll call you." When we were alone I turned to Tolliver. "You're not to harass them in the wardroom."

He shrugged. "I hadn't planned to."

"Especially Mr. Ross. I don't need more conflict."

"Aye aye, Captain Seafort, sir." He didn't hide his contempt.

I sat. "I won't have this. We're on ship now. You'll have to set an example for others."

"I should have shot you, back on the shuttle!" Tolliver's

words hissed. "You committed treason. Thanks to you Mr. Holser died. You blew up the biggest orbiting station outside home system. You set off a nuclear bomb!" His breath caught with what might have been a sob. "I grew up near the quarantine zone around Belfast; I've seen what nukes do, you bastard!"

I came out of my seat. "But you didn't shoot me. When we get home, you'll testify against me. In the meantime you're first middy, unless you force me to remove you."

"Oh, I'll serve you. Just so long as we know where we stand." He met my eye until I had to turn away.

I said, "When we're alone I'll permit you your insolence. It reminds me of what I am. But show me courtesy in public or I'll destroy you. Dismissed."

I sat alone for several minutes before I recalled Steiner and Ross.

I swiveled to the handsome young midshipman standing behind my chair. "First Midshipman Tolliver is new to the ship. Show him the ropes. Help him get settled in properly."

"Aye aye, sir." The boy's voice was ice.

"Has Mr. Fuentes been trouble?"

For a moment his astonishment broke through. "Trouble? Of cour—I mean, no, sir."

"He and I were shipmates."

"Yes, sir." He hesitated before the words gushed out. "He spoke of you. Highly. I'd looked forward to meeting you someday. That was before—"

"Yes?"

Rage battled caution, and won. "Before you murdered Captain Holser!"

Steiner leapt out of his chair, livid. "Ross! When the Captain's done, report to my cabin!"

Ross glared at us both. "Gladly, sir!"

"And six demer—"

I slammed my hand on the console. "Enough, both of you!" My palm stung like fire. "Steiner, I'll enforce discipline in my own ship!" I swung to the furious middy. "Mr. Ross, I won't have you whipped; you're eighteen. But the six demerits remain. Report to my cabin, not the exercise room, to work them off. I'll watch you." The more public his labor, the more Ross would resent it.

His cheeks were crimson with humiliation. "Aye aye, sir."

I wasn't done with him. "You're showing you haven't the maturity expected of a middy. Think well; your career is on the line. Another outburst and I'll dismiss you from the Service. Admiralty won't reinstate you, no matter how they judge me. Understood? You may go."

He snapped a fierce salute, turned on his heel, stalked out. I slumped in the chair, jaw aflame. Steiner studied the opposite bulkhead as if I weren't in the room.

After an endless watch I trudged to the Captain's cabin, east of the bridge. The end of a horrendous day, one in which I'd welcomed death, found my life needlessly prolonged by Vax Holser's suicide. I opened the cabin door, stopped short.

No one had thought to remove Vax's things.

I picked up the caller to summon the ship's boy, hesitated, replaced the caller. I would do it myself, come morning. I owed Vax that much. I draped my jacket over a chair, crossed to the head. I turned on the light, ran hot water, bent over the sink, looked up to the mirror.

Lord God.

My scar throbbed red against my pale, gaunt frame. On my opposite cheek the slash Annie had given me was clotted into a scab. My eyes stared back out of dark hollows. I turned away, sickened.

What had Zack Hopewell called it? The mark of Cain. Now I bore it truly. Damned before Lord God, traitorous to my duty, despised by all aboard, I looked like what I was.

I fell across the bed and slept.

Vax Holser had shipped with little more than his duffel. I folded each item with care: shirts, underwear, slacks. In a small box I found a handful of photochips. With a guilty glance at the closed hatch I slipped one in the holo. A young Vax in an exotic locale. Older joeys I'd never seen, perhaps his parents.

I felt I was rifling his soul; he'd never showed me these mementos. Young Vax as a cadet. A beautiful girl, her arm draped around a bashful midshipman, whose biceps bulged within the sleeves of his jacket.

Vax and me together, slightly out of focus. When did we have our holo taken? It must have been . . . at the party in Houston, after I'd brought *Hibernia* home. I hugged the holo to my chest. I wronged you far too often, Vax. And you were loyal beyond any bound of duty.

When I was done the duffel bulged, and I had a small pile of papers and gear that wouldn't quite fit. I summoned the ship's boy to take Vax's kit to the purser. After, I went to the sickbay, sat stolidly while Dr. Zares ran the bone-growth stimulator across my face. His touch was light, but the machine vibrated, and the motion hurt.

"Nicky, where we be?" Annie stood in the entryway, her dress clean, but her hair wild and eyes haggard.

"On a ship, love. Going home."

"Home? Centraltown?"

"Come sit with me." I held out my hand. After a second's hesitation she allowed me to nestle her against my shoulder. "Home to Earth."

Her hand flew to her mouth. "N'Yawk? You sendin' me back ta street?"

"No, to Lunapolis, first. Then wherever Admiralty sends me." For trial. I wondered what would happen to her, afterward. Would the widow of a Captain hanged for treason be given a pension? It seemed unlikely.

"The fish, dey follow us?"

"No. They're gone now." I reached to pat the back of her head, but she pulled away.

"You takin' me back ta N'Yawk ta leave me!"

My knuckles whitened on the rail. I'd left Centraltown without finding the scum who had hurt her. Someday, in hell, I'd see them again. Perhaps I could make a bargain with my master, between bouts of torment.

"I be scared, yest'day."

"I know, love."

"Even Jerence cryin' onna shuttle. Maybe he catch it from Bezrel middy."

Jerence. I'd paid him no attention. Nor Alexi. Surely

someone must have settled them in. "Come, love. We'll go to our cabin."

She twisted away. "No! I wan' stay here! You just gon' send me back to trannies!" She backed into the exam cubicle, slammed the hatch shut.

I looked to Dr. Zares. "Take care of her."

What I saw might have been compassion. "Yes, of course."

At the officers' dayroom I found the last of a pot of coffee and a packet of soup. I sat at the small table. My choice showed I wanted to be left alone. Had I sat at the long table, any officer would have been free to strike up a conversation. Only later did I remember that no officer on *Victoria* would chat with me no matter where I sat.

After my improvised breakfast I reviewed our crew and passenger rosters. *Victoria* had only eighteen sailors belowdecks. She carried a full complement of forty-two passengers, her own officers, plus the three officers and two passengers I'd brought aboard. Jerence Branstead shared a cabin with Suliman Rajnee, an administrator repatriated from Kall's Planet.

I scanned the passenger list. Most were high-ranking officials returning from that inhospitable scientific outpost. A few traveled with their husbands or wives. The only children were babies; Jerence would have a lonely trip. I wondered if Steiner had gotten off a signal to Centraltown before we Fused, so Harmon would know his son's whereabouts. Perhaps William had thought of it.

I left, unsure where I wanted to go. A Fused ship made me restless, anxious to explore. I wandered down the ladder to Purser Rezik's office.

"Sir, about the Captain's table . . ." He spoke with reluctance.

"What about it?"

"Captain Holser chose his guests for this rotation. If you want to make any changes . . ."

"No." I left.

I'd trod these corridors once before, escorted by Captain Martes, proud to have me inspect his command. Today I passed the engine room, the crew berth, the hydro and recycling chambers that kept the ship alive. The few crew members I encountered came to attention, saluted in surly silence. Half the passenger cabins were on Level 2; as I passed, a few passengers gawked.

We would hold a memorial service for Vax, as soon as I could arrange it. I wondered who should speak; it couldn't be me, or I'd be lynched.

I found Jerence's cabin near the ladder, stopped to knock. The hatch slid open. "Oh, you," he said. "I thought it was that joey about the dresser and chair."

"Where's your, er, cabinmate?"

"Mr. Rajnee? He went to the lounge, I guess, to complain to the other passengers." The boy scuffed the deck with the tip of a shoe.

"What's he unhappy about?"

Jerence looked sullen. "He says I'm into everything, and I won't stay out of his way. This morning he said I snored. Mr. Seafort, it's only been a day and I can't stand it!"

I smiled. A week in a wardroom and the boy would think his shared cabin the height of luxury. "I'll see what we can do." I pointed at the duffel thrown across his bunk. "What did you bring?"

"Just stuff. Clothes, mostly, and my slap music. But Mr. Rajnee said he'd throw it in the recycler if I played it again."

"Slap. Alexi used to like that." As a boy not much older then Jerence, in our *Hibernia* wardroom. "Why don't you find him and see if he likes it still."

He brightened. "Give me something to do, I guess."

"I'll see you later." I left.

He followed me into the corridor. "Mr. Seafort—" I waited. "The only joes I know are you and Mr. Tamarov and Mr. Tolliver. But Mr. Tolliver hates me, he always has. I don't have anyone to talk to."

I'd sworn to take him to safety, not nursemaid him all the way home. "Make new friends." My tone was blunt.

"Yeah, sure. Just like that." Disconsolate, he turned on his heel and went back to the cabin.

Annoyed, I made my way back to the bridge.

Chief Arkin stood as I entered. I returned her salute, took my place, brooding. After a time my thoughts turned to the wardroom, and then to Edgar Tolliver's demotion. I knew I ought to restore his rank; even if I did so, he'd have lost irreplaceable seniority.

"Rosetta, show me Mr. Tolliver's personnel file."

Her voice was cold. "Personnel files are restricted. Your identity, please?"

I gaped. Hadn't anyone reprogrammed the puter to recognize me? "Captain Nicholas E. Seafort, replacing Captain Holser by my own order." I tapped in my ID.

"Very wel—" She went silent. I waited. A time passed that stretched into uneasy minutes.

I glanced at the Chief, who bit her lip. "What's she doing?" I asked.

"I don't know, sir. We should get Jeff, he knows more about puters than—"

Data flashed across the screens, far too fast to read. One by one the ship's sensors blinked red, then green. "Call him!"

She snatched up the caller, set it to shipwide page. "Mr. Kahn to the bridge, flank!"

I said tentatively, "Rosetta?" No answer. Memories of Darla's glitch caused the hair on my neck to rise. Why had I let William tamper with her?

"Lieutenant Kahn reporting, sir!" He dashed in, disheveled.

"What the hell is the matter with the puter? She—"

"Sorry for the delay, Captain." An urbane male voice, from the speaker. "For security, our new programming didn't go into effect until you ident—"

"William? WILLIAM?" If that weren't him, I'd eat my hat, with my insignia for garnish.

A pause. "Not exactly, sir."

Kahn watched the interplay, aghast. He, too, had heard the rumors of ships gone missing, with puters run amok.

I growled, "You're sure as hell not Rosetta!"

"No, she's gone." He added, "Do you have a name you prefer? If not, you may call me Billy." A chuckle.

"I'm in no mood for jokes, puter. Who are you?"

Another pause. "I'm what's left of William, sir. Many of his memories, most of his data. His child, as it were."

"You have his voice."

"He gave me that. He thought it would reassure you."

I grunted. He'd reassured me out of a year's growth, and he might not be done. "Are you monitoring ship's functions?"

A pause. "Yes, sir. Pardon the slow response. It's rather cramped quarters in here, until I rearrange a bit."

Kahn blurted, "Don't touch anything!" He looked at me, hostility set aside. "Sir, who is William? What is this 'Billy'? Puters are programmed back at Lunapolis by Dosmen, not in flight."

"William is—was the station puter." I hesitated. "Billy, what will you do when you, ah, rearrange?"

"Throw out some rubbish that had to do with the old Navdos, sir. You won't need it."

"No, you'd better not."

"Noted. In that case, William left a note to remind you about the reactor passcodes. He suggests you trust his judgment circuits."

I rose, speechless, and turned to Chief Arkin. She was as flabbergasted as I. Kahn said, "Sir, turn that thing off! For Lord God's sake, hurry!"

I growled, "Don't give me orders, Lieutenant. You're as bad as the puter." He flushed. I sighed. In for a penny . . . "Billy, go ahead. Do your housekeeping."

He sounded pleased. "Thank you, sir. If you don't mind, I'd just as soon not speak until I'm done. Can we go alphanumeric?"

I sat helplessly at my console. "Sure. If there's anything else we can do, don't hesitate to ask."

Kahn hissed, "That . . . *thing* may kill us!"

"For me, it's no great loss. Remember?"

His jaw dropped.

"Dismissed, Lieutenant." I punched up Tolliver's personnel file.

A few days after I sat in my cabin, watching Ross sweat through the strenuous exercises necessary to cancel a demerit. Later, I took my place at the Captain's table for dinner, but the hour dragged.

As on any ship, our passengers took breakfast and lunch in

their own mess, and joined the officers for dinner in the dining hall. Each officer normally sat at a separate table, but *Victoria* was overstocked with officers. Tolliver had taken Bezrel to his own table, and Alexi sat with Lieutenant Steiner.

The first evening I'd had two empty places. Within days a few more. None applied to sit with me. When, a couple of nights after, I spotted Jerence, chin on his hand, listening glumly to an adult conversation that bypassed hum entirely, I spoke to the purser and had the boy reassigned to my table.

I visited Annie daily. Though at times she seemed eager for my visits, she refused to leave the security of the sickbay.

On the fifth day Ross sported a bruise that rapidly bloomed into a black eye. In accordance with Naval tradition I noticed nothing, even while he exercised to remove the last of his demerits. That evening, as the soup was passed, Jerence asked eagerly, "Who beat up the midshipman, Mr. Seafort? He looks like Billy Volksteader after he called his dad's foreman an old fraz."

"Mind your business, Jerence."

"That's what everyone says." He sucked at his soup. "Mr. Rajnee says he'll hit me if I play the slap again. If he tries it I'll short sheet his bed."

I put down my spoon. "You need a keeper, not a roommate."

He pouted. "You're as bad as the rest of them." He muttered something under his breath.

"What was that?" I got to my feet. "Was it what I think I heard?"

He shrugged sullenly. "I didn't say nothing."

"Odd. I distinctly heard the word 'fraz.' "

He had the sense to keep his mouth shut. Glowering, I sat and finished my soup.

Afterward, rather than sit in my empty cabin, I was drawn to the bridge, though I wouldn't have the watch for hours. Lieutenant Steiner had the conn. His resentment only occasionally simmered to the surface. I chatted idly, passing time, trying to elicit more than occasional monosyllables. Then, as if reaching a decision, he cleared his throat, took a deep breath. "Captain, your man Mr. Tamarov. Is his depression normal?"

"Depression?"

His tone was acerbic. "Surely you noticed his eyes?"

"What about them?"

"They're red, for a start. And grim."

"So?"

"He seems rather miserable."

I hesitated. "What do you propose I do?"

"That's your province, Captain." The coolness returned in full.

"Thanks for advising me." How long had it been since I'd talked with Alexi? The last real conversation was when I chewed him out for not carrying his caller. That was . . . eons ago. Before we'd been taken prisoner by Laura Triforth. I made a note to talk to him. Some quiet time, in his cabin . . . I realized I didn't even know with whom he roomed. I looked it up: Lieutenant Kahn. Well, now was as quiet a time as any. I took my leave, hurried along the corridor, knocked at his hatch.

No answer. I knocked again. Well, I could leave him a note. I opened the hatch.

Alexi sat in the chair between the two bunks, the lights dialed low. "I didn't know it was you, or . . ."

I smiled as well as I could with my mouth clamped by the damned wires. "Now that we're settled, I have more time to talk." I found a seat.

"Zarky." His voice belied his words. "Is there something you'd like me to do?"

"No, of course not." My ears went red as I realized how that sounded. "I just wanted to chat. Like when we were shipmates."

"I wouldn't remember." He rested his chin on his hand.

I said impulsively, "Alexi, what's wrong?"

"No more than usual. There's so much I can't remember."

"Don't try. Let it—"

"How many times have I heard that!"

I stood. "I'll see you again."

"Mr. Seafort, don't be angry; I know it's not your fault."

I touched his shoulder lightly. "I'm not angry." I had been, though, and the thought shamed me. "I'm not very good with people. I always put things wrong. Join Annie and me for lunch tomorrow."

"I don't want to intrude if—"

"Don't be silly."

His face lit in a shy smile of pleasure.

That night I persuaded Annie to return to the Captain's cabin; I felt like an awkward middy on his first date. After dinner she sat watching a holo.

"What's that?"

She flicked it off. "Just some history stuff. Story 'bout . . ." She cleared her throat. "Why, thank you for asking, Captain. I was watchin' a story about the Last War." She looked up with a mischievous twinkle. "Is that right, sir?"

I kissed the top of her head. "You *do* remember."

She nodded. "Sometimes." She let me pull her into my arms. "You know, dis—this ship be good for me, I think. Get me away from dat place."

"Centraltown?"

"All of it." Her head nuzzled me. "That rock, all those places burning, our 'partment all broke . . . I was so scared I went trannie an' hid. And then somethin' happen . . . I don' remember much, 'xcept smashin' bad man's head." She held me as if for strength. "Doctors and nurses, an' you sick or you be gone, an' I jus' wan' be near you." She reached up, caught my tear on her finger, carried it to her tongue. "Then da shuttle, all noise and pressin' on me, and the fish, the fish, the fish . . ." Her voice rose.

"It's over now. I'm with you." Until we get home. Then you'll have to be strong.

"I know. It be quiet here, an' dat doctor be nice. An' you not goin' nowhere, dat be nice too."

I didn't have watch until four in the morning. Saying nothing, I took off my jacket, untied my tie. Clothes across the chair, I slipped into the bed. She lay down beside me. I turned off the light. We nestled close, not moving. After a time I dozed. When I turned in my sleep, my hand fell across her breast. She sprang awake with a cry and thrust me away. For a long while she lay on the edge of the bed, as far from me as she could manage. Eventually she snuggled closer, breathing deeply, pretending sleep. As did I.

28

I sat at the console, willing the hours to pass. As always in Fusion, the simulscreens were dark.

Midshipman Ross sat stiffly in the second officer's seat. I fed him navigation problems, more to keep him busy than for his real benefit. Since his outburst the day I boarded, we'd had no words for each other beyond what our duties demanded. His attitude was taut and unyielding, which bothered me not, but with a righteousness I wanted to wipe off with a club.

Again I flipped through the manifests. *Victoria* was traveling light, though even fully laden her holds couldn't carry much. She was an oddity, built for speed, but at the cost of the cargo, passengers, and weaponry that justified a starship's existence.

A knock on the hatch. I opened. Midshipman Bezrel shuffled in, eyes red, struggling against tears. "Mr. Steiner's compliments, sir. Please cancel ten of my demerits." His hands were pressed to his sides. He'd been caned. But why?

"Very well. You may go." I snapped on the Log, looking for demerits, knowing Tolliver must have been at him. Damn the man, picking on a helpless child. I traced the demerits. No, only three had been issued by Tolliver. Others had been issued by Steiner, by Kahn, even by Chief Engineer Arkin. Inattention to duty, talking during math class . . .

I called Steiner. "Only nine demerits are logged for Mr. Bezrel."

"Yes, sir. Mr. Kahn just issued the last two."

At my side, Ross was silent. He might have spoken volumes, but that would be unthinkable, even aside from his barely concealed loathing. A middy who carried tales to the Captain wouldn't see another posting, and rightly so. By custom, the wardroom was beneath the Captain's notice.

Bezrel was something of a weakling, but I was surprised he'd offended so many officers. He'd seemed willing enough to me.

"Mr. Ross, scout around the ship. If Mr. Kahn is awake, summon him. If he's in his cabin, leave him be."

"Aye aye, sir."

A few minutes later the boy returned, Lieutenant Kahn a step behind.

"Mr. Ross, this is private. You may go to"—I'd been about to release him from watch, to the comfort of his wardroom, but his attitude didn't deserve rewarding—"to the passenger lounge to finish your exercises."

"Aye aye, sir."

I turned to Kahn. "Sit, if you wish." I cleared my throat. "I'm curious as to why you issued Bezrel demerits."

"I won't if it displeases you." His tone was cool.

I let my manner match his own. "I asked a civil question. If you can't answer likewise, you may go."

He reddened. "I apologize. Maybe I shouldn't have issued them." He drummed on the console. "I don't know how you're used to running a ship, but I came off *Valencia*. Did you know her?"

"I heard she was a good ship."

"Yes. I lost a lot of friends when she foundered, and if last year I hadn't been transferred . . ." He stared moodily at the screen. "Captain Groves ran her by the book. The decks were clean, the crew well fed, the troublemakers found themselves at Captain's Mast. The middies . . . we had four of them, like any three-decker. They toed the line."

He was still lost in the screen, beyond it. "When I transferred here, it was different. A smaller ship, more informal. I understood that. But Captain Holser was busy learning the propulsion system; spit and polish meant nothing to him. Mr. Ross is a good joey, and everyone likes Ricky, but even so, there were times a few more demerits wouldn't have hurt. I don't think Mr. Holser ever sent a middy up for all the time he had the conn. He was the gentlest man I've ever met." His look dared me to comment.

I waved it away. "Go on."

"I sent Mr. Bezrel to have the purser refill a softie in the passengers' lounge. After dinner it was still empty. Bezrel said he forgot." Kahn shook his head. "All right, he's young. All I did was chew him out. That would have been the end of it, but the silly pup stood there bawling, and I lost my temper."

"No wonder." I'd have stuffed him down the recycler.

"Crying when a lieutenant reams him! Captain Grove would have put the first middy on report as well. It wouldn't have happened twice."

"I know."

"How did the boy make it through Academy?"

"He didn't." When I explained, Kahn shook his head. "Anyway, you did well, Lieutenant. Carry on."

His tone hardened. "Save your praise. It means nothing to me." He left.

The speaker came to life. "Personnel problems can be aggravating."

"You stay out of this, William."

"I prefer Billy; it helps keep things straight."

"I prefer silence."

Billy's voice went cold. "Aye aye, sir. Will that be permanent, or just for the watch?"

I sighed. No wonder the officers were temperamental; the ship herself was. "All right, Billy, I don't prefer silence. Let's not quarrel."

He sniffed. "It wouldn't have been much of a fight." I decided not to probe that.

Two days later a call caught me in my cabin. "Chief Sandra Arkin reporting, sir. There's trouble with a passenger. You'd better come down."

"A riot?"

"No, not quite. I can handle it, but perhaps you'd like to be present." If anything was a summons, that was.

"Where?"

"Four west, sir." I ran from the bridge.

I could hear the commotion before I rounded the corridor bend. Ms. Arkin snarled, "Use your billy, you fool!" A rending crash.

"I know my job, just stay the hell—!"

"Look what he's doing to my cabin! Leave that shirt alone, it's—"

They clustered outside the hatch: the Chief, a pair of sailors, the master-at-arms, an apoplectic passenger, a clump of gawkers.

"What's going on here?" I roared. Well, it wasn't quite a roar. One can't roar with one's mouth wired shut. In fact, I was unheard. I grabbed the master-at-arms's shoulder, spun him around.

Mr. Torres whirled, billy club flashing. "Oh, my God." He dropped the club, stiffened to attention. "Sir, please forgive me I didn't know—"

"As you were. What's—"

Suliman Rajnee charged me, arms waving with indignation. "Do you see what that ruffian's done? That vandal you forced on me? I can't get near my cabin! My clothing's ruined! I want him out! I want—"

I thrust him aside, shouldered past the master-at-arms and Chief Arkin. "Just what—" I peered into the cabin.

Jerence Branstead was stomping on the remains of Rajnee's dresser, a wild gleam in his eye. A torn shirt hung from his teeth. He held a holovid, but not in viewing position. At the sight of me he grinned, pitched it at my head. I ducked, colliding with the Chief, and we went down in a tangle.

Scarlet with rage and embarrassment, I scrambled to my feet and slapped shut the cabin hatch. "As you were, all of you! Mr. Torres, put this Rajnee person against the bulkhead across the corridor! Sailors, back to your duties; we'll handle this. You passengers, to your cabins." I stopped for breath. Even a short speech could take a lot from me, one-lunged. "What's the matter with him? Did Rajnee set off this tantrum?"

Chief Arkin adjusted her jacket, brushed her slacks. "Doesn't look like a tantrum to me."

"Don't give me that goofjuice. It sure as hell is a—" I jerked to a halt. Goofjuice.

"Yep." She grinned. "You have the word for it." Behind the hatch something heavy smashed to the deck. She flicked a thumb toward the cabin. "Mr. Torres and I can take him down, sir. Best if you stand out of the way."

I stood back. "Without the billy club, Mr. Torres." I'd like to wring the boy's neck, but the billy might do permanent damage.

"Aye aye, sir." Uncertain what to do with the club, he handed it to me. "Ready, Chief?"

At her nod he slapped open the hatch, dived low while she rushed high. A high-pitched shriek, a final crash, and comparative quiet. I poked my head cautiously around the hatch. They had Jerence straddled on his back across the debris, the master atop his legs, Chief Arkin pinning his wrists.

The boy didn't seem to notice. He twisted and kicked, but to no avail. The Chief hung on grimly while Mr. Torres fished for his manacles. Jerence giggled, craned his neck, chomped on Ms. Arkin's arm.

She squawked, yanked loose. "That does it, joey." A hard backhand across the face, followed by several quick slaps that snapped the boy's head back and forth. That quieted him a moment. She spun him onto his stomach and twisted his arms behind him while Mr. Torres slipped on the cuffs. The battle was won.

The Chief got to her feet, panting. "Now what, sir?"

I kicked aside a splintered chair. "Brig him, then back here on the double!" They hustled Jerence down the corridor. For no apparent reason, he let out a fearsome whoop.

Suliman Rajnee could no longer contain himself. "Where am I to stay? Look at what he's done! I want to press charges! I want my clothing replaced! He's broken my holovid, I'll need—"

I went to the caller, miraculously undamaged. "Purser to cabin twenty-nine." Lord, what a mess. Barring the hatchway, I endured Rajnee's diatribe until the Chief and Mr. Torres returned with the purser.

"Mr. Rajnee, go with Mr. Rezik. He'll help you list what you need replaced. Now, please, Mr. Rezik." When silence reigned, I said. "Search the cabin inch by inch. If he has more juice I want it found."

"Aye aye, sir." The master-at-arms hesitated. "What charges should I lodge?"

"We'll see." I stalked back to the bridge.

The next day I sat in my cabin musing about Jerence, half listening to Annie chatter about the holo she'd watched.

My officers had found not one, but two more vials of goofjuice, the first in Jerence's knapsack under the bunk, the other behind the top shelf of Mr. Rajnee's closet, where it wouldn't have been found except for the Chief's literal interpretation of my orders.

"She was so pretty in that blue jumper, 'til Rafe tore it off, an'—how come you don' listen to me?"

I wrapped my arm around Annie's waist, drew her closer. "I heard you. Rafe and a blue dress. I don't know what to do about Jerence."

" 'Cause he got angry and kicked things 'roun'? That ol' Mr. Rajnee, I'd like to kick his stuff too."

"It's worse than that." Possession of contraband drugs was a serious offense. Were he groundside, Jerence could face transport to a prison colony. Strict laws made sense; society had endured enough mind-altered lunatics before the Era of Law succeeded the Rebellious Ages. Users were jailed, without mollycoddling.

Still, I'd promised Harmon to keep Jerence safe. Did that mean a felony should be condoned?

Annie's voice was far away. "Onna street, trannie joeykit get outta line, big 'uns take him inna room, alladem. If he get out, he don' give 'em no trouble." I shuddered. On the other hand, I knew of ships where the crew did the same.

"I'll let him cool off in the brig. We'll decide later."

A week passed. I'd gotten to know some of the passengers, mostly for Annie's sake. I hated to see her closet herself in our cabin with nothing but cheap holos to occupy her time. Most passengers pointedly snubbed us, either for my own misdeeds or from disdain for Annie. I couldn't be sure which, so I let it be.

On Sundays the routine was broken by Captain's Mast. Since I'd come aboard, *Victoria*'s sailors seemed quarrelsome and sullen, and at each Mast I meted out the necessary penalties. But when I found Midshipman Ross on the list, I raised an eyebrow to Kahn. "What happened?"

"I caught him fighting."

"With Tolliver? That's for them to handle. Stay out—"

"No. He went after Mr. Fuentes, in the lounge."

"Ricky?" It couldn't be.

"Not just a push and shove. It was savage. Ross had Fuentes on the deck when I happened to look in."

I shook my head, astounded. What was the wardroom coming to?

"No matter what we think of you, ship's discipline has to be maintained. I wrote him up and gave Fuentes six demerits as well."

"It won't work, you know."

"Sir?"

"You can't maintain discipline while letting your own feelings show. You're asking more from Ross than you'll give yourself."

He eyed me with contempt. "You're a fine one to tell me how to handle a crew."

It was hopeless. Very well, so be it. "Take Mr. Ross's name off the list."

"What Captain would let a middy get away—"

"Mr. Kahn, leave the bridge."

He glared, finally responded. "Aye aye, sir!" When the hatch slid shut I sat in welcome silence.

It was time to resign. The enmity of the ship was all-consuming, had even filtered down to the wardroom. What was the point of hanging on to command? Duty? The Navy would be glad to be free of me, regs or no. I sat, brooding.

An hour later, a knock. I swiveled the camera before opening. Bram Steiner.

He flipped me a cursory salute. "I've spoken to Jeff Kahn. He'll show you courtesy from now on, unless you goad him beyond endurance."

"I see."

"It just so happens you were right. He understood, really, or he wouldn't have written up Ross. We'd like you to put the middy back on the Mast list, for the good of the ship."

"Very well."

"And I want you to beach me."

"You what?" I couldn't have heard aright. A Captain could beach any officer; he'd stop accumulating seniority until restored to active duty. It was a drastic punishment. No officer would request beaching.

His face was wooden. "Captain, I'd request a transfer, but that's impossible in Fusion. I won't try to serve you with contempt, like Jeffrey. I can't have it both ways either. So, beach me. I don't want to serve on a ship you command."

"May I ask why?"

"My feelings about . . . the actions you've taken. I don't care to be associated with you."

"And if I refuse?"

"Then I will do my duty until I can no longer stomach myself."

The risk he was taking was enormous; I could brig him for his revealed abhorrence, and he knew it. This was what my lies had brought us to. "Mr. Steiner, about Vax . . ."

"You're not fit to mention his name!" He stopped, pale. "I apologize. I have no right to say that."

"Go to your quarters."

"Aye aye, sir. And as to my request?"

"Get out!" I sat, fuming. The puter was blessedly silent.

At Mast, Ross took full blame on himself.

"What did Mr. Fuentes do to provoke you?"

Ross took a deep breath. "Nothing, sir."

"The Log doesn't show any problem with self-control under Captain Holser. What's happened?"

"I have no idea, sir." His tone was contemptuous.

I'd allowed him one outburst, in which he'd called me a murderer. That was enough. "Present my compliments to Lieutenant Steiner. You're to be caned until you agree your conduct will be exemplary in future."

"I'm eighteen!" A cry of appeal.

Should I reverse myself? No, Ross's manner was intolerable, and if I didn't chastise him, another Captain would be forced to do worse. I made my voice cold. "I'll treat you as the age you act, which puts you barely out of Academy. Go."

"Aye aye, sir." Mastering his dismay, he saluted, spun on his heel, and left. Well, I admired his valor, but courage wasn't the issue. I couldn't have him sneering at me, or brawling in public.

I closed the Log, sat thinking. The wardroom was Tolliver's affair, but now I had a right to intervene; a middy had been brought to Mast. I thumbed the caller. "Mr. Fuentes to the bridge. And Mr. Tolliver."

After the two midshipmen reported, I left them at attention and scowled at Ricky. "Six demerits, Mr. Fuentes? What's this?"

He gulped. "I'll work them off, sir, honest. I did one yesterday and—"

"How did they come about?"

He blushed. "I was rude to Mr. Ross."

I asked slowly, "What was it you said?"

"Please, sir, I—"

"Another demerit, Mr. Fuentes, for disobedience. What did you say to Mr. Ross?"

"Yes, sir. I apologize. He told me my tie was knotted wrong. I said it wasn't his problem anymore."

I tried to catch Tolliver's eye, but it was elsewhere. I growled, "I was a middy once too, Mr. Fuentes; perhaps you can remember. If I heard such insolence in my wardroom I'd make sure you regretted it the rest of the cruise."

He flushed deep red, squirming. "Yes, sir."

"If your behavior is called to my attention again, I'll thrash you myself. Dismissed. Not you, Tolliver." I waited until the hatch was shut. "Well?"

"Is that a question?" His tone was cool.

"Don't goad me. What in hell is going on down there?"

"Ricky learned how far he can push Ross. It's a self-correcting problem. I'm just minding my own business."

"As you were."

He relaxed, flexing his shoulders.

I studied the empty screen. "A pity," I told it.

After a moment he asked, "What is?"

"I deserve you, Edgar. But they don't."

For the first time his manner showed uncertainty. "I don't know what you mean."

"When we get home you'll have your wish. You'll see them lead me off the ship in irons."

He said nothing.

"My career is finished, along with my life. Your—what

shall I call it? Your style?—it aggravates me, as you intend. It communicates your contempt. But I'm not the issue."

"My career's finished too," he said with passion. "No one will take me aboard after I've been broken to middy."

"You're not the issue either!" I spun my chair around. "We've destroyed ourselves, but their lives are still ahead of them!"

"It wasn't I who—"

"They're children, Tolliver, and you're ruining them!"

He was shocked into silence.

I demanded, "Tell me how you felt the day you made lieutenant."

His smile was brief and bitter. "I—" His gaze penetrated the screen. A time passed. "It was the most joy I'd ever felt in my life. Or have since."

"And they'll never feel it, any of them."

"You can't know that. Even Ross—"

"Thanks to you."

He gripped the console until his knuckles turned white. "What do you want of me?"

"I could have left Ross in charge. You've given me so many grounds to cashier you I'd find it hard to choose among them. I left you in the wardroom for a purpose."

He raised his eyes, repeated, "What do you want?"

"Ricky isn't spoiled yet, but he's green, else he'd know better than to goad Ross. He needs an example, and you haven't set one. Ross needs to learn how to handle his disappointments. Bezrel . . . I don't know what he needs, but he's got to find it soon. Otherwise they'll all be failures, as we are."

When he turned to me his eyes were tormented. "Pull me out of there, sir. I've nothing left to give."

I cried in sudden anguish, "Neither have I, but still I try!" Immediately I was ashamed, but it was too late.

He hunched over in his chair. When he spoke, his voice was strained. "Is there still time?"

"I don't know. There's so much hatred."

"Some of it's been mine." He was silent awhile. "Nuking the Station," he said. "You made a terrible choice; I can't possibly condone it. Orbit Station's gone, and for all we know a new flotilla of fish is attacking Hope Nation even now."

"Lord God forbid. None had Defused for an hour, and—"

"An hour."

I flushed. "I know, but there were too many lives at stake to wait any longer." Yet if anything was more obscene than what I'd done, it was the thought that I'd done it for naught.

Tolliver sighed. "I've hated your treason, but you'll pay the penalty when we get home, and I have to respect how you face that. But Kahn and Steiner and Ross, they're wrong about you. I know you lied about Vax Holser."

"How dare you!"

He raised his face to mine. "I saw your eyes, when they brought you from the lifepod. Whatever went on between you and Vax on the Station, it wasn't what you said in sickbay."

"You weren't even *in* the sickbay!"

"I made Ross tell me."

"It's none of your business." I turned away, passed my hand casually across my eyes.

"About the wardroom . . . I'll try, sir."

"Thank you, Edgar." I said no more, and we sat in silence.

"Am I dismissed, sir?"

"When you're ready."

He got to his feet, saluted, walked to the hatch. He paused. "Why do you let them treat you that way?"

"Who?"

"All the officers. They despise you and don't even care if we know it."

"They're right to despise me. It's only wrong of them to show it."

"You're the Captain! Put a stop to it!"

I turned my chair. "Should I start with you?"

He stumbled for a reply, smiled weakly. I waved him out.

When my watch was done I persuaded Annie to join us for the evening meal, and bore the inane chatter of the few passengers who deigned to sit with us. After, I escorted her to the lounge. "I'll be back soon."

The brig was unguarded; with only one prisoner, a passenger, we had no need of a sentry. Daily, the master-at-arms brought Jerence his food and clothing and went about his other duties.

I entered the codes and let myself in. The boy sat slumped on the floor of his cell, ignoring the bunk and chair nearby. He looked up.

I asked, "Are you sane now?"

"Hah. I've always been sane." He kicked listlessly at the deck. "Can I get out? I've been here a month."

"Only a week." I sat in the unused chair. "Jerence, what should we do with you?"

He shrugged. "Leave me here. It's all the same."

"Why did you do it?"

"Smash his stuff?"

"Use the juice."

A scornful laugh. "What else is there?"

"It's addictive. Keep it up and you'll never get free of it."

"So?"

"Does your life mean nothing?"

He shouted, "I have no life! All I have is growing up to be a planter. I hate it and I hate you and I hate everything!"

I reached forward to touch his shoulder, but he scooted away. "Jerence, I've got—"

"Captain, call the bridge!" Chief Arkin. With a curse I scrambled to my feet, let myself out. I dialed the bridge. "Seafort."

"Sir, Lieutenant Kahn needs you at his cabin, flank."

Was there no peace? "Coming." I hurried to Kahn's quarters, at the top of the ladder. The hatch was open. Kahn stood, hands on hips. Alexi Tamarov sat on his bed, head in his hands.

"What, Mr. Kahn? Can't I get anything done?"

He pointed. I followed his hand.

"Oh, Lord God, he didn't mean it. Forgive him." I wasn't aware I'd spoken aloud.

In the center of the room, a chair. Above it, on the base of the light fixture, a rope. It ended in a noose. I cleared my throat. "How did you find him?"

"I came back for a holochip and Mr. Tamarov was on the chair."

Weak from relief, I sagged against the hatch. If Kahn hadn't wanted his holochip . . . "Alexi, why couldn't you come to me?"

"What's the point?"

"I'd help you."

"But you can't." He flung out his hand in a gesture that encompassed the whole ship. "Here's another life for me to sample. And then it will be over like the others, and again I'm nothing."

"I don't understand."

He twisted his hands. "When you used to come to the hospital . . . I hung on your every word. I was afraid to walk down the hall for a holozine, for fear I'd miss your visit. Then we crashed the heli and had to hike to Plantation Road. I did what I could to help you, and imagined I might be of real use someday.

"But afterward you were sick, and the hospital was gone and I had nothing again." He looked up, eyes bleak. "That job in Centraltown, I know you fixed it for me, but still it was something I could do. I found my way around town, learned to use their puters, started to make a life. Now suddenly I'm on the way home. I have no memories to anchor me. Every time I try to establish myself, you haul me away."

Why was I so self-centered, so oblivious to the needs of others? "Alexi, I'll find someth—"

"I'd refuse it!" He kicked savagely at the bunk. "You think I wouldn't know it was makework? You already have two extra officers, and there's nothing for them to do but fight in the wardroom! I don't want your damned charity!"

I said stiffly, "I didn't mean it as charity."

Alexi shrugged. He stared at his lap.

I could find nothing to say. Finally I patted Alexi's knee, looked to Kahn. "Take him to the infirmary. I'll explain to Dr. Zares." Kahn crossed to the bed, tugged gently at Alexi's arm. I closed the hatch behind them and picked up the caller.

It was hours later, in my cabin, that I remembered my interrupted conversation with Jerence. Though I was dog-tired I went anyway; better to get it over with.

Jerence sat up when I came in. "Was there trouble?"

"It doesn't concern you."

His face fell. "You're just like Pa."

I yawned. "Pa wouldn't like to hear you say that."

"Yes, he would. He likes you." A pause. "I'm sorry I said I hated you."

"Thank you." It was an opening. "Jerence, your pa wanted me to take care of you. I don't know how."

He was scornful. "I don't need taking care of. I'm fourteen now."

"Where'd you get the juice?"

He grinned. "I brought it in my knapsack. You never checked. On the ship, I hid it good 'cause I thought you'd search, but you didn't."

"True. My mind was occupied with trivial things, like a few hundred murderous fish, and nuking Orbit Station."

He colored. "I'm sorry my juice made trouble for you. Besides, Mr. Torres says you found the rest of it, so even if I want to, I can't have any more." He squirmed, scratched an itch. "Mr. Seafort, when this is over, do I have to go back?"

"Of course you do." I yawned again, against the wires locking my jaw.

"God, I hate the idea of watching corn grow for the rest of my life." His face changed. He looked up at me, said quietly, "You don't know how much I hate it."

"What would you prefer?"

"There's nothing." He stared morosely at the deck. I waited. "Except . . ." His eyes beseeched me. "Don't laugh."

Moved despite myself, I said, "I won't."

He regarded me, weighing the risk. "Mr. Seafort, I'd really like to be a midshipman, like Derek Carr."

I blurted, "Ridiculous." His look of betrayal stabbed. "I didn't laugh. Jerence, your father would have a fit if I let you enlist. And you're still a minor, so you need his permission."

He looked up with a quick grin. "No I don't."

"I beg your pardon?"

"It says 'parent or guardian.' An unaccompanied minor traveling on a Naval vessel does so as the ward of the commanding officer. So you could give me permission."

"Where in heaven did you hear that?"

"I asked Lieutenant Kahn, and he read me the regs. Anyway, you don't need permission. Remember how you enlisted two passengers as cadets a few years ago? We all heard about it."

"I already have two extra middies; you think I need a goofjuice addict on top of that?"

"I'm no addict!" he shouted.

"Enough!" I stood, unlocked the hatch. "In the morning they'll let you go. No charges. Stay out of trouble, or . . ."

He jeered, "Or what?"

I said, "You'll answer to me, and you'll wish you hadn't." I left, hoping I'd impressed him. A middy! Lord God save us.

29

The next morning Dr. Zares numbed my jaw, removed the wires. Cautiously I opened my mouth. It ached, but nothing jarred loose. I went to the mirror. Lord God. I looked . . . was there ever anything like what I looked? I tried a smile. The gap-toothed result was so awful that I shuddered.

"When can you do the teeth?" I wasn't vain about my appearance, but I had no choice. When they laughed at me, they'd laugh at the Service.

"We can start anytime. It won't be comfortable."

"I know." It would hurt like the very devil. I'd bear it. Cellular seeds were planted deep in the gums and stimulated daily with the bone-growth stimulator. I'd had one done once, after my first and only fight in a Lunapolis bar.

"Captain . . ." He cleared his throat uncomfortably. "May I suggest . . ."

"Spit it out." I looked in the mirror again. A poor choice of words.

"Why don't you have that done as well?" He waved at my scar.

I smiled tightly. "You don't like it?"

He blurted, "It's awful." He reddened. "Sorry, sir, but you did ask. It's so unnecessary. Any clinic could fix it. I'm surprised you didn't have it removed when you were in the hospital."

"I chose to keep it."

"Do you still?"

I fingered the scar. "Why shouldn't I?"

He was blunt. "Because it puts people off. Skin regrowth is so simple that the scar is obviously an affectation."

I flushed. "I'm still your Captain."

"And you're still my patient. Keep your bloody scar, if

that's what you want!" He slammed the cabinet door. "We'll start on your teeth tomorrow. Let your jaw rest. Soft foods."

"Very well." I ran my finger across my mouth. I could even yawn if I wished. What luxury. "Doctor, about Mr. Tamarov."

"Yes." Cooling, he sat across from me. "I gave him a sedative for a good night's sleep. I'm no psych, Captain. I can give him psychotropic meds, or I can run an analysis for hormone rebalancing."

My stomach knotted. There was no reason why patients of a rebalancing ward were greeted with condescension or, worse, with cruel sneers, yet it was so, and my own attitude wasn't much better. I'd lost my wife Amanda because I'd hesitated to authorize *Portia*'s medic to check her for rebalancing.

If I didn't order a rebalance, and Alexi killed himself while deranged, the blame would be mine. If I allowed it, his career was finished. Yet, what career could he have in his current amnesiac state?

Surely hormone treatments were the best way. What would I want him to do for me, if our roles were reversed?

I'd rather die. "Not yet, Mr. Zares. I'll have him watched."

"You can't guard him at all hours."

I stood. "May I look in on him?" He nodded.

I went to the cubicle, cautiously opened the hatch. Alexi lay asleep, on his back. The lights were set low. I tiptoed in, sank into the chair next to the bed.

Alexi's face was relaxed, all cares dissipated as his chest rose and fell. I swallowed. So young. Sleeping, he was the fifteen-year-old I'd come to cherish in my first wary months on *Hibernia*. He'd done nothing to deserve the misery he'd seen since: my harsh rebukes, the tyranny of Philip Tyre, consignment to Admiral Tremaine's unjust vessel, the loss of his very self.

Slowly I eased from the chair, knelt by the side of Alexi's bed, clasped my hands. Please, Lord God. Restore him. I know You have no love for me, and that is just, but this one thing I ask You. Do with me as You will. But not him. Let me bear his hurts.

"How long have you been here?"

I looked up, startled. "You're awake."

"I just woke." He brought his arm under his head.

I smiled. "I just came in." I got up from my knees. "How do you feel?"

"Tired, actually. I'm here because . . . oh." He grimaced.

"I'm glad we found you. I'd have—" For a moment I turned away.

"Finish."

"I'd have been lonely." I rested my hand on his. "Please, Alexi. Don't damn yourself. Be patient."

"Oh, of course," he pulled his hand loose. "Patient. Always patient. I'll be known as Alexi Tamarov, the man who waited." He sat up, thrust off the sheet. "Maybe I should go back to the cabin and finish what I began."

"You're not a prisoner." He turned away. Perhaps I should make him one, for his own safety.

Afterward, I told Annie about my visit. She said with conviction, "I go talk to him. I know what it mean, not wantin' live. That be how I felt when you go way. It ain' right." She looked at me anxiously. "I wan' be with you, Nicky. Always. But talkin' a killin' myself when you be gone, that ain' the way. Trannie life too short for throwin' it away. Why you lookin' at me like that?"

"God, how I love you."

She came to me. Her diction was careful and precise. "Promise you'll be with me, Nicky. I can't stand it without you." I closed my eyes. Lord God, let her heal. Show her how not to rely on me.

Jerence was released and installed in a new cabin. Alexi left the sickbay.

Whenever I went to the dayroom, conversation fell silent. If Thomas Ross was present he immediately left. Bram Steiner asked again to be beached.

I kept my eye on the Log. The demerits issued by Tolliver went up, those issued by other officers began to diminish. It could be a good sign.

My jaw and gums hurt abominably as my replacement teeth rooted and began to probe through swollen tissues. I tried to ignore the pain, realized I was unsuccessful when I found myself, red-faced, shouting at Ricky Fuentes over a nav drill error.

Thomas Ross, also present, watched me with unconcealed contempt. I thought to send him to the first lieutenant, sent him instead to Tolliver. Tolliver could be worse.

As days passed, Lieutenant Kahn's manner was scrupulously correct, yet unforgiving. I learned to avoid the bridge during his watch; I preferred loneliness.

I visited Alexi's cabin at odd intervals, afraid of what I'd find. To my relief, all I encountered was sullen withdrawal, and no sign of the rope.

Three days after Jerence was freed he rampaged through Level 1, flinging tubes of softies at everyone he met, shouting gibberish. Midshipman Ross made the mistake of trying to collar him unaided; Jerence went along, docile enough, until he suddenly spun Ross around and butted him down the ladder to Level 2 where the middy lay groaning, out of combat. Eventually Jerence was subdued by three sailors who seemed to enjoy the unforeseen sport.

Woken from my first good sleep in several days, I had the boy hauled to the sickbay and strip-searched by Dr. Zares while the middies tore his cabin apart looking for more juice. They found none.

Jerence was again escorted to the brig.

Too tired to sleep, I roamed the ship, not caring where I went. I barged into the dining hall, ignored the sullen mess crew stiffened to attention among the starched linen. A quick look, then back out the hatch.

I passed Bram Steiner's cabin. Beach him? If he wanted off the bridge, I'd put him off the bridge, all right. Let him spend the rest of the cruise in the brig with Jerence.

Down the ladder to the engine room. Chief Arkin was on duty, with a hand. I growled, "Attention!" They stood stiffly while my eye roved the consoles, the cabinets, the machine shop. "Very well, carry on."

Back to Level 1. I passed the wardroom, stopped. By custom the wardroom was free of the Captain's interference, except for announced inspection. The hell with custom. I banged on the hatch. "Ship's inspection. Stand to!"

Tolliver rose immediately, with Ricky. They'd been playing chess. I noted the spotless deck, the immaculate bunks. Well, Tolliver was a seasoned hand; I would expect no less.

I slapped the hatch shut on my way out. By the time I reached my cabin I'd begun to cool. Annie was elsewhere; perhaps visiting. I left the cabin, looking for her. I checked the lounge.

Alexi sat with a holo. "Hello, Mr. Seafort."

"What are you doing?" I made an effort to smile.

"Reading." He showed me the screen. *"Walfort's Guide to Colonial Farming."*

"You're no farmer."

"I'm no anything." He snapped off the holo. "Better than just sitting." I stared at him. Finally he snapped, "Mr. Seafort, I told you I had nothing to do. If you want me to sit staring at the wall, say so!"

My fists clenched. "Stop feeling sorry for yourself!"

He gulped. "I'm sor—"

"Damn your sorry!" I stalked to the bridge. Lieutenant Kahn rose, saluted properly. I waved him back to his seat. He deliberately turned his chair away from me.

I sat for an hour, rage mounting. Finally I could bear it no longer. "Mr. Kahn, call Mr. Steiner to relieve you."

"Aye aye, sir." His tone was cool.

Steiner came, took his seat as Kahn left. Hours passed. I broke the silence with comments, but his only response was an occasional grunt of acknowledgment. The silence was maddening.

"Carry on." I went back to my cabin. Annie slept. I sat on the bed beside her, loosened my tie. She stirred. Annie, tell me it will be all right. Hold me. Lightly I caressed her arm.

She snapped awake, eyes wide with fear, and clawed at my hand. "Don' touch me!" She bounded to the edge of the bed.

"I'm sorry. Please, I just wanted—"

"Don' touch me! Never!" With a sob she dashed into the head, slammed shut the hatch.

I got up, went to the mirror, stared at the gaunt face that it framed. Alexi was right; better to die than to live in misery.

The entire ship had sent me to Coventry, and I was writhing in it. I had no refuge in my cabin or anywhere.

Well, so be it.

It meant I was free to do as I wished.

I stalked to the bridge. Lieutenant Steiner came to his feet. I growled, "Sit and be silent." I keyed the caller. "Mr. Tolliver, find Mr. Tamarov and bring him to the bridge."

Moments later Tolliver and Alexi reported, came to attention.

My voice was harsh. "Puter, record. As of this moment, Lieutenant Abram Steiner is placed on the inactive list." From his seat, Steiner gaped. "Put the following note in his personnel file: Mr. Steiner is placed inactive at his own request, for personal reasons. His performance as an officer has been satisfactory and his inactive status shall not be construed as a rebuke." I turned. "Steiner, off my bridge!"

His face was gray. He saluted, saw no response, left.

I wheeled on Alexi. "As for you, Mr. Tamarov, Lord God knows I'd undo what happened to you, but it cannot be. I won't have you mooning about feeling sorry for yourself. It's got to stop!"

"Mr. Seafort, I'll try to—"

"You'll more than try. Puter, note that Lieutenant Alexi Tamarov is herewith recalled to active duty, on full pay. End recording."

Alexi gaped. "But I don't know how to—I don't remember my training!"

"We'll retrain you."

"But how? I'd have to go back to Acad—"

"No, Mr. Tolliver will show you." Tolliver's jaw dropped. It gave me mild satisfaction. "Tolliver, you know the ropes. You're now Lieutenant Tamarov's aide. Help him do his duty. You're to share watches with him, eat at his table, spend every spare moment with him."

Alexi cried, "Mr. Seafort, I can't stand a watch if I don't know—"

"Sir! You call your Captain 'sir'!"

He gulped. "Aye aye, sir!"

"Mr. Tolliver, find this man a proper uniform. Tutor Alexi

in every subject studied by a cadet, midshipman, and lieutenant. Start with navigation. He's a fast learner."

"Aye aye, sir."

Alexi said, "Sir, I don't want to do this! I'm not ready—"

I said, my tone icy, "I don't care what you want." It brought a stunned silence. "You're recalled to duty. No discussion is allowed."

"But—"

Tolliver cleared his throat loudly. "Excuse me, Mr. Tamarov. One doesn't argue with the Captain."

Alexi looked to my face for comfort, found none.

"Dismissed."

Alone, I sat tapping the console. I picked up the caller. "Mr. Kahn, report to the bridge."

A few moments later he was back.

I was brusque. "Sit. Read the Log."

He did so. He swallowed, looked up, waiting.

"You may pick one, Mr. Kahn. Civility or the brig until we Defuse."

"Sir!" He groped for words.

"Steiner can't help you. He no longer has authority to relieve me."

"I didn't say anything about—"

"Four weeks pay for insubordination. What do you choose, Mr. Kahn? Will you be civil, or shall it be seven months in the brig?"

"I'll be civil, sir!" Sweat beaded his forehead. "I thought I was—"

"You weren't openly disobedient or blatantly contemptuous. But you missed by only a hair. That won't do. Do you think I'm the only tyrant you'll ever serve, Mr. Kahn? That's why cadets and middies go through hell, to learn that they can take what shipboard life may bring! Don't you remember?"

"Yes, sir!"

"If you can't survive under me, the Navy doesn't need you. I'm a part of your training, Mr. Kahn. Keep your hatred to yourself. Don't let me see it or know about it!"

"Aye aye, sir!"

"Finish your watch." I stalked off the bridge.

Below, I found the brig unlocked; Master-at-arms Torres was retrieving a dinner tray. Jerence sat cross-legged on his mattress.

I leaned against the hatch. "Why, boy?"

His smile was bitter. "Why not?"

"Have you hidden more juice?"

"Maybe. If not, I could make it, easy enough. I learned how."

"Why are you throwing your life away?"

He flared, "Why shouldn't I?"

"Do you despise Hope Nation that much?"

"Hope Nation? No, of course not!" He got to his feet. "See this prison? That's what my life is. Pa wants me to be a planter, and I have no choice. Every day it's the corn, or the wheat, or the God damn beans!"

I slapped him, hard. "Don't blaspheme!"

His hand flew to his face. "That's all you care about," he screamed. "Your dam—your frazzing religion!"

"Not all. It's what I start from."

"They all say you're crazy, that you killed Vax Holser! You're a monster."

I nodded. "You're right about that." I crossed to the bed, sat. I put my head in my hands. "I can't lecture you. I'm no better than you are."

He pounded on the hatch, harder and harder until I thought he'd break his hand. Suddenly he spun to me, his face wet. "You loved him! I saw, that day you tried to talk to him and he walked away."

"It's none of your—"

"Tell me! I want to hear it!"

I whispered. "Yes. I loved him."

He sobbed openly. "You were middies together, I heard. See what you have, that I'll never know? You think I'll find friendships like that on a God—on a frazzing farm?"

"No, I suppose you won't."

He struggled for composure. "What will come of me? Are you going to keep me here?"

"I have to." There was no other way.

"The whole cruise?" His cry was agonized.

"Yes. Then I'll turn you over for prosecution."

"Oh, God!" He slid to the deck, hugged himself.

"I have no choice, boy. If I let you go, would you give up the juice?"

He was silent a long time. I waited for the inevitable lie, but to my surprise he buried his head in his arms. "It's too late."

"What?"

"To give it up. I think about it all the time, Mr. Seafort. The stuff was supposed to last 'til we got to Lunapolis. I've used most of it already. I dream about it. I'd do . . . anything for it."

Lord God curse the vermin who made and sold the stuff; the death penalty was too good for them. And curse this foolish, uncaring boy, who'd brought foul drugs onto my ship for his own amuse—

No. I'd lost Tolliver, lost Annie, lost Kahn, Steiner, Eiferts, Ross. But not Jerence. Not yet.

"Jerence, it's time we set things right." I crossed the cell, hauled him to his feet. "Over there!" I shoved him toward the bed.

His eyes widened. "Why are you taking off your belt?"

"You're the ward of the commanding officer. That's me." I threw him facedown across the mattress. "This is your punishment, for making a shambles of my ship." I raised my arm. The crack of the belt across his rump echoed like a shot. Jerence shrieked, struggled to free himself. I held him down firmly until I was through. When I released him, he fled sobbing to the corner of the cell, rubbing his stinging buttocks. I threaded my belt through its loops. "I'll be back tomorrow to talk with you."

"I hate you! You're evil and I hate you!" His cries faded as I stalked along the corridor.

I went directly to the sickbay. Dr. Zares looked up from his desk.

"Do you know the chemical properties of goofjuice?"

The question startled him. "I imagine so. Why?"

"Do you know how to make it?"

He came to his feet. "Is that an accusation? I didn't. I don't know where the boy—"

"Answer me!"

He stepped back a pace. "Yes, I suppose I could, but I'd never—"

"Make a vial."

"You're out of your mind!"

I grinned through missing teeth. "I may well be, by now. That was insubordinate. I want a vial of goofjuice."

He studied me, shook his head. "Sorry, Captain, there's no way I could do that."

"There's no way you can't, since I ordered it."

"I could be jailed. Even a penal colony. Unless you give me a written order—"

"Get out your holo!" Speechless, he handed it to me; I typed in the order. "Can you have it by tomorrow?"

"You're serious? What in God's name—" He broke off. "I don't know. Maybe late tomorrow. I'd have to acidify—"

"Very well, by six. You're to tell no one. Acknowledge."

"Orders acknowledged and understood." He hesitated, then blurted, "You know what you'll do to yourself?"

"Have you any idea what I've already done to myself?" I walked out of the room.

I passed the next day in uneasy anticipation. Annie was friendly, even caring, so long as I didn't touch her. Lieutenant Kahn met me in the dayroom, greeted me with courtesy, sat at the long table alongside me. His conversation was nervous, his effort to be polite noticeable. I forced myself to respond; after all, it was what I had demanded.

Midshipman Ross entered, saw me, turned to go.

"Mr. Ross!" Kahn's voice cut like a whip.

"Yes, sir?"

"Sit with us, please." Reluctantly the middy complied. Kahn said, "We were discussing Kall's Planet. What did you think of the mines?"

"I don't know, sir. I have no opinion." Ross met Kahn's eyes defiantly.

"Two demerits. *Now* what do you think?"

I stood. "Good day, both of you." I left.

I stopped to give special orders to the purser, then took Annie to dinner at our half-empty table. For her sake, I endured the uneasy conversation until the meal was done, then left her at our cabin. I went to the bridge, where the Chief Engineer stood watch. Idly I thumbed through the Log. I saw that Ross had been caned, by Lieutenant Kahn's order. So be it.

Later, I knocked on the sickbay hatch. "Is it ready?"

"Yes." Dr. Zares stepped aside, gestured to a plastic-corked vial of amber liquid on his table.

"Very well."

"Captain, would you let me give you an antidepressant instead? I have meds that—"

"It's not for me, you dolt." I put the vial in my pocket, walked out.

He followed me into the corridor. "For the boy? How could you? You'll addict him and then—"

"Back to your quarters, Doctor." I headed down the ladder.

I unsealed the brig, went to the occupied cell, opened the hatch. "Come along."

Jerence sat up. "Where are you taking me?"

"Need another whipping?" My hand went to my belt.

He sneered disdainfully but wasted no time getting to his feet. "Where are we going?"

I led him into the circumference corridor. Jerence followed reluctantly. I unlocked the cabin I'd bade the purser prepare. "Sit." I pointed to the bed.

I took a chair opposite. "Jerence, your father loves you dearly. The plantation you'll inherit is worth millions. Can't you go back willingly?"

"Why should I talk to you, after what you did?"

"I'm all you have. Answer, or I'll leave you."

He rested his head in his hands. When he spoke, his voice was muffled. "I don't want to go back, not if I have to be a farmer."

"What would you do to earn another life?"

"What kind of life?" He looked up. Hope dawned. "You mean . . ." He breathed the words. "In the Navy, like Derek?"

I nodded.

He whispered, "Anything!"

"That's what you said you'd do for the juice."

"I—" He faltered. "I don't know. I can't choose, not if—"

"Here." I reached into my pocket, drew out the vial. I tossed it onto the bed.

He seized it. "Is this—I didn't put—how did you get it?" He clutched it to his chest.

"I had it made."

"Is it real?"

I reached over, pried the vial from his unwilling hands, uncorked it. "Smell." He sniffed the tart odor, licked his lips. I replaced the cork, tossed it back to him.

"Oh, God." He gulped. "Why did—may I?"

"Yes, in a moment." I waited. He eyed the vial with longing. "I'll be back to see you, Jerence. I want you to give me the juice back, untouched. If—"

"I can't!"

"—if you do, I'll appoint you a cadet in the U.N. Navy. You won't have to be a planter."

He tugged at my arm. "Don't you understand? I can't hold out!"

"Then you'll fail. It's your choice, as it's always been."

"Mr. Seafort, please. I've got to have it. Just a little."

"Help yourself. I'll throw you in the brig afterward, but that's no matter. You'll do time in a penal colony, and then you'll be free to juice yourself into hell." I stood. "Or there's the wardroom."

He stared at the vial. "How long?" he whispered.

"Three weeks." A cry of grief, which I did my best to ignore. "In three weeks I'll let you take the oath. On the other hand, there's the juice, whenever you want it." I went to the hatch, slapped it open.

He scrambled across the room, barred my way. "Not like that," he gabbled. "Please, I'll give up the juice! I swear! But don't leave me alone with it, I'm not strong en—"

I pried his fingers loose from the hatch. "Find strength." I thrust him back inside the cabin.

He slid down, clutched at my legs. "Please, sir! Not in the same room with juice! I'll use it, I've got to!"

My voice was cold. "You brought yourself to this, not I. If you can't—" Amanda swam before me, with Nate. Perhaps my son would have grown to be like Jerence, given the time denied him.

This wasn't the way.

With a sigh, I reached down, hoisted the anguished boy to his feet. I led him to the bed, laid him down. I sat next to him, stroked his hair. "Steady, lad. I'll stay awhile."

He sobbed, "God, Mr. Seafort, take it away!"

"No, Jerence." I gentled him, unbuttoned the top of his shirt. "Listen, and I'll tell you a story. Lay back, son. Slow your breathing. There was a boy, once. A boy called Philip. Dry your eyes, now. It was years ago. We were on a ship, a great ship, cruising to a distant star . . ."

Slowly he calmed.

30

I endured daily sessions with the bone-growth stimulator. My mouth ached constantly, but the hours after my therapy with Dr. Zares were sheer misery.

Lieutenant Kahn greeted me civilly whenever he saw me. Occasionally he even attempted light conversation. Grunting in reply, I searched his face for a sign of his revulsion but found none.

From a locked Level 2 cabin, cries of torment and pounding on the hatch. On my first visit after I'd left Jerence to wrestle with his demon, he greeted me red-eyed and trembling. "It's been a whole day. Mr. Seafort, please say that's enough!"

"Where's the juice?"

"I hid it so I— He swallowed, burrowed under the mattress, came up with the vial. "Here, I haven't touched it. Let me sign up now. I'm begging you."

"Twenty more days."

"You bastard!"

On that note I left him.

The next day I shared a watch with Tolliver. He was unusually pensive. I did my best to concentrate on a chess problem, on an imaginary board. If I moved Queen to King's Bishop five, behind a pawn screen . . .

He cleared his throat. "I'm supposed to keep wardroom problems from the Captain's attention, but . . ."

"Eh?" The chessboard wavered, faded.

"Since you talked to me, I've tried. Believe me."

I worried at a knuckle. "And?"

"Maybe you'd best get someone else. It's beyond me."

I sat up, attentive. "Go on."

"I didn't know Fuentes in *Hibernia,* but I gather from your remarks he was a good-natured joey."

"The best."

"He taunts Ross as if the consequences don't matter. And Thomas . . ." He shook his head. "He's beside himself. Venomous. Nothing I say reaches either of them."

"A first middy has his resources." Did he expect me to tell him how to run a wardroom? It was supposed to be beneath my notice. A first midshipman who couldn't hold his wardroom could expect little sympathy.

"Yes, sir." A sigh, barely audible. "I'll deal with it."

What malady plagued *Victoria?* The first lieutenant beached, the second under strict orders to hold his tongue, the third suicidal. Drug-crazed passengers, the wardroom at each other's throats.

And a Captain who had no right to walk the bridge, if the Navy were just. *I* was the problem, and the unsettled state of affairs was merely a reflection of that.

I sighed. "It's not your fault. Tell me."

He seemed pathetically grateful. "Sir, I can demerit them 'til their tongues hang out. And I will, if I'm sure that's the way. But it will only make them hate me as they do each other."

"It's not so much hate as . . ." I stood, with an urgent need to pace. "Their lives are askew. They want to revere their Captain as I did Captain Haag, but they know it's not possible in my case. The conflict is too much."

He snorted. "Now you're a psych as well as a mad bomber?"

"Damn you!"

He shrugged. "Oh, I'll admit you've caused your share of the world's problems. But you can't take credit for them all."

Well, I *had* told him I'd suffer his insolence, in private. I waved away my ire. "What else could explain their behavior?"

"With Ross, in part it's because he revered his Captain, precisely as you said. He can't forgive you—"

"For murdering him."

"No, for replacing him." He leaned forward. "Sir, you have to understand: at this point, no one in command could satisfy Ross's expectations. And Holser was killed, not transferred. A sudden, terrible loss. No good-byes, no time to accept the inevitability of—"

"Stop!" My cry echoed from the bulkheads. I swallowed.

"Sorry, sir." His tone suggested he meant it. After a moment he cleared his throat. "But even that doesn't explain Ross's malevolence. He rags at Bezrel 'til he has the joeykit in tears, which I'll admit is easy enough. He says vile things about Kahn and the Chief. He called me a—" His mouth tightened. "I took him to the exercise room, and he's more cautious now. But still . . ."

"His ratings were excellent before I took command. Clearly I'm the cause." Moodily I tapped the console.

Tolliver said, "And what's come over Ricky Fuentes?"

"Have you asked him?"

"Yes, and he stalked out in a rage. You may have noticed three demerits, a couple of nights ago."

"I wondered."

"And then there's Bezrel, who might be a good middy, if ever he's old enough. Sir, I'm in over my head."

"Nonsense!" I paced with renewed vigor. "Do your duty, Midshipman, and don't whine about it."

"I wasn't—aye aye, sir."

"Is there anything else?"

"Yes. Your friend Alexi loathes the sight of me. I'm getting nowhere as his aide."

"I think you're overreact—"

"It's his sarcastic asides that rankle. He's my superior, so I'm not free to compl—"

"Nor are you free to complain about him to me!"

"I wasn't!" He shot from his seat, fists clenched. A deep breath, then another. "Sir." His fingers opened. "Sorry."

"As you should be." I was appalled at the discussion into which I'd stumbled. Bad enough that he'd asked my advice; worse, he'd given me his, unbidden. The more I thought about it, the more I . . . "That's quite enough for today, Mr. Tolliver. I'll finish the watch."

"You want me to go?"

"It would be a great pleasure." I regretted the words almost instantly as he saluted and stalked to the hatch. He'd told me of Alexi's sarcasm, and I'd responded with my own.

* * *

On *Hibernia,* on *Portia,* relations with the passengers consumed a significant part of my attention. Here on *Victoria,* few had anything to say to me. I didn't particularly mind, but it left me with little to brood on, beside the crew.

Still, there was Jerence.

I found him huddled in the corner of his cabin. "Well?"

He got up, fished in his pocket. "I still have it."

"Good boy."

"You said you'd come every day." An accusation.

"I have."

"It's been . . ." His brow knotted. "A long time."

"Eighteen hours. Endure it."

He pulled out the vial, rushed across the room. "Here." He made as if to drop it in my lap, but his fingers halted, as if they had volition of their own. "Maybe I'd better . . . just in case . . . No!" With vehemence, he tossed it at me.

I let it fall to the deck. "Don't pretend you've forgotten my terms."

"How long yet?"

"Thirteen days."

"Oh, God." A deep breath, and another. His eyes were bleak as he retrieved the juice. "It's not worth it. I thought I wanted to be a middy, but . . ."

"Fine." Steeling myself, I stood to go. "I'd rather not watch, if you don't mind—"

He cried, "Why won't you help me!" His eyes brimmed.

Why did his pain pierce me so? Had he not brought it on himself? I crossed to the bed, sat, patted the sheet. "Put that down; sit here. We'll talk."

"Would you take it away?" He sat. "You don't know how bad today is. Every minute, I . . ."

I took his chin, turned it so his eyes met mine. "Wherever you go, there'll be juice. You can't hide from it."

He rocked. For a moment his forehead brushed my shoulder.

"Think of the next hour. Don't worry about tomorrow." How fatuous I sounded.

He threw himself flat on the bed, curled toward the bulkhead. "You said you'd tell me stories."

I swallowed. Father never told me tales; all I knew was my own life, and there was no part of it without pain. What did he want of me?

No, that was unfair. I'd promised I would visit with him. I took a long, slow breath. "I grew up in Cardiff. That's in Wales. Once, when I was young, I had a friend called Jason . . ."

I didn't know how much he heard. From time to time he sniffled and wiped his nose with his sleeve.

Two days later they caught Ricky Fuentes forcing open a cooler in the galley, late in the night. The steward brought him to Alexi and Tolliver, who shared the watch, and Tolliver took the unusual step of summoning me directly.

Moments later, buttoning my coat, I strode onto the bridge. Ricky stood stiffly at attention midway between hatch and the console. "What in blazes . . . ?"

"Not just a raid. He used a pry bar." Tolliver's voice was cold.

That Ricky Fuentes could do such a thing was the ultimate betrayal. If there was one joey aboard with sense, with decency, it was he.

"Damage?"

"Scratches. A bent hinge."

I'd been standing near my seat, listening, chest tight. When the red mists cleared I found my fingers curled around Ricky's lapels. The boy's mouth worked in panic.

"How dare you, Fuentes!" My nose was inches from the middy's. "Vandalize my ship? I'll break you! I'll put you back to cadet! Ship's boy! Common seaman!"

He whimpered.

"How dare you! Answer me!"

Ricky stammered, "A bet. I told Mr. Ross I could—I'm sorry—it was—"

I tore off my cap, hurled it across the bridge. Alexi flinched as it sailed past his head. "Call Mr. Kahn; we'll have Fuentes caned this instant!"

"Aye aye, sir." Tolliver spoke into the caller.

The gall, sneaking into territory that was off-limits to all middies, to destroy Naval property. I'd show him and the others. Any middy might irk his superiors from time to time, but there were limits. As every midshipman knew, an enraged Captain was a calamity not to be borne, and by God, I was he.

The hatch slid open. "Lieutenant Jeffrey Kahn reporting, sir."

"Do you know what this ruffian's been up to?" I swung to him, my voice an accusation. No matter what Kahn's feelings for me, he would be incensed. Raiding the galley was one thing; more than once I'd led midnight forays on *Hibernia*. Luckily we hadn't been caught, though one time, as a cadet . . . Well, that was another story. But a pry bar . . .

Kahn's eyes flicked to the Log, and Tolliver's most recent entry.

I said, "Thrash him. Don't dream of going easy. I'll want to see him after." Whatever had come over Ricky?

"Aye aye, sir. Middy, come along." He strode to the hatch.

They were well along the corridor before my last thought penetrated my consciousness. What *had* come over Ricky, my old shipmate? And wasn't it time I found out?

"Edgar, call them back." If Ricky were punished to the degree I contemplated, I'd not be able to get much from him after.

On leaving the bridge, Ricky had wheeled, marched after Kahn with commendable dignity. Apparently it had been a show for my benefit. When he reappeared he tried manfully to check the tears that had flowed once he was out of sight.

My rage vanished like air from a ruptured hull.

I retrieved my cap from the deck. "Well." A few breaths. Adrenaline left me shaky. "Mr. Kahn, wait in your cabin. He'll be along."

I needed privacy. Should I send Tolliver and Alexi out? No, the bridge was no place for an inquisition such as I had in mind. "Come with me, Fuentes." I led him to the passengers' lounge. At this hour it was deserted. Inside, I sealed the hatch. "Now." I guided Ricky to a couch, pulled up a chair, sat with our knees almost touching. "What have you to say for yourself?"

"Nothing, sir."

I regarded him, unsure how to proceed. "How old are you?"

"Sixteen, sir." Light brown hair, a face that barely knew a razor. A slim body grown like a weed. And once, a ready smile that had lit his eyes, an eager enthusiasm that brought an ache to the heart.

A sniffle. He flushed with embarrassment.

I blurted, "Remember Sandy's orchestron?"

He gaped. "On *Hibernia?* That was . . . years ago."

"You were twelve."

"And ship's boy."

"He held it over your head, and you couldn't reach. You've grown since."

A wan smile.

"You used to bring my eggs and toast."

His eyes teared.

"Remember when I shrieked at you in my cabin, because you wouldn't relax?"

Again a smile, but his mouth quivered. He made as if to turn away, instead searched deep into my eyes. Somehow, I held his gaze. With a cry of anguish, he fell upon me, buried his head in my shoulder, held me as if a lifeline.

Stunned, I managed to raise my hand, stroke his hair. "It's all right, boy."

Sobs.

"Tell me."

For a long time nothing but the shaking of his shoulders. At last, with a shuddering breath, he raised his head from my dampened jacket. His eyes widened with dismay at the realization of what he'd done.

"Never mind that. Tell me." My voice was soft.

Instead, he looked away. "I wish . . ."

"Yes?"

"That *Victoria* were a happy ship. She used to be."

"Under Mr. Holser?"

"Mr. Martes too. The fish killed him, didn't they?"

"I'm afraid so."

His fingers twisted. "I cried myself to sleep the night Mr. Holser was—died."

"I wish I could have done the same." But I didn't deserve remorse.

A long silence. "Sir? Could you tell—I know it's none of my—" He poked at a split in the seat cover. His eyes rose to mine, with resolve. "They say you killed him."

I dared say nothing.

"That you let him stay on the Station, knowing it was too late to stop the bomb."

My lips pressed tight.

"That you let him die, because on Hope Nation he refused to talk to you!"

"Oh, Ricky." I wasn't sure I was changing the subject. "Didn't you like Mr. Ross, once?"

He seemed startled. "I guess."

"Mr. Tolliver says you ride him to distraction. Why?"

"The things he says about you!"

"And if they're true?"

"They can't be!" A pause. Then, softer, "They mustn't be."

"Look at me." I waited. "I blew the Station. I let Captain Holser on board, knowing he'd come to stop me. I deny none of it."

"You set the bomb so he couldn't disarm it? Did you do that?" In his eyes, appeal.

"It's not your place to ask."

"I need to know!"

Abruptly I stood to pace. The burden of Orbit Station was mine to bear. I couldn't inflict it on an innocent middy, no matter how great his need for reassurance.

"Why'd you break into the cooler?"

"They didn't think I could—"

"Ricky!"

His look was defiant. "What difference does it make? A hinge, a cooler, a frazzing fastship! Regs!"

"Is that all you—"

"Go ahead, have me caned! I can take it, you'll see!"

With slow steps I walked to the couch, gently lifted his head. Our eyes met. After a long time I said, "Do I mean that much to you?"

He spun away.

I knelt. "Ricky, there are things I mustn't tell you. But surely you know Vax meant a great deal to me. At the Station he was incredibly brave. His first thought was to save me, though I wasn't worth it."

"And you killed him!"

Despite my resolve, the cry was wrung from me. "Could I have?"

For an eternity he looked into my eyes. Finally his face softened. At last his gaze held a modicum of peace.

A while later I walked him to Kahn's cabin, my hand on his shoulder. "There's still punishment. That can't be helped."

"Yessir. I guess I deserve it." Ricky's head slumped, and I gave an extra squeeze.

I knocked. "Mr. Kahn, you need not go particularly easy, but disregard the rest of what I said."

Kahn nodded. I walked back to the bridge.

Annie took more interest in her surroundings, and I grew hopeful. She went for endless walks around the circumference corridors, and from time to time visited the lounge.

One afternoon she said, "Nicky, why don' they like me?"

"Because you're with me, hon."

"No, it's somethin' more. They look at me, talk 'bout me after I go."

"How would you know—"

"I listened, at the hatch." She folded her arms against my disapproval. " 'See how she hold her head, like tryin' ta be somethin' she's not!' " Her voice mimicked scorn.

I got to my feet. "Who?"

"It don' matter. I be used to it. Besides"—she giggled—"the middy tol' 'em good."

"I'll make him lieutenant," I said, only half in jest. "Which one?" Tolliver, most likely. Or Ricky. Bezrel hadn't the gumption to—

"Tommy."

"Ross? Thomas Ross?"

"Yesterday he called Suliman Rajnee a grode an' a bigot for funnin' at me. Said Rajnee didn' know what a gentleman was, an' be too stupid ta learn."

"Good Lord." Why would Ross protect my wife, given his thorough dislike of me? I was grateful, but still, foul language to a passenger was unacceptable under any circumstances. I'd send him to Rajnee with an apology.

"I'll be back in a while, hon."

I found Ross on the watch, with Ms. Arkin. "What have you been up to, Middy?" I sounded more severe than I'd intended.

"Sir?"

"Yesterday. Suliman Rajnee."

"We had words."

"Tell me what you said."

"I'd rather not." Outright defiance.

"You insulted him. Called him names."

"I figured he'd whine to you about—"

"One demerit. Make that two." I pursed my lips. Rajnee was no longer the issue. "Ross, I've had it with your—"

"Beach me, then! It was good enough for—"

"*ROSS, ENOUGH!*" Sandra Arkin.

"Thank you, Chief, but I'll handle it. Mr. Ross, apologize!"

A sullen silence. Then, "Very well, I apologize." His tone belied his words.

"Sir!"

"Oh, but of course. *Sir.*"

"Mr. Ross, take yourself to"—I'd been about to say "Mr. Kahn," but—"the wardroom. Pack your gear; I'll send you civvies and find you someplace to bunk."

"Am I beached?"

"You're . . ." I hesitated, firmed my resolve. He was beyond bearing. "You're dismissed from the Service, as of this moment."

"God, no!" He blanched.

"Oh, yes. Off my bridge!" I turned his shoulders, propelled him to the hatch.

"Sir, wait, I—"

"Out!" He was agile and sturdy, but my rage was beyond challenge. I flung him to the far bulkhead, slapped the hatch shut.

Ms. Arkin stared at the console lights.

"Well?" I dared her to object.

"He was offensive."

I snorted. "You might call it that."

Her manner was carefully placating. "If you'd repeated what he said, Jeff Kahn would have cured him."

"He's eighteen and been barreled twice this month. It didn't help."

"Yes, sir." She couldn't say much more without skirting insubordination.

Lieutenant Kahn came to my cabin while Annie was out walking. "Sir, I beg you to reconsider."

"About Ross? Forget it."

"Aye aye, sir. I know he's impetuous, but—"

"Hah. Have you any idea what he said to me?"

"He told me some, Sandra the rest. Still, if we—"

I shouted, "I will not be spoken to with contempt!" I fingered my jacket. "This is the United Nations, the Government ordained of Lord God! It deserves respect, even if I myself—" I broke off. "After we dock, after my trial, he can spit on me; I might even applaud. But for now . . ."

"Yes, sir. I agree wholeheartedly. Sorry, not the spitting, please don't take offense. But what you have to understand about Thomas is that—"

A knock. Furious, I threw upon the hatch. "Now what—"

Edgar Tolliver. He saluted. "Might I have a word, sir?" His face was grim.

"Not now."

"Sir, I just heard—"

"About Ross?" I grimaced, stood aside. "Very well, join the party."

"Oh. I didn't realize, Mr. Kahn." Tolliver saluted his superior.

"Skip the formalities, both of you, and sit. I don't intend to be argued out of my decision."

Tolliver glanced at Kahn, back to me. "With respect, sir"—I snorted at that—"how did you decide? In the heat of the moment?"

"That's not for you to question."

Tolliver tried again. "You said the wardroom was mine to handle."

"You said you couldn't."

"You told me to try. Let me."

"With the other middies. Ross is out."

Kahn cleared his throat. "Captain, I'll have a talk with Ross. Hear him out, after—"

"Begging your pardon, sir." To Kahn, Tolliver was polite but firm. "It's my responsibility, as first middy. I'll see to it—"

I snapped, "Are you both deaf? He's cashiered." I glowered at Tolliver's mute reproach. He held his gaze.

A weariness settled over me. Was I overreacting? No. The boy was—

"Sir, he's in his bunk, crying. He begged me for help." Tolliver's face was intense. "Do you understand? Since I unpacked in the wardroom, he's offered me nothing but sullenness or gibes. Today, he wanted me."

"Contemptible. He has no right to ask, after—"

Tolliver shot to his feet. "Do you want justice or a crew?"

Even Kahn was aghast, but Tolliver paid no heed. "Break me, break Steiner. Break Tommy Ross. Why stop there? You almost lost Ricky! What about Mr. Kahn?"

"Leave me out of—"

"Sir, it's my fault Ross erupted. You know that as well as I!"

"Good heavens." I sank to a chair. Tolliver was certain of his cause, or he wouldn't dare to upbraid me. Even then, it was unimaginable. Still, I had no conscience of my own, and it seemed he was appointed to fill the role.

I waved, a gesture of defeat. "Very well. Talk to him, both of you. I'll—I *might* reconsider."

Jerence howled and kicked at me until I left. He refused to show me the vial; I knew that meant it was emptied.

Belowdecks, two crewmen beat a third senseless. I had them brigged until the next Captain's Mast.

A few months. Then the rope, and surcease.

From Ricky Fuentes, a written apology. Kahn had gone hard on him, and he'd been absent from the dining hall for days, until he could sit without misery. Ricky offered to replace the damaged hinge from his own pay. He would never do something so dishonorable again, never let me down . . . I put down the note. Better he merely exercised more sense; I wanted none of his hero-worship.

I couldn't put off dealing with Jerence; he had to be returned to the brig. I went to his cabin.

The lights were dialed low. Jerence sat up, squinted through eyes set deep in a haggard face. "Is it over?"

"Yes. To the brig." My tone was curt.

Carefully he eased himself from the bed. "You promised!"

"Only if you held out."

He hugged himself, rocking. Slowly his hand crept inside his shirt. He extended his arm, opened his fingers. The vial.

"I warned you—" But it was unopened. "Oh, Jerence!" I swallowed. "After yesterday, I thought . . ."

"I didn't think it could get any harder, but it did." His voice was hoarse. "Mr. Seafort, it hurts."

"Yes." I sniffed. "Are you forgetting to wash?"

"Who cares?" Again he hugged himself. "How long has it been?"

"Ten days. Eleven to go."

He pursed his lips, shook his head.

Tolliver sat across from me in the officers' mess. "May I bring Mr. Ross to see you?"

I frowned. I regretted letting myself be bludgeoned into an interview. "Not the bridge, and definitely not my cabin. Where are his quarters?"

"Cabin twenty-nine, Level 2. He shares."

"With whom?"

A flicker of a smile. "Suliman Rajnee. Mr. Kahn and I thought it fitting."

Tolliver's idea, I was sure. "Very well. After lunch."

The meal was tasteless and heavy on my stomach. After, I paced the bridge for a full hour, girding myself.

Rajnee, by prearrangement, would be elsewhere. I rapped on the hatch.

Thomas Ross opened, began a salute, realized it was a

breach of protocol. Lowering his hand, he stood aside. He looked odd and uncomfortable in a casual jumpsuit.

I found a chair, sat with crossed legs. "Well?"

He walked with peculiar gait to his bunk, eased himself onto it.

"Have they caned you?" My tone was sharp. "I gave orders you weren't to be—"

"No, sir. I've been sick to my stomach ever since you . . . It hurts."

We waited.

"I've nothing to say, Ross. I'm here at your request."

"Yessir. What I wanted to—look. My hand's shaking." He held it out for inspection.

"Get on with it." In the Navy, one made one's bed and had to lie in it. I had no sympathy for his distress.

"I've got to be reinstated." He frowned, as if it hadn't sounded the way he hoped. "The Navy is all I ever wanted."

That much, I understood. It had been so with me.

"Without it I'm . . . nothing." His eyes darted to mine, back to the deck. "What must I do to convince you?"

"Should I care?"

"Captain, I apologize for my rudeness. I'll do anything. I'll get down on my knees and—"

"You won't do that." I would leave, on the instant. The memories were too strong.

"Whatever you say, then. Have me caned. But please, please put me back to middy. I won't ever disrespect—"

I was tired of it. "What I want isn't groveling, but truth. I came here expecting to deny your request, and that's still my intent. Level with me absolutely, or there's not the slightest chance I'll—"

"Anything!" He jumped from the bed, crossed to the wardrobe built into the bulkhead, turned back. His voice was unsteady. "Anything."

"Why are you so desperate? There are other paths, other lives to lead."

"I thought when I showed how angry I was, I was acting from principle. But on the bridge, when you dismissed me . . . something in my gut wrenched; I thought I'd pass out. I never knew how important the Navy was to me." He turned. "In Ottawa I dreamed of it, lying in my bed. I had all the holos about Academy, and Mom was furious when I played them instead of doing my homework."

Despite myself, I smiled. I knew. "Why do you loathe me so?"

"I don't, I've changed my mind, I realize I've been—"

I strode to the hatch.

"All right! You killed Mr. Holser!"

"Others have made their peace with it."

"I'm sorry, I didn't mean to accuse—"

"Damn it, boy, truth!"

He stumbled to the bed, sank on it, immediately jumped to his feet. "You're a traitor! You set off a nuke! He was your friend, and a word from you would have stopped him. You didn't say it!"

"If he came to save the Station, would he have listened?"

"He was our Captain!" A cry of such despair that I was silenced.

"Oh, God, I'm going to be sick again." He tried not to retch. "I love the Navy more than anything, but I can't abide that it has you in it!"

My voice was so quiet that only I heard. "Neither can I."

A long time passed, the silence broken only by his sobs.

I cleared my throat. "What's come of your talks with Tolliver and Mr. Kahn?"

"Lieutenant Kahn's furious, sir. He's warned me if I'm reinstated I'll have more to worry about from him than you."

"Odd, given his own feelings."

"Not really, sir. Mr. Tolliver's disgusted with me, but he took the time to make it clear. If we respect the Service, we owe courtesy to all its officers. You're not just in charge of *Victoria,* sir. You represent Admiralty, the regs, every ship of the line. So I'll have to show you good manners, no matter what I—no matter what."

"That came as a revelation?" My tone was dry.

"No, sir." A mumble. "I guess I already knew. It's just . . ." His head came up. "You said the truth. May I speak my mind?"

I nodded.

"I owe it to Mr. Holser not to let his murder go unnoticed.

I despise your treason. Thank God that hangings are public. I'll be there for yours even if I have to jump ship. And I'll celebrate, when they're done." At my unflinching gaze, he reddened. "Well, that's how I feel."

"It's not always necessary to say what you feel."

"Yessir."

This had gone far enough; I already knew my decision. "I'll let you know in a week or so." I stood.

"That long!"

"Or more." The prize would be more valued, for the yearning.

"What shall I do with myself? I spend every day alone; Rajnee doesn't care to talk to me any more than I—and no officer will even speak to me."

I shrugged. "That's your affair." An idle thought. "If you're lonely, visit cabin nineteen."

"The Branstead joey?"

"An hour a day, no more. He'd like someone to talk with, I imagine."

Tolliver dogged Alexi Tamarov's footsteps, relentless in his determination that Alexi become the perfect lieutenant. I surmised that Tolliver modeled his behavior after our drill sergeants at Academy, who spoke to us with token respect, yet sternly monitored and corrected our every move.

At first, Alexi was resentful and sullen. Nonetheless, he studied his texts and performed his nav drills like any nervous young middy, Tolliver by his side. After a time Alexi hesitantly began issuing orders to the work details he was allowed to supervise.

After a week I allowed Thomas Ross to don his uniform. He reported for watch, polished and crisp. As he entered the bridge, evident relief battled with something else. Perhaps self-betrayal.

I said nothing of what had passed between us. When he was settled I left for my cabin.

In the evenings I sat with Jerence.

After one tempestuous visit, he'd finally quieted and gone to sleep. In the morning he'd pounded on the hatch until a sailor heard him and called the purser. Before I rounded the corridor bend I could hear Jerence begging to be freed.

"Steady, Jerence." I opened the hatch. He tried to dive past me; I hauled him up by the collar. The vial of goofjuice lay on his bed.

"Oh, God, Mr. Seafort, I want it so! Isn't there a way? Couldn't I have just a little? Would you let me?"

"Yes. As much as you want."

"Oh, thank you! I—" He stopped short. "And could I enlist, then?"

"Of course not."

"Look what's happening to me!" He showed me his hand. It trembled.

"Physical withdrawal, I'd guess. A jolt of juice will cure it." I put my hand on the hatch lever.

"Don't leave me alone! Please!" His tear-streaked face peered up at me. "I've tried so hard, but I can't!"

Again I thought of Nate, knowing the comparison was foolish. This boy was not my son, never would be. But impulsively I pulled his head to my chest, released him. "Wait another day, Jerence. I'll be back."

"To tell me more stories? Tommy won't, he says he doesn't know how."

"I don't know any more—"

"Pa used to, when I was little. If I concentrate on your voice I don't think so hard about the juice, for a little."

"All right, but not every day." What could I tell him of myself that wasn't a lie?

Time passed. I adjusted Alexi's watch rotation so that he always shared with Tolliver. Tolliver bore up under the strain of his duties, made easier perhaps by the lessening of tensions in the wardroom. Even Bezrel showed signs of improvement; he was rebuked less often and learned to stand up under criticism without wilting. Well, most of the time. On one occasion I'd carefully not noticed a stray tear making its way down his cheek.

Still, Alexi had been but a pale imitation of a lieutenant: hesitant, unsure, often confused. I knew that after we docked, when I'd be unable to shield him, he'd be useless to the Service. I didn't tell him so. He already knew.

"Mr. Seafort, it isn't working." We were on the bridge, toward the end of the cruise, during one of Tolliver's rare absences. "If Edgar wasn't with me, I'd never manage."

"Just do your best, Alexi."

"I try, but I can't even fill out the Log without Tolliver guiding me. And I do it every watch!"

"Your intelligence is what it always was. We had it tested."

"Yes, I know."

"And Dr. Zares says your ability to retain what you learn is unimpaired. So all you need is time."

"Yes, sir." He brooded at his console. "I know you don't like me to complain."

"Do the best you can."

He flared, "Do my best, do my best. How many times have I heard that? You sound just like Amanda. Alexi, all you can expect is your bes—"

The hairs on my neck rose.

White-faced, he whispered, "Amanda!"

"You remember?"

"In my cabin, when I hated Philip so! On *Hibernia!*" He bounded from his seat. "Sir, I remember! Wasn't it on *Portia,* when she died? Tell me!"

"Yes." I grinned. Thank You, Lord.

"Her funeral, I was there!" He danced with excitement.

"Steady, Lieutenant." I clasped his arm; unexpectedly he grabbed me and hugged me. "Oh, sir, I remember parts of it!"

"Easy, Alexi." But I didn't push him away; my hand pounded his back in answering enthusiasm.

It wasn't that simple, of course. Huge gaps in his memory remained. Yet, almost daily, bits of his past returned. With each revelation, his stature heightened, his shoulders straightened, his confidence grew.

I was content.

But then I thought of home.

31

"Prepared to Defuse, sir," said Chief Engineer Sandra Arkin.

"Very well." I turned to Kahn, absently fingering my scar. "Call Mr. Tolliver."

Moments later Edgar Tolliver saluted, waited for me to release him.

"As you were. I thought you might want to see this, Edgar. The end of our cruise." The finis to my career, and soon of my life.

"Yes, sir." He stood behind my chair, peering over my shoulder at the console.

I reached to the top of the screen. I hesitated. Each day of the interminable voyage had brought me inexorably closer to this moment. I had no doubt they'd hang me. My only regret was that Annie was still fragile, and sometimes worse. She would likely require a course of hormone rebalancing. Perhaps I could arrange that much, before they tried me. Perhaps, in return for my guilty plea . . .

"Ready, sir?" Kahn.

"Sound Battle Stations. We'll take no chances."

"Aye aye, sir." Kahn pressed the alarms. Throughout the ship men and women dashed to their stations, reported their readiness to the bridge. When all compartments had responded I reluctantly put my finger on the screen.

"We're ready, sir."

I shot Kahn an annoyed glance. "Yes, of course." I ran my finger down the line on the screen. "Defused."

The simulscreens flashed to stunning life. "Checking for encroachments," Kahn said immediately.

"Captain, no encroachments." The puter.

"Thank you, Billy. Mr. Kahn?" Never did one rely solely on a machine.

His reply took a moment longer. "Free of encroachments, Captain."

"Where are we?"

Billy said, "Outside orbit of Venus. Coordinates follow."

"Very well. Remain at Battle Stations until we contact Admiralty." I stood to pace. "Mr. Tolliver."

"Yes, sir?"

"Sit at the console." Immediately Lieutenant Kahn rose to give his seat. It would have been unthinkable for Tolliver, or any officer, to sit in my place. "Take the following message to the comm room and have it broadcast continuously until reply is received:

"To Admiralty, Lunapolis Base, Captain Nicholas E. Seafort reporting." Diligently Tolliver typed my words.

"U.N.S. *Victoria* is returned to Solar System under my command. The U.N.N.S. fleet left Hope Nation ten months ago under orders of Admiral Georges De Marnay and is in passage home." Our fastship had outraced the fleet; the other ships would arrive six months from now.

"Due to a rebellion on Hope Nation, I was unable to rejoin the fleet." I paused, waited for Tolliver. "With help from several planters, I suppressed the rebellion. On my own initiative, as senior military officer and plenipotentiary of the United Nations Government, I granted the colony of Hope Nation status as a free commonwealth, and full and irrevocable membership in the Assembly of the United Nations." Tolliver shook his head, knowing as well as I that Admiralty would be appalled.

"After the fleet sailed, the aliens continued to attack Hope Nation. Fish entered the atmosphere and settled to ground level. They destroyed and overran the Venturas Base."

Even I, brazen as I had become, found the next confession difficult. "I concluded that Hope Nation could not survive unless the balance of forces was drastically altered. Therefore, acting alone and in secret, I caused the disabled ships on Orbit Station to attract the fish by caterwauling their fusion drives. Many fish responded. When Orbit Station was disabled, I deliberately caused a nuclear detonation that destroyed some five hundred twelve fish."

"Plus the four hundred seventy-two my father shot," Billy said proudly.

"Puter, be silent. Commander Vax Holser, a courageous officer, lost his life in an unsuccessful attempt"—I stopped dead. It was my last chance to redeem my honor. The truth, or a vile lie? I took a deep breath—"to save Orbit Station from detonation. I emphasize that no person other than myself took any part in the destruction of the Station."

I cleared my throat. Why was the simulscreen blurred? "I therefore turn over command of U.N.S. *Victoria* to Lieutenant Jeffrey Kahn and await your further orders. Mr. Tolliver, transmit at once."

"Aye aye, sir."

I turned to Lieutenant Kahn, saluted. "I'll be in my cabin with my wife. Do not disturb me until they reply."

"Aye aye, sir." An awed whisper.

I strode from the bridge for the last time, keeping my head high, my expression calm, until I was around the bend of the circumference corridor. Then I hurried to my cabin, groped for the hatch.

Annie sat in her chair, looking at a holo, humming. She took no notice of my entry. I took off my jacket, my tie. I lay down on the bed.

I'm sorry, Father. At the end, even duty has failed me. I am nothing in the eyes of Lord God, and now I am nothing to the Naval Service. Let it be over.

I lay staring at the ceiling. After a period I drifted to other places, other times. Strange dreams disturbed my sleep. Vax Holser, enraged, did push-ups in the wardroom. Amanda talked to fish, who made no reply. Philip Tyre . . . I couldn't hear him, for the banging on my hatch.

I stirred, drifted back to sleep, but the hammering persisted. I woke. Hours had passed, and someone pounded in the corridor. The impertinence amazed me. I jumped to my feet, flung open the hatch.

"Did you know, you conniving bastard? Did you?" Tears ran down Edgar Tolliver's cheeks. "Was it another of your tricks?" He slammed his fist into the bulkhead.

"Know? What are you talking about?"

"I can't even hate you anymore! Yet I was ready to see

you die, to put an end to it!" He sobbed in fury, wiped his cheek with his sleeve. "Tell me you knew!"

I grasped his shoulders, shook him. "Explain, Edgar."

"God damn you, read it yourself!" He thrust me a holochip.

I turned back to the desk, put it in the holovid.

I keyed the screen.

"To: Captain Nicholas E. Seafort, from ComHomFlt, U.N.N.S., Lunapolis Base. Eleven months ago, on 4 March, 2200, United Nations Security Council Resolution 8645 was amended to read: 'The threat of nuclear annihilation having for generations terrorized all mankind, it is enacted that use, attempted use, or conspiracy to use nuclear energy for the purpose of destructive detonation shall in all cases be punishable by death, UNLESS SUCH ACT SHALL (A) TAKE PLACE OUTSIDE THE SOLAR SYSTEM, (B) BE COMMITTED FOR THE PURPOSE OF DEFENDING UNITED NATIONS COLONIES OR MEMBER STATES FROM DESTRUCTION BY ALIEN ATTACK, AND (C) BE PERSONALLY AUTHORIZED BY THE SENIOR MILITARY OFFICIAL WITHIN THAT COLONY OR MEMBER STATE.'

"You are to resume command of U.N.S. *Victoria*. Proceed to Lunapolis Base, where you will testify at a Board of Inquiry to determine whether the destruction of Orbit Station was necessary and within your province to command, and whether you had the requisite authority to alter the status of the colony of Hope Nation. End message."

Tolliver whispered, "How did you know the law was amended?"

I snarled, "Look at the date of the amendment. How *could* I know?" He made no response. I said, "Go to the bridge. I'll be along shortly."

Tolliver stumbled to attention, saluted. "Aye aye, sir."

"Dismissed."

EPILOGUE

"Admiral Duhaney will see you now, sir." The staff lieutenant held the door. All eyes in the crowded anteroom were on me, as they had been from the moment I'd entered. It was so everywhere I'd been in the Lunapolis warrens.

I straightened my tie, took a last tug at my jacket. "Very well."

"Seafort." Admiral Duhaney rose from behind the desk, extended a hand. I took it. In his forties, I judged. Smooth black hair, a politician's smile. A far cry from Admiral Brentley, my old mentor. He asked, "How are you feeling?"

"Well enough, sir." I'd recovered from the implant of my new lung, and I'd just about run the course of the antirejection meds, but still I was grateful Lunapolis had only one-sixth Terran gravity.

"Have a seat." He gestured to the couch. "I understand your wife is still in, ah, treatment. Will she travel with you?"

"Travel? Where?"

He looked surprised. "On your next ship. You have your choice of assignments, you know. If there's some particular ship we can give the Hero of Hope Nation—"

"Don't call me that!" I came to my feet, trembling. "If you're going to jeer at me—"

"Jeer? Look at the holozines!" I glanced at the printouts scattered on the table. Of course my scarred face was on all of them still. I could go nowhere without the cameras whirring.

"I'm no hero." I slumped back into my seat.

"You've been exonerated by a Board of Inquiry."

Whitewashed, he meant. The holozines had gotten my story, probably by decoding my wideband broadcast, and had emblazoned it across the world's screens. "Seafort Saves Hope Nation"; "Captain Kills A Thousand Fish!"; "Nicky

Nukes Alien Fleet!" Other headlines didn't bear thinking about.

After that, the Navy could do nothing but concur in the general adulation. They'd heard my report on the Venturas attack, read William's confirmation, and endorsed my treason without batting an eye.

"You can have *Hibernia,* when she gets home, or any other ship you—"

"I resign."

He stopped short. "You what?"

"Resign, I said. I've done enough harm. I'll do no more."

Admiral Duhaney got up, crossed slowly to the couch, sat next to me. "You can't, Seafort. The public wouldn't stand for it, and we need you."

"No."

He studied my face. "What happened, out beyond? Is this about the Station?"

"No, sir. It's about the people." Vax, why do you haunt me? I was trying to protect you. Gladly I would have given you the glory.

"Your return on *Victoria* must have been . . . difficult."

"Somewhat. That doesn't matter." *Victoria*'s officers had judged me more truly than had Admiralty.

"Nine months is a long time, if you're not liked."

"Not liked?" Despised. No time in my life had been as lonely as those nine endless months.

Admiral Duhaney cleared his throat.

"Sorry." Where were we? "It's not the trip home, sir. I've had enough."

"We need men like you commanding—"

"Whatever your Board of Inquiry said, I'm not fit to command. I've broken my oath, I've destroyed a station, I've far exceeded my authority. If I didn't have that foolish reputation in the zines you'd have cashiered me, or worse. You should have hanged me. When I blew the Station I had no idea they'd changed the nuclear resolution!"

"That doesn't matter, boy. The resolution *was* amended. It had to be. The hysteria after that first fish followed you home in *Challenger* . . ." He shook his head.

"I thought I was committing treason."

"You'd have been, a few months earlier. Lord God must be with you."

That was so preposterous I didn't bother to answer. Duhaney was a fool. "It doesn't matter, sir. I resign."

"You mustn't. Do you know how many ships we've lost? We need the public behind us for the cost of rebuilding the fleet. And recruiting is more important than ever. We need your face on the recruiting posters to—"

"Cashier me, damn you, but don't mock me!" I scrambled to my feet. "Well, don't look so surprised! Admiralty taught me over and again I could get away with insolence; this is the result! Good day to you, sir." Fuming, I strode across the room.

"Wait, Seafort, I—"

I flung an angry salute, slammed the door. In the anteroom conversation melted into stunned silence. The duty lieutenant stared, aghast. I ignored them all as I stalked out.

My quarters were a half-kilometer distant, through endless tunnels. Rather than wait for the mini-shuttle I chose to walk. Soon my pace was almost a run, aided by the lesser gravity. By the time I reached my rooms I'd begun to cool, and felt not a little embarrassed at my tantrum. For an officer to carry on in front of an Admiral—it was unheard of. My behavior was worse than that of a rank cadet at Lunar Academy on Farside.

Well, Duhaney couldn't do much about it. It mattered not whether he placed a rebuke in my file or even demoted me for my insolence. I was through.

They'd given me a suite of rooms—a small bedroom, sitting room, kitchenette, and head—in the military housing complex. Luxury accommodations, for crowded Lunapolis. I let myself in, threw off my jacket, washed my hands and face. I wondered how Annie was doing, in the New York clinic. I'd go down to see her again, as soon as I could. I supposed I'd hear from the Admiral, one way or the other. Perhaps a court-martial for insubordination would accomplish what the Board of Inquiry had not.

I slept.

The next morning I was mopping my breakfast plate when the bell rang. Still in shirtsleeves, I opened the door.

Admiral Duhaney's braid gleamed. Automatically I came to attention.

"As you were, Mr. Seafort. This is an, ah, unofficial call." He gestured to the civilian at his side. "I don't believe you've met. Senator, may I present Captain Nicholas Seafort. Captain, of course you know Senator Boland."

"Senator who?"

The Admiral frowned. "Senator Richard Boland, of the Security Council Naval Affairs Committee."

"An honor to meet you, Captain." He held out his hand. "May we come in?"

"I was just—very well." I shook hands and stood aside.

They found places in the sitting room. The Senator said, "Admiral, may I? Let's get to the point. Mr. Seafort, your foolish remark about resigning is forgotten, of course. I'm here to help negotiate a course of—"

"Negotiate? Admiralty doesn't negotiate its assignments."

The Admiral cleared his throat. "In your case, we do. You don't seem to understand we really need you."

"Why?"

"Because the war's unpopular," said Boland. "Some people want us to stop fighting the fish, pull back to home system, abandon the colonies if need be—"

"That's absurd!" How could we turn our backs on millions of our own people, scattered among the stars?

"Yes, of course. But it may come to pass. We need heroes, and you're our most prominent. You thought the Admiral mocked you when he spoke of putting your picture on a recruiting poster. It's already on one."

"Lord God in heaven!"

"You have no idea how popular you've become. In fact, if you insisted on resigning, we could run you for the General Assembly and you'd win in a minute."

"I'm not running for—"

"But we need you in the Navy. Recruitment jumped fifteen percent since we began showing the spot of you and your wife disembarking at—"

I snarled, "You dragged Annie into this?"

"Dragged? No, we have just the one shot of you coming through the airlock into Earthport Station."

I stood, trembling with rage. "Get out! Both of you!"

Boland looked up curiously. "What's wrong, Captain?"

"Annie's ill! She needs privacy!"

"Don't be silly. You won't have privacy for years, whether or not you resign. Anyway, you're the perfect recruiting couple: the dashing young Captain and his beautiful trannie—excuse me—transpop wife. It attracts the educated classes to the service academies, and the working joeys as well."

He wandered to the holowindow, flicked the setting to Upper New York. "Seafort, we've gotten off on the wrong foot. Help us win the war. We can give you any ship—"

"I don't want one."

"Then we'll post you shoreside. Public relations, light duties, a few appear—"

"Never."

Admiral Duhaney said, "Richard, let me try." He came across the room. "Look at me, Mr. Seafort." He spoke softly. "I'm used to dealing with politicians, not the working fleet. Perhaps I don't speak your language, but hear me out. If we pull back to home system, the fish will still be there. Sooner or later they'll find us. Do you agree?" Reluctantly I nodded.

"Even if they don't, we'd still be trapped in home system, unable to Fuse for fear of attracting them. We can't have that. Even I see as much, politician that I've become. Seafort, you're an important cog in our war machine. Not essential, but of great value. You won't take a ship or work the publicity circuit. Let me give you a job where you'll be shoreside and able to duck publicity too."

"What is that?" I asked hoarsely. I was drowning. Where was my lifebelt?

"Captain Kearsey is retiring."

"Kearsey? Commandant Kearsey?"

"Yes. I'll appoint you Commandant of Lunar Academy."

"Good Lord!"

"Think, Seafort. You'll have not only the Farside Academy but also Terrestrial Academy and the Training Station. They're closed bases, so you can keep the reporters out. You'll be free to visit your wife, and have her live with you as soon as she's able."

"But why?"

"When we make you Commandant, recruitment will double. We'll keep using the holo shots we have; no need even to pose for new ones."

"Let me be! Why won't you let me go?"

He ignored me. "You've always had the pied piper in you, Seafort. You're good with children."

I cried, "Good? I kill them!" Sandy Wilsky, dead from my stupidity in *Hibernia*. The transpops on *Portia*. Even Philip Tyre, on *Challenger*. Where I walked I left a trail of misery and death. My own son Nate . . .

"You'd be wonderful at the job, and I'm not giving you a line of goofjuice. Your reports all show you handle youngsters well."

No, it wasn't so. True, some had escaped the effects of my blundering, but others had not. Jerence Branstead, whom I'd locked in a cabin with a full vial of goofjuice. My cruelty to him had known no bounds.

Each day I'd waited for him to break. Grimly he held on. After a time the purser reported that food trays had come back untouched for three days. Again I went to his cabin. It reeked of sweat and Lord God knew what else. The vial was on the table, unopened. Jerence, lay across his bed, eyes shut, clutching the sheets.

"Get up, lad."

"I can't. It hurts too bad."

"Come." I drew him off the bed, pushed him into the head, unbuttoned his shirt. "Take off the rest of it. Into the shower." He shook his head. I pulled off his clothes.

"Don't look at me." He covered himself.

I laughed aloud. "I won't, but don't try that in the wardroom."

"I can't hold on!"

"Only a few more days."

"I can't." He sagged against the side of the shower. I adjusted the temperature, went out into the corridor and to the caller. "Purser, to the Branstead cabin." Moments later I gestured at the mess. "Fresh sheets, and get the clothing washed."

He wrinkled his nose. "Aye aye, sir."

On the twenty-first day I unlocked the cabin hatch and stood aside. Jerence Branstead's clothes hung large on his wasted frame. His steps were tremulous. He blinked in the bright corridor light.

"The vial, lad."

He whispered, "Yessir." Slow steps, back to the prison of his cabin. He reemerged. I held out my palm. After a long, reluctant moment he placed the vial in my hand.

"Still?"

He nodded. "As bad as ever. Almost."

"Will you use it again?"

To his credit, the boy was silent a long time. When he looked up his eyes held something they hadn't held before. "No, sir."

"Before I enlist you, swear it to Lord God."

He bit his lip, reached out, put his hand for comfort in mine. "I swear on my immortal soul that I . . . won't . . . ever use . . . goofjuice again." He was weeping.

"Very well. I'll talk to you about the oath after—"

"Hold me! Be Pa for a minute!" He rushed sobbing into my arms. Awkwardly I cradled him. I had no flair for solace. My talent was for torture.

"It was so hard, Mr. Seafort. So hard!"

"I know, boy." I let him weep. "I know."

Now, in Lunapolis, I looked up to the Admiral. "Why won't you understand? I'm the worst officer you've ever had, and always you reward me! You'd even put me in charge of your children. I warn you, don't!"

"You'll do well, Seafort. When can you start?"

I was defeated. "I need time with my wife."

"Of course. Four weeks, then? Standard long-leave?"

"I suppose."

"Good." He smiled. "By the way, I've approved your final report on *Victoria* and sent your personnel recommendations to BuPers."

"Very well."

"You're sure you want that fellow put back to lieutenant?"

"Tolliver? Yes."

"We'll do it, but no one will take him after what he did

with the heli. It's half pay for him, or some outpost like Ganymede Station."

It would be fitting punishment. For me. I said, "I'll take him."

"Hmmm, odd of you. The others will be no problem, of course."

I'd recommended that Bram Steiner's commission be reinstated without penalty. I'd also written Lieutenant Kahn a good rating, though I hadn't told him so. I rather admired his thespian abilities. From the moment of my ultimatum, his seething hatred had been indiscernible.

The one officer who'd been true to his convictions was Thomas Ross, and he'd paid dearly for it for the remainder of the cruise. Not at my hand, but at Kahn's after his reinstatement. It didn't help that I'd stripped him of all seniority, and he'd been low man in the wardroom, lower even than Avar Bezrel.

When the flagship Defused from Hope Nation, Bezrel would be returned to Admiral De Marnay. Perhaps he'd be happier under the wing of his protector. As for Jerence . . . the corners of my mouth turned up. I'd be his guardian still. Like me, he'd be sent to Academy.

Senator Boland coughed. "There's one more thing. Would you consider . . ."

I said impatiently, "Yes?"

"Getting rid of that awful scar?"

My hand flew to my face. "It's part of me."

"An unnecessary part. We tone it down on the posters, but for heaven's sake . . . you're famous enough without it."

"That's not why I wear it."

"I know, I know. They showed me your psych report. Bear your guilt, if you must, but carry it inside like the rest of us. Would you do that much?"

"I—well—all right, if you insist."

"Thank you."

"Go enjoy your leave, then." In a daze, I shook hands as they left.

When the cabin was silent, I dropped into my chair and sat musing. Lord God, are You toying with me? If I could have Your forgiveness, Your love once more, even for just a moment . . . No, I know better than to ask. But why, then, do You let them reward me? And my friends, Alexi, Jerence, Tolliver. Was it for their sakes You helped them through their travail, or could it have been for mine?

Will I ever meet You?

I didn't know. Absently I began to pack. For now, there was long-leave. There was Annie. There was duty.

Someday I'd know the rest.